COGNAC VIXEN

PUSHKIN BRATVA
BOOK 2

NICOLE FOX

MAILING LIST

Sign up to my mailing list!
New subscribers receive a FREE steamy bad boy romance
novel.

Click the link below to join.
https://sendfox.com/nicolefox

ALSO BY NICOLE FOX

Corrupted Angel (Book 1)

Corrupted Queen (Book 2)

Corrupted Empire (Book 3)

De Maggio Mafia Duet

Devil in a Suit (Book 1)

Devil at the Altar (Book 2)

Kornilov Bratva Duet

Married to the Don (Book 1)

Til Death Do Us Part (Book 2)

Heirs to the Bratva Empire

Can be read in any order!

Kostya

Maksim

Andrei

Princes of Ravenlake Academy (Bully Romance)

Can be read as standalones!

Cruel Prep

Cruel Academy

Cruel Elite

Tsezar Bratva

Nightfall (Book 1)

Daybreak (Book 2)

Russian Crime Brotherhood

Can be read in any order!

Owned by the Mob Boss

Unprotected with the Mob Boss

Knocked Up by the Mob Boss

Sold to the Mob Boss

Stolen by the Mob Boss

Trapped with the Mob Boss

Volkov Bratva

Broken Vows (Book 1)

Broken Hope (Book 2)

Broken Sins *(standalone)*

Other Standalones

Vin: A Mafia Romance

Box Sets

Bratva Mob Bosses (Russian Crime Brotherhood Books 1-6)

Tsezar Bratva (Tsezar Bratva Duet Books 1-2)

Heirs to the Bratva Empire

The Mafia Dons Collection

The Don's Corruption

COGNAC VIXEN

One evil stepfather.

Two ex-fiancés fighting to claim me.

Three beautiful words: "Happily ever after."

I ran from my old life because the monsters in my past thought they could own me.

For one brief moment, Ivan Pushkin gave me a taste of a happy ending to my story.

But now, those same monsters are back to finish the job.

Francia wants me dead.

My stepfather wants me married.

And the Sokolovs want me chained to them forever.

The only thing between me and them is Ivan.

But there's stuff between me and him, too.

Lies. Secrets.

Heartbreak. Hope.

This whole thing started with a sip of cognac.

Is the man who poured it my hero…

Or my villain?

COGNAC VIXEN is Book Two in the Pushkin Bratva duet. Ivan and Cora's story begins in Book One, **COGNAC VILLAIN!**

1

CORA

The moment the silhouette appears in the doorway at the top of the stairs, my heart sinks.

"Don't look so fucking grim," Mikhail scolds as he saunters down into the room. "Your fiancé has come to claim you at last. You're going home."

I don't know where Mikhail plans to take me, but it won't be *home*. And he sure as fuck isn't my fiancé.

"I'm not going anywhere with you," I spit with as much venom as I can muster. But it's hard to sound tough when your hands are still bound to a chair. "Where did Francia go?"

She left as soon as Mikhail showed up without so much as a goodbye. I wonder what could be more important than keeping two women prisoner in this dank, depressing basement.

His eyebrows spring upward. "You'd prefer to be down here with that crazy bitch over me?"

"You're the one working with her."

"Means to an end, darling," he drawls. "Francia is simply a means to an end."

I'm the "end" he's talking about. But whatever Mikhail is hoping will happen here today, he's mistaken. I refuse to let Mikhail fucking Sokolov be the end of my story.

I scan the dungeon again. There are two doors: the main one Mikhail just came through and the locked side door where Francia dragged Jorden's unconscious body through earlier. Aside from those, there's no way out. Not unless I can kill Mikhail and use his dead body like a battering ram. Which, hello—hands still bound in chains here.

"If Francia is a means to an end, what is Jorden?" I ask. "You haven't checked on her in a while. She should be awake by now."

At least, I *hope* she's awake by now. If she isn't, I'm not sure what that means for her survival. Can people die from chloroform or whatever the hell they used to knock us out?

His eyes dart to the door and his jaw flexes. "Gone."

My entire body goes cold. "… Gone? What does that mean? She isn't gone. She's—"

"*Alive* and gone," he corrects wearily, as if feigning human emotion is exhausting for him. Poor guy. No one ever has enough pity for sociopaths. "She isn't useful, so we pawned her off. The going rate on pretty women with no family to search for them isn't bad. You should remember that. If I get bored with you, you'll end up in the same place."

She's alive. I should be relieved, but it's cold comfort if the rest of what Mikhail is saying is true.

Jorden, my best friend, trafficked to some sicko who thinks they can own a human being. Jorden, the life of the party who just wanted to be taken care of and loved, sold off to God only knows who. The horror of it is too much to process. Like so much else about this experience, I bottle it up and shove it down deep.

Ivan will come for me. When he does, he'll save Jorden, too.

As if he can read my thoughts, Mikhail shifts closer to me. He kneels down, his bony arms on his knees, his skin so pale it practically glows in the gloom.

"Is that *hope* I see in your eyes?" Mikhail twists his face to the side. "Unbelievable. After everything, you still think Ivan Pushkin will come save you."

"I *know* he will." I lift my chin, refusing to sink to Mikhail's games. He wants to drag me down, but I can't let him.

Mikhail studies me for a moment longer. Then he laughs.

The sound of it sends goosebumps shivering across my skin. It's repulsive. I can't believe I ever spent a single second by his side. That I tucked my arm through his and let him lead me through dinner parties. That we stood in a jewelry store and chose a fucking *wedding ring.*

"You've always been delusional, Cordelia. Your expectations for your life are childish. Like you think you live in some fairytale."

"If you think you're the Prince Charming, you're out of your fucking mind."

He bares his teeth and his fist clenches. For a second, I think he's going to hit me. Then Mikhail relaxes. He eases back and smiles. "You also overestimate your value. Most women know when they're being more trouble than they're worth. You have never been a good judge of that."

"If I'm so much trouble, why are you here?" I rasp. "Why not let me go?"

"Because I don't mind working for what I deserve. You're like a wild horse. You need to be broken before you can be put to your proper use."

His eyes smear up and down my body. I fight back another shiver.

"I'm not yours to train."

"Oh, really?" he snorts. "Who do you belong to, then? Ivan?"

Yes. The word echoes through my hollow chest so loudly I'm sure Mikhail can hear it.

"I don't belong to anyone."

"You don't belong to Ivan, that's for sure," he snarks. "If you did, he'd be here now to save you, wouldn't he? But no—just like always, you were difficult. You pushed back against his control and you and I both know that Ivan has no interest in someone he can't control. He doesn't want a wild horse; he wants a docile little show pony."

I blink back the tears suddenly collecting in my eyes. "That's not true."

"But it is." He kneels down again, his face twisted into a horrifying mask of faux sympathy. "Ivan announced to the entire underworld that he wanted a simple business arrangement for a marriage. He wanted a woman who knew how to follow orders and wouldn't get in his way. He wants a woman like *Francia*."

Jealousy flares in me. "Fuck you!" I strain forward, rubbing my already-raw wrists against my bindings. "You don't know Ivan. Not the real him. You don't know anything about us."

Mikhail barks out a laugh. "'*Us.*' Fucking delusional. Ivan doesn't love you. He never loved you. The bastard isn't capable of it."

"And you are?"

He considers the question for a moment. "No, probably not. But I hold tightly to what is mine. Whereas Ivan is already moving on. Why should he care about you when there is another woman willing to fill your position?"

I want to ignore him. I *should* ignore him. Mikhail is trying to get a rise out of me. He's trying to break me down.

But I think back to all those times where the truth hit me—when I was forced to realize that there are so many other women better suited to Ivan and what he wants. Francia, as crazy as she may be, is one of those women. She doesn't want love; she wants power. Ivan can give her that and more.

Mikhail stands up and pulls out his phone. "No word from Francia yet. Maybe she's busy securing the deal." He winks at me suggestively and my stomach bottoms out.

The thought of anyone touching Ivan is too much to think about.

He wouldn't do that to me, I think. *He's going to save me. He'll come for me.*

I repeat the words to myself again and again, clinging to the warmth of the thought even as a chill I can't fight seeps into my bones.

2

IVAN

"You want me to marry you; otherwise, you'll kill Cora." It's not really a question, just a repetition of the absolutely batshit nonsense spewing out of Francia's mouth.

The truly crazy part is that Francia doesn't look nearly as deranged as I know she is. The bitch is watching me with an easy smile like she just asked how I take my coffee.

"I'm glad we're on the same page. I hate repeating myself." She looks down at her watch. "You have five minutes to decide."

I can't decide something like that in five minutes. I'm going to need five years just to wrap my head around the clusterfuck of this situation.

Up until a few hours ago, I had never bothered to think much about Francia. She was Cora's friend. Someone I needed to protect to fulfill my deal with Cora. To make Cora happy. I never paid her any mind.

That was my first mistake.

While she cowered in the shadows, unnoticed and unwatched, Francia was busy betraying *everyone*. She lied and deceived us all and now, Cora is in danger.

My fault, my fault, my fault.

Guilt thrums through me. I can't believe I doubted Cora. In the midst of it all, I thought maybe she was behind this. Maybe she was a spy who had betrayed me. I didn't let myself think that *I* was the one who had failed *her.*

Now, her life is in the balance—and it all hinges on what I decide in the next five minutes.

"Tick, tock. Tick, tock." Francia clicks her tongue as her head sways back and forth. I'd love to rip it right out of her smug mouth.

"Give me a fucking second alone to think," I growl.

She flips her dark hair over her shoulder and backs away. She's trying to play it off, but I scare her.

Good.

"It's Cora's life you're gambling with," she says flippantly. "Throw it away if you want. I don't care. But if I don't call my associates within five minutes, they've been instructed to kill her and send you her pretty little head in a box."

My vision is gone, replaced with white, blinding rage. I have to fight to stay standing and not lunge down the hallway for Francia's throat.

"Take your time. Not too much of it, of course." She drags her thumb across her neck with a ghoulish smile. "But don't worry—I'll watch the clock."

I'm still staring unseeing at Francia when one of the Bratva soldiers grips my elbow and pulls me away. I expect him to take me to a nearby room, but he starts jogging down the hallway. At the end, we take a left and then we're at an emergency exit door. Whatever alarm should be blaring now that it has been opened is silent.

And Jorden is lying on the concrete just outside.

"What the fuck, Yasha?"

My second is at his knees next to Jorden's limp body. She's conscious, but barely. "I got the text while Francia was giving her speech. The security team spotted Jorden in the alley. No fucking idea where she came from."

I scour the alley for any sign of a second body, even though I know there won't be anything to see. If there was a sign of Cora, the team would have relayed it to me by now.

Yasha helps Jorden sit up. "Can you hear me?"

Jorden's eyes roll around in her head like marbles. It looks like it takes all of her energy to force out his name. "Y…asha."

He crumples at the rasp in her voice. "I'm here."

I ignore their happy little reunion. "Where the fuck is Cora?"

We don't have time for this. I can hear Francia's voice in the back of my head. *Tick, tock. Tick, tock.*

Jorden shakes her head, but doesn't say anything.

"That's not good enough. Speak! Where is she?"

"She's hurt," Yasha snaps at me in a surprising show of frustration. "She needs a doctor."

I know he's right, but the fact Jorden is this out of it sets off a flurry of alarm bells. If she's this bad off, how much worse is Cora?

"She needs to tell me where Cora is. Maybe you weren't paying attention, but unless you want Cora's head overnighted to my doorstep, I need to find her. *Now.*"

Jorden flinches against Yasha's chest and he wraps his arms more tightly around her. When he looks at me, his eyes are granite. "Back off, man."

Second-in-command, best friend all my life—none of that matters right now. I'm about to tell him exactly what happens to insubordination in the Bratva when Yasha turns back to Jorden and strokes her cheek gently. "Jorden. Jorden. Do you know where Cora is?"

Her eyes focus on him and I watch as she settles into the safety of his touch. "I don't—No, I don't—I woke up alone."

Fuck.

"Where?" Yasha presses gently. "Where did you wake up?"

She shakes her head. "Dark. I think I p-passed out a few times. I'm not sure if I... Maybe someone carried me. It's all confused and I—They hit me."

She presses her scalp and winces. Yasha studies the spot and looks at me, his eyes wide. "She needs to get to the doctor. They fucking clocked her, Ivan. She could have a concussion or bleeding in her brain."

I know he's right, but I'd let every goddamn person in the world die a million times over if it got me even half a step closer to Cora.

"Do you know anyone who might—" I grit my teeth and start over. "Did you see anyone? Mikhail Sokolov? Or Alexander McAllister?"

Jorden frowns. "Mikhail. Cora and Mikhail…"

I lean forward as her voice trails off, hanging on every word. "Cora and Mikhail *what*?"

Yasha gives me a warning look, but I ignore him. Now is not the time for his puppy love. Not when Cora's life is on the line.

"She hates him," Jorden mumbles. Her eyes are starting to flutter. She's fading fast. "She hates… I don't know who. I can't—What did you say?"

"I have to get her to a doctor," Yasha barks. "Now. No more questions."

He cradles her in his arms and stands up. And there's no point arguing. Jorden is already unconscious again, her body sagging against Yasha's chest. Now that she's off the ground, I can see the blood matting the hair at the back of her head.

Did they hit Cora, too? Is she unconscious in some dark room? Is she crawling towards what she hopes is safety, praying I'll be there to rescue her?

The questions torment me. They torment me enough that I know exactly what I have to do.

"Take Jorden to Dr. Popov," I tell him. "We're done here anyway."

Yasha hesitates. "What are you going to do?"

Whatever it takes to keep Cora safe.

"I'm going to marry Francia."

3

IVAN

"No!" Yasha shakes his head. "No. I won't let you marry that psychotic—"

"I don't have a choice."

"You always have a choice! You're Ivan Pushkin, for fuck's sake. There is always a way out."

Yasha isn't prone to idealism. It's one of the many reasons I chose him as my second. But he knows what my job is. What my job *truly* is: I'm a man who knows how to make the tough calls other people are too afraid to make.

This is one of them.

"She played us, *sobrat*. Francia played us all for fools. The only way to save Cora now is to give her what she wants."

"No. There has to be another way."

"Not one we can figure out in—" I glance at my phone. "Two minutes."

My heartbeat ramps up, matching pace with the seconds ticking past. Time is running out fast.

Jorden stirs in Yasha's arms. She grabs his shoulder and tries to sit up, but she is weak. She can barely hold on.

"Relax," Yasha reassures her. "I have you."

Her head swivels to me, her gaze glassy. "Cora... You need her. She talks about... you two. Two... together."

"Get her to the doctor, Yasha. She isn't making sense."

Except she is. I know what she's saying as well as Yasha does. But it's not possible. Cora and I can't be together. Not in this lifetime. I'd rather break her heart and save her life than doom her to dying because of me.

"When we find Cora, she'll be destroyed if she finds out—"

"She'll be dead if I don't do this," I bite back. "It doesn't matter anyway. I never wanted a wife."

Yasha gives me a knowing look. "C'mon, Ivan. That was different. That was before. Now—"

"Now, I'm going to marry Francia and save Cora's life. What's one bride compared to another?" My words are ice-cold, but Yasha doesn't look convinced. Neither am I. He opens his mouth to respond, but I shake my head and point down the alley. "Go. Now. Jorden needs you."

If the situation was any different, I know Yasha wouldn't leave. He'd stand here and fight as hard for me as I would for him. But Jorden has slipped into unconsciousness again. Blood from the wound on the back of her head has soaked into his shoulder. She needs medical attention.

So, with a drawn-out sigh, Yasha gives me one final look and then turns and carries her down the alleyway.

When I get back inside, Francia is waiting for me. "I was getting nervous you'd made a run for it," she titters. "It wouldn't be that surprising, I suppose. I never understood your interest in Cora."

"Don't you dare say her fucking name."

The words tear out of my throat. Francia is smart enough to press her lips together and stay quiet.

"I have demands," I add.

She arches a brow. "I thought I was the one making demands."

"We've entered negotiations," I tell her. "You made a demand; now, I'm countering. Do you want to hear it or not?"

"By all means. But know that you only have…" She looks at her watch. "One minute."

Sixty seconds to negotiate the rest of my life. No pressure.

"If you're going to marry me, you will play the role of the traditional Bratva wife."

"Meaning…?"

"You are to be seen, not heard." *Though I wouldn't mind if she wasn't seen, either.* "You have no power over any part of the Bratva—that remains fully in my control—and we live in separate wings of the house."

She frowns. "Were you and Cora living in separate wings?"

"Cora wasn't my wife."

In my head, I add, *She was more than that.*

What I had with Cora is more than anything I'll ever have with Francia. The fact Francia thinks I'll ever treat her the way I treated Cora shows exactly how delusional she really is.

She hums, considering. "Is that all?"

"I also want proof that Cora is alive. Now and whenever I request it from this moment forward."

"As you wish." Francia's mouth pinches into a sly grin. She slowly slinks forward, moving closer to me than she ought to dare. "I can't demand that you love me, Ivan. But once you see how perfectly I fit into your world… once you see me carry your children… who knows what might happen?"

Not that. Not ever.

I decide right here, right now, that I will never touch Francia. Fuck my lineage. Fuck the Bratva. I'll leave it to Yasha's children in my will if I must. But I will never lay so much as a finger near Francia—unless it's to rip her still-beating heart out of her chest.

As the vow crosses my mind, Francia extends her hand. "Do we have a deal?"

"One more thing." I reach out and snare Francia's wrist from mid-air. She yelps as my hand swallows up her finger and yanks.

"What the fuck are you doing! That is—"

"Not your ring," I finish.

I step back and open my palm to reveal Cora's engagement band shining in the palm of my hand. It looked wrong on Francia's finger. It looks wrong here. It belongs in one place only.

I look up at Francia as a storm cloud settles on her brow. She's a vengeful bitch—that much has become blindingly obvious. If I'm going to navigate this relationship, I have to play it right. Carefully. I need her docile until I'm ready to make my next move. So for now, that means forcing little white lies down her throat one by one.

"You don't want a hand-me-down, do you?" I croon. "I'll get you your own ring. One that suits you."

Preferably one tied to a cement block that is well on its way to meeting the bottom of the ocean.

Revenge fantasies are the only thing that will get me through this relationship with Francia, however long it has to last. Because outwardly, I'll have to play my part. I'll have to ease Francia's vindictive side and lure her into a false sense of security. Until I can find Cora and kill everyone who played a part in separating us.

Francia's smile grows slowly. Then she nods and pulls out her phone. "I like white gold. And big diamonds. Spare no expense."

"I never have."

"That's what I like to hear." She presses her phone to her ear. "It's done."

Then she has the audacity to wink at me. Like this chapter is finished.

But nothing about this is done.

We are just getting started.

4

CORA

Mikhail can't shut up. He's incapable of it. So I do my best to tune him out.

As he rattles off all of the ways that I'm ill-suited to be with Ivan, I count stones in the grimy wall across from me. While he keeps blabbing, I twist my wrists against my bindings until I nearly cry out from the pain. I'd rather sever my own hands with nothing but friction than spend another second in the same room with Mikhail Sokolov.

Thankfully, before I can get that far, Mikhail's phone rings.

"Finally!" A wicked smile twists his pale face. "Francia must finally be done with him. That didn't take long, did it?"

He's a liar. Nothing he's saying is true. He doesn't know what happened between Francia and Ivan any more than I do.

Still, the words stick their landing in a deep, jealous part of me. I turn away so he doesn't see me cringe.

He presses his phone to his ear and turns towards the wall, the smile disappearing from his face. "Well?"

I watch him carefully, but I can't hear anything. This room is soundproof. Airproof, too. The stone walls and floor are stifling, swallowing any drop of sound that might try to make its way to me.

Mikhail nods and hums. He lets out a few "Okays." None of it is useful. None of it eases the burning need to know where Ivan is and why he isn't here with me.

But the longer I wait, the more Mikhail's words slither behind my weakening defenses.

Ivan chose Francia. He saw the way she manipulated his security and played her role. The fire he saw in me? It burns ten times brighter in her. She is everything I could never be: a fierce Bratva wife. An asset to his empire.

He's going to choose her and this will be the end of me.

I sit straighter. Is this how I die? In the dark at the hands of Mikhail Sokolov? I literally can't think of a worse ending.

Then Mikhail turns back to me. His expression is unreadable, but he thrusts the phone towards my ear.

I look up at him, ready to ask what he's doing. Then, without warning, he grabs my arm and twists.

Fire shoots up my injured wrist. My shoulder blade burns and my forearm scrapes against my bindings. I cry out and try to pull away, but it only makes it worse.

Mikhail lets go of me with a laugh, the phone back against his own ear. "How is that for proof of life?"

My body still aches, but it dulls in the rush of relief. Ivan wanted to make sure I was alive. He cares. He isn't going to leave me here with Mikhail. He's just making a deal and then he'll get me out. I'll be saved.

By the time Mikhail is tucking the phone back in his pocket, I've convinced myself that this is almost over. If I just hang on for a few more minutes, Mikhail will untie me and hand me over to Ivan. I'll go home with him. *Home.* To his mansion, his bed. I'll be safe and warm wrapped in the heat of his body.

Jorden went through a phase a few months ago where she wouldn't shut up about manifesting. *Just tell the universe what you want and boom, presto-change-o, you'll get it.* I'm trying to believe in it, clicking my little ruby red slippers together and praying for Ivan to come bursting through the door.

But it stays shut.

And Mikhail's grin grows wider.

"Oh, you poor thing. Is that *still* hope I see on your face?" Mikhail gives me a sarcastic pout. "Ivan is not coming. Is that what you were imagining? He isn't coming for you."

It takes everything in me not to dissolve into tears.

Mikhail senses the weakness and draws closer. His voice is a low, insistent hiss. "Are you finally realizing that you were nothing more than a pawn in Ivan's game? He never cared about you. You were just the latest woman in a long line of them, willing to suck his cock whenever he felt the need." I turn my face away, but Mikhail grips my chin and forces me to look at him. "Ivan Pushkin never gave a fuck about you and now, he's going to marry Francia. You were nothing more than a distraction."

I want to push back against what he's saying, but I don't have the energy. Not when everything he's saying lines up so perfectly with what I've felt all along.

Ivan needed someone else. Someone better.

Now, he has that.

He has Francia.

5

IVAN

I watch Francia talk on the phone. Her voice is an annoying drone, like a mosquito's. She isn't saying anything useful.

The deal is done.

You know what to do.

As we agreed...

All I can think about is how close I am to Cora. She's one phone call away. Right there, on the other end of this line. This is the closest I've been to her in days and I still can't touch her. Can't see her.

Is she conscious? Is she alive? I don't fucking know.

The wrongness of not being with her settles in my veins. Especially as Francia hands me the phone.

Her lips are pursed. She's smug in her success, however temporary I intend for it to be. She wouldn't look so pleased if she knew all the sick fantasies swirling in my head. Most of them end with her in several distinct pieces.

I snatch the phone away without touching her hand and press it to my ear.

At first, there is no sound. No distinguishing background noise to clue me into where they might be holding Cora. I press the phone harder to my ear, desperate to hear anything. I'm about to reveal exactly how desperate I am and call out Cora's name...

Then I hear something.

Shuffling. A struggle. Chains rattle and feet skid across a hard floor. But all of that is background noise to the main event.

Cora's scream.

I know Francia can hear it through the speaker. She's watching me carefully, but I keep my *pakhan* mask on and up even as I want nothing more than to rip it off and howl in rage. I'd smash Francia's fragile skull against the wall if I thought it would help. But whoever she's working for would kill Cora regardless. Francia has planned for that contingency. She is crazy enough that she's willing to die before this mission fails.

I'm not willing to let Cora suffer the same fate.

So I bite my tongue and listen to her scream.

When she stops, she's panting. Another voice comes over the line. A sneering voice I recognize all too well. "How is that for proof of life?" Mikhail Sokolov asks.

This "proof of life" just secured Mikhail's painful death. If it's the last thing I ever do, I'll make him pay for hurting her. He'll regret touching Cora for the rest of his short, miserable existence. I'm going to make sure of it.

Francia's dark eyes are narrowed on me. I can't tell if this was part of her plan or not. It wouldn't surprise me if Mikhail was going off-book. He has never been one to follow strict orders. Growing up the spoiled only son of a maniac will do that to you. But Francia is inscrutable.

It doesn't matter. She'll die either way. Just like him.

I meet her eyes as I speak to Mikhail, my words slow and even. "I'm going to say this once, so you better listen."

"God, you really think you control us all, don't you?" he snarks. "You are not my—"

"If Cora screams like that again at any point between now and the end of time, I am going to burn your world to the ground."

Mikhail has gone quiet. Francia's lips purse, but she refuses to break eye contact with me. She knows as well as I do that the power balance between us is in flux. She has the upper hand now, but she'll have to maintain it.

And I plan to make her fucking work for it.

"She isn't yours anymore," Francia spits, a hard edge to her voice.

"I'm not saying this because she's mine," I explain to them both. "This is because you made me an oath. Cora lives. Period. If you fail to fulfill your promise, I'll kill you both."

She arches a brow. "I guess you've always been a softie for women suffering, haven't you? Your sister, Katerina…"

I don't react. Tossing out Katerina's name is her way of pushing me off-balance. But I'm immovable.

Soon enough, I'll kill her and Mikhail. I'll wipe every last Sokolov off the face of the earth. I'll get Cora back and I'll spend the rest of my life making this up to her.

Until then, the game is on.

Francia blows out a casual breath. "Well, I guess we're all done here. Unless there's anything left you want to discuss...?"

I don't respond, but she carries on anyway.

"I'll take your silence as a 'no.' So that's that. I'll be at your place in"—she checks her watch—"an hour? I guess it's *our place* now, isn't it?"

Fuck, no. Never.

"That will take some getting used to." She smiles and reaches out. Her hand strokes the air over my arm, not comfortable enough to touch me just yet. "For both of us."

I step back, putting more space between us. "Don't forget the details of our arrangement. You'll have your wing. I'll have mine."

She rolls her eyes, but keeps a fake smile on her face. "I'll be home in an hour. I have a few things to pack up first. Are you going to be there to carry your new bride over the threshold?"

"I'll be there to watch," I say flatly. "And unless you manage to break both your legs in the next hour, I'm sure you can walk in by yourself."

Francia's face is tight, but she forces out a laugh. "See you soon, darling."

"Too soon," I mutter.

If she hears me, she doesn't show it. She sashays down the hallway and leaves me alone, my knuckles white around her phone.

6

CORA

I don't even have tears to blink back.

The storm of faith and fears and courage and doubt that has raged through me for hours is suddenly quiet... which, in a weird way, is the worst feeling of all.

"I almost preferred when you had a little hope," Mikhail comments. "It was more interesting."

I look up. Mikhail is watching me with a pout. He looks like a child staring down at the ruined tangle of their Slinkie. He's destroyed my hope and I've destroyed his sadistic fun. The two offenses don't seem anywhere close to equal, as far as I'm concerned.

"Ah, well. Onward and upward."

He walks around my chair and fiddles with the chains on my wrist. When he sees my cuts, he winces and pokes at the raw, oozing skin. It takes everything in me not to cry out in pain again.

"That's gross. You should really clean that up before it gets infected. I have a lot of big plans for you." Suddenly, his breath is hot against my ear. "Many of which involve your hands."

The thought of whatever else Mikhail has planned is enough to make me hurl. "If you don't get me something to eat soon, there won't be anything left of me, big plans or not."

The chain around my wrist clatters to the ground. As soon as I'm free, I clutch my hands to my chest. I don't need to look at the damage to know it's there. The cool air hisses against the exposed flesh like rubbing alcohol. If I look down, I might pass out. And I don't dare to be that vulnerable with Mikhail.

"Patience," he croons, walking around my chair to face me again. "I'm taking you home."

Home? For one solitary second, I think he means my home. Ivan's home. Then that fairytale fractures into a thousand, razor-sharp pieces.

"Do you mean… Do you have a house? I thought the Sokolov estate was where all of you lived together."

Maybe that would be for the best. Mikhail's rotten apple did not fall far from his daddy's fucked-up tree, but if we are surrounded by Mikhail's younger sisters and the household staff, maybe that'll at least keep him from going completely and totally apeshit. If nothing else, it'll be nicer accommodations than this foul, cobwebby dungeon.

Without warning, Mikhail grabs me by the elbow and hauls me onto shaky legs. He doesn't grab me by my wrists, which is the only mercy he has shown me in… well, *ever.*

"As fun as it would be to take you home with me, I'm a man of tradition."

I frown up at him, waiting for understanding to click into place.

"I'm not taking you to my home," he explains. "I'm taking you to *yours*. I need your father's permission, after all."

There it is. Understanding. It clicks into place like the cocking of a gun.

"Alexander?" I rasp. "My… my parents? You're taking me to my parents."

Francia admitted she sold me out to my stepfather. I was just so distracted with everything else that I forgot.

Mikhail slides closer to me. Instinctively, I jerk back from him. But he holds me still with a strength that his thin arms shouldn't be capable of.

"Your mother and stepfather will be *so* happy to hear our big news," he drawls through clenched teeth. "They always loved me."

"They loved your *money*."

He shrugs. "Close enough."

"Don't you care about… about anything? They only want to work with you because you're rich. They don't even know you. Wouldn't you rather marry someone who actually loves you?"

I feel like a cornered gazelle pleading with a lion for my life. Even as I know it won't do any good. The same way I was raised to be prey—to stay quiet and obey—Mikhail was raised to be a predator. He is doing what he was taught.

"I'd rather marry someone who can give me what I want."

"Which is what, exactly?" I ask that as if I have anything at all I could give him.

He smiles and strokes a callused finger down my jaw. I turn away, but he forces my face back to his. "I want everything Ivan Pushkin has."

Any ember of hope that might have survived snuffs out.

I turn towards the door behind me. The place where Francia dragged Jorden. If she was still back there, we could have tried to fight Mikhail together. We could've tried to escape and—

It doesn't matter. It's impossible. Then and now.

Jorden is gone and I don't need to try anything to know that Mikhail isn't going to let me escape this time. More than that, my stepfather won't, either. I've fooled them all before. They won't sit back and let it happen again.

Mikhail brushes a thumb over my lower lip. I taste the salt from his fingertip. "Don't look so glum, Cordelia. I'll make sure you're taken care of."

"In exchange for what?" I ask. "I know you well enough to know nothing comes cheap."

He smirks. "All it will cost you is your worship."

I blink, stunned. "Pardon?"

"Treat me as your god," he says casually. "Whatever I say is gospel. Whatever I want, you give me. Live and die by my desires and I'll make sure you have every extravagance you could ever want."

Ivan. I want Ivan.

But I don't have to ask to know Mikhail will never give me that.

"If you don't..." He lets his voice trail off as his eyes scrape over my skin. Being under his gaze feels like lying naked on an exam table. He might as well be standing over me with a scalpel. "Well, as disappointed as I'd be to see it happen, you can be replaced, sweetheart."

"You can't kill me. That's what Ivan asked for, right?"

He snorts. "Ivan didn't ask for a fucking thing. He doesn't care what happens to you."

"Then why haven't you—?"

"Killed you?" Mikhail's hand slides to my throat. "Because I'm having too much fun. If you want to live, make sure it stays that way."

I swallow, my throat bobbing against his palm. I don't want to think about what Mikhail's version of "fun" looks like.

Then Mikhail drops his hand and steps back. "So you have a choice: come with me willingly and live. Or come with me unwillingly and die."

Not much of a choice. But in this world of prey and predator, I shouldn't be surprised. All we can do is play the roles we've been given. No matter how hard I fight or how fast I run, this is where I always end up. This is the choice in front of me.

And I'm so, so tired.

I lower my head and nod softly. "Okay."

"What?" Mikhail calls loudly. "I couldn't hear you."

I look up at him. The words lodge in my throat, and I have to force them out. "I'll come with you. Willingly."

A slow smile spreads across Mikhail's face. He brushes my cheek with his cold, clammy hand. "Now, *that's* a good girl."

Mikhail leads me through the side door where Jorden was taken and out into the alley, where a car with tinted windows awaits us. He opens the door and pushes me into the backseat with a hand on my head. Then he pauses for a moment with an easy smile smeared across his face. "Things are finally going to work out the way they were always supposed to, Cordelia."

He slams the door closed, leaving me alone. I see him standing outside on the phone, but I can't hear anything. It's a good thing. I need these quiet moments to focus on my situation. To sort out the jumble of panicked thoughts in my head.

No one is coming to save me. That much is stupidly clear by now. So if I want to get out of this and rescue Jorden, I have to figure out how to save myself.

When I do, I'm going to escape this city—this life—and start over. There's nothing and no one here for me.

Everything I loved has been taken.

7

IVAN

Once Francia leaves, I'm tempted to drop her phone on the tile floor and crush it. If I can't break her, this worthless piece of shit is the next best thing.

Then I hear voices.

Distant, tinny voices, coming through the phone's speaker.

I look down at the screen and see that the call is still connected. Slowly, I raise it to my ear. My entire body tenses when Mikhail's voice cuts through the silence.

"So you have a choice," Mikhail is saying to someone else. His voice is soft. He must not be holding the phone to his mouth anymore. "Come with me willingly and live...or come with me unwillingly and die."

He isn't stupid enough to kill Cora. Not after the threat I made.

But she doesn't know that.

There's a long pause. I hold my breath as the seconds pass, waiting to hear the fire in Cora's voice. Ready to hear her tell Mikhail exactly where he should shove his threats.

Instead, she responds in a voice so shattered, it's a wonder the phone is even able to catch the pulverized pieces. "Okay."

"What?" Mikhail barks back. "I couldn't hear you."

He's not going to be able to hear anything when I rupture his eardrums. The fucker. Kidnapping her, threatening her, and then demanding enthusiasm as she bends to his will... I file this away as yet another reason why I won't offer him any mercy when the time comes. See how he likes begging with enthusiasm for a quick, painless end to his miserable life.

"I'll come with you," Cora rasps. "Willingly."

There is no fire in Cora now. Only icy resignation.

She has to know I'm coming for her. That I'd do anything to get her back. But unless she's putting on the performance of a lifetime, it doesn't sound like she has any hope of that.

Cora has given up on me.

But I'll never give up on her.

"Now, *that's* a good girl," Mikhail croons.

My entire body clenches against the false tenderness in his voice. I'm going to make him regret every threat. Every single word.

Voices are replaced with rustling and footsteps. They're on the move. My standards are so low that I'm just glad Cora isn't screaming.

"Things are finally going to work out the way they were always supposed to, Cordelia," Mikhail says.

A car door closes and then Mikhail's breath crackles through the phone's cheap speaker. "Wouldn't you agree, Ivan? Everything is happening just as it was supposed to."

I freeze. It wasn't an accident. He knew I was listening.

Motherfucker.

I hesitate. Maybe it would be better to make him think I never heard him. That his performance was for nothing.

In the end, I can't bite my tongue. "Everything will happen exactly as it's supposed to," I confirm. "But it hasn't happened yet. I'll let you know when it's time."

He chuckles. "You're right. It hasn't happened. Because I haven't tasted Cordelia yet."

My chest tightens with pent-up rage.

"I've waited for so long." Mikhail practically moans. "She'll be so fucking sweet. I bet she moans pretty, doesn't she? I bet she sounds delicious."

"Her name is Cora," I growl. "If you touch her, I'll—"

"You'll what? Tattle on me? Do you think Francia cares what I do to Cora? So long as she stays conscious, I've kept my word. Even then, Francia would be fine if I flayed her alive. She has a bit of a jealous streak. Be on the lookout for that."

My hand is shaking. "Don't fucking touch her."

"Where shouldn't I touch her? Specifically?" he asks, amusement dripping from every word. He wouldn't be so amused if he was standing in front of me. If he could see the murderous look on my face. "Should I avoid her tits? What about her ass? Oh, I know: I bet you want me to keep my fingers away from that sweet little cunt between her legs.

You want that all to yourself, I assume. You've always been territorial."

I've endured physical torture less painful than this. But if I let myself crack now, I'll never be able to piece myself together now. For the sake of this mission—for Cora—I have to keep it together.

"But Cordelia is no longer yours to claim," he tuts. "She never was. From the very beginning, the bitch was mine."

"When Cora had the choice, she ran from you. She didn't think twice."

He ignores me, carrying on like I didn't say a word. "And now, I have her back. Soon enough, I'll have her in every way imaginable. I'll break her until it's *my* name she screams when she comes. Until she can't even walk straight, let alone run back to you."

I should know better than to let this stupid, petty motherfucker get to me. But I'm seeing red. It takes every ounce of my restraint to stay quiet and let Mikhail prattle off his taunts and jeers.

"Are you finished?" I ask once the line goes quiet.

"No," he sneers. "I'll finish inside Cora later. But I'm done talking for now, if that's what you meant."

Fucking g'andon. "If you hurt her, you'll answer to me, Mikhail. And I'm—"

"What? You're breaking up," he lies. "I can't hear what you're—"

Then the line goes dead.

This time, I don't hesitate. I hurl Francia's phone against the wall. It shatters into pieces, taking a chunk of the wall with it.

But it isn't enough.

I roar, my voice echoing down the long corridor. I yank a fire extinguisher from its cradle, leaving a gaping wound in the drywall. I kick through a wooden door and rip an exposed air duct down from the ceiling.

I rage and destroy and break shit until my chest is heaving and there are so many cuts up and down my arms that I don't know where the imagined pain stops and the real pain begins.

Francia and Mikhail and whoever else is working with them are going to regret crossing me. I'll track them down. I'll chain them up. And only once I've emptied my near-bottomless rage on them will I give them the mercy of ending their lives.

8

CORA

The sun has no business shining on a day like today.

Golden light streams through the car's windows as Mikhail pulls into the long, familiar driveway I ran down years ago. It was nighttime the last time I was here. The windows on the front of the house were dark except for the one next to the front door. That lone light glowed, one single window like an open eye watching me flee down the driveway with nothing except what would fit in my ratty old backpack.

As I turned my back on Alexander McAllister's house, I swore to myself it would be for the last time.

But here I am again.

"Does it look how you remembered it?" Mikhail is grinning, watching me through the rearview mirror. "It's been a long time since you've been home. Your dad will be happy. He's missed you."

"Alexander isn't my dad."

Mikhail stretches an arm across the passenger seat and looks back at me. His nose wrinkles. "You could use a shower. And a change of clothes."

"Next time you kidnap someone and hold them captive, keep them at the Four Seasons then," I snap.

His eyes narrow for only a second. Then he chuckles. "Alexander will understand. As soon as you open your mouth, he'll know exactly why it looks like you were dragged through a sewer."

Mikhail climbs out of the car and comes around to the back door. He opens it, but I stay put.

I can't force myself to move. Can't bring myself to slide across the seat and closer to Mikhail. A single inch closer to the house I've spent years running from is an inch too far.

He looks in at me through the door, his smile gone. "You promised, Cordelia."

"Promised what?"

He arches a threatening brow. "You'd come willingly. If I have to force you, you won't like how things end up."

I don't think I'll like how things end up either way. But I slowly scoot my way across the seat and press my feet flat onto the pavement. I'm hungry and tired. The world spins as I stand up, my knees threatening to give way.

"Come on." Mikhail tugs on my arm. "We're running late."

"I thought Francia was in charge."

He stops and looks back at me. "No one is in charge of me."

He says it softly, as if he doesn't want anyone else to overhear. Probably because Mikhail and I both know he has never been in charge. His entire life has been him buckling under the leadership of his father. Now, it's Francia. Maybe Alexander. Perhaps both. He's a little fish in a sea full of sharks.

Which is why my true fear doesn't kick in until he opens the front door of my stepfather's house.

It smells exactly like I remember. Like bottled cinnamon and mint. My mom always loved potpourri. As a kid, I tried to eat a glittery decorative pinecone and shredded the roof of my mouth. I ate nothing but applesauce for a week.

The scent of it now makes me nauseous.

I only have a second to take in the staircase, the foyer, a glimpse of the den. Then Mikhail clicks his tongue in irritation. "This way." He yanks on my arm again, dragging me up the stairs towards Alexander's office.

The only time he ever asked me to meet in his office was when I was in trouble. Like the time I broke school dress code and wore a skirt that was half an inch too short. Or when I got caught sneaking out to meet a boy Alexander had not expressly approved of.

He wanted to control what I wore and who I spoke to. He wanted to groom me into the quiet, obedient pawn he needed.

Admittedly, he got close. But close isn't good enough. Not when it comes to crushing a human spirit.

Alexander left a little too much of my willpower intact. By the looks of it, he's fixing that mistake now.

Mikhail doesn't knock on the office door. He just yanks down on the handle and shoves it open. And that is how I see my stepfather for the first time in three years.

In the blink of an eye, the door is open and there he is, standing in the middle of his office and staring at me. His hair is a little thinner, but I can tell by the swoop in his bangs that he's trying to hide it. Otherwise, he looks the same. Dark suit, white collared shirt, clean-shaven face. It's like no time has passed at all.

Except his mouth is hanging open slightly. He looks almost as stunned to see me as I am to see him. Like he didn't really expect me to walk through this door today. Maybe he never truly thought he'd win one over on Ivan.

He quickly schools his expression into a much more familiar scowl. "You're late."

"Thank your daughter for that." Mikhail pushes me into the room and slams the door closed.

I look around in vain hope for my mom. Not that she would do anything to stop what's happening even if she was here, but I can't bring myself to give up the hope that she'll finally step up and be the mother I deserve.

I'm still trying to find my bearings and get my footing when Mikhail pushes me again. He hits my shoulder, shoving me towards the chair directly across from the desk in the middle of the room. I barely catch myself from falling.

"Idiot!" Alexander barks. "Careful with her."

Is that concern in his voice? Is he feeling protective of me? It would be the first time. But at this point, anything is possible.

"She's valuable," he continues in a placid drawl. "The more you beat her up, the less she's worth."

Ah. There it is. *Welcome home, Cordelia. Nothing has changed a bit.*

Mikhail shifts behind me and gathers my stringy hair in his hands. He lays it over my shoulder as I fight hard not to cringe away from his touch. "I just have to keep her alive."

"No, you just have to keep your fucking hands off of her."

"But she screams so pretty." Mikhail's fingers dance over my throat. "How could I not want to hear it all the time?"

My stepfather sighs. "You can hear it as much as you want once she is officially yours. Until then, hands off."

Finally, my brain unlocks. I clear my throat and lean forward. "But the wedding is—The wedding was called off. It was in the paper."

I wondered how he and my mother would handle my disappearance. Whether they'd call the police and organize a search or simply try to sweep it under the rug. In the end, there was a small correction issued in the society section of a paper no one under the age of seventy-five read.

I hoped that would be the end of it, but based on the way Alexander is looking at me now, I know exactly how wrong I was.

When I first walked into the room, Alexander studied me. His eyes roamed over me, calculating, checking to make sure all the pieces were accounted for.

Now, he looks directly into my eyes. A chill runs down my spine. "I did the best damage control I could, given the circumstances," he rasps. "But now, you are going to fulfill the commitment you made."

"I never made a commitment! *You* made one on my behalf."

"And he'll fulfill it," Mikhail chimes in. He moves around my chair to stand next to my stepfather, sneering down at me with pure contempt. "I've been clear since the very beginning, Cordelia: you were promised to me. You belong to me."

It's one thing when you have to sit and listen to a lunatic babble. But when everyone else starts agreeing with him? When person after person spouts the same story? It's hard not to feel crazy.

I turn back to my stepfather. "You can't be serious. My mom would never—"

"Your mother wants what is best for this family," Alexander snaps. "What is best for this family is for you to follow through with your commitments. You were young and wild before, but now, you're—well, older, if nothing else. And you're back. You're back and ready to fulfill your promise."

A desperate laugh squeezes out of my lungs. "You can't just rewrite history like this. I'm not some press release you can edit to your liking. You've got to be kidding."

"No one is laughing," Mikhail interjects.

"I am!" I raise a hand in the air. "I'm laughing my ass off. Because you must be insane to think I'm going to marry—"

A scream slices through the room and makes my blood run cold.

I whip around, trying to see where it's coming from. Then I see Alexander is holding his phone. "Who is that?" I ask. Even though some part of me already knows.

The screen goes black and he pockets his phone. I want to claw it out of his hands and scream into it. Can she hear me? Is she on the line or is it a recording?

"You've always lived under the delusion that you have a choice, Cordelia. You don't."

"Who was that?" I ask again. "Who was screaming?"

My stepfather's face creases. Faux concern is etched in the lines of his face. "Your little friend won't fare so well if you give us any more trouble."

"Jorden," I breathe.

They have Jorden.

Mikhail told me she was sold off to someone, but he didn't say who. It's not a stretch that she was sold to someone they know. Someone sick enough to send them clips of her screaming.

What did they do to make her scream like that?

My stomach twists. I want to drop to my knees, but I know it won't help. "Don't hurt her."

"I knew I'd need an insurance policy."

"Don't hurt her."

"Then don't make things difficult."

"What do you want from me?"

"What I've always wanted." He reaches out and plucks a strand of hair away from my face. "A quiet, obedient daughter."

Bile rises in my throat. I want to spit it at him. He deserves worse than that. But Jorden's scream is still echoing in my ears.

My decisions don't just affect me anymore. If I don't do what they ask, not only could I die, but I could take Jorden with me. I'd never forgive myself for that.

"Are you going to be a good girl and do as you're told?" he asks.

In the end, Alexander is right. I don't have a choice. I never have.

I lower my head and nod slowly.

He presses a kiss to the top of my head. "I always knew you'd come around."

9

CORA

I stumble out of Alexander's office on numb legs and move in a stupor down the hallway. As I pass by the front door, I pause. Just a moment. A half-step of hesitation.

Then I keep going.

There is no escape. Even if the opportunity arises and I can run through an unlocked door or slip through an open window, they have me by the throat.

They have Jorden.

So I duck my head and keep moving, plodding the well-worn path up the stairs to the second door on the right.

When I open the door, I see that my bedroom looks exactly the same as it did the day I left. Every book in its place on the little white shelf in the corner. Every necklace hanging from golden hooks on the wall. Every fuzzy, flower-shaped pillow on my bed.

It's all the exact fucking same.

Like none of the years in between ever happened.

Tears well in my eyes, and for the first time all day, I can't stop them. I press the door closed quietly and lean my forehead against the wood. Tears roll freely down my cheeks, though I choke down the sobs so they can't hear me fall apart.

It's not as if I've spent the last three years missing this room. Every second that I was forced to live in this house, the only thing I imagined was getting away.

But seeing it perfectly untouched—like they always knew I'd be coming right back—is just a little too much for me to process right now. The future has never looked so bleak.

I take a few deep breaths and let the tears stop on their own. I'd hate to get all cried out so early in this nightmare. I'm sure horrors aplenty await me.

I run a hand down the lime green paint on the walls, smiling sadly at Teenage Me's design aesthetic. My mom hated it.

"Alexander has an interior decorator," she argued when she saw the gallon of neon paint I came home with. "Let Jennette design your room. That way, it will match the rest of the house."

That was the problem: I didn't *want* this room to match the rest of the house. In here, I wanted to feel like I was a million miles away. Like I was in my own world. One where Alexander McAllister didn't exist. And when I couldn't pretend I lived somewhere else, I poured my feelings into journal after journal.

I drop down on my knees in front of the bookshelf. Tucked behind a row of *Babysitter's Club* books are three tattered diaries. I gingerly pull one out and flip open the cover.

The first entry doesn't have a date or a greeting. It's just chicken scratch penmanship blurred in places by little drops of water. I must've been crying when I wrote it.

I have no clue who would choose to live in this hell. My mom is brainwashed and no one seems to see what is happening to me. Alexander is making me break up with Trent because his family isn't nice enough. His dad is a dentist! His mom works at our school. I don't even know what that means. "Nice enough?" Before Mom met Alexander, we weren't "nice enough," either. We were living on the streets. Mom and I ate at soup kitchens. Does Alexander know that? Maybe I should tell him. Maybe then he'd kick us out. I'd rather eat garbage than spend one more night around his fancy dining room table.

When I close my eyes and focus, I can see Trent's face. He was a blonde-haired, blue-eyed boy on the lacrosse team. He had acne and a scruffy goatee, but I thought he looked like a Calvin Klein model. I was in love.

When I asked my mom if I could meet Trent at the movies, Alexander took one look at Trent's last name and shook his head.

"You aren't going anywhere with him."

I turned to my mom for backup, but she wouldn't look at me. Sometimes, I knew she disagreed with my stepdad, but she was too scared to say anything.

I flip through the journal, reading entry after entry of me pouring my heart out on paper. There were moments of levity. Brief glimpses of the life I managed to eke out for myself amidst Tsar Alexander's tyranny. But mostly, I prayed for a good man. One who was bigger and stronger than Alexander and would take me away.

"You're wasting your ink," I mumble to my past self.

The only reason I got out of this mess the first time is because I left all on my own. No man ever showed up to whisk me into the sunset.

Ivan came close, though.

The thought of him has tears pressing against the backs of my eyes again, and I fight them back. Ivan is gone. He isn't coming back.

As soon as the thought crosses my mind, I hear someone in the hall. Just like that, I change my tune. *Ivan. He's here. I'm being rescued.*

Then the door opens and it's Mikhail.

That ought to teach me to pin my hopes to pipe dreams. But somehow, I doubt it. My heart has always been a little too tender for this world.

Mikhail wrinkles his nose and looks around. "Remind me not to let you make any design decisions."

"I was a teenager." I casually close my journal, trying not to bring too much attention to it. The last thing I need is my heartfelt words in the hands of Mikhail Sokolov. He has enough of me in hand as it is.

"It doesn't matter," he says. "You won't be here long anyway. Your dad and I were just talking."

My jaw clenches, my molars grinding together.

Alexander is *not* my dad. But my correction would fall on deaf ears, so I swallow it down and practice suffering through Mikhail's bullshit in silence. I'll be doing a lot of that, it seems.

"I found you a year ago, you know?"

I snap my attention to him, eyes laser focused. "No, you didn't."

"You dropped four letters from your name, Cordelia. You didn't flee the country. Of course I found you."

It sounds so stupid when he says it like that. I thought I could escape.

"I thought... I thought you found me because of Ivan. Because of the party and—"

"I found you way before that," he scoffs. "And when I saw the dingy shithole you were living in, I was positive you'd come crawling back."

He's wrong to call it a shithole. Sure, my little studio wasn't in a great part of town, and yes, I had to caulk around the pipes in the bathroom so my neighbor couldn't watch me through the gap, but it wasn't a shithole. It was modest. Affordable.

It was freedom.

Or at least, that's what I thought then. Now, I see it for what it really was: a delusion.

"I don't get it," I whisper. "Why did you wait for me? Why spend all of this energy on me? Your daddy could have picked another bride for you."

Mikhail's lip curls up in barely-restrained rage. "Because you were *promised* to me, Cordelia. And I always get what I deserve."

What he deserves is a ride down a slide made of razor blades into a pool full of lemon juice, but I bite my tongue and meet his eyes. If I have to figure out how to live in this world, I'm not going to spend my days staring at the ground.

If they want to hold my prisoner, they'll have to look me in the eyes.

"I had no idea I was such a prize," I drone. "Seems like you'd want a wife who is more interested in interior design and pretty dresses."

He sighs. "That would be the easier choice. Fuck knows plenty of women have offered themselves up. I sampled many of them. But they didn't hold my attention."

"Is it because they were willing? Consent can be so boring." The question sounds innocent, but I can tell by the flex in Mikhail's jaw that he knows I'm goading him.

He kneels down in front of me and grips me hard by the chin. "When I was twelve, my dad took me hunting. It's a Sokolov tradition. Our family's yearly excursion. To reconnect with nature, earn our place in the hierarchy of things. All that bullshit."

I try to turn away, but he holds tighter. His face is so close to mine that I feel his every exhale on my skin.

"The first year, I went all day without hitting a single target. Just before sunset, my father shot a coyote in the leg. Once it was crippled and unable to move, he let me shoot it in the head." He sighs. "When they asked me if I wanted the animal stuffed and mounted for my room—"

"And you complain about my design choices," I mutter.

His mouth ticks up in a flash of amusement before he continues. "I declined. It didn't feel right. I didn't earn it. But the next year… the next year was mine. I tracked a herd of elk for hours. And when my father warned me against taking my shot, telling me it was too risky, I pulled the trigger. And I went home with the biggest kill anyone in our family had bagged in decades."

"Am I supposed to be impressed?"

Mikhail's eyes flare for a second. Then I'm snatched off the floor and thrown flat against the wall. His hand is banded around my throat so tightly I can't breathe. Black dots form on the edges of my vision.

"I don't need you to be impressed," he growls. "I don't need anyone to shoot you in the leg and cripple you for me, Cordelia. Because I've tracked you down. I've cornered you. And whether you like it or not, you're going to be the prettiest fucking trophy I've ever caught."

I stretch onto my toes, straining for air. For just a single breath.

Just as I feel my eyes rolling back in my head, Mikhail lets go.

I slide down the wall, gasping. But he doesn't let me get far. Before I can fall to the carpet, he pins me to the wall with his body. I feel every inch of how much he's enjoying this moment against my thigh.

"I waited for you, Cordelia," he whispers harshly, "because I don't want a half-dead coyote. I don't want some simpering, easy whore who has been delivered to me on a silver platter. I want to work for it."

"First time for everything," I rasp.

His body shoves even closer to mine as he glares down at me. "One day, you're going to give me everything I want. You're going to hand it to me with a smile on your face. And that's when I'll know I've won. But until then…" He slides his hand down my waist and grips my hip. "… I'll take what I can get."

The reality of what he's going to do slams down on me like a cartoon anvil hanging over my head.

Mikhail is going to rape me.

Here and now, in my childhood room, he is going to rape me.

With rough hands, he hitches my leg over his hip and grinds into me with painful thrusts. His teeth scratch across my neck and my collarbone hard enough that I'm sure he's drawing blood.

"I thought you wanted to earn it," I gasp, doing my best to hold him off.

He fists my shirt in his hands. I hear stitches popping. "I will. I'm going to."

"Then don't take it now."

I'm about to black out with panic. I can feel my mind slipping away, tucking into some secret, safe space in my brain. I can't fight him, so I have to get through this. I have to grit my teeth and bear it.

But Mikhail's grip loosens.

I peek an eye open. I wouldn't say it is remorse on his face, but it's a new expression I haven't seen before. And I jump on it.

"If you're so sure you're going to win me over, then wait," I say, breathless. "You've waited this long. Give it some more time."

He huffs in frustration. "I've been too patient."

"Doing this now will only make things harder. I'll... I'll never forgive you."

He looks down at me, and I can see in his pale eyes that he really thinks there's a chance I won't always hate him. The psychopath thinks he has a shot at winning me over one day.

That scrap of insanity is scarier than anything else that has happened so far.

He lets me go and steps back. There's a bulge at the front of his pants that I pointedly ignore.

"Remember this," he says. "Remember that I... I controlled myself. I waited."

Like fuck he did. The only reason he isn't raping me right now is because I stopped him.

But I stay quiet and nod. "Okay."

He reaches out and cups my cheek. His palm is clammy against my skin, and I want to cringe away. But I don't. I need him to believe there's hope.

"You're right. The wait will make it so much better, Cordelia." He drops his hand and backs away. He stops in the doorway, his eyes trailing over me one last time. "I'll see you soon."

The moment he is gone and the door closes, I drop to the floor.

All the panic I bottled up and shoved down comes racing to the surface. I cry into my sleeve and bite back loud, heaving sobs.

I knew there was a good reason I was saving my tears.

After what could be minutes or an hour, I shift to my knees and crawl back to my bookshelf.

The journals aren't the only things I kept hidden. I pull out several books from the first shelf and run my hands along the underside of the wood. After a few swipes, I feel it. Just where I left it.

I peel off the brittle tape and a weight lands in my palm. I close my hand around the polished wood handle.

I stole this letter opener from Alexander's office years ago. It was the only weapon-like thing in the house I knew he'd never miss.

I take a practice swipe through the air, imagining the thin blade slipping into Alexander's carotid or jabbing between Mikhail's legs.

It's not much, but I know now that no one is coming to save me. No one is going to get me out of this. All of the tears I shed and letters I wrote didn't do a damn thing.

I'm no princess and there is no happy ending waiting for me. It's just me versus the world I left behind.

So I might as well be armed.

10

IVAN

The shades are pulled down over the glass door and a "Closed" sign hangs in the window. Still, I knock.

There's a security camera hanging just above the door. I know I'm being watched, but I don't look at it. I don't need to. Because the door will open for me in three, two, one…

"Mr. Pushkin!" Kieran's voice is muffled by the glass as he fumbles frantically with the shades and the lock. "I didn't realize you were coming in today. You didn't call. I would have had the door open and unlocked if you'd—"

He opens the door. "Hello," he repeats, beaming at me with the smile he reserves for his highest-paying customers.

I tilt my head in greeting. "Kieran."

"I would have had the shop ready for you if you'd called ahead. Where is your lady? Is she with you or—" He looks past me to the sidewalk. Then his eyebrows jump. "Or is this a surprise for her?"

His words land like a fucking knife to the gut. I remind myself that Kieran doesn't know. Of course he has no idea what just happened. He can't fathom the guilt and rage tearing through me right now.

Which is why I clench my fist at my side instead of wrapping it around his throat.

"I'm alone and I need a favor."

Kieran must pick up on the shaky control I have on my temper because he steps aside immediately and ushers me inside.

The shop is dark, but the little bit of sunlight coming through the blinds glints off the gold edges of the display cases. I can almost close my eyes and see Cora standing in this shop mere weeks ago.

She thinks I chose her gaudy engagement ring that day as punishment, but it was because that larger-than-life jewel was the only thing in this entire shop that could even begin to complement her the way she deserved. A beautiful woman needs a beautiful ring. Which means Cora deserves a fucking planet made of diamond.

Kieran flicks on a light. The memory dims and fades.

"I hope nothing serious is wrong," he says with a frown. "If there's trouble with your ring, you know I will do everything to keep my best customers happy. Whatever you need—a rush job or a replacement jewel—I'm happy to—"

"I need you to hold onto this for me."

I place the ring I just snatched off of Francia's finger into Kieran's palm.

His eyes widen. "Does your fiancée not like it? If she is unhappy, then I can make something else. A custom order. No cost."

My fiancée is almost certainly unhappy. But not for any reason Kieran could possibly imagine.

"I just need you to hold onto it for me," I tell him. "I need you to keep it hidden and tell absolutely no one I was here."

Kieran closes his fist around the ring and nods. "Of course. Anything, Mr. Pushkin. I'll keep it in my safe. I'm the only one who knows the combination."

"Good."

"Do you know how long you want me to keep it?" he inquires.

Until I can slide it back on the finger where it rightfully belongs.

"Not long," I tell him. "It'll be any day now."

I can only hope it's the truth.

Just as I climb back into the car, my phone rings. Yasha's name flashes on the screen.

"Has Jorden said anything useful yet?" I ask when I answer.

"She's still unconscious, but I'll let you know," Yasha replies. "Have you murdered Francia with your bare hands yet?"

"Not quite, but I have a lifetime of opportunity ahead of me. I'll let you know."

He curses under his breath. "I can't believe you're going to marry that bitch. I should have seen her coming. Why the fuck didn't I see her coming?"

I've asked myself the same question over and over again. "We got distracted."

I'm sure that was Francia's plan. She sent Cora and Jorden to my party hoping I'd pay attention to one of them. That was her way in… and I fell for it—for Cora—hook, line, and sinker.

Yasha sighs. "Jorden trusted her. Cora did, too. I never even thought to look."

"Feel free to make up for lost time and find out everything you can about her then. I'd like to know the woman I'm in bed with."

There's a pause. "You aren't actually going to get into bed with her, are you?"

Just the thought makes me cringe. "Fuck no," I snarl. "She is going to have her own wing of the house. I might even put a brick wall up between us. No love. No fucking."

"You should have killed her," he grumbles. "I mean, I know it wasn't an option. But I wish it was."

"You and me both." I sigh wearily. I've never felt more exhausted in all my life. "Do you have an ETA on when Jorden might wake up?"

"Not yet. She'll be okay, though," he says. "Dr. Popov said she needed stitches and she's concussed, but the only reason she's asleep is because she's tired and dehydrated. As soon as she gets some rest and fluids, she'll be fine. She might have information."

That would be a lucky fucking break. But if the last twenty-four hours have taught me anything, it's to not hold my breath.

"Oh, and, um…" It's not normal for Yasha to sound nervous, but he's clearly beating around the bush right now. "Popov also mentioned that Jorden is going to need, like, a guardian. Or someone to watch her. You know, since she has the concussion. So I thought—"

"Stay with her."

"Really?" He sounds astonished. "Because there is so much going on. I totally get that I'm needed back at the base. You'll be busy with Francia, so someone has to keep the search alive. I can do a lot from the medical bay, but I could do more if I was there on the ground. So if you want me—"

"I want you to stop talking. I told you to stay with Jorden, so stay with her." It's the meanest I've ever sounded while delivering good news. "If she wakes up and has information, I want it as quickly as possible."

What I don't say is that I saw the way Yasha cradled Jorden in that alleyway. I heard the way he snapped at me for being too rough with her.

It's the same way I would have snapped at him when it comes to Cora.

Yasha has never been in love before, but I think Jorden might be changing that. And as cold and unfeeling as I am, I don't want to be what stands between Yasha and the woman he loves. Especially when I don't think there is much Yasha can do to help me right now.

Where Francia is concerned, I'm on my own.

"Okay," he says. "Thank you. I'll stay here and handle whatever. Anything you need, I'm available. I'll look into Francia and see what I can dig up. But what else is there? What's your plan?"

That's a great question. All I've done so far is react to the situation in front of me.

Francia disappeared, so I went to look for her.

Cora was kidnapped, so I rushed to save her.

Francia threatened Cora, so I did what I had to do to keep her alive.

Now, finally, it's my turn to make the first move. And there is only one thing that makes sense.

"We find Cora."

Yasha sighs. "Yeah. That's what I want, too, man, but... I have to be honest, I don't know how to do that. Francia slipped under all of my radars. We had an inkling the Sokolovs were involved, but I never picked up on Mikhail specifically playing a role in all of this. And Cora's stepdad has been elusive. Alexander McAllister never came up on any of my searches. If he's working with Mikhail again, they could be hiding Cora anywhere. I don't know where to start."

"The usual suspects won't be of any help. Mikhail has obviously kept his part in all of this quiet, so there won't be any rumblings about it in the usual places. And we can't march into Konstantin Sokolov's office without warning again."

Especially if what I did to help Katerina escape has made its way back to Konstantin. He will not be pleased with me after hearing that news.

"So we go to a new source," I continue. "To the person who will have more dirt on Cora's mom and stepdad than anyone else."

"Who would that be?" he asks.

"Cora's father."

11

IVAN

"No."

I'm not often stunned, but hearing my house manager defy a direct order is stunning. There's no other way to put it.

"Excuse me?"

Niles lifts his chin. "I said... I said no, sir. I respect you, Mr. Pushkin. Deeply. But I will not work for *that woman.*"

I know he remembers Francia's name. Niles never forgets a damn thing. So if he's not using her name, it's for a very good reason. Probably because saying it three times might summon her like Beetlejuice.

While I was negotiating with Francia, talking to Mikhail, and leaving Cora's ring with Kieran, Yasha called to fill Niles in on the last twenty-four hours. Apparently, the man took the news of Francia's betrayal about as well as the rest of us.

I sigh. "If I could have Cora back here right now, I'd..."

Well, I'd lock her in my room and never let her out. I'd tangle her in my sheets and wrap her in my arms and we'd never come up for air. Niles would have full run of the mansion. He'd never have to take care of me again because I'd be extremely well cared for.

But instead of all that, I say simply, "This is what I have to do to make things right."

His teeth click together so hard the soft line of his jaw quivers. "She betrayed Ms. Cora. This woman you're bringing in here hurt my mistress." His face flushes. He's embarrassed by his own devotion to Ms. Cora, but that doesn't stop him. "I won't lift a finger to serve anyone who hurt Ms. Cora. That woman could be on fire and I wouldn't bother to spit on her."

"Holy shit," I snort, biting back a laugh. "And I thought what you said about Konstantin Sokolov after his first visit here was bad."

Niles' hesitant smirk dissolves into a deep frown. "That man hung his jacket on my head like I was a coat rack. When I corrected him, he apologized with a one-dollar bill. They can both share a room in hell."

Niles knew in two minutes what it took my father until... well, until never to realize: the Sokolovs are not to be trusted.

I know he's once again right about Francia.

But that doesn't change what has to be done.

"I don't want to deal with Francia in my house any more than the rest of you. I'm the one who has to fucking marry her. If she is ever on fire, I'm probably the one who lit the match."

His brow furrows in concern. "There has to be a way out of it. You deserve better than her. You deserve…"

His voice trails off, but we both know what he was going to say.

Cora.

I'm flattered he thinks so. The trouble is, after the fuck-ups I've made the last couple days, I'm not so sure Cora deserves me.

She deserves safety. Protection. Things I can no longer offer her.

"What any of us may or may not deserve doesn't matter. Francia is moving in today. That is the decision I made. Now, I need you and everyone else to figure out how to make it work."

Niles stiffens. I see his sense of loyalty fighting against his honor. He really might rather quit outright than serve Francia.

Then, finally, his stiff posture relaxes just a fraction of an inch. "I'll do my best, sir."

"Your best has been good enough so far." I clap him on the shoulder and turn towards the door. "Help her get settled and—"

"She can't stay in Cora's room," Niles interrupts. "She can live in this house if you allow her to, but I will not put her in my mistress's room. Not after what she has done."

His loyalty is a testament. To Cora's influence, but also to the man himself. The old coot will have a home in my Bratva for as long as he wants it.

"She'll sleep in the East wing," I agree. "I'll leave it to you to choose her room."

Finally, Niles shows a sign of amusement. Whatever he has planned for Francia, I know she won't like it.

But all work and no play isn't good for my household staff.

I'll let them take their vengeance where they can.

I make sure I'm not around when Francia arrives. I hear the crunch of wheels on the pavement outside and the shuffle of movement deep in the house, but I stay in my office. She can carry her own ass across the threshold. Fuck knows I'm not going to do it.

The only time I'll carry Francia anywhere is to an exit. Preferably in a body bag.

As the minutes tick past, my fingers itch to do something. To stay busy. I want to text Yasha about anything he may have found out about Marcus St. Clair in the ninety minutes since we spoke, but I know it's too soon for that. Besides, I don't want to do anything that Francia could walk in and see. The bitch doesn't need any more leverage.

So I dig through my top drawer and find the Save the Date mock-ups Anya sent me last week. Actually, she dropped them unceremoniously on top of my laptop and said, "Pick your favorite."

I swiped them away. "I can't."

"Yes, you can," she complained. "Testosterone may make you an unbearable asshole, but it does not make you incapable of having an opinion about design. So pick your favorite and then I'll tell you if you're right."

I stacked them up and handed them back to her. "My favorite is the one you choose for me."

She'd love to walk through my office door and see me flipping through them now. Unfortunately, when my door opens, it isn't my sister in the doorway.

"This is ridiculous!" Francia shrieks.

I keep my eyes down. The first Save the Date looks like the announcement for a baby's baptism. There are winged cherubs and laurel branches and cartoon white roses around the edges. I loathe it.

I slide it to the back of the stack and study the next one.

"What's ridiculous?" I drawl with as little concern as humanly possible. It's easy, because I truly do not care.

She stomps into the room, her heels clicking across the hardwood floor. "I told you when I'd be here."

I glance at the clock hanging on the wall. "You did. You're very punctual. Good for you."

I don't need to look at her to feel the heat of her glare searing into the side of my face.

The second Save the Date template looks like it's for a destination wedding. Too much blue and gold. Cora and I have never been to a beach together and we wouldn't get married on one. I slide it to the bottom of the stack.

"I told you when I'd be here," she repeats, the words practically vibrating out of her. "But no one met me at the door. Your butler left my bags—"

"House manager."

An exhale hisses between her teeth. "What?"

"Niles is the house manager." He already hates Francia, so he might turn homicidal if she refers to him as my "butler."

"Well, your house manager hasn't managed a fucking thing since I've been here! He left my bags in the driveway and showed me to a broom closet instead of a bedroom. It was barely big enough for a twin-sized mattress! This is absurd."

I bite back a smile. Niles really is a gutsy son of a bitch. I know exactly which room she's talking about. It actually was a broom closet, at one point. The thought of Francia sleeping with the spiders and cleaning product is exactly the kind of mood boost I needed today.

Then Francia snatches the stack of Save the Dates out of my hand.

"Your staff is treating me like trash and you can't even look at me. What are you going to do about this?"

Any whisper of a smile is gone from my face now. I turn towards her slowly, looking at her for the first time since she barged into my office. And my blood is fucking *boiling*.

The fact that sometime in the last hour Francia decided to dress in a full evening gown, diamond earrings and an up-do included, is not helping matters. Does she think we're heading to our wedding today or does she dress like the Queen of England every afternoon?

"I told you you'd be sleeping in another wing of my house. You agreed to—"

"I didn't know you expected me to squeeze myself into a fucking shoebox! I saw Cora's room," she snaps. "I *know* there are bigger rooms here. I want to stay in one of those."

The last time Francia was inside my house was when she was lying to all of our faces. If only I'd known who she really was then, I would have killed her on sight. No hesitation.

"All of the main bedrooms are in the West wing of the house. You are staying in the East wing."

"Then put me on the West side," she grits out. "I'm not sleeping on a twin mattress like some peasant brat at summer camp."

"Then don't sleep."

Hang upside down like the life-sucking vampire you clearly are.

She inhales sharply. "Despite this morning, I wanted today to be pleasant."

And I want Cora to be standing in front of me, whole and unharmed, while Francia's head is mounted on a spike in my front lawn.

"We don't always get what we want."

She leans forward, eyes wide. "*I* do. And I want the room Cora had."

"No."

The air between us ripples with tension, but neither of us break eye contact. "All it takes is one phone call," she whispers. "One text. And Cora is gone."

I fucking hate that Francia's threat tempers the rage boiling inside of me, but how can it not? Cora is in danger. I have to act to keep her safe. That means denying myself what I want more than anything—to have Francia's hot blood dripping down my hands while she gasps for her last breath—and sticking to the plan.

"You can't sleep in Cora's old room because it's not tradition."

She frowns. "But Cora—"

"Was never my real fiancée. You are." It's a lie disguised as the truth. Cora was closer to being my wife than Francia will ever be. Even if I do have to go through with an actual wedding with her, I will never care about her in the ways that count.

"What does that have to do with anything?"

"It means that we have to do things the right way," I tell her. "Or as right as possible under these circumstances. We can't cohabitate until the wedding."

She snorts. "This isn't the Dark Ages. And I know you are no saint. Plenty of women have 'cohabitated' with you."

"None of them have ever lived with me."

Until Cora.

Which is why I won't let Francia prance around my house and play Housewife. That role is reserved for one woman and one woman only.

"I'm not going to be disrespected by your staff and you. If I want to sleep in whatever room I want, then—"

"Then you'll be breaking the agreement you made."

Her mouth closes slowly. "How?"

"You agreed to fulfill the role of a Bratva wife," I remind her. "That means submitting to all of my desires. Right now, I desire tradition."

She wants to argue, but she knows I'm right.

I reach out and pluck the Save the Dates out of her hand and drop back down into my chair.

She watches me flip through the stack for a few seconds before she lets this battle go and forces lightness into her voice. "Already prepping for the big day?"

If by "big day" she means the day that I get to obliterate her from the planet and be with the woman I actually care about, then…

"Yes," I tell her. "I'm looking forward to it."

12

CORA

I wake up to silence. No one is standing over me with an ax and a ghoulish smile. No one is dangling my best friend's fate in my face. No one bursts in and rips my curtains open and orders me here and there.

That all comes as somewhat of a surprise.

Half of my night was spent tossing and turning, imagining the torture that was waiting for me in the morning. Would Mikhail come back and try groping me again? Maybe I'd wake up with Alexander sitting on the edge of my bed, stroking my hair away from my forehead like a stepdad from a *Dateline* episode.

But there's nothing. Just the sound of birds singing outside my window.

"We fucking get it," I mumble at the sparrows, rolling over and pulling the covers over my head. "You're happy. Don't rub it in."

I stay buried under the covers for as long as I can until finally, I sigh and get up. I didn't bring any clothes with me, but someone clearly prepared for my arrival. All of my favorite clothes from high school are still hanging in my closet. But next to those is a stash of brand new items with tags attached. They're all in my current size. One pair of jeans, a few t-shirts, and hanger after hanger after hanger of demure, girlish dresses.

I try not to think about what it means that someone bought these clothes, knowing I'd be held prisoner here. Whoever it was had some skewed expectations. No way I'm pulling a June Cleaver and showing up to breakfast in a floral print dress. If that's what Alexander wants, he better get out his lobotomy equipment.

But even prisoners need to eat. So after I steel myself for whatever my captors have waiting for me, I creep down the stairs towards the kitchen for something to eat. Coffee, at least.

I don't see anyone in the sitting room and I can't hear any voices. Maybe if I'm lucky, I'll pour myself a cup of coffee and grab a banana without being seen. A few more hours alone in my room sounds nice.

But luck hasn't been on my side recently. Actually, Lady Luck has been a stone-cold bitch who seems to get her shits and giggles from kicking me when I'm already way down.

So I guess I shouldn't be surprised that, the moment my toes touch the hardwood floor of the entryway, my name is called from the dining room.

"Cordelia," Alexander says like he has been expecting me. "We're in here."

I don't know who "we" is, but I don't want to be included in the group. It is firmly Me versus Them.

Caffeine-less and stomach growling, I stand tall and walk into the dining room.

Then my past wallops me over the head with a chair.

"Mom…"

My mom is here. She'll save me.

Except my mom is wearing a string of pearls around her throat that might as well be a dog collar. She looks at me with a pleasant smile on her face. No concern. No fear. She just smiles at me blankly, like some kind of robot hand-programmed by a psychopath.

After the hellish twenty-four hours I've had, there isn't a mother in the world that would do anything but run to their kid and hold them in their arms.

But my mother doesn't move.

She isn't going to help me do a goddamn thing.

I clear my throat and try to take in the rest of the room through the sheen of tears. "Good morning."

Alexander smiles and gestures for me to take the seat next to him. The seat between him and Mikhail.

"It's a full house today," I mumble.

Mikhail stands up and pulls out my chair. "We've been waiting for you to start breakfast."

"No one told me. I slept in. Yesterday was… hectic. I needed the extra rest this morning."

He shoves my chair up to the table a little too hard. My ribs pinch against the edge and I have to slide away to catch my breath.

Without warning, Alexander claps his hands.

I jolt in surprise, but no one notices because the door to the kitchen opens and three maids hurry out carrying trays of fruit and pastries. Another has pitchers of milk and orange juice in her hands.

"Wow."

Alexander's smile slips. "What is so surprising? Was Ivan not feeding you breakfast?"

My mom is staring down at her lap and I get the sense I've done something wrong. But I'm not sure what.

"No, we had breakfast. I just don't remember there ever being a full kitchen staff here first thing in the morning. We always ate—"

"That's what happens when you don't keep in touch," he snaps. "Things change."

Yeah, and apparently, the main thing that must have changed is the number of zeroes in Alexander's bank account. When I last lived here, he would hire temporary staff to impress dinner guests. After that night, I'd never see them again. Now, there are three—no, *four* women dishing out sliced fruit and pouring glasses of milk.

Mikhail is looking from me to Alexander with a slightly puzzled furrow between his brows. Is this little show for *his* benefit?

Maybe my two co-abductors aren't as honest and open with each other as I thought.

I file the information away for later and grab a croissant from the center of the table. These people may be monsters, but nothing can get between me and a flaky pastry.

We eat in silence. Alexander waves his hand and requests a coffee refill. My mom picks at the three strawberries on her plate for fifteen minutes before she dares to grab a spoonful of blueberries for seconds.

The only time Mikhail says anything is to make a comment under his breath as I reach for my third croissant.

"You haven't had any fruit, Cordelia."

Without breaking eye contact, I pluck a banana off the table and peel it. He finally looks away when I wrap my lips around the tip of it.

I know I shouldn't play with fire. Not after what happened in my room yesterday. But after years of freedom, it hurts to feel the invisible chains around my wrists again.

Speaking of chains, I look over and see my mother staring wide-eyed at my wrist. At what her husband and Mikhail did to me.

I didn't exactly have access to a first aid kit last night, so I did my best with hand soap and bits of a washcloth I ripped into strips. They fell off while I was sleeping and I woke up with no bleeding, so I didn't bother covering them up. Now, I'm glad I didn't.

If my mother has deluded herself into thinking I'm here by choice, then hopefully, my scabbed-over injuries can be a wake-up call to her.

"Is something wrong, Mom?" I ask.

She blinks and looks towards Alexander in a panic. But he isn't looking at her—he's watching me.

Mikhail pushes my arm under the table and wraps his hand around my raw wrist. He squeezes the freshly-closed cuts until a whimper is forced out of my throat.

Then he chuckles to the rest of the table. "Cordelia has forgotten her manners while she was away."

"I hate how—" My mom stops and clears her throat. "I always hate the adjustment period after being away. The week after a vacation, I'm always a mess. It's hard to get back into a routine."

I've never had a great poker face. This moment is no different.

I just stare at my mom, mouth open because I can't believe what she just said.

Is she comparing me fleeing my home in the middle of the night and changing my name to protect myself from *her* husband... to a vacation?

I pick my jaw up off the floor and push away from the table. "Yeah, I agree. Such a strange transition. It's a bit of a culture shock to go from being your own person and having freedom to being forced into—"

"Cordelia!" My name rings across the table. Alexander doesn't quite have the bass necessary for his shout to be truly intimidating. Not the way Ivan can make it feel like the world around you is thundering without even raising his voice. But he gives it his best shot. It's enough to interrupt me mid-sentence.

My mother drops her eyes to the table. She has never looked less impressive to me. So small. So meek.

Before I left, I had some compassion for her. I viewed her like a person trapped in a cult. Someone with the best intentions who couldn't see the damage being inflicted around them.

But she can see it all now… and she's still here. Even when her own daughter is collateral damage.

I run my tongue over my teeth and turn to Alexander. "Yes?"

"I'd like to speak to you in my office," he grits out. "Now."

"I'm not finished eating."

I reach for another croissant, but Mikhail grabs my wrist again. He jerks my arm back and twists. We knock over a glass of juice and a bright orange stain spreads across the white tablecloth.

"Let her go," Alexander orders.

Mikhail squeezes harder. "I'll let her go when she shows me that she can behave herself. I might have to carry her in—"

"Let. Her. Go." There is no question in my stepfather's voice. No request.

It's an order.

And Mikhail follows.

He drops my arm and slowly settles his hand in his lap. But he doesn't take his eyes off of me.

Alexander walks to his office at a fast clip. I follow, feeling Mikhail's gaze on me the entire time.

Whether they know it or not, they just revealed a gaping crack in their facade. I make a mental note to poke at it later.

13

CORA

I walk into Alexander's office, but weirdly, it's empty. I'm just starting to turn around in confusion when the door slams closed behind me.

"Whoa. What the—" I whip around to see he's lurking next to the entrance like the boogeyman.

"You don't have a knack for details." He carves his way across the room towards his desk. "You are so focused on yourself that you don't see the larger picture."

I nod sarcastically. "You're right. I've been way too self-centered during my abduction. How are *you* doing?"

His upper lip curls. "You've never understood the stakes, have you, Cordelia? Do you think I *enjoy* making you hate me?"

The silence goes on for so long that I realize he actually wants me to answer.

"Yes," I say with a humorless laugh. "Yes, I do. I think you enjoy it very much."

He sits back, his hands folded in his lap. "You're wrong. You're wrong about everything."

"Then enlighten me!"

I'd love nothing more than for all of this to be some big misunderstanding. If Alexander revealed himself as the hero of this story and could justify all of his actions, I would be the first to shake his hand and ask for forgiveness.

But that isn't going to happen.

Sometimes, the villain is just the villain. Simple as that.

"I have to marry you to the Sokolovs to form an alliance between our families," he explains.

"Yeah, I gathered that much on my own. But thanks for the help."

His nostrils flare, but he carries on. "When this all started, you were so young. Your mother and I decided that marrying Mikhail Sokolov was the best thing for you. He would be able to take care of you and give you a comfortable life."

"I didn't want to marry him!"

"You didn't know what you wanted!" he snapped. "If I'd let you do what you wanted, you would have ended up a pregnant slut with no prospects."

I blink at him. "You're... you're kidding, right? I didn't even have my first kiss until I was eighteen!"

He leans in with a smile. "You're welcome. I kept you safe, Cordelia. The same way I protected your mother."

"Brainwashed my mother, you mean."

"Call it what you want, but the two of you were days away from eating out of a garbage can when I took you in," he snarls. "I vowed to take care of you both, so that is what I did. Mikhail was a good choice. But then you fucked everything up."

"I saved myself."

"You embarrassed the Sokolov family!" he roars. "Do you have any fucking idea how much damage you caused? I got you connected to the only son of one of the richest men in the city and you ran off on him."

I roll my eyes. "Then Mikhail's daddy should have found him another willing wifey. There were plenty who would've waltzed in with eyes open."

"Not for men like that." He shakes his head. "You embarrassed him. The only way to right the wrong was to get you back. If Mikhail wanted to recover his reputation, he needed you to come back on your knees."

"Yeah, well, don't count on it."

"You still don't—" He growls in frustration. "I was building a career before you threw everything away. When you disappeared, I had to start over from nothing. You didn't just ruin Mikhail's reputation; you destroyed *my* good name."

"What good name?" I spit.

Before the words are even fully out of my mouth, Alexander's hand cracks across my face.

"Watch how you talk to me, Cordelia. I don't stand for disrespect."

He shakes out his hand like it stings a bit. I want to ask if my face hurt his hand, but I don't feel like getting slapped twice before I've even had a sip of coffee.

"I've done well for myself while you were away," he says. "In some ways, you leaving helped. I talked to everyone imaginable trying to find you and it put me in touch with all kinds of people: lawyers, doctors, politicians. I have info on everyone. And information sells."

"If that's true, you wouldn't need to sell me," I mumble.

He narrows his eyes in warning. "Well, there's a limit to who I can sell *that* kind of thing to. People like Konstantin Sokolov aren't going to trust just anyone. They like to keep things in the family. So creating a foothold there would be helpful. Plus, you *were* promised to Mikhail, Cordelia. What good am I if I don't prove myself to be a man of my word?"

"So all of this—tracking me down, holding me prisoner, marrying me off to Mikhail—this is all so you can be a professional gossip?"

"Fixer," he corrects icily. "I'm a political fixer. It's a whole lot more than gossip. I clean up messes. I take care of problems."

I feel his eyes on me. He doesn't need to say I am a problem he will take care of in order for me to understand that is exactly what he means.

"The job is underworld-adjacent, given the somewhat questionable favors I have to pull from time to time. But I don't want to work near the Sokolovs; I want to work *with* them. I'm seeking a promotion."

I snort. "Entering into a life of crime is a real step up. Congratulations."

He leans back, relaxed now. Slapping me must have consumed some of the rage he'd been carrying. "You have no vision, Cordelia."

"Stop calling me that."

"Stop living in a fantasy," he bites back. "Your name is Cordelia. You're marrying Mikhail Sokolov. These are the realities of your life and the sooner you come to terms with them, the better off you'll be."

I stand tall and proud. "I'm going to escape and live free again. The sooner *you* come to terms with that, the better off you'll be."

Alexander arches a graying brow. "Are you still waiting for Ivan to come and save you?"

"No."

Yes.

I wish I didn't, though. I want to cut that useless hope out of me, but I don't know how. Some part of me will always be waiting for him, I think. Some part of me will always believe.

"You're a terrible liar, Cordelia. I can see it in your eyes. You think Ivan Pushkin is going to rescue you." He shrugs lazily. "Maybe he'll try. He's put forward more of an effort than I thought he would. He bartered on your behalf."

I frown. "He has?"

The crack in my facade allows a flood of baseless hopes to come rushing in. *Maybe his relationship with Francia is all part of some deal. Maybe everything he has done is to keep me safe.*

"Ivan is as good as *pakhan* in the Pushkin Bratva now," Alexander says, ignoring my question. "The fact that you have a connection to him is useful for me. It gives me some leverage there."

"No one has leverage over Ivan. He'll destroy you."

He turns to me, eyes narrowed. "Then why are you here with me instead of there with him?"

Alexander thinks he has made a good point. I can tell by the smug expression on his face that he thinks he has won.

But the only reason I'm not with Ivan right now is because I *chose* to leave.

I found out about Katerina going missing and I doubted him. I threw away everything I'd learned about Ivan in a second and fled from him and his house—right into the arms of the people I ran from in the first place.

This is all my fault.

Alexander sighs and waves me towards the door. "Go eat and shower. You look like a wreck."

"I didn't realize my prison cell had a dress code."

"Oh, it doesn't. But the cameras are unforgiving." An oily smile slips across his face.

I don't want to give him the satisfaction of asking, but I can't stop myself. If there are cameras in my bedroom or somewhere else in the house, I need to know. "What cameras?"

"You're going to go shopping with your mother. A proper girl's day out so you can pick out some new clothes."

"I have clothes upstairs."

"Clothes you left hanging in favor of jeans and a t-shirt." His lip curls in distaste. "I'll have the staff wrestle you into dresses if I must, but I'm going to be kind and let you pick something you might like."

I want to laugh in his face. Sending me dress shopping with my mom is the furthest thing from kind. It's actually a nightmare.

"Then," he continues, "you and Mikhail have a lunch date."

"In public?"

People. Freedom. I could escape. I could yell for help, and—

"Unfortunately, poor Jorden won't be joining you," Alexander adds. "She's… occupied."

There it is. The not-so-subtle reminder of why I won't be escaping anytime soon.

They'll kill her if I try.

"I'm here," I tell him icily. "You are holding me prisoner and I'm going to marry Mikhail. Why do we have to parade around the city together? Isn't this enough? Is your victory over me not complete until you've rubbed my nose in it?"

"Not everything is about you, Cordelia," he drawls. "This is tactical. The more people who see that my prodigal daughter has returned home, the harder it will be for Ivan to make a move."

Is that a concern? Does he think Ivan might come to rescue me? If so, he might as well save his worry. Ivan isn't coming for me.

These men are going to use me as a pawn in their own greedy games.

Unless I make it stop.

Just like he did at the start of breakfast, Alexander claps his hands again. "Now, go. I'm busy."

I give my stepfather one final look before I leave his office. He's regal behind his desk, comfortable and relaxed. Nothing about my presence unsettles him. He doesn't think I'm capable of fighting back.

Good.

When I do, he'll never see it coming.

14

IVAN

I've lost count of the days since I've seen Cora.

It's hard to keep a reliable record of time when every second feels like an hour. The nights are an endless stretch of tossing and turning. I spend them replaying the last couple weeks in my mind again and again.

What could I have done differently?

Everything.

Who should I have killed?

Everyone.

That's the conclusion I reach every goddamn time. If it would mean keeping Cora safe and with me, I would have destroyed the world. I still might, if that's what it takes to get her back.

Francia, to her limited credit, has kept a low profile. It's not for my benefit; she just knows that I am one outburst away from snapping her spine like a stick over my knee.

The only reason she is even still breathing is because she knows where Cora is. All it would take is one whisper from her and Cora could be gone. Lost to me forever.

So I've let her putter around and play House, even when it makes me feel fucking murderous.

I avoid her and try to stay busy. Yasha is still with Jorden. She's out of the hospital now, but she needs around-the-clock care. "The doctor is still worried about her sleeping," he said when we talked last night. "Someone needs to be there to watch over her and make sure she… sleeps."

"Then I'm not sure you're the right guy for the job."

"What?" he snapped, already frothing at the mouth with jealousy. "Why not? Who else should it be?"

"Probably someone who doesn't want to keep her up all night."

It took him a couple seconds to get the joke. Even when he did, he didn't laugh. I don't blame him. Nothing seems particularly funny anymore.

So as long as the world is on fucking fire, at least one of us should be with the woman we want to be with.

Suddenly, my office door flies open.

"Where is she?" Yasha asks. No knock. No greeting.

I frown. "I thought you were with Jorden."

He waves me away and slams the door shut behind him. "She's fine. She told me to come, actually. I was going to call, but she thought I should show you in person."

"Show me what?" I growl.

Instead of answering, Yasha pulls a rolled-up newspaper out of his back pocket and throws it on my desk. "This."

The newspaper is folded in half. An article about a record-setting fundraiser for a children's hospital fills the bottom half of the page. I have a feeling that slice of wholesome good news isn't what Yasha wanted me to see. So I flip the paper over…

… And nearly crumple it in my fist.

Cora fills the upper quadrant of the society page. Her dark hair is pulled into an elegant low bun just underneath today's date in the top right corner. She has on a simple green dress —the same shade of emerald as her eyes—and heels. She looks like the housewife in a 1950s vacuum commercial.

Except there is no pearly white smile on her face. No full, pink cheeks. No joy. Her face is long and drawn. There are bruises under her eyes and she looks frail. I'm not sure if it's possible to actually become noticeably thinner in a week, but she looks like she's wasting away.

I don't have to wonder why. The answer has his arm looped around her waist.

"Mikhail."

I throw the newspaper off my desk. If I look at his plastic smile or his hand clutching her shoulder for another second, I'll explode.

"For someone in the middle of an abduction, he isn't in hiding," Yasha says, pointing out the obvious.

"Of course not. Mikhail wants everyone to know they're back together."

Back together. I'm still trying to get used to the idea that Cora was ever engaged to Mikhail.

That night I caught him cornering her at The Coop, I had a feeling there was more to the story. At the time, I thought that, at worst, he was targeting her because he thought I was responsible for his sister's disappearance. I figured his only connection to Cora was through mine and Katerina's engagement.

But there was so much more going on that I missed. So much more that Cora didn't tell me.

I blow out a breath. She's alive. This photo proves it. That's something to be grateful for, even in the midst of this shitstorm.

"Do you think it's a jab at you?" Yasha asks, tipping his chin towards the picture.

I shake my head. "If anything, it's a compliment. He's worried about me. He's like a dog pissing on the street corner, trying to mark his territory."

"I guess that makes sense." Yasha grabs the paper and scowls at the image. "He's trying to insulate himself with witnesses."

"As if they could save him," I mutter.

The fact that he thinks any amount of social pressure could stop me from getting to Cora is laughable. He has no idea the beast that he poked when he fucked with me.

He thinks these photos will save him, but I can see how tired Cora looks. How weak she is. If I needed more motivation—which I certainly fucking did not—I have it now.

I snatch the newspaper out of Yasha's hand and study the picture again. This time, I look at the background.

The photo is a close-up. Nothing more than a few letters from a sign behind them is visible. And the description is useless.

I throw the newspaper back down on my desk. "We need to find out where they've been. I need a team trailing them."

"Done."

"Let me know if—"

"There's something else," he interrupts. "Before I saw the paper, I was going to call and tell you the news." He smirks, clearly proud of himself. "I got us a meeting. With Marcus St. Clair. He's expecting us."

I try not to let my emotions get too out of hand. It might be nothing. He might not have any useful information for us.

But at this point, I'll take any lead I can get.

I push back from my desk without hesitation. "Then what the fuck are we standing around for? Let's go."

15

IVAN

I feel the air change the moment we step out into the hallway. I'm pretty sure I smell sulfur and brimstone, too, actually. Which makes sense, because—

"Ivan!" she calls out.

Yasha curses behind me as I look down the hall at Francia.

She's standing at the mouth of the hallway, blocking the exit. Her hands are on her hips and a sickly sweet smile twists her face.

I never found Francia attractive, but she was a cute enough girl. Innocuous. Now that I know what she's really like, though, it's as if I can see through the optical illusion. Whatever trick she uses to look nice and normal doesn't work on me anymore.

All I see is the desperate fucking ghoul underneath.

"Where are you two off to?" she asks.

It's the first time I've stood face to face with her since she moved in. Last night, I brushed past her in the kitchen. She was at the table eating what looked like warmed-over slop. I breezed past and went to my room where Niles had left me a plate of steaming hot beef and broccoli with a chocolate souffle for dessert.

I need to talk to Niles about the piss-poor job he's doing making our new house guest feel welcome. Maybe give him a raise.

"Out," I growl at her.

It's as much as I'm willing to say. It's already more than she deserves. She should be grateful.

"Do you know when you'll be back?"

"No."

I gesture to Yasha and he slinks away, keeping his face low and guarded so she doesn't see his vicious scowl.

Francia hurt Jorden, too. Yasha is every bit as furious at her as I am. I position myself between them so he doesn't do something stupid—even though I'd love nothing more than for him to do something really, *really* stupid.

But instead of moving out of our way, Francia steps into my path as we near the end of the hall. "I'm asking because I had plans for dinner."

"I don't see what that has to do with me."

"We haven't had dinner together all week."

"I'm eating just fine."

"If you don't like the meals your chef cooks, we can fire him," she suggests. "I haven't been thrilled with his cooking, either."

"*We* aren't firing anyone. *I* am happy with my staff."

She sighs. "Fine. But you can't eat out for every meal. All that salt and cholesterol is bad for your heart."

I try for a fake smile, but it ends up as more of a grimace. "I suggest you worry about your own heart."

Francia steps closer and smooths her hands across the collar of my shirt. "You're so sweet to worry about me, Ivan. Believe me, I take *very* good care of myself. My body is a temple, after all. I want the worshipers to enjoy the view."

She gives me a sultry smile. My stomach physically turns.

"I didn't realize Satanists worshiped at a temple," Yasha muses from off to the side. "Is that why you look like a goat?"

I have to stifle my laugh with a cough, but Francia isn't fooled. Her face and neck turn angry shades of red as she looks past me to my second, who is wearing his usual shit-eating grin.

"I think there's a bit too much male influence around here." She snaps her eyes from Yasha back to me. "You've been living like you're in a frat house for a long time now. I think this place is ready for a long overdue shake-up."

"Are we still talking about your body temple?" Yasha asks. "Or...?"

"I'm talking about the house." When her eyes land on me, they soften again. "I have some ideas for redecorating. The house should feel more like *us*."

Unless she's envisioning flames shooting out of the walls, brimstone scent in the oil diffusers, and torture devices in every bathroom, I'm not sure how she's going to capture our "vibe."

"I've put together some ideas for a design revamp. I wanted to show you what I'm thinking over dinner," she finishes.

It's not as if I'm in love with the design of the mansion. Much of it was done under my father's leadership. He passed the buck onto designers and let them craft a beige palace.

But Francia is overstepping by a fucking mile. She's trying to carve out a place for herself here. If she manages to do that, I'll have no choice but to burn the house down once I've disposed of her. I do not intend to let anything of her linger once this shit is all over.

"All design decisions go through Niles," I lie.

Niles will hate me for sending Francia his way, but I'm more liable to strangle her with a curtain than choose a fabric color with her.

Her jaw sets, her already thin lips disappearing in an angry line. "Fine."

I move to walk past her, but she shifts into my path again. "Also, I want to be introduced to the other Bratva wives."

Unexpectedly, a laugh bursts out of me. Her eyes narrow and there isn't a cough big enough to disguise the fact that I just cackled in her face.

I control myself and shake my head. "No. No, that won't be possible."

"How am I supposed to acclimate into this world if I don't know anyone? You don't take me anywhere," she complains.

"I've been cooped up in this house since I got here and I don't know anyone. I need to make friends if I'm going to..." Whatever she was going to say, Francia thinks better of it. "I need friends so I don't go crazy."

"Too fucking late," Yasha mumbles.

Francia starts to look at him, but I drag her attention away. "People at the top don't have friends."

She gestures to Yasha. "Then explain *him*."

Yasha wags his fingers at her from under his own chin. "I defy explanation."

"He is my second-in-command. He works for me."

"Well, I don't have a staff," she whines. "Everyone here works for you."

"Which you agreed to."

"I agreed to be the Bratva wife. So let me be one. I want to meet some other women who can relate to what I'm going through."

"Good luck with that," Yasha guffaws. "I don't know of any other Bratva wives that abducted their predecessor and held them ransom so their new husband wouldn't murder them the first chance he got."

If looks could kill, Yasha would be a smoldering hole in the carpet by now.

"No, I suppose not." Her gaze flicks back to me. "Maybe that's why you seem unfamiliar with the concept that *Cora's life is in my hands*. You've never seen or experienced this kind of thing before. If you don't cooperate with our deal as it was laid out, then I can make sure she suffers... or worse."

I positioned myself between Yasha and Francia to keep the peace, but it is Yasha's hand fisted in the back of my shirt that acts as the only thing keeping me from throwing myself at Francia. My chest rises and falls in ragged gasps. I blink away the hatred blinding me and try to think clearly.

She's right. With Cora in her control, she has me by the balls.

I have to be more careful.

"I am cooperating with our deal," I tell her icily. "I'm saving you embarrassment."

"You think I would *embarrass* you?" she practically shrieks.

"The *pakhan's* wife wouldn't be caught dead fraternizing with 'lessers' in the family," I lie. "I'm not going to introduce you to them—because you are above them. It would make you look weak. Is that what you want?"

Francia studies my face, searching for signs of my deception. She must not find any because she shakes her head. "No, I don't."

"I didn't think so. Now if you'll excuse us," I purposefully sidestep her and move into the entryway, "we have things to take care of."

Get away. Get away now. Before you strangle this fucking bitch and throw Cora's life in the balance.

Suddenly, her hand wraps around my bicep. On instinct, I jerk my arm away. Francia frowns, but recovers quickly. "I am tired of being cooped up. Maybe I could come with you."

"No!" This time, it's Yasha with the outburst.

We both turn to him and he swallows. "I—I'm in charge of security and it wouldn't be safe to bring you along."

"Are you doing something dangerous? If so, I deserve to know what it is. I live in this house, too. If my fiancé is going to get hurt, then I—"

"Every day is dangerous for Ivan," Yasha says. "It's even more dangerous for his… his woman."

He stumbles over the descriptor the same way I do. It's just plain fucking wrong. Francia is not my woman.

"You are safe when you're here. I can keep a closer eye on you and make sure nothing happens to you. It's—It's my duty to protect you." He bows his head slightly. "Even if I don't want to."

Francia's mouth twitches at the last little barb, but it actually serves to make the rest of Yasha's message seem genuine. Despite his own feelings about her, he feels it is his duty to protect her. How noble. It's his loyalty in action.

It's also utter bullshit. But based on the sparkle of surprise in Francia's eyes, she doesn't know that.

She sighs. "Okay. Then I suppose I'll stay here."

I nod and move towards the door, but Francia reaches out one last time. Her hand swipes over my shoulder. "Be careful."

I don't bother to respond.

As we walk through the door and to the car, I want nothing more than to go back inside and shower. I want to scrub the feel of Francia off of me—with bleach at the least and with fire if necessary. I want to forget she ever existed.

Not much longer until I can.

16

IVAN

I spot Marcus St. Clair the moment we walk into the cafe.

He chose an upscale spot downtown wedged between corporate office buildings. People in suits and ties charge through revolving doors and bark loudly into cell phones.

But Marcus is sitting in the empty restaurant with his hands folded politely on the table in front of him. His green eyes—the exact same shade as his daughter's—study us as we arrive.

He stands up to greet us, radiating suspicion. "Hi," he says, hand extended. "Marcus St. Clair. Nice to meet you."

I shake his hand firmly. "Ivan Pushkin." I watch carefully, but I don't register any recognition of my name in his eyes.

"And I'm Yasha. I arranged the meeting."

Marcus nods at my second and gestures towards the table. The moment we sit down, he leans forward. "So, are you lawyers for Alexander McAllister?"

I look at Yasha. "I thought you spoke on the phone."

"We did," Yasha says softly.

"And what did you talk about?"

"You want to meet concerning my daughter, Cordelia," Marcus says. There's a bite to his voice. He doesn't like being talked around. Yet another trait he shares with his daughter. "In my experience, that usually means Alexander has something to do with it. I haven't spoken to Cordelia in... well, it's been a long time."

Marcus says it matter-of-factly. No sense of shame or disappointment. Just a truth he's acknowledging: he hasn't played a role in his daughter's life.

And he doesn't seem to care.

But he really fucking should.

"If you haven't spoken to your daughter, when was the last time you spoke to Alexander?"

"Even longer," he says with a scowl. "Alexander likes to send in other people to do his dirty work. People like you."

Yasha sits taller, locked and loaded to inform Marcus exactly how wrong he is. But I subtly wave him off.

"What kind of effort have you made to see your daughter?"

Marcus scoffs. He crosses his arms over his chest and I can tell exactly how well made his shirt is. It's tailored for him and the cotton is thick. Proof enough that he's doing well for himself. Just like Cora said, her father had more than enough money to take care of her and her mom.

But he didn't.

Because of that, Cora ended up in the hands of Alexander. Her entire life was derailed. As glad as I am that it brought her to me, it also stole her from me. This man should have protected her, but he abandoned her.

I want to know why.

"Cordelia hasn't missed me." There's anger in Marcus's voice, but I get the feeling that there's more happening here that I don't understand yet.

"You think your daughter doesn't want to know you."

"I think no one has made any effort to include me, so I haven't made an effort to be included," he spits. "I thought maybe, once Cordelia was an adult, she would reach out and we could—well, it doesn't matter. She didn't. I assume she's doing fine and I leave it at that."

Marcus twines his fingers together, his jaw working back and forth.

I get it now: there was no shame in his voice a moment ago because he's *livid*. Whatever this man has been through, he is pissed that he doesn't get to know his daughter.

Now, *that* I can work with.

"If that's what you think, then I'm glad you agreed to sit down with us," I say. "Your daughter is not doing well, Marcus. She's not doing well at all."

His brow lowers. He looks from me to Yasha, suddenly tense. "What are you talking about?"

"We don't work for Alexander," Yasha explains. "I told you that we wanted to talk to you regarding Cora and Alexander, but—"

"Cora?" He frowns. "Who is that?"

"Your daughter," I explain. "She changed her name after she ran away from Alexander the first time."

"I didn't know she—Hold on. The first time? She ran away more than once?" He blinks, processing. Then his eyes go wide. "Is she alive?"

"She's alive," I reassure him. "And she ran away once before, but I'm hoping she'll do it again. Because as of now, Alexander has her back."

Marcus leans forward. His nostrils flare as anger burbles out of him. "What has he done?"

Oh, yeah. I can definitely work with this.

"Cora is set to be married off to a psychopath in the criminal underworld against her will," I tell him coolly. "It's why she ran away the first time. Alexander is using her to form alliances for his own benefit."

"That isn't—for God's fucking sake, that isn't legal! That can't be—Why didn't she come to me?" It seems more like a question he's asking himself than one he expects an answer to.

"Because you abandoned her and her mother."

Marcus turns on me, eyes narrowed as he hisses, "I *never* abandoned her. Ever. Evaline ran around behind my back and hooked up with Alexander. I was willing to make things work for Cordelia's sake, but Evaline divorced me. Then she took my daughter and ran."

"Cora thinks you hung them out to dry."

He chuckles darkly. "Yeah. Evaline and Alexander made sure to paint that picture of me. But he's the one who abandoned them. He told Evaline that he'd never speak to her again if she didn't pack up Cordelia and leave me. So she did. But Alexander didn't give her anywhere to go."

Cora told me about the months she and her mom spent on the streets. How desperate they were to find shelter and food.

I frown. "Cora thinks that Evaline met Alexander later on. After they were already homeless. She told me that they met and then he took them in."

Marcus shakes his head. "No. Alexander wanted her dependent on him. He wanted to make sure she burned every other bridge in her life before he finally let her move into his house. She chose living in the fucking gutter over being with me. She stole my family away in the dead of the goddamn night." He blows out a breath.

"Why would Evaline do that to her daughter? Things must have bad between you for her to—"

"They weren't," he bites out. "We weren't always the happiest, but I took care of her. And Cordelia, too. She left because Alexander is a snake who knows how to prey on weak people."

"Did you try to get them back?"

"I fought for custody. I tried, anyway." He shakes his head, a shadow falling over his face as the memories roll back. "Alexander has friends in high places. When I tried to take them to court, men showed up at my house with documents saying that I gave up my rights to Cordelia. I never signed them, but it was my signature forged right there at the bottom of the papers. And if I tried to fight it, I knew how I'd end up. The threats were vague, but they were clear enough."

I know Alexander is a political fixer, but it sounds like he had a lot of power even a decade ago. How much more powerful is he now?

"What have you been doing since the last time you spoke to her? Haven't you wondered what is going on in her life?"

He drags a hand over the back of his head, ruffling hair the same shade of chestnut as his daughter's. "Of course I did. But I didn't feel like I had an option to know anything about her. So I tried to move on. I got remarried. I lived the best life I could and hoped, since I couldn't look for Cordelia, that she would look for me."

I can't think of a single threat that would ever keep me away from Cora. There is nothing anyone could say or do to make me stop chasing her. To make me let her go.

As if he can read my mind, Marcus leans forward. His eyes— Cora's eyes—bore into mine. "If I'd had any idea what Alexander had planned for Cordelia, I never would have stopped fighting. I truly thought she was happy there."

Marcus isn't perfect, but he cares. On some level, he cares about Cora and what happens to her.

Right now, that's good enough for me.

"Cora is not happy there, which is why I need to get to her. *Now.*"

Marcus nods. "Absolutely. If there's anything I can do, then I'll—"

"Tell me everything you know about Alexander McAllister."

He pauses and sighs. Then he starts to talk.

As it turns out, Marcus has less information than I hoped. He scribbles Alexander's address down on a napkin as well as a few other businesses that are connected to him—lawyers and accountant's offices, mostly.

But it's a start.

Though, as he starts to slide the napkins towards me, he stops. "Just one thing. A favor."

I eye the napkin. "Ask."

"When you find Cordelia, I want to meet with her." He lowers his gaze to the table. Finally, a sign of the shame I wanted to see before. "I want to apologize to her. I should have fought harder. I should have—ah, fuck, let's just leave it at. There's a lot I want to say to her.'"

"I won't make you any promises."

Marcus frowns. "But she is my—"

"She's her own woman," I interrupt, my voice sharp. "It will be her choice if she meets with you or not. But I'll pass the message along."

He sighs, but nods slowly. "That's fair. I only want to see her if she wants to see me, too. I don't want to be like Alexander."

"Nobody does," Yasha mutters.

"I couldn't agree more." Marcus slides the napkin over, meeting my eyes. "Give him hell."

As we leave the cafe, the napkin tucked in my back pocket, I feel something I haven't felt in days.

Hope.

17

CORA

I lean against the dressing room wall and watch the bubbles float to the surface of my champagne flute.

A stack of dresses in every imaginable cut, shade, and material are piled on the bench next to me. Looking at it makes my eyes cross. My mother and a pair of her friends are hunting down more things for me to try on from the showroom floor, so I close my eyes and try to absorb the peace and quiet while I can.

It doesn't last long.

I hear the gaggle of voices drawing closer and I toss the rest of my champagne back. Mom told me I shouldn't partake when we arrived, so I've been drinking a bit every time she's out of the room. There's a healthy buzz percolating under my skin now. It's better than the fear and uncertainty that has been stabbing at me since the moment I woke up in that dank basement with my wrists bound.

"Here we go!" Mom sing-songs, pushing back the curtain so the attendants can cart in another metric fuck-ton of fabric. "More options."

"*Every* option," I correct. "This has to be most of the store."

A blonde woman Mom introduced as her "dear friend" laughs from the hallway. "If you want the store, you can have it. God knows Alexander can afford the bill."

My mom chuckles, but it doesn't reach her eyes. Pink rises in her cheeks.

I take her blush as confirmation that I was right about the four staff members serving us breakfast this morning: Alexander doesn't have the money for them or any of this. It's why he needs me to marry Mikhail.

"If Alexander won't buy you what you want, ask Mikhail," a dark-haired woman suggests. Her name rhymed with Stella or Stacy or something like that, but her coiffed updo looks like devil's horns so I've been calling her "Satan" in my head.

"That's true," the blonde woman agrees. "Mikhail isn't lacking for anything, either. I can't believe he hadn't been snatched up yet."

Satan elbows Blondie, who seems to realize what she said all at once.

"But obviously, it's because he was waiting for you," she adds quickly. "True love is worth waiting for."

Looks like I'll be waiting forever, I think miserably.

Still, Ivan's face flickers in my mind. I see him every time I blink. Haunting me with what I can't have.

My mother has kept herself busy since the moment we arrived at the store. Now is no different. To avoid looking at me, she occupies herself by hanging each item of clothing from a bar on the wall. But she glances over at her friends. "Mikhail is very patient. And generous. I couldn't be happier with the match."

Right on cue, her friends *ooh* and *aww* over this make-believe version of Mikhail. "Much better than that awful Pushkin brute—" Satan starts to say before realizing she's crossed a line and clapping her hands over her mouth.

My mom's hands go perfectly still over the linen dress she's holding. She's so pale I think she might pass out.

Then she quickly spins to me, her gaze fixed somewhere over my shoulder. "Here, Cordelia. Try this on."

It's an order. *Change the subject. Now.*

While the women quickly launch onto the safer ground of floral arrangements and color themes for the ceremony, I try on ten more outfits that I don't even see. It wouldn't matter if I did—before I can even attempt to form an opinion, my mom or one of her ridiculous friends makes up their minds for me and then I'm being unzipped and shoved into the next thing.

This is how they break you, I think. *They make fighting back and having your own opinion so exhausting that it's easier to let them have control.*

By the end of it, we have a tidy stack of things laid up in the back corner that are Alexander-approved. My mom hands them to Satan and Blondie to take to the front of the store.

"If it had been me, I would have done a lot more damage," Blondie says with a wink. "There's always time, though. We'll come back later and I'll teach you my ways."

"Not if I can help it," I mutter.

They don't hear me, but I catch my mom's eye in the mirror and I know she did. She turns away and starts gathering all of the rejected clothes into a pile.

It's strange to watch her move around me. Both so familiar to me and completely unrecognizable. I'm standing one foot away from her and yet I miss her more than I have in years.

"Mom." My voice cracks. I know she hears it.

She stiffens but doesn't turn to me.

"Mom, just… just let me go," I whisper. "Tell Alexander that I got away. I slipped through an emergency exit and you lost me. I'll disappear."

I can't do any of that. Alexander still has Jorden. If I run, they'll kill her. It's why there aren't guards with us right now. He doesn't need them.

But it's a test. What will my mom choose? Will she try to protect her daughter from the horrors headed my way?

Or will she drag me along and toss me into the flames?

Her jaw flexes as she stands tall and turns towards the doorway. She checks to make sure her friends aren't nearby before she looks over at me. "That isn't what Alexander wants."

"Yeah, I know," I snap. "Because what Alexander wants is insane."

"Being taken care of by a good man is not insane."

"Thinking Alexander is a 'good man' is, though. He's a monster!"

She shakes her head. "You're only saying that because you don't know what it's like not to have a safety net. Even when you left, you knew you could always come home."

"Home?" I spit. "His house was *never* my home. I can't be safe with a man who treats me like cattle. Like a bartering chip."

I can practically see my words bouncing off the shield Alexander has built around her. "He takes care of us, Cordelia. Alexander is doing what is best for us—for *both* of us. Without him, we'd still be on the streets."

There isn't a single part of her that thinks she can take care of herself. Jorden always waxed on about wanting a sugar daddy, but it's because she wanted a break. Not because she wasn't capable.

But Alexander has fooled my mom into thinking she can't do a single thing for herself.

"I'd rather be on the streets than in prison," I hiss. "That's what this is for me, Mom. A prison."

She lifts her chin. "I'm sorry you feel that way."

I pause, waiting for her to say something else. Waiting for her to show some kind of concern for her only daughter. Even just a tiny little smidge of sympathy.

But there is nothing.

I knew a long time ago that my mother was brainwashed, so I'm not surprised. But that doesn't make her response any less painful.

Hat the Brat pokes her helmeted head of hair into the dressing room. "They are ringing you gals up. Someone better get out here and pay before I throw a few things for myself on the pile."

"Right? If I was twenty years younger and twenty pounds lighter, I'd steal all of Cordelia's clothes for myself!" Mom laughs giddily and turns to me, no sign of our previous conversation on her face at all except for the slightest glimmer in her eyes. "Never forget how lucky you are, darling. It all fades in an instant."

Go ahead. Fade.

I won't complain.

18

CORA

Sometime during dinner, someone delivered all of the clothes I bought this afternoon to my room. I shuffle through the hangers and don't recognize anything. I'm sure I tried it all on, but it was a blur. Even now, the dresses might as well be identical prison jumpsuits for as different as they look to me.

I slam my closet closed and flop down on the bed.

Dinner was slightly more bearable than breakfast, but only because no one spoke. Not a single word. Alexander and my mother ate in stony silence. I wanted to probe them to see if they were in a fight. I'm finding weaknesses between Alexander and Mikhail already, so maybe finding a few between Mother and Daddy Dearest could be useful, too.

But the silence was nice.

At first, I thought being locked away in a room by myself was torture. Now, it's preferable. There are no mind games when I'm alone. No one tries to bend me to their will. It's peaceful.

So I guess I shouldn't be surprised that fate says, *Oops, never mind,* and my bedroom door swings open.

I go from relaxed to a ready position in record time. My heart slams against my ribs, adrenaline pumps through my veins.

But it's only a maid. She's young. No more than twenty-five. Her blonde hair is twisted into a braid on the top of her head. She's wearing a black dress that covers her from neck to knee just like Alexander orders.

"Excuse me, miss," she says, inclining her head slightly. "I'm just here to change the sheets."

"Someone was in my room earlier today." I gesture to the closet. "If my sheets needed changing, they would have done it then."

"It's a normal part of the schedule. Just a blanket refresh."

She takes a step into my room, but I move towards her, blocking her path. "I'm fine. I don't need new blankets."

What I need is five minutes to myself without any surprises.

"It will only take a moment."

All at once, my annoyance shifts to awareness.

Something is wrong.

She isn't supposed to be here. Did Alexander send her? Mikhail? Francia? Someone worse?

I throw out an arm so she can't pass. "Who are you and what do you want?"

Her cheeks flush and she speaks even more quietly. "I want to help you…with your blankets. That's all."

The way she says it sets off even more alarm bells. "No."

"Miss Cora," she says so softly I can barely hear her, "if you'd just let me in, then I'll—"

"I'm not letting you anywhere," I bark. "I don't know who you are or what you want, but if you don't leave then I'll—"

I'll… what? Yell for Alexander? If this woman is here, it's probably at his bidding. She's probably going to slip some kind of powdered drug on my pillow to knock me out so he can do God-knows-what to me.

Before I can finish the thought, the woman reaches into her pocket.

I take a step towards my bookshelf so I can snatch my letter opener out of its hiding place, but then I stop.

The maid pulls a phone out of her pocket. She taps a single button and presses the phone to her ear. "Here is Cora, sir."

Cora. Not Cordelia. *Cora.*

Then she holds the phone out to me.

I stare at it like it might be radioactive. In the end, curiosity gets the best of me. Gingerly, I press it to my ear. "Hello?"

There's a single beat of silence before three little words crack my heart wide open.

"Cora." The deep rumble of his voice is as familiar to me as my own. "It's me."

Ivan.

I drop to my knees.

19

CORA

The maid checks the hallway and then closes the door behind her.

I'm still on my knees. My legs are weak and wobbly, but my grip on the phone is crushing. My mouth opens and closes around silent words I can't speak.

I miss you.

I need you.

Where are you?

Come save me.

Finally, I rasp out, "It's you."

"It's me," he repeats. "I'm sorry it took so long."

Tears sting my eyes, but I blink them back. I don't know what this conversation is about yet. Last I heard, he's engaged to Francia. I've learned better than to jump to conclusions.

"What is this, Iv—"

"Don't say my name," he barks.

I snap my mouth closed.

"Don't risk it," he adds a bit softer. "In case anyone is listening."

"Are you worried what your new fiancée will think if she finds out?" More venom than I expected leaks from my voice. Apparently, losing a game of musical fiancés will do that to a girl.

I use the anger to force myself back to my feet. I need to be ready for whatever is coming next.

Ivan has the audacity to chuckle. "I knew you'd be pissed about that."

"Pissed? I'm not 'pissed'; I'm devastated."

"Cora." He sighs.

The pity in his voice makes me feel physically sick. "I trusted you and you lied to me. You got engaged to the woman who wanted to kill me."

I make it sound personal, but I'd be just as broken if he was engaged to some random girl I'd never seen before.

It wouldn't matter who he was with—it would always feel wrong.

He should be with *me*.

"It's more complicated than that. It was the only way to save your life. Why the fuck else would I ever want to be with Francia?"

Mikhail's words in that basement dungeon come back to me.

Ivan Pushkin never gave a fuck about you, and now, he's going to marry Francia. He said she would have been the better choice all along. You were nothing more than a distraction.

"She knows how to play the game better than I do," I say softly. "She has connections and she wants a business arrangement. That's what you—"

"I didn't want you to actually answer the question. Fucking hell, Cora," he breathes. "I'm not with her and I never will be. Not in any way that matters."

I want those words to be true more than I've ever wanted anything.

But I've been deceived too many times. Tricked and lied to too often to trust anything.

Even Ivan.

Especially Ivan.

He exists in a world I barely understand. As far as I know, this could all be another manipulation.

"Are you okay?" he asks gently. "Has anyone hurt you?"

I look down at my wrists. They've scabbed over, though still tender to the touch. But beyond that...

"No. No one has hurt me," I say. "Not physically."

He breathes out and it sounds a lot like relief. That alone goes further than anything else he has said to making me believe that he actually cares.

Even if he can never love me—even if I'll never be his wife— at least he cares whether I'm safe. That's more than can be said for any other man in my life, including my own father.

"I'm sorry it has taken so long to get in touch with you. It took a fucking eternity just to figure out where you were being held. Then I had to get someone on the inside to make contact."

I glance over at the maid. She is standing against the door, her eyes fixed on the floor.

"Why did someone need to make contact? What is this about?"

"Because I need you to know that I'm going to get you out of there, Cora."

I'm asleep. I'm dreaming. That is the only way those words are coming out of Ivan Pushkin's mouth right now.

"I'm going to get you out of there and send you... God, so fucking far away," he continues. "I'll get you away from this city and these people—from me. Where you'll be safe."

Just like that, the dream pops. "You're going to send me away?"

"Halfway around the world if I have to. Whatever it takes to keep you safe."

Okay, so this doesn't seem like a trick, but it also isn't the romantic rescue I was hoping for.

"I don't want that," I protest. "I don't want to be sent away."

"It's the only way you'll be safe, Cora."

"I don't care about being safe if I'm not—" *If I'm not with you.* I swallow down the words. "Even if that is what I wanted, it's impossible. I can't leave."

"The fuck you can't," he growls. "I'm going to get you out of there. No one is going to stop me."

"Jorden."

He hesitates. When he speaks, his voice is icy cold. It sends a shiver down my spine. "Is Jorden involved in this shit, too? Was she working with Francia? If she is involved, you need to tell me everything—"

"No, no. She isn't involved. She's a victim," I tell him. "But they have Jorden. If I escape, they'll kill her."

"Who will kill her?" he asks.

I bite my lip, guilt rising up in me. "I should have told you about all of this that night at The Coop. I should have told you before that probably. But I was... I was running away. I was trying to hide. I didn't think—"

"Mikhail."

"Yeah." I sag, head dipped low. "Maybe if I'd been honest about everything from the start, you could have stopped this before it started. But now, it's too late. Mikhail has Jorden and he is going to kill her if I don't marry him."

"Mikhail does not have Jorden."

I stand tall, my every cell at full attention. "What?"

"Mikhail doesn't have Jorden," he repeats.

"But... I heard her. There was a scream, and—How do you know?"

"Because she is with Yasha right this second."

I stare at the wall as reality shifts around me.

"Fuck," I hiss.

One scream through a tinny cell phone is all it took for me to buy into Alexander's version of events. That is all it took for me to go quietly. To do what I was told and obey without question.

I could have plowed through my mother and her two friends at the shop and sprinted down the sidewalk this afternoon. I could have screamed for help when Mikhail and I walked to lunch.

"I could have escaped so many times," I grit out. "I'm going to kill them. All of them."

"Cora, wait."

I walk to the bookshelf and pull out my letter opener. The maid is still in the room, but if Ivan trusts her, then I guess I trust her, too.

"I'm tired of waiting," I say. "I'm going to—to—shit, I don't know! Force my way out?"

He snorts. "With what? Do you even have a weapon?"

I look at the tiny blade. When I close my fist, it barely sticks out of my hand. "I have a letter opener."

"You and a two-inch dull blade against the world?" He laughs. "Why am I not surprised? But if you stop and listen to me for a second, I think I have a better option."

"A better option for what? Is the maid you sent in here armed with something more deadly than a cell phone?" I look over at the woman and she finally meets my eyes. She gives me a quick shake of her head.

Guess not.

"I have a better option for getting you home," he clarifies.

Home.

God, I want that so bad.

Ivan clears his throat. "I'll get you out of Alexander's house and get Francia out of our lives. But I need you to be patient."

I cling to the phone with both hands. "I can't. I need to get out of here."

"And you will." He says it with so much certainty that it's almost impossible not to believe him. Yet some part of me really can't see beyond these four walls. Some part of me refuses to think I'll ever escape.

Tears well in my eyes. I swipe them away, grateful Ivan can't see them. "Alexander is scary. I know what he's capable of now. I don't want to be here any longer than I have to."

"If I could get you out right now, I would. But…" He growls in frustration. "I'm going to get you out, Cora. And you aren't in there alone. I have people watching over you."

I look over at the maid again. As if she can hear Ivan, she nods her head at me.

"But we have to get off the phone now."

"No!" I know I sound like a child. *Just one more minute.* But that's how I feel. Small and helpless. Even if he can't be here in person, having Ivan in my ear is better than nothing. I feel safe.

"It will look suspicious if she's in your room too long," he explains. "I'll call again soon."

"You promise?"

"I swear it, *solnishka.*" His voice is low and serious. I want to wrap up in it like a blanket. "I won't leave you there. I'll get you out."

I nod, tears clogging my throat.

"I need you to trust me."

I swallow down my emotions. "I do. I trust you."

He doesn't say anything else as the maid takes the phone and slips out of my room.

20

IVAN

I've held countless lives in my hands. I've been responsible for ending them. For saving them.

But nothing compares to hearing Cora admit that she trusts me.

I hang up the phone with a new weight on my shoulders and an ache below my belt. Since the moment Cora was taken, I haven't been able to think about anything except getting her back. I've been solely focused on finding her and making sure she is safe.

Now, I know she's alive. For the moment, she's safe. And she trusts me. I'm going to get her out of Alexander's house and when I do…

I'm going to reclaim every last fucking inch of her.

All the sexual frustration I've ignored and shoved down for days bubbles up in one instant. I shift in my seat, trying to ease the pressure of my rock-hard cock against my zipper.

"I have to let her go." I say it out loud, as if my dick might listen to reason and go limp with disappointment.

But if anything, the understanding that I can't keep Cora makes me want her even more.

"Maybe just one more time," I whisper to myself. "It will be a goodbye."

My cock jumps at the truly terrible idea even as my mind knows there will be no walking away from Cora. If I get her back in my bed, even for a night, I'll never want to let her go.

Her soft body in my sheets. Her smooth skin against mine. The burning heat of her desire on my tongue.

Without really meaning to, I slide my zipper down and let myself spring free.

I've never met someone who can make me lose control the way she can. No other woman has ever made me want to throw away everything I have and everything I've built just for one more taste of her.

I drag my palm up my length, groaning as I imagine Cora sprawled on my mattress. A sheen of sweat glistening on her skin. But as I get closer, she rolls to her belly and angles her hips up.

Take me like this, she says. *I'm too tired to sit up. But I need you.*

God, I need her, too.

I've memorized the feel of her hips in my hands. The weight of her body as I drag her against me and thrust inside of her.

One stroke, two, three… It doesn't take much and I'm already on the edge. Already trying to drag out this imaginary moment for as long as I can. Because this is the only relief I'll get until Cora is actually back in my arms.

Until I can hear the soft noises she makes in the back of her throat when she's close.

Until I can feel her body grip me as pleasure explodes inside of her.

"Fuck!" Heat erupts out of me, spilling down my hand as the image fades. As the dream slips away.

I don't deserve one more night with her. I'm not sure any man does.

But I'm going to take it anyway.

As soon as Cora is out of Alexander McAllister's house and safe with me, I'm going to take one last selfish night with her to burn through as much of the insatiable desire in my chest as I can. Then I'm going to send her away where she'll be safe. Safe from me and Alexander and Francia and Mikhail and Konstantin and anyone else who wants to hurt her.

But I can't let her go without one more taste.

21

IVAN

I slept in an empty bed for years before Cora. It was by choice; I didn't want anyone in my space, especially when I was asleep. I never trusted anyone enough to let them close while I was so vulnerable. Until her…

Now, though, when I feel her side of the bed dip, when I feel a hand snake around my waist… I welcome it.

I don't even mind that she woke me up from a damn good dream as her hair whispers over my chest.

In the dream, Cora and I were out on a date. The restaurant was loud, but the world around us was dark and hazy. Indistinct. No one else mattered. I couldn't see them. Didn't want to.

There was only her.

She wasn't sure what to order, but I told her exactly what I wanted. "And what is that?" she asked, a knowing smile teasing the corners of her full mouth.

In answer, I spread her on the table in front of me. I ran my hands up her thighs and dragged the tiniest pair of panties I've ever seen down to her ankles.

I devoured her right then and there, not stopping until she'd fallen apart twice and begged me to stop.

"I can't take anymore," she panted. "It's too good."

When I let her up, she slid off the table into my lap. She wrapped her legs around my waist…

Now, I'm awake. And ready to bring those dreams to life.

"I was dreaming about you," I murmur into the dark.

Sharp nails drag down my abs, a little too painful to feel good. She breathes out.

"Are you trying to tell me you want it rough tonight, then?" I ask with a smirk.

She answers by pressing her lips to the jut of my hip bone. Her breath is damp against my skin. And her lips feel rough, not nearly as soft and smooth as I'm used to.

I never thought I'd say the dream was better than reality, but…

Suddenly, she cups her hand around my dick, but she moves too quickly. Her hand slaps my balls and the haze of sleep burns up in a second. I jolt up, eyes wide.

"What the fuck, Cor—"

Except the woman kneeling between my legs is *not* Cora.

All at once, everything feels wrong. The sharp nails, her damp breath, even the way she smells—some deep, musty stench instead of the bright fruitiness I'm used to…

Francia smiles up at me.

"Get the fuck out of my bed!" I roar.

Her eyes widen in panic, but I don't stop. I can't. Not until she is out of my bed. Out of my room.

"Out!" I rip the covers off and shove her off of the mattress. "Get off of me. Get the fuck away!"

"Ivan, wait—" She scrambles to get her feet under her, but I keep shoving her towards the door.

She pulled me out of a dream and into a nightmare. If I hadn't opened my eyes, how long would it have taken me to realize? How long would the she-devil have been in my bed? How far would she have gotten?

Anger burns through me. She isn't moving fast enough.

Because she isn't running for her life.

I grab her arm and drag her out of my room and into the hall.

"I'm leaving!" She tries to pull out of my grip. "I'm out of your room, Ivan. Let me go."

But I don't. I can't. I want to drag her straight out of the front door. I want to kick her to the curb in nothing but the clothes on her back. Or, really, the clothes *not* on her back.

Because she's wearing a tiny silk slip with lace cutouts on her hips and chest.

"This is just a misunderstanding," she whines.

Like hell it is. There is no misunderstanding the way she's dressed. The way she touched me.

I grit my teeth in an effort not to twist her arm out of the goddamn socket. "I fucking told you there would be no touching. No love. No sex."

As we cross the entryway and move into the opposite wing of the house, I see a few staff members poking their heads out of the shadows. Some guards are taking note of what's going on between us.

Good. If they wanted to know Francia's place in this house, this is it. Cowering at my feet like a dog.

When we get to her door, I finally let her go. She drops to her knees and looks up at me beneath lowered lashes.

Even now, she's trying to seduce me. The games never stop with her.

"I didn't come into your room to do… *that*. I came to talk to you."

"Most people use their mouths for talking. Not their hands."

"I came to talk to you, but then I saw you." Her eyes glance down at my crotch. "I wanted to give you some relief. You liked it at first."

"I assure you I didn't."

"Tell that to your dick," she whispers. "You got *hard* for me."

Before the words are even out of her mouth, I snatch her off the floor and pin her to her bedroom door with my forearm barred across her throat. She yelps, but then goes perfectly silent as I crowd into her space.

"That was not for you," I growl. "It will *never* be for you."

She frowns. "If it's not for your wife, then who is it for?"

I don't answer the question because we both already know the answer.

Francia's scowl deepens, but I lean in closer. "If you ever sneak into my room again, I'll kill you."

With that vow hanging in the air, I turn and march back to my side of the house.

22

IVAN

The knock at my office door is so soft that I almost don't hear it at first.

Then the knob turns.

I assume it's going to be one of the new maids. To save my staff from needing to interact with Francia quite so often, I hired a few extra sets of hands. They are young and skittish. I'm sure being ordered around by Francia all day has something to do with that. You have to be meek and mild to deal with her all day without committing homicide.

Instead of one of the new maids, however, my sister slips silently through the door.

"Anya? What are you doing?"

She quietly presses the door closed behind her and then turns to face me. "Avoiding your new roommate. She was in the sitting room. I had to crawl on my hands and knees through the entryway."

"Since when do you knock on my office door?"

"Since I heard storming into your room uninvited is worthy of a death threat these days."

I'm not surprised the story of me putting Francia in her place is making the rounds. I knew we had an audience. I'm glad we did. Francia might try to get her revenge, but at least everyone knows where I stand where she is concerned.

"I thought I told you to quit gossiping with my maids. Who do I need to fire?"

Anya smirks. "Niles."

I fold my hands over my stomach and kick my feet up. "Bullshit."

"I'm serious!" she insists. "It was Niles. He told me all about your little late night run-in with your darling betrothed."

I shiver at the pet name. Francia is a lot of things, but she is sure as fuck not my darling anything.

"Even for you, that is impressive. You must have really worn him down to get that kind of gossip out of him."

"Pfft, yeah right," she snorts. "Niles couldn't wait to tell me all about it. He might have even giggled a little bit." She smiles at the memory, which is a welcome sight. There hasn't been much to smile about for either of us in too long.

Then her smile fades. My sister shifts closer to my desk, her hand flat on the wooden top. "How are you doing?"

"Don't say it like that."

"Like what?" She pulls back. "I'm worried about my brother."

"You're saying it like I'm terminal."

"You are. Kind of." She wags her brows playfully. "Terminally *in love*." Just like she did as a kid, Anya makes kissy faces at me until she can't help but laugh at herself.

I roll my eyes. "Are you done?"

"Done with the air kisses? Or done teasing you?" she asks. "Because I'm done with the air kisses *for now*. But I will be making fun of you every day for the rest of your life. Or my life. Whichever comes first."

"If you don't stop being annoying, then the end of your life is rapidly approaching."

She grins, proud of herself, but holds up her hands in surrender. "How about this?" She leans forward, face flat and expressionless. In her most robotic voice, she asks, "How are you doing, IvanBot?"

"Better," I declare. "And I'm okay. How are you?"

She sinks down into the leather chair across from my desk and sighs. "I'm okay, too. Scared, but we don't have to talk about that. We'll keep it light and fun. Otherwise, bored. I miss planning your wedding to Cora."

"My *fake* wedding to Cora."

She waves me away. "Yeah, yeah. I know it was all fake, but coming up with the designs and the colors was so fun. It felt real."

It did. But it's never going to happen. This is something even Anya won't be able to charm into existence.

"You can help Francia with her planning. I'm sure there are ice sculptures to commission and you'll need to give the Bolshoi Ballet time to choreograph a special number for the reception."

"Don't remind me," she grumbles. "She's left me three messages."

"She actually called you?"

Anya nods. "She wants us to go out for lunch so we can 'get to know each other.' I'd rather gargle bleach. Also, I know plenty about her already. Like, I know she's a fucking psychopath, for starters. I also know I wish she was dead." She raises her brows in challenge. "Should I keep going?"

"You're preaching to the choir, *moya sestra*." I grimace. "If I'm not careful, she's going to plan this entire wedding behind my back. I'll walk out of my room one day and find myself in the middle of the ceremony."

"I doubt it. She'd need help to plan a ceremony and she isn't getting any of that from anyone around here. Niles said her breaking into your room sealed the deal for a lot of the staff. They hate her."

"That could be a problem."

Anya frowns. "How is that a problem? It's a good thing. Francia is insane. Now, people realize that."

"You're right. She's insane," I say slowly. "Which means I don't have any fucking idea what she'll do when she realizes her plan isn't working out. She could attack my staff. She could hurt Cora."

"She wouldn't do that." Anya looks at me with wide eyes. "…Would she?"

"I can't be certain," I admit. "Which is why, aside from last night, I've tried to keep her calm. I need her to be placated so I can do what I need to do."

She nods sadly. "That makes sense. If you need anything from me, just let me know. I'm happy to—" Anya stops when she sees my face. The offer to help lodges in her throat. Then she shakes her head vehemently. "Nope. Nuh-uh. No way. I didn't mean it. I don't want to help. Find someone else."

"She already asked to meet up, Anya. It's the perfect plan."

"Yeah, except for the part where I have to be *anywhere near Francia.*"

"It wasn't a question, Anya."

My sister groans and melts out of her chair until her ass hits the floor. "This is going to be terrible."

I nod. "Probably."

"What if I take her for a drive and then pull over to stretch but forget to put the car in park and 'accidentally' send her over a cliff?"

"It's a good plan up until the point where Alexander and Mikhail find out about her death and kill Cora in punishment."

Anya snaps her fingers. "Dang. I'll keep brainstorming."

I lean over my desk and clap my sister on the shoulder. "You can brainstorm while you take Francia out to lunch and pick out some jewelry."

"Jewelry? We're going shopping together now, too?"

"Francia is like a dragon. Or whichever mythical creature likes shiny baubles. Point is, I want her to be so busy guarding her hoard that she doesn't see me coming."

"Fine. But I'm buying myself something, too."

"Go for it," I tell her.

"It's going to be big. And expensive. Like, a necklace that needs its own private security. We'll need to inform NASA of the purchase 'cause they'll be able to see it from space."

"I'll call the International Space Station right now and let them know."

She narrows her eyes at me. "You're no fun."

"And you're not getting out of this no matter how many threats you make." I give her a tight smile. "Francia is currently in the sitting room, if you want to go make plans with her."

Anya scowls and waves goodbye with one very specific finger.

23

IVAN

The moment Francia and Anya disappear down the driveway, Yasha arrives. "They're gone?" he asks.

"For now. But we don't have endless time."

I've swept my bedroom and office for cameras and microphones countless times since Francia moved in. I'm confident she isn't recording any of my conversations. The only danger left is that she could somehow eavesdrop on my meetings herself. Hence getting her out of the house.

Despite what Anya probably thinks, I'm not just sending her out on the town with Francia as some kind of twisted punishment. She's giving us vital time to plot and plan. She's getting us one step closer to Cora.

When we get to my office, I lock the door while Yasha spreads out a stack of papers he brought with them. A few of them are large, architectural plans sketched out in graphite.

"Alexander's house," he explains.

"That didn't take long."

He smiles. "Fun fact: the night security guard at City Hall is easily bought with a couple courtside basketball tickets and a crisp one-hundred dollar bill."

"Hopefully, Alexander's staff can be just as easily bought."

"So far, so good," Yasha says. "The main problem is that Alexander hires and fires maids so fast. One of the maids said that he canned her without paying her a cent. The cheap asshole. I covered her lost wages with a little bonus in exchange for some tales of her time in the McAllister household."

"That explains why he needs Cora so badly. He's broke."

It's an explanation, but there is no excuse for what he's done. And there sure as fuck will be no salvation.

"When we're done with him," Yasha snarls, "he'll have a lot more to worry about than his lack of money. Lack of a head, for instance."

I laugh grimly.

Then we buckle down and get to work.

Aside from the maids we've planted, Yasha has access to one of the security cameras. It's an exterior angle, but it gives us an idea of who is coming and going from the house. Mainly, the answer is Mikhail Sokolov.

"He isn't there in the evenings," Yasha says. "As much as I know you want to kill him—"

"You don't have any fucking idea how much I want to kill him," I growl.

"Well, regardless, we should probably wait until he isn't around to go in and get her."

I grimace but nod. "The fewer casualties, the better. I don't want them to be able to tie any of this back to me. Not if Alexander is half the fixer that Cora's dad thinks he is."

"That's another thing." Yasha straightens up, wincing as his back pops. We've been bent over my desk for a long time. "I've been thinking about what Marcus said. I didn't realize exactly how much sway Alexander has over... well, everybody."

"So?"

He runs a hand over the back of his neck. "I want to get Cora out of there as much as anybody, but we have to do it in a way that won't ruin the rest of your life. Or the rest of my life. Or the rest of *her* life."

"I know. We get in; we get out. No casualties if we can help it."

"I think we need to hit pause on any rescue plans until I can get more security in the house. If we just—"

"No."

The word rips out of me before I can even understand what Yasha is saying. It's an instinct.

Leave Cora in the hands of my enemies? No.

Be apart from her longer than necessary? Never.

Abandon her after I promised I'd get her out? *I don't fucking think so.*

"I know, I know." Yasha has his hands raised like he's trying to ease me off a ledge. "We need to get to her as soon as possible."

"Not as soon as possible," I correct. "*Immediately.*"

"But we don't do any good if we barge in there and are unprepared. Which is why I want to get some more cameras put in place. I already have one of the maids on the inside working on it. If things go our way, it will only add a day or two to the plan."

"And if they don't go our way?"

Yasha hesitates. "Things will go our way. They always do."

"If things always went my way, Cora would be in my bed and Francia would be in a shallow grave."

"Both of those things are going to be true, brother," Yasha says softly. "I'm going to make sure of that."

In the end, my good sense wins out. I nod reluctantly. "Get the cameras up as soon as possible. Cora is scared. I want to get her home."

Yasha frowns at my word choice. I do, too. It's the second time I've slipped up like that. This can't be Cora's home. No matter how much I want it to be. I'm to free her from the hellhole she's trapped in—but after that, if I want to keep her safe…

I have to let her go.

Before Yasha can say anything, my phone rings. He leans over and checks my screen to see Francia's name. "Speaking of the devil. Not to say we were talking about her. Just that she is, you know, the devil."

"Maybe Anya actually tried to push her off a cliff."

Yasha's eyes widen. "Was that her plan?"

"I guess I'll find out." I press my phone to my ear. "This is Ivan."

"I know who you are," Francia croons. There's no sign of anger in her voice. After last night, I expected a freeze-out. Apparently, Francia has other ideas. "I wouldn't be calling if I didn't."

"Who is this again?"

She laughs. "Don't tease me, Ivan."

"What do you want?"

There's a beat before she answers. "You."

I tense. The urge to throw my phone through the nearest window grows stronger.

"You here with me," she continues quickly as her jokey seduction attempt falls flat. "At lunch."

"I wouldn't want to interrupt the sisterly bonding." Or be in the proximity of both Francia and a steak knife. Seems like a recipe for disaster.

"No fear of that. Anya left after the jewelry store."

I grit my teeth. "Why is that? The plan was for the two of you to have lunch."

"And I changed the plans," she says cheerfully. "I want to go out on the town with my fiancé. Unless you have something more important going on?"

"Actually," I hedge, "I am busy."

"Too busy for me?" she asks, her voice pouty. "If you don't want to come, I guess I could check in on how Cora is doing."

Hearing Francia say her name sends me to my feet. My hackles rise. It's a threat; we both know it. She's threatening Cora so I'll cooperate.

Which means she's up to something.

"Fine," I grit out. "Text me the address. I'll be there."

"This is going to be so fun!" she gushes. "See you soon."

I hang up and take a deep breath. Then I crack open one eye to look at Yasha. "Just a few more days?"

"Two, tops," he confirms. "She'll be out of our lives soon."

If I have anything to say about it, Francia will be out of everyone's lives soon. The world will thank me.

24

CORA

Every single person who lays eyes on Mikhail seems to instantly sense that he's stuffed to the brim with shit.

The people he smiles at as we walk down the sidewalk. The hostess he slides a twenty-dollar bill to so she can give us a table near the windows. The waitress who blushes when he compliments her perfume.

"Write down the name of it for me," he tells her with a wink. "I'd like my fiancée to smell that good."

The woman looks at me, embarrassed that my "fiancé" is flirting with her in front of me. If only she knew how much worse it could get.

Mikhail's mask is thin. Even before I knew how deep the rot in him went, I had a bad feeling about him. I knew right away that we couldn't get married. It was some survival instinct in me that came to life whenever he was around. A radar that went *ping* whenever I was in the blast radius of the self-centered asshole.

As soon as the waitress walks away, Mikhail leans in close. "Remember what I said this morning, Cordelia. *Smile.*"

Considering he burst into my room and started to talk to me before I was fully conscious, I don't know why he expects me to remember anything he said.

Though I do, of course. It's hard to forget when someone threatens to torture your best friend.

"Up. Get dressed," he'd barked, throwing a dress on top of my comforter. "We're going out."

"I don't feel well," I said.

It wasn't entirely a lie. After I hung up with Ivan last night, I spent the rest of the night crying quietly into my pillow. When I woke up this morning, my eyes were raw and puffy.

He grimaced at me. "Yeah, you look like shit. Put some makeup on. There might be pictures."

I shook my head. "I don't feel well. I'm not going with—"

Suddenly, he leaned in close, his words ripping out in a harsh whisper. "Unless you want me to go spend my new free time with your little friend instead, you'll get out of this bed and do exactly what I say. *Now.*"

I knew it was bullshit. Ivan has Jorden. Mikhail and Alexander have been lying to me about holding her captive to control me. If I wanted to, I could have told Mikhail to fuck off and pulled the covers over my head. I could have gone with him and then ran at the first opportunity. The control they had over me is gone now. I'm free.

Except I promised Ivan I'd wait. I told him that I trusted him and I'd let him try things his way.

So, reluctantly, I dragged myself out of bed, stepped into my dress fit for a garden party from a patriarchal wet dream, and did as Mikhail said.

A few hours later, I'm still doing as he says.

I give him a pointed look and smile. "How is this?"

"Much better," he says approvingly. "You're not half bad when you put a little effort in."

"Wish I could say the same," I mumble.

He snaps his gaze to me, annoyance burning in his eyes. Then our waitress reappears with our drinks and the name of her perfume on a tiny square of cardstock. I ignore her and take a sip of my iced tea.

If she actually wants him, she can have him.

Besides, there's more than enough going on around us for me to focus on instead. The world is big, but the world of rich, privileged socialites in this city who can afford to go out to lunch in the middle of a weekday is small. The room is filled with people I half-remember from my old life. People I've seen at fundraisers and weddings who don't know a damn thing about me beyond the name of my stepfather.

Some glare, though. At least a handful of women in this room must have been at Ivan's party the night he and I met. And now, it is painfully clear they can't believe I'm sitting here with Mikhail Sokolov instead.

Mikhail places both of our orders without asking me what I want. Just as the waitress leaves, a couple takes her spot. The guy is my age with a trendy haircut and a pink and green plaid polo tucked into his trousers. But the girl is young. Ridiculously young.

"Mikhail! Hey, man. How's it going?" the guy asks. His arm is around his date's waist, holding her close like he's worried she might run off.

Mikhail stands up and shakes the man's hand. "Geoff, how have you been?"

They fall into an easy conversation about business or world domination or the size of the sticks up their respective asses or something. So I smile at the girl.

"Hi."

She gives me a tight-lipped smile and a nod. That same instinctual radar that warned me away from Mikhail all those years ago pings again.

Something isn't right here.

I smile a little wider, trying to communicate to her that I'm a safe space. I'm friendly. "What's your name?"

"Lucy." She folds her hands in front of her nervously and now, I'm convinced she's no older than seventeen.

"Nice to meet you. I'm Cor—Cordelia." I correct myself clumsily. Mikhail is too busy snickering with Geoff to notice. "Are you two here together?"

She purses her pale lips and nods once.

"Dating or—?"

"Engaged." She holds up a small hand with an oversized diamond. The ring is gorgeous, but it looks like costume jewelry on her thin finger.

"Oh, wow. Congratulations."

I must not look as cheerful as I sound because Lucy frowns. "Thanks. You, too."

I shake my head. "I'm sorry. Me, too? For what?"

"Your engagement," she says like it's the most obvious thing in the world.

I guess it is. Or it would be—if Mikhail and I were actually engaged. He didn't even organize a sham proposal to accompany our sham engagement. I still don't have a ring on my finger.

I chuckle. "Oh. Right. Yes. Of course."

"It's probably a lot to keep track of," she says softly.

My brows pinch together. "I'm not sure I know what you mean."

She glances over at Geoff and Mikhail. Both of them are busy assuming they are the center of the universe, so they aren't paying any attention.

Lucy looks back to me and leans in. "It's probably hard to keep track of your engagements. You've had so many."

I pull back and her expression is neutral, but I feel the venom from her words.

"Oh. I don't—That wasn't—" I fumble for something to say, but I don't know how to recover from this. Or how to explain the last few weeks of my life. Instead, I blow out a breath. "How old are you?"

Her brow arches sharply. "Old enough to know you're a fucking idiot."

I blink at her, stunned. She glances at Geoff. When he looks over, she smiles pleasantly. But the moment he looks away, her gaze snaps back to me. "No person in their right mind would give up Ivan Pushkin. You're the dumbest woman alive."

There are a million things I should say, but all I can manage is, "I didn't give him up."

Her eyes narrow further. "Then you weren't worth his time. Which makes you the most pitiful woman alive. Have fun with that."

Bitch.

I tell myself to give her grace. She's young, probably being manipulated by this douchebag named Geoff, and has been brainwashed to think that her only worth comes from marrying someone with money.

But I can't say any of that. Not right now. Not when Mikhail is standing two feet away. Not when I'm supposed to be playing my role to perfection.

Instead, I smile at her and turn to the side. "And you have fun being repeatedly cheated on by a man named *Geoff* for the rest of your life."

Her mouth falls open, but before she can say anything, I lay a hand on Mikhail's arm. "Excuse me—I'm going to the restroom."

His eyes flare. He doesn't want me out of sight, but he can't say that in front of his acquaintances.

His teeth clench as he grimaces. "Hurry back. Our food will be here soon."

I slip away and move towards the back of the restaurant. I feel eyes on me as I walk, but I don't stop and talk to anyone. Mikhail's goal in bringing me here was for the two of us to be seen. And we've been seen. Goal accomplished. Now, I need five minutes in a quiet room to decompress.

The women's bathroom is a right turn and a long hallway away from the dining area. Just turning the corner takes some of the weight off. I sag into my bones, dropping the facade I've been clinging to for dear life all morning.

When I step into the restroom and bolt the door behind me, I release a soul-deep sigh.

Whatever plan Ivan is working on, he better make it happen fast. I don't know how much more of this I can take.

The fake smiles. The fake people. The metaphorical knife twisting in my ribs.

Mikhail is content just to trot me out like a show pony—for now. But it won't be long before he tries to corner me again. Before he wants way, *way* more than I'm willing to give.

I won't be able to fake a smile through *that*.

No, if Mikhail tries to touch me again… I'll kill him before I give myself over.

For now, though, I don't have to kill anyone. Right now, the goal is to get through lunch without wanting to kill *myself*.

I shake off the dark thought and turn to at least wash my hands before I walk back into the arena. But just as I reach for the water, there's a knock on the bathroom door.

"Just a second," I say sweetly.

Whoever it is knocks again. Three times. Hard.

I clear my throat and speak louder. "Someone is in here. Just a second."

Again, three more knocks.

My heart rate spikes. I turn to face the door in mute horror. I don't say anything. I just stare at the wood and the laminated sign reminding employees to wash their hands.

Another knock.

Suddenly, I'm certain I know who it is.

Geoff and Lucy must've walked away, and now, Mikhail has come to find me. He's outside the door, and the moment I open it, he's going to push me back inside and punish me for walking away from him.

I just swore to myself I'd kill him if he touched me, but I don't even have my purse with me. Unless I can figure out how to turn a roll of paper towels into a weapon, I'm unarmed and backed into a corner.

My breathing is coming fast and heavy. I feel panic taking hold.

What do I do? How do I get out of here?

Then the knob turns.

25

CORA

I hear my name. *My* name. Spoken by a voice I'll have to die to forget. And maybe not even then.

"Cora."

Without another thought, I unbolt the door and throw it open.

Ivan pushes through the door and locks it behind him in an instant. He does exactly what I worried Mikhail would do, but instead of panicking, I throw myself at him.

I plaster my body to Ivan's in every conceivable way, trying to touch as much of him as I can. The more of him I touch, the less likely it is that this is some kind of vivid daydream.

If every part of me touches every part of him, then this has to be real.

"Ivan," I breathe.

Help me, is what I'm really saying. *Save me.*

His hands smooth across my shoulders and down my spine. My face is pressed into his chest as I take deep breaths of him. We're in a public restroom, but he smells like fresh air. Like nighttime and sandalwood.

I squeeze my eyes closed just in case this actually is a dream. If it is, I never want to wake up.

"Cora." He curls a hand around the back of my head and runs his fingers through my hair.

"How are you here?"

"I was on my way to meet Francia for lunch. I saw you walk past the back door." He chuckles to himself in disbelief. "I thought it was a dream."

Cautiously, I crack one eye open and peek up at him.

His eyes are bright, cloudless. He's staring down at me like he can't believe I'm in his arms. For some reason, that is enough to convince me this *is* real. Because I would never in my wildest dreams imagine Ivan could look quite this stunned.

He's here.

Ivan Pushkin is standing in front of me, alive and real.

The enormity of it slams into me and, before I can stop myself, I hook my hands around his neck and kiss him.

His mouth fits against mine the way I knew it would. Then his tongue swipes across my lower lip and there is suddenly nothing at all comfortable about the gnawing ache in my stomach. One flick of his tongue and my body is on *fire*.

"I missed you," I gasp against his mouth. "I want you."

I arch against him. I feel how much he wants me pressed against my stomach. I slip my hand between us, stroking him roughly.

"Fuck." He presses his stubbled cheek against mine. His breathing is heavy in my ear.

I am cataloging every detail of this. Of *him*. The million tiny things I didn't know if I'd ever experience again.

It all feels so precious. But I can feel it slipping through my fingers. Time is short and I don't want to waste a second of it.

I stroke him again, drawing a deep groan from his chest. Then I move to unbutton his pants.

But Ivan grabs my wrist. "We can't. Fuck, I want to, but—" His forehead drops to mine. I look into his eyes, but the amber is gone, devoured by dark desire. "When I'm inside you again, Cora, I'm going to take my time. It's something that can't be done in a few minutes. I need hours. Days. A whole fucking lifetime."

My whole body warms. I trail my hand over his chest and cup his cheek. "You can't talk to me like that and expect me to wait."

He huffs out a soft laugh. "Who said anything about waiting?"

I'm about to ask what he means when he spins me around and presses me to the tile wall. Slowly, *so slowly*, he kisses his way down my body and drops to his knees.

A dark tendril of hair falls over his forehead as he looks up at me.

I'm absolutely positive there is no sight more beautiful in all the world than this mountain of a man on his knees.

Then he pushes my dress up around my waist and I can't savor anything. I don't have the brain space for it. All I can focus on is the heat of his breath against my damp panties. The scrape of his beard against my inner thigh.

He hooks my leg over his shoulder and I melt back against the wall. I'm balanced between him and the tile, which is good, because I don't think I can stand on my own.

Then he shoves my panties to the side and I moan.

Suddenly, I realize that there is no way I'll be able to get through this without screaming. There is no way we can do this without me alerting every human within a ten-mile radius that Ivan is eating me out like his life depends on it.

"Wait!" I tug on his hair, trying and failing to pull him away from the ache between my thighs. "Wait. I can't—I'll scream, Ivan. I can't—"

He reaches up and presses a palm flat over my lips. "Save your screams, *solnishka*. Save them for when they count."

I kiss the tip of his finger just as he kisses my clit. He flicks his tongue against me and then delves deeper. He tastes me in long strokes, lapping from top to bottom and bottom to top and kissing every point along the way.

I writhe under his touch. "Ivan," I gasp, raking my fingers through his silky soft hair.

He strokes his hands up and down my thighs. He reaches under my dress and grips my waist. One hand curls over the lace of my bra, kneading my breast.

He's everywhere all at once. All I can do is press back against the wall and take it.

"You taste so fucking sweet," he growls. I feel the vibration at my core. Goosebumps sprout across my skin.

"I need you," I whimper, clutching my leg around his neck to draw him closer. "I need you inside of me. I need to feel you. I need—"

Ivan slides a finger inside of me. It isn't what I meant, but I gasp anyway. My hips jerk, taking in even more of him.

"Like that," he says. "Ride it, Cora."

I grind myself against his hand, slowing slightly as he adds another finger and then a third.

He pumps his hand into me and flicks his tongue across my clit. His other hand is still kneading my breast, working me from every angle.

I don't want it to end.

The last few days have been a nightmare. I was beginning to worry that the rest of my life would be stumbling through the darkness, desperate to find the light.

But here it is. The light.

"I'm so c-close." I tug on his hair and arch against his mouth. "I'm so… Right there… Please don't…"

Ivan hooks his fingers inside of me, setting off nerve endings I forgot existed, and *boom,* I explode.

Pleasure overflows from me in mindblowing pulses that take my breath away. There's no lung capacity left for me to scream. It takes every bit I have just to keep breathing.

I squeeze my eyes closed as the world spins out of control.

Gently, he works me down from the climax. His fingers slow and his tongue eases me down. Finally, he works my leg off of his shoulder and lowers my dress. All I can do is collapse into his arms, a puddle of Cora left behind where prim and proper Cordelia was just a few minutes ago.

"What about you?" I whisper into his chest.

"If you think that wasn't for me, then you're fucking insane." He grips my chin and kisses me. His lips are slick with me and I press into the kiss harder.

His tongue slides into my mouth. I start to lose myself in him. But now, the frenzied desire has passed and my mind has a little more room to think clearly.

I pull back, pressing a hand to his chest. "Don't ruin my makeup. I have to—I have to go back out there."

"Leave it," he orders. "Let me take it off. Let me take everything off."

"Mikhail is here," I protest. "He's right out there in the dining room. If he sees me like this, he could... I don't know what he'd do."

He growls. "Nothing. If he touches you, I'll kill him."

"Funny. I just thought the same thing before you got here." I press my cheek to his chest and listen to the consistent thudding of his heart. "I want to stay here with you. But he's out there. Waiting."

Ivan strokes my hair. "Francia is probably here by now, too."

That means we should leave. The rational part of my brain is shouting at me. *You should go before you run out of time.*

If Mikhail comes looking for me, there is nowhere to hide Ivan. He should get out of here while he still can.

"Oh," I say, an idea taking root. I can't believe I didn't think of it sooner. "You should... Oh my God, take me with you! Right now. Ivan," I gasp, grabbing his hands, "let's get out of here. We can leave and—"

"If there was any chance I could get you out of here today, I wouldn't have touched you." He grips my hips in frustration. "I would have waited until we were back at my house. In my bed."

My skin heats again. It's good to know he was thinking clearly, at least. As soon as I saw him, I had to touch him. I forgot about everything and everyone else.

"Why is there no chance?"

"I have no idea how many guards Mikhail has with him and I'm by myself."

My hopes deflate. "There are at least five Sokolov guards with us today. Maybe more."

"I could call in a team, but there's so much we wouldn't know. I'm not going to escape with you into a situation I haven't scouted. I'm not going to risk your life like that. Not when I have a better plan taking shape."

I fall against him, my forehead pressed to his chest. "I want this to be over, Ivan. I don't know how much longer I can do this."

He takes a deep breath and then pulls me away. He leans down and looks into my eyes, his mouth a serious slash. "You are Cora fucking St. Clair."

"That doesn't mean anything."

"It means *everything*. Everything, Cora." He squeezes my shoulders. "You are going to clean yourself up and walk back in there like nothing happened."

I shake my head. "I'm not like you. This isn't my world. I don't know how to do any of this."

"You are. It is. And you do." He presses a kiss to my forehead, his lips lingering there before he finally pulls away. "I have to go. But I'm going to see you soon."

Instinctively, I dig my fingers into his arm. Gently, he pries my hands away and wraps his fingers around mine for one brief squeeze.

Then he's gone.

And I'm all by myself again.

26

CORA

It takes a full thirty seconds after Ivan has left the bathroom for me to feel the small lump he left in my palm.

I open my hand and find a necklace. It's a circular locket with intricate designs worked into the gold. It looks like the petals of a peony. It looks like the engagement ring Ivan gave me.

I glance down at my left hand. For as much as I hated the gaudy ring at first, I miss it now that it's gone. I hope Francia isn't wearing it. If she is, I'll make sure she chokes on it before she dies.

I flick the tiny latch on the locket and it springs open. A tiny strip of paper falls out. I unfurl it with trembling fingers.

Wear this and I will always find you.

Tears burn the backs of my eyes. I press the locket against my chest and try to gather up these last few minutes I had with Ivan. I want to hold them close and use them to help me make it through the next however many days I have left in this prison.

Then I hear Ivan's voice in my head.

You are Cora fucking St. Clair.

He has a plan and I am stronger than I think. So I take a deep breath and get to work.

I flush the strip of paper down the toilet and drop the locket into my pocket. I can't walk out wearing a piece of jewelry I didn't have going in. I'll figure out how to make sure it can hang proudly around my neck soon.

Until then, Ivan told me to clean myself up. I turn to the mirror and—*holy hell.* My lipstick is smudged around my swollen mouth, my eyeliner has gone smokey, and my hair is falling out of the loose bun I had it twisted into.

As quickly as I can, I clean up the blurred edges of my makeup and redo my hair. It's not perfect, but Mikhail has been so busy showing me off that he hasn't really bothered to look at me.

But as soon as I step into the restaurant's dining room, Mikhail is waiting by the hallway. He grabs my arm and pulls me towards the back patio.

"We're leaving," he hisses.

I feel like I'm suddenly standing under a black light, signs of Ivan blazing across every inch of my skin. He's going to smell Ivan on me.

He'll see what I've been doing. He knows.

I take a deep breath and do my best to look confused. "What? We haven't even eaten yet."

He spins around so he's in front of me. His pale face looks yellow in the direct sunlight. "Where were you?"

I snap, "I was in the bathroom. Can I not even go to the bathroom by myself now?"

His hand tightens around my wrist, but his eyes shift over my shoulder towards the dining room. People are watching us. He loosens his grip and smiles.

"Where the fuck were you, Cordelia?"

"I just told you: I was in the bathroom, Mikhail."

Is Ivan somewhere behind me? Can he see me right now? The urge to turn around and find him is strong, but I shove it down.

Instead, I pat Mikhail's forearm as gently as I can bear to. "Did something happen? Is everything okay?"

He frowns at my gentle touch. Then he follows the line of my arm up, up, up. For the first time all day, he looks at me. Really *looks* at me.

Then he grabs my hand and pulls me out of the restaurant.

I struggle to keep up with his long strides. "I'm in heels," I remind him. "Can we slow down? Where are we—"

We duck behind a tall hedge and he turns on me. "Did you know he would be here?"

Warning bells blare so loud I can barely hear him. Can barely think. "Who?"

His top lip sneers. "Ivan."

I knew that's what he was going to say, but my stomach still bottoms out. I hope it adds an air of authenticity to the shock I smear across my face. "What? He was—He was here? Today?"

His pale eyes narrow. "Yes. He and Francia showed up together moments before you walked out of the bathroom."

"Then how would I know he was there?"

He stares hard at me for a long time. I hold my breath until, finally, Mikhail turns away, though he keeps a hand on my arm. He leads me to the waiting car and herds me into the backseat.

I feel the distance growing between Ivan and me. It hurts, like a chain set into my ribcage with fishhooks.

I ignore the ache. At least Mikhail isn't interrogating me anymore.

But the moment he closes his door, he's on me again. His fingers are clenched around my forearm with bruising force and I can't twist away.

"Ow! You're hurting me."

"You'll suffer worse than this," he croaks, "if you ever so much as breathe the same air as Ivan Pushkin again."

"You're the one who made me come here for lunch! I would have stayed home if you hadn't made me go."

He scowls, but there's no denying that's exactly how it went this morning.

"If you're so worried about everyone knowing I belong to you, why don't you just get me a dog collar?" I add sarcastically. "You could put your name and address on the tag in case I get lost."

"A leash might not be such a bad idea. Disobedience should be punished."

My stomach turns. The way he talks about me like I'm barely human is terrifying.

But I can use this.

"I don't know if I'd even mind a leash," I mumble. "Then maybe women like Lucy wouldn't give me so much shit."

His anger gutters out. "What did Lucy say?"

That I'm an idiot for giving up Ivan.

She wasn't wrong, but I can't say that. That won't help my argument at all.

"She noticed I didn't have a ring on and wondered how serious we really were." I sigh. "That's why I went to the bathroom. I didn't want to talk to her anymore."

I watch as the words land exactly how I planned them.

Mikhail twists his lips in thought. "There's a ring, but it's going to take time to have it finished and resized."

"If you really want to convince people we are together, get me another piece of jewelry in the meantime. A bracelet or…" I pretend to waver, thinking. "A necklace could work. It's not so far off from a collar."

I look out the window, feigning boredom. Pretending like my heart isn't about to hurl itself out of my chest.

"I was under the impression you didn't want people to think we were really together. You're still waiting for Ivan Pushkin to come save you from my evil clutches, aren't you?" he drawls.

It's a trap. He's so twisted, he might actually like if I fall into it. That way he'd have an excuse to punish me. Not that he needs one.

I snort. "I've given up on men—*all* men. My relationship with Ivan was never real. Maybe I deluded myself into thinking it was real, but…" I shrug. "He's with Francia and he isn't coming for me."

Mikhail's hand loosens on my arm. "If you've given up on men, why do you want people to think you're with me?"

I look up into his pale eyes. We're closer than I thought. I can see the blue veins running under his skin. The desperation burning in them.

"I may not have chosen to be here, but if I have to, I don't want to be at the center of the rumor mill. I want to be left alone. If selling your version of the story does that, then so be it."

It's a blend of my truth and the reality Mikhail wants. A compromise of sorts. I just hope he takes it.

He lets out a slow breath, his eyes roving over my face. Then, without looking away, he barks at the driver, "Stop at a jewelry store on the way back. Any store. I don't care which."

I fight back a smile as the words from Ivan's note flicker in my mind. *Wear this and I will always find you.*

I hope to God he meant it.

27

IVAN

We're back at the mansion and things are going poorly.

Francia slams her hands on the dining room table hard enough that the empty glass next to her setting crashes sideways. One of the new maids jolts to get it, but Francia scares her away with a skin-melting glare.

"Leave the glass. Just bring out the food. *Now.*"

"There's an appetizer first," the maid says shakily. "A house salad and—"

"It's the middle of the fucking afternoon and we still haven't eaten. I don't want a salad—I want lunch. Bring it."

The maid's mouth opens and closes. She glances at me for help.

The staff just found out twenty minutes ago that lunch at the restaurant was canceled and they needed to have a full lunch ready for us by the time we got back home. Francia doesn't seem to grasp that roast duck isn't the kind of thing you throw in the microwave on short notice.

"Skip a few courses and let's get to the entree as quickly as you can," I tell her. "Let's get this show on the road."

The woman nods and hurries out of the dining room with Francia calling after her, "*Now,* you listen? That's what I said!"

"I think it's more about the way you said it."

Her attention slides to me. "How did I say it?"

"Like a rabid dog," I say flatly. "Maybe we shouldn't go out if it's going to upset you so much."

She frowns. "I'm not upset about going out. I'm upset that we *couldn't* go out."

"I still don't see why not."

Her eyes widen. "You don't see why not? I suppose that makes sense. You apparently 'didn't see' Cora today, either. Like I believe that."

"I didn't see Cora," I reiterate. "Even if I had, I wouldn't have made a huge scene the way you did."

"I didn't make a scene."

I snort. "You screamed at the hostess and stormed out of the restaurant."

After I left Cora in the bathroom, I snuck out through the back patio door and walked around to the front of the restaurant to meet Francia. She was all smiles, clinging to my arm and grinning at everyone on the street like she was in a fucking pageant.

Then we walked inside.

Mikhail sprang out of his chair the moment he saw me in the waiting area. I caught his trail across the dining room out of the corner of my eye. But based on the way Francia's face tightened, I know she saw all of it.

We barely made it through the doors before she was stomping back out onto the sidewalk, looking a hell of a lot less pleased than she had when she'd gone in.

That was all fine with me. I'd already gotten exactly what I wanted from our lunch date. More than I ever could have bargained for, actually.

"I didn't want to sit around while people whisper about you and your ex," she hisses. "Our first outing together can't be a double fucking date."

"It would put to bed a lot of rumors swirling around right now."

She unfolds her napkin with a quick flick of her wrists. "Putting anything to bed is what I'm worried about."

The memory of Cora wrapped around my neck, her pussy quivering against my lips, roars to life in me. It's the fight of my life to keep from grinning like a lunatic.

Francia is still staring at me when I hear the front door open.

"Who is that?" she asks.

I don't say anything because I already know. There are only two people who barge into my house with any regularity—and Yasha doesn't usually wear high heels that click across the entryway.

Francia starts to stand just as my sister appears in the doorway. When she sees who I'm sitting with, her smile curdles.

"Great timing, Anya." I wave her in. "Join us. Sit down."

"I'd hate to interrupt. Anyway, I was actually just dropping by for—There's a dress upstairs in the guest room. I wanted to wear it."

"It's great that you're here!" Francia crows. "I wanted to talk more about the wedding planning."

Anya is still creeping around the edge of the dining room. As if she might be able to slip back into the shadows and escape. "I sent you an email. Did you get my email?"

Francia frowns. "No."

"Oh. Maybe I forgot to send it." She chuckles at herself. "I am so scattered. Very busy recently. I should leave and check and then I'll send it and—"

"Or we can talk about it now." Francia pulls out the chair between us. "Sit."

Sensing she's lost this battle, Anya reluctantly sits down. Under the table, she kicks my ankle. I just smile back at her over my ice water.

"Like I told you the other day, Francia, I'm not really great at the whole wedding planning thing. I don't have the head for all of the details and the color schemes."

"You planned your own wedding, didn't you?" Francia asks. "I saw an article about it in the paper. It looked beautiful."

"Years ago." She waves a hand dismissively. "Which feels more like a lifetime ago. And it was kind of out of necessity."

"Yeah, because you fired the wedding planner you originally hired," I added. "You told me she couldn't capture 'your vision,' so you'd have to do it yourself."

I feel another hard, sharp kick under the table. My ankle will be bruised, but having Anya here as a buffer between me and Francia is worth it.

Francia arches a brow. "It sounds like you really know what you're doing. And I know you are the one who organized Cora's bachelorette party. And you arranged for her to try on wedding dresses here at the house."

"Most of that was Ivan's doing." Anya turns to me. "Right, Ivan? You arranged most of that."

I clap my sister on the back. "Don't be modest, Anya. That was all you."

"Great. Then you can help me, too." Francia really is shameless. Most people would pick up on the very obvious hints Anya is dropping, but either Francia is clueless or she's in deep, deep denial. "I'm imagining a garden party for the bachelorette. And I'd like Ivan to be there with me."

"Not much of a bachelorette party if I'm there."

"Then don't call it a bachelorette party." She reaches over and lays her hand on top of mine, her finger tracing my knuckles. It's like trying to hold perfectly still as a tarantula crawls across your skin. "Call it a celebration of love."

Anya snorts so hard she almost chokes.

Francia snaps her attention to her. "What's so funny?"

"I'm sorry, but… love?" Anya laughs again and looks between us. "You two aren't in love. You're just… you're not. You have to know that, Francia."

"The only thing I know," she spits, "is that I'm not going to sit here and be disrespected in my own house."

Anya's mouth falls open. *"This isn't your house!* What the hell is wrong with you?"

"Out." Francia stands up, finger pointed towards the door. "If you can't respect me, then—"

"If that is your bar for who is allowed in your house, it's going to be a long, lonely life."

Francia exhales sharply. She makes me think of a bull before it charges. "Get out right now."

"Are you trying to throw me out? You can't throw me out. This is my brother's house."

Francia lifts her chin. "This is *our* house and you're not welcome here."

Anya stares at her for a few seconds, a smile slowly spreading across her face. Then she shakes her head. "You're actually deranged. Full-on unhinged. Like, have you considered seeing a specialist? Books could be written about how absolutely, banana-pants crazy you are."

Francia takes a step towards my sister, her eyes narrowed to slits like the snake she is. "Get out of my house before I—"

I'm on my feet and standing between her and Anya before she can even get the words out.

"It's my house. I choose who stays and who goes."

She stumbles back and glares up at me. "You'll let her talk to your wife like that?"

"You aren't my wife."

"Yet," she adds with a sneer.

Ever, I think with a scowl.

Instead, I just shake my head, too tired to even fight about this. "Anya stays as long as she likes."

Anya cackles and then flops back down in her chair and kicks her feet up on the table. "Amazing. Suddenly, I'm overjoyed to be here. Maybe I'll stay for dinner, too."

Francia starts to argue, but I push past her towards the balcony.

"Where are you going?" she hisses at my back.

I don't answer. I just walk onto the patio, letting the doors close behind me.

Silence. Blissful silence. The sun is sinking lower in the sky. It's well past lunch and dipping into mid-afternoon now. There's a breeze rustling the plants in the garden beds and whirling under the overhang.

But I don't feel it.

I don't feel anything.

Numbness has been seeping into me bit by bit, piece by piece, for days. Every second Cora is away from me, it spreads further.

Is this what I felt like before I met her?

Now, I'm back here—back with Francia—and I can't even bring myself to care that she and Anya are yelling at each other in the other room. I don't care that she thinks she lives in my house. She can have the house. I'll give it all to her.

I just need Cora.

I had her in my arms only a few hours ago. I held her and tasted her. Now, it's hard to convince myself any of it was real. It's hard to convince myself that I'll ever get her back.

I close my eyes and blow out a long, deep breath.

Fuck that.

I stare out at the lawn until the tightness in my chest eases. I don't know how long it takes, but by the time I'm done, the shouting inside has stopped. Either Francia and Anya have solved all of their problems or one of them is dead. I should probably go see which it is.

I head back into the dining room, expecting there to be bloodshed. Instead, Francia and Anya are sitting perfectly politely at the table. It takes me a second to see why.

My father is standing in the doorway.

"This is becoming a real family affair," I say with a grimace. "Will you be joining us for lunch, too? Or do you—"

He cuts me off. "I should have figured. You've turned us into a laughingstock, but you're having brunch. Typical." He throws a crumpled-up piece of parchment at me. "Konstantin Sokolov just sent me his son's engagement announcement."

I knew it would be coming out sooner or later. After our almost-run-in this afternoon, I'm not surprised. Mikhail was shaken and wants to stake his claim.

If he'd seen what Cora and I got up to in the bathroom, he wouldn't have bothered.

She's mine.

Otets turns back to me. "You put that little bitch on my payroll. You tied her to our family name. And then you let her go? You fucking let her humiliate us. You let her make an embarrassment of you."

Francia stands up. "Hello, Mr. Pushkin. My name is Francia. I'm Ivan's fiancée."

Any sane person would see the vein throbbing in my father's forehead and stand down. But it's already well-documented that Francia is not a sane person.

My father looks her up and down. His lip twists into a sneer. "*Another* one?"

Francia frowns. "I'm sorry. Another what?"

He ignores her. "Ivan, are you fucking kidding me? This isn't a brothel. You don't get a harem. Pick one woman and be done with it."

He wants to get a rise out of me, but he has no clue the favor he is doing me. I'd love nothing more than for Francia to be kicked down a peg. He's saving me the effort of doing it myself.

"I'm sorry we haven't been able to meet yet," Francia continues obliviously, "but I'm excited to join your family. I hope that we can get to know each other and you'll see—"

"Don't tell me what I'll see," he barks. "I know what I see. Another useless leech."

"My parents are lawyers." Francia's voice is shaking, making her argument sound even weaker. "I'm not—I can bring value to—"

"If you want to bring something, bring me a drink," he barks. "The men are talking."

Anya is trying so hard not to laugh I'm worried she might give herself a hernia. I have to admit, this is the first time I've ever been glad to have my dad turn up unexpectedly.

Francia looks distinctly less happy about it.

She snaps her mouth closed, but I can tell by the set of her jaw that she'll have plenty to say about this later.

28

CORA

I stand in front of the full-length mirror in my bedroom and try my hardest to recognize the woman staring back at me.

The dress Alexander chose for me to wear tonight is a ruffled eyesore. I look like a pastel piñata. It's really fitting, actually. They don't physically hurt me, but I'm taking an emotional beating from every side.

I reach up and grab the gold locket around my neck. I squeeze the metal until it's warm in my palm. I can't tell where I stop and it begins.

Mikhail will look at it and think it's the one he bought me. I was pleasantly surprised at how close of a dupe I was able to find at the random jewelry store we stopped off at after leaving the restaurant.

But the moment I got to my room, I hid Mikhail's locket behind the loose piece of trim in my closet and swapped it with Ivan's.

Wear this and I will always find you.

God, I hope he's right.

I still have my hand wrapped around the necklace when my door explodes open. "Are you ready?" my stepfather barks.

I slowly drop the necklace and lower my hand. The last thing I want is to look guiltier than I already feel.

It's hard because Alexander has been especially keyed-up today. He isn't ever pleasant, but he's been on the warpath all afternoon.

"Is anyone ever truly ready to meet their in-laws?" I drawl.

He jabs a finger at me. "None of that smart mouth at dinner. You smile. You nod. You look pretty."

"Hard to do in this dress."

His eyes narrow. "If you can't handle—"

"Just getting it all out of my system." I lower myself into a deep curtsy. "I'll be on my best behavior, Master."

He sneers and opens his mouth to say more. But before he can unleash his nerves on me, my mother moves behind him and places a hand on his shoulder.

"She knows what to do, Alex. It will all be okay."

He shrugs her hand away. "I remember a similar sentiment the night before she ran away. Maybe you don't know your daughter as well as you think you do."

Alexander tosses one final glare in my direction before he storms into the hallway to snarl at the temporary staff he's hired for the evening. He's brought in at least ten new hires to fill out the decor. God forbid Konstantin Sokolov see that this house runs with only two permanent indentured servants.

"You really should try to cooperate, Cordelia," my mother says softly.

I almost forgot she was standing in the doorway. I've gotten good at tuning her out. Survival instinct has me dividing everyone into friends or foes. Who is here to hurt me and who is here to help me? My mother is doing neither, so as far as I'm concerned, she might as well not exist.

"I'm in the dress. I'm going to dinner. I don't know what more he wants from me."

She sighs. "He's stressed. If you could not talk back, then it would make things easier."

"Easier for me or for you?"

A crease forms between her brows. She looks older than I remember. Like she's aged ten years in the last three. "Why can't it be both?"

"They're here!" Alexander roars up the stairs at us. "Get down here. Now!"

She half-turns towards the command, but then stops and looks back at me, waiting.

I don't let Alexander's order rush me. I consider her question seriously. "Maybe it used to be possible. At one point, you and I could both benefit from the same outcome. But now... I can't win if my enemy succeeds. And you're with the enemy."

She blinks like I physically hit her. Her mouth falls open. Before she can gather the words for whatever lie she is about to tell, I brush past her and head towards the stairwell.

If I'm going to make it through tonight, I need to focus my energy on the players that matter.

Just as I reach the foyer, my mother not far behind me, Alexander reaches for the doorknob. His eyes sharpen on me. One silent final warning to behave.

I take a deep breath as he pulls the door open.

Let the games begin.

Before the appetizers can even hit the table, Konstantin Sokolov has offended me in every way that matters.

"If things had happened like they ought to have," Konstantin says, referring for the fifth time to me running away to avoid marrying his son, "then I wouldn't be worried. But she's past her prime. If we want healthy offspring, they need to get married and get started as soon as possible."

Past my prime? I'm twenty-four, for fuck's sake!

Then again, I don't want to be in my prime. Not for Mikhail Sokolov. Not for being used as a breeding cow for his psychopath babies.

So I bite my tongue and drown the words. I wish I could literally drown them, but Alexander already silently warned me off of any more water. When the maid refilled my glass for the third time, Alexander glanced over and shook his head. But I think he'd rather I drink than say what is on my mind.

Which is that Konstantin Sokolov is going to need more than a woman in her prime to have sex with Mikhail if he wants grandchildren. Because as it is, one look at his mean, pasty son has me dryer than the Sahara. I can practically feel my ovaries shriveling up. Nine out of ten fertility doctors recommend against trying to reproduce with men you despise on a visceral, physical level.

"We announced the engagement today, but left the wedding date unspecified since the situation is... unfolding." Mikhail looks down at me and I realize I am "the situation."

"'Un*willing*' is more like it," I mutter.

No one seems to hear me because, right as I speak, the kitchen doors open. Four women I don't recognize and one I do march out carrying baskets of bread and salads. There's one server for each person at the table. Because that isn't ostentatious and obnoxious in the least, right?

If Mikhail and Konstantin are impressed by Alexander's show of wealth, they hide it well. Better yet, everyone is so focused on the food being placed in front of them that no one notices a small phone being dropped into my lap.

The young maid doesn't look at me or signal to me in any way. She simply places my starter course on the table and then drapes a cloth napkin in my lap, discreetly covering the phone. Then, without breaking rank, she disappears into the kitchen with the others.

"That's why we're here," Alexander says to the table. "To hammer out the details of our families becoming one. I'm sure we can handle that over four courses."

Four more courses? I can't sit here for four more courses! Not with this bomb in my lap.

My heart is thundering. I take a bite of bread, but it turns to cement in my dry mouth.

Is the phone from Ivan?

Or is it a trap?

Maybe Alexander and the Sokolovs are testing my commitment. Maybe they are testing me to see what I'll do when presented with a way out. Will I take it or will I obey?

"I don't want to wait four courses; I've waited long enough," Konstantin says. "I don't see what we're doing with this dinner in the first place. It's a waste of time. It should be a wedding rehearsal."

"If we rush it, it looks like we're scared," Mikhail offers.

He looks down the table at me for only a moment. Does he know what's hiding in my lap? He has to know. *He can see right through me. He sees the terror burning under my skin.*

Then I see it. The ghost of what he felt in the restaurant is written all over his face. The panic at seeing Ivan there. The fear that I am slipping through his fingers.

What would he think if he knew he'd never had me in his grasp in the first place?

Konstantin sighs. "I suppose. But the wedding should happen as soon as propriety allows."

Alexander mulls over the thought. "We could fast track things a few weeks. The main concern would be the investment. Putting a rush on some of these things will be costly and the benefit I'm expected to get out of it—"

"The cost is of no concern to me," Konstantin snaps.

Great. Glad we got that settled. Now that money isn't a concern, maybe they can be concerned about the abduction and forced marriage.

I can't even be bothered about that right now, though. Not with this cell phone of unknown origin burning a hole in my lap.

They ramble on, talking about wedding dates and optimal times for me to be impregnated, but I'm so distracted I can't be as disgusted as I should be.

I need to get out of here.

I need to see what is on this phone.

I finish my salad in record time, shifting the phone towards the built-in pockets of my dress each time I reach down to wipe my fingers on the napkin. By the time the salad is gone, the phone is safely tucked away. The three glasses of water I chugged before the starters arrived are also sitting heavy in my bladder.

"Are there any hereditary conditions we should know about?" Konstantin asks. He looks at my mom, studying her. "Her mother looks fine enough, but what do you make of her father? Is he unwell? I don't want to invite any disorders or diseases into our family line."

Yes, what a shame it would be to tarnish their long history of sociopathy with a dose of sanity. Can't have anyone with a conscience breaking into the fold.

"Our genes are strong enough that I'm not concerned." Mikhail smirks. "Impregnating her won't be a worry, but whether she can carry a Sokolov baby full term is. Sokolov mothers tend towards anemia. We suck our mothers dry, apparently."

I want to throw up in my mouth. Maybe that's what's wrong with the entire family. They are all parasites. If I'm not careful, Mikhail will latch onto me.

Alexander laughs like Mikhail just said something funny. Like making a crack about how the women in the Sokolov family get ill and die while Alexander is actively marrying me *into* that family isn't cause for concern.

I guess, for him, it isn't.

"We can schedule a physical if you need, but there has never been anything out of the ordinary with Cordelia's health. Has there, Evaline?"

My mother shakes her head. "No. She's healthy as a horse."

"I can pee like one, too," I interrupt.

It's the first time I've spoken the entire meal. All eyes turn to me. My mother's face is bright red and Alexander looks livid.

Apparently, a sense of humor is not a welcome quality in a bride. Ah, well, nevertheless. He told me to be on my best behavior. This is the best I've got.

"I need to use the restroom," I correct, my voice meek and dainty. "If you could all excuse me."

The phone sits against my thigh like a brick. I feel the weight of it bringing my skirt down on the right hip. I shift that side away from the table as I slide out of my chair and make for the door.

"Cordelia." Konstantin Sokolov's voice rings out across the dining room. "Stop. Turn around."

My heart gallops uncomfortably in my chest, but I turn slowly.

Oh, fuck.

I chose wrong. This was a test and I failed it. What comes next? How bad will it hurt?

Four sets of venomous eyes are locked on me. I can feel sweat dripping down my spine.

"Yes?" I croak through a dry throat.

Konstantin's eyes narrow. His gaze sweeps me up and down slowly. Finally, he turns back to Alexander. "She's too thin. See to it that you fix this before she carries a Sokolov."

Relief mingles with disgust as they all turn their attention back to the table and each other, looking away as though I don't even exist.

It's a good thing. It means I can slip out of this room and to the bathroom with the contraband in tow without being noticed.

But it still makes me feel small. Insignificant.

I'm thin because humans don't usually fare too well in captivity. We need joy and sunlight and hope to thrive. None of which are available in the McAllister household. And I have a feeling the Sokolov estate is even bleaker.

By the time I get to the bathroom, I'm shaking with adrenaline and fear and anger. *So much anger.*

At first, I wanted them all to ignore me. Now, the way they talk around me, planning my future, arranging when I'll have children… It makes me sick.

I don't know how much more of it I can take.

I take a moment to pee—I really did have to go after three cups of water—before I pull the phone out of my pocket and finally dare to look at it.

There's a text message from an unknown number.

It's me. Use this phone if you need it. I'm here.

Ivan. He smuggled a cell phone to me through another one of the maids. But he's never felt farther away.

Before I can decide what to text back, there's a knock on the door. I lock the screen and shove the phone in my pocket.

"Hello?" I call.

"Just checking on you," my mother says softly through the door. "We're waiting on you for the next course."

I haven't been gone for more than ninety seconds. Was she listening to my flow from the outside of the door? *She finished peeing and flushed, so only twenty more seconds for washing hands, which means...*

I want to cling to the promises Ivan has made me. I want to believe that he is coming for me and that this will all end.

But that's hard when my world is no bigger than this beige half-bath. As much as I want to deny it, *this* feels like my future.

Not Ivan, but Mikhail.

Not hope, but hate.

Not love, but fear and pain and being forced to give birth to a new generation of people who will grow up in this toxic cycle and suck me dry from the womb and then drop-kick me into an early grave.

I blink back tears and open the bathroom door.

29

IVAN

The audio is coming through crystal clear.

When Cora left the restaurant, the necklace was shoved in her pocket. Everything was muffled and unintelligible. But she must have figured out how to display the necklace without raising eyebrows. Because I can hear every word.

Every disgusting, horrendous word.

Konstantin Sokolov hasn't changed a bit since he and my father arranged for me to marry Katerina. "The goal of any marriage is healthy offspring," he'd said, gesturing to his barely twenty-year-old daughter. "No woman will give you higher quality babies than Katerina. She's ready for this."

Of course, Katerina wasn't ready for it. For any of it.

She ran away the same way Cora tried to. She started over.

The difference is that Katerina is still free. Without his prized offspring, Konstantin has set his sights on Cora. She is his only hope to have heirs. Because no one in their right mind would marry Mikhail Sokolov.

And Konstantin knows it.

"The wedding should happen as soon as propriety allows." It takes me a second to realize that is Konstantin's voice in the present and not from my memories.

I bring my phone closer to my ear, trying to catch every word.

"We could fast track things a few weeks," Alexander snivels. "The main concern would be the investment. Putting a rush on some of these things will be costly and the benefit I'm expected to get out of it—"

Konstantin cuts him off. "The cost is of no concern to me."

Liars. The cost is the only thing that matters to any of them. They are all looking at their bottom lines all the time. The moment this union doesn't bring in enough money or ensure enough power, it will be dissolved.

I hear Cora sigh every so often. Her breath rumbles against the speaker, sending a blast of static. The reminder that she is alive and breathing is calming.

Which is good—because nothing else about the conversation is calming.

It's the world's most boring boxing match. These two preening idiots squaring off, circling each other while they try to make sure they are each getting the better end of the deal.

Konstantin wants to know Alexander's fixer business is on an upward trajectory. Alexander wants to know that selling his stepdaughter will guarantee Konstantin Sokolov's continued business moving forward.

It's not dinner conversation; it's a buffet of the thoughts of insecure men. Men who have nothing better to do than sell their sons and daughters into joyless marriages while they count their coins.

At one point, I could have been one of them. If it hadn't been for watching my own sister suffer… If I hadn't been engaged to Katerina, who literally begged me to help her get free… Maybe I would have turned into one of these manipulative ghouls who treat the people around them like kindling for the fire.

But now, there is Cora.

With Cora, it isn't just about setting her free and helping her escape this world. It's about destroying any world that would ever want to keep her down.

Mikhail's voice breaks me out of my thoughts. The audio jumps and then picks up. "Impregnating her won't be a worry, but whether she can carry a Sokolov baby full term is."

My knuckles go white as I grip the phone.

The thought of Mikhail even being in the same room as Cora is enough to make me want to drive across town and drag Cora out of there, body count be damned. But the thought of him touching her… *impregnating her…* there isn't a violent enough word for what it makes me want to do to him.

Maybe that anger is why I didn't hear the footsteps in the hall until the knob is turning.

I swipe out of the audio app and place my phone face down on my desk just as Francia stomps into my office.

"I will not live like this, Ivan!" she screeches. "I will *not* live like this. I refuse. This treatment is—is—It's unacceptable!"

Her hair is in a sweaty, frizzy mess around her head and she's panting. She must have marched here all the way from her wing of the house.

"Ah, yes. Of course." I fold my shaking hands on top of my desk and nod. "I can see how living in a mansion with two maids assigned to care for you, around-the-clock protection, and a live-in chef could be unacceptable. How dare I make sure your every need is met?"

Francia stares daggers into me, but all I can think about is Cora locked away in her room. She has no freedom, no connection to the outside world beyond the phone a maid will hopefully be delivering to her soon, and she's withering away with every passing day.

She's completely alone, trapped in that room with men who don't deserve to breathe the same air as her.

And I'm here… listening to Francia complain about the accommodations she stole from Cora.

Without looking at my unwelcome bride, I grab my phone and fire off a text to Cora's burner number.

It's me. Use this phone if you need it. I'm here.

I want Cora to know she isn't alone. No matter how she feels right now, I'm going to come for her. I'm going to get her out of there.

When I look up, smoke might as well be pouring out of Francia's ears. "There is more to a life than amenities, Ivan," she spits. "I don't care what the thread count of my sheets are if you can't even make it through a single conversation with me without grabbing your phone. I don't care about a jacuzzi tub if no one in this fucking mansion respects my role as your wife."

"We aren't married."

"Yet," she hisses. "We aren't married *yet*. But we will be, and being treated like a second-class citizen in my own home is not what I signed up for."

"Guess you should have read the fine print." It's a struggle not to laugh in her face. "You aren't dead. You could be dead. I suggest you keep that in mind and you'll be more grateful."

She blanches, but doesn't back down. "I'm a Bratva wife. I should have some power."

"I'm sorry the reality isn't living up to your fantasy."

"This isn't about some fantasy I have, Ivan! I'm not a little girl with stars in her eyes. I'm not *Cora*."

Her name hits me like a bolt of lightning. I go rigid. I feel every breath. Every inhale and exhale.

I've toed the line between pushing Francia away and drawing her in. I've held my tongue and let her buy new pillows for the sitting room. I've sat back and let her play House, all so she'd think there was even the vaguest chance that I could come to accept her as my wife.

But now... fuck it.

"No," I snarl, my voice pure venom. "You're not. You're a fucking business deal and not a goddamn thing more. If you're alive to say, 'I do,' then that is good enough for me. Beyond that, you're useless to me."

Truthfully, I have no intention of ever letting this bullshit get that far. But I don't need to reveal all of my cards at once. Not when a peek at this hand is sending Francia into shock.

Her eyes are wide as she blinks at me, silent for the first time in a long time. Thank fucking God.

"You wanted a strong, capable bride." Her voice is unsure like she hasn't fully convinced herself. "You wanted a partnership. That's what you said. How can this be a partnership if... if I'm disrespected?"

"I'll make sure you are respected in public," I tell her. "It does me no good if you are a laughingstock amongst our peers. But in this house, I won't lift a finger to make your life easier. I won't go out of my way to make sure the staff cuts the crusts off your sandwiches or makes your bed."

"But... but we're engaged! I—"

"You forced me into this marriage," I remind her icily. "If you thought I would take kindly to that, you severely underestimated me. And if you don't like the way things are going here, you have no one to blame but yourself. The moment you decided to double cross me, this is the life you signed up for. You are my bride, not my beloved. And you never will be."

I expect Francia to throw another fit. To scream and shout until she gets her way.

Instead, she glares at me for one second, two, three... Then she turns and twirls out of the room, leaving as silently as she came.

Konstantin Sokolov wants to bump up their time frame. Well, I have yet another great reason to bump up mine.

Francia is not going to quit this easily.

30

FRANCIA

I thought he would come around.

Cora is wide-eyed. Naive. She doesn't know how to take care of herself. How can Ivan think she'll be able to take care of him? She is a helpless little girl trapped in a useless woman's body.

I hate that I was right.

I hate that I knew Ivan would choose her. All I had to do was send her teetering in his direction and he fell for her.

No—he fell for *me*.

Everything he wants is because I told him to want it. So why can't I make him want this? Want *me*?

I lift my chin as I pass through the kitchen. The maids think they are hiding well enough in the pantry, but I can see the light coming from under the door. Tittering. Mocking me.

I'll come back for them later.

Right now, I need to take care of my husband-to-be.

Men know what they want, but they have no fucking clue what they *need*. Ivan needs a real woman. He needs a partner who can carry the weight of power alongside him. Cora would buckle under the strain. She can't do for Ivan what he needs. She can't do what I'm going to do for him.

He'll see it. I know he will.

Ivan will open his eyes to the prize standing in front of him or… or I'll get rid of him, too. I'll get rid of everyone in my way.

The phone rings six times before there's an answer. "You know I'm busy," he snaps. "What do you need that is so—"

"Get rid of her."

There's a pause. "Who?"

"You know who," I hiss. "Who the fuck else? I want her out of the picture *now*."

There's a long pause. I sigh. Another man who doesn't know what he needs. Do I have to do fucking *everything* around here?

"Francia, there are things in motion that can't be rushed. We have to go through the proper channels and—"

"Shut the fuck up and do what I tell you. Get rid of Cora."

He starts to say something, but the retort is lost as I hang up the phone.

"Ivan doesn't know what is best for him, but I do," I whisper. "I'm going to be his queen whether he likes it or not."

31

CORA

The moment I'm alone in my room, I tear my frilly dress off and kick it into the corner.

I feel filthy. Like I've spent the last two hours wallowing in the mud with pigs.

In a lot of ways, I have. Alexander, Mikhail, Konstantin—they're all pigs. The only worth I have in their eyes is the ability to look pretty and procreate. They don't care if I'm happy. They don't give a shit if I'm fulfilled.

If the last two hours taught me anything, it's that if I stay here, I'll end up like my mother. A weak, simpering woman clinging to the arm of a heartless bastard.

I go into my ensuite bathroom and scrub the makeup off of my face. It takes two passes before the eyeliner and mascara is finally nothing more than a slight smudge around my eyes. Usually, I'd try again, but what does it matter? Who is going to see me? No one I care about impressing.

When I'm done, I pad back into my empty room, grateful to be alone. But still, I wish I was somewhere else. With *someone* else.

It's me. Use this phone if you need it. I'm here.

Ivan's text pops into my mind at the same moment I see my dress crumpled in the corner.

The rest of the dinner was such a nightmare that I almost forgot about the phone he sent me. I hurry across the room and dig through the swaths of fabric before I feel the piece of plastic.

I rest back on my ankles and open the phone. My message to Ivan is still in the text box unsent.

Don't forget about me, Ivan. Don't leave me here. Thank you for this, but please come—

All of those same feelings still burn inside of me, crying out for anyone to hear. But now, there is something else, too. A need.

I delete the message and draft a new one.

I wish you were here. Right now. In my bed.

I send the message and then scramble back onto my mattress, waiting for his reply. I don't have to wait long.

Say more.

My fingers tingle with anticipation. **Do you remember that bag of sex toys you made me buy?** I ask.

Of course I remember.

My body remembers, too. A shiver works its way down my spine. I remember trying to chase the ache inside of me, trying to get Ivan out of my head, only for him to show up in my shower. I can still feel the way he shifted behind me. The way his body fit against my curves. He brought me to the brink with his hands and the toy and the raw sexuality that no one else on earth can hold a candle to.

I blow out a shaky breath. *I want you to tie me to your bed and use them on me.*

I send the message before I can doubt myself. For the first time in days, the walls of my room disappear. The cage around me falls away and I float off somewhere else.

I stare at the screen, waiting for his text. Instead, the phone rings.

As soon as I accept the call, the deep timbre of his voice cuts through the silence. "Don't say anything. I don't want them to hear you."

My mouth is already half-opened, but I close it.

"Cora," he breathes. Even the way he says my name is foreplay. I feel the vibration of it in my toes. "Slide your hand between your legs."

My heart jolts. I grip the phone tighter. Sexting was one thing, but hearing Ivan say all these dirty things right in my ear is different. I'm not sure if I'm ready for—

"Stay quiet," he reminds me, as if he can read my thoughts. "And let me make you feel good."

I blink back the sudden threat of tears. No one seems to care about what I want or need.

Except Ivan.

He cares.

So I let him.

I slide my hand between my legs, curling my palm over my heat.

"Run your middle finger over your slit."

I listen, my breath hitching as I follow his orders.

"I love that sound," he growls. "I love when you fall apart just a little bit for me. Push your panties to the side and do it again."

It's my own hand moving my panties to the side and dipping into my arousal, but it feels different. I'm at Ivan's mercy. I'm frozen, waiting for his next direction, aching for him to let me go further.

"You're wet, aren't you?" He hums like he knows the answer. "Circle your clit, Cora."

I gasp again, shocked at the jolt of pleasure that shoots through me. Ivan moans, too. The fact he's enjoying my pleasure makes it so much better.

"Keep going," he says. "Don't stop touching yourself. I wouldn't. If you were in my bed, I would wrap your legs around my head the way I did in that bathroom. I would lick you and suck until you were quivering. Are you quivering, Cora?"

I nod, my breath catching with a gasp in my throat.

"Good girl. Touch yourself for me, Cora. Take what you want. Take what you deserve."

He's breathing heavily in the phone. I imagine his hot breath on my neck. On my breasts. I imagine Ivan's familiar weight on top of me.

There are so few reasons to feel good in my life as it currently stands. So few moments that belong exclusively to me.

But *this* moment does.

This is mine and I'm going to take it.

I arch my back with a gasp. "Like that," Ivan encourages. "Don't stop."

So I don't. I keep circling and stroking until the heat blooming in my core flares and then explodes. Tendrils of it expand to my fingertips and my toes. I feel my heartbeat between my legs, pulsing and thrumming with life.

I whimper with the effort it takes not to cry out.

Ivan groans in my ear. I hope he's finding release, too. I wish I could talk to him. I wish I could take him to the same place I am.

"Fuck, Cora," he pants. "You are... You're incredible. My *solnishka.* My little sun in the darkness."

I've never gone from arousal to tears quite so quickly before, but I sniffle and swipe at my eyes.

"You're going to get out of there," he says softly. "Captivity is nothing but a state of mind."

It's been impossible to latch onto hope the last few days. But hearing how much Ivan believes in me, I can't help but believe in me, too.

I will get out of here.

No matter what happens, I'll get out of here.

Or I'll die trying.

I wake up to a crash. I'm out of bed and on my feet before my mind can catch up to what my body is doing.

There was a bang. A loud bang.

And voices.

I blink into the dim light filtering through my curtains and see people moving into my room.

"What is it?" I rasp. "What is going—"

Someone clicks on the lamp next to my bed. I hiss away from the sudden brightness.

"Come on, Cordelia. It's time to go." I don't need my vision to know that is my mother's voice.

"Mom?" My eyes are starting to adjust. I can see Alexander standing in the hallway. He has his hands folded behind his back, his eyes cast towards the stairs. "What's going on? What is—Is everything okay?"

She moves towards me, reaching for my arm. "We'll talk about it. You just need to come with—"

"No!" I jerk back, smacking into the wall behind me.

She lowers her head, brows pinched. "Cordelia, don't make this harder than it has to be."

"Make *what* harder? I don't even understand what is happening! Why are you here?"

My mom opens her mouth to respond, but another voice cuts in. "If you can't control your daughter, then I will." Mikhail steps into my room, and I swear a dark cloud of sulfur rolls in behind him.

I'm wearing a cotton t-shirt and flannel shorts, but I might as well be naked for how exposed I feel. I wrap my arms around myself. "You shouldn't be in here."

"I go where I want." He holds out a hand. "Come with me or I'll have to make you."

I recoil from his touch. "Alexander, this is your house. You can't—Tell him to leave."

I hate that I'm turning to my stepfather for any help, but he's the only one who can stop this. I know the relationship between him and the Sokolovs is all fucked-up. Maybe if I can poke at that connection, he'll stop whatever this is.

"It's late, Cordelia," he sighs. "Don't be difficult."

I didn't know I still had the capacity to be shocked by these people, but here I am. I'm stunned. There's no humanity in them. No empathy.

"I don't even know where I'm going. Someone tell me what's happening!"

Maybe if they tell me what is going on, I can stop it. Maybe I can get out of this.

But even as the thought crosses my mind, something inside of me knows it isn't true.

"It's actually great news." Mikhail smiles. Silver moonlight glints off of his teeth, turning them into fangs. "You and I are getting married. Tonight."

32

CORA

"Married?" My hand shifts up to squeeze the locket resting against my collarbone.

The phone Ivan gave me is wedged under my mattress. There's no way I can get to it and text Ivan in time.

Even if I did text him, I know what would happen.

He'd rush into the house to save me unprepared. He'd try to fight, but Alexander and the Sokolovs would be ready for that. He would die. And it would all be my fault.

So I can't text Ivan.

But I also can't leave with Mikhail.

Once we're married, death will be the only way out: either his or mine. Divorce won't be an option.

"You knew this was coming. Don't act surprised," he says.

"It's the middle of the night. Of course I'm surprised!" I spit. "Plus, tonight at dinner you all said it would be a few weeks. You said—"

"We have new information now."

It could be my imagination, but Mikhail's face seems to sharpen. The angles of his face turn ominous. I've never enjoyed looking at Mikhail, but I've also never found him scary.

Right now, though, he's terrifying.

He reaches for me, snagging the sleeve of my t-shirt just as I dodge out of the way. "Come on, Cordelia. It's time to go."

"No!" I crawl over the bed and make for the door, but Alexander is still there.

"You aren't getting out of here, Cordelia," he says. "Not until we let you."

"Not until we drag you," Mikhail amends.

I spin around and look to my mother. This is it: her last shot to be maternal. To take care of me. To save me. *Please*, my eyes beg. *Please don't let them do this.*

Her lips purse. I can see her writhing under the uncomfortable pressure. She doesn't want to be here doing this.

But then she looks away.

My mom doesn't mind that I am in danger; she minds only that she is uncomfortable. Her entire life has been about taking care of herself. And that won't change anytime soon.

Mikhail walks around my bed towards me. "Let's go. It's time to—"

Just before he can grab me, I turn and lunge for my bookshelf.

How many times have I practiced sliding the letter opener out of its hiding place? Countless. I've pulled it out just to make sure it's still there. To console myself with the thought that I have a backup plan in case everything goes sideways.

Well, things aren't just sideways—they are upside fucking down.

I crash into the white set of shelves, crying out at the pain in my shoulder. But there isn't time to stop. To hesitate. Because Mikhail is on me.

His cold hands wrap around my ankle, tugging me back.

But I grip the shelf with enough force that I think my fingernails might crack and kick my legs. I flail and flop until Mikhail can't hold me.

I crawl forward and swipe my hand under the shelf. For one panicked second, I think it might not be there. Despite how many times I've double- and triple-checked, I imagine hitting nothing but dead air.

But then my hand wraps around the now-familiar wooden handle. I rip the letter opener free of the tape, whirl onto my back, and hold the blade in Mikhail's direction.

He pulls back in shock that quickly turns to rage. "What is that, Cordelia?"

"I'm not going with you," I grit out. "You can't force me into this. You can't drag me out of bed in the middle of the night and have a shotgun wedding."

"Can't I?" He smirks. "I'm not sure if you heard me the first time, but I can do whatever the fuck I want."

I shake my head. "Not me."

His smile widens. *"Especially* you."

I tighten my grip on the letter opener, but it doesn't matter. Before I can say anything else, an arm swipes out from behind me and knocks my only weapon out of my hands.

I scramble after it, but Alexander kneels on my chest, pinning me down.

"I can't breathe!" I gasp, clawing at his thigh. "Get off of me!"

He looks down at me, his eyes cold. "Are you going to cooperate?"

A sob wrenches out of my tight chest. "Please, Alexand—I can't—You're suffocating me."

"Are. You. Going. To. Cooperate?" he repeats slowly.

I want to refuse, but my vision is narrowing to pinpricks. Black is creeping in, a growing circle of darkness swallowing my sight.

If I refuse, he'll kill me. I know it.

"Yes," I rasp in a desperate attempt to breathe. "Yes, I'll cooperate. I'll—Please. I can't—"

His knee lifts and I inhale greedy lungfuls of air. I flop back on my floor, my head pressing into the plush carpet. Sprawled out and oxygen-starved and defenseless.

"That's a good girl." Mikhail grabs my arm and yanks me to my feet.

I wobble as the blood rushes out of my head, but before I can even regain my footing, Mikhail is dragging me towards the door.

For a few stunned seconds, I let him. There's no use in fighting. Alexander, Mikhail, and my mother are all here and they all want me to get married to Mikhail. No one is going to help me.

Then I hear Ivan's voice in my head. *Captivity is nothing but a state of mind.*

The moment I decide I'm caught, it's over.

I have to fight.

"Wait." I don't jerk out of Mikhail's hold, but I lay a hand on his wrist. I slow him down. "Wait a second."

"You aren't getting out of this, so shut up and come—"

"I'm not trying to get out of it," I lie. "But I... I don't want to get married like this."

He rolls his eyes. "If you wanted romance, you shouldn't have started our wedding day by shoving a knife in my face."

"I don't need romance, but we can still make this nice, right?" I brush my thumb along his wrist.

Mikhail looks down at our hands. I expect him to twist away from me. Surely he'll see right through my games and demand that I shut my mouth, right?

Instead, he glances up at me. "What did you have in mind?"

I release his wrist and throw my arms wide. "Not getting married in my pajamas is a start."

He looks me up and down. "I don't care what you're wearing. All I need is a signature."

"And consummation," I blurt. My face flushes deep red, which I'm actually grateful for. It makes me look every bit the literal blushing bride. It sells my lies.

Mikhail frowns.

"After the wedding," I explain softly, stepping closer to him. "If I have to do this, I want it to be memorable. I want it to be nice. We should try to start our marriage off on the right foot."

His mouth twists down even further. "Why would you care?"

"This may not be love, but I still have my dignity." I lift my chin and press my shoulders back. "I want to shower, clean myself up, and choose something nice to wear. Right now, I'm braless in ripped pajamas. Is that how you imagined your wedding night?"

Mikhail probably imagined his wedding night with torture racks and whips. Or, no—that's too exciting for him. More likely, it involved joyless missionary sex until he finishes and rolls off of his bride. I'm sure that's his fantasy.

I don't plan to fulfill it.

"I suppose not," Mikhail admits. He considers it for a few more seconds and then nods. "Okay. You can have an hour to get ready."

An hour. Maybe that'll be enough.

I'll be alone and I can text Ivan. I can tell him what is going on. Maybe he'll have time to rally his forces and stop this. Maybe he—

"But your mom will stay here with you the entire time," Mikhail adds.

Just like that, my hopes crash and burn.

"I'd be happy to," my mother says.

There's some pride in her voice. It must feel nice for her to be useful after so many years spent as little more than a lawn ornament. *Is that what I have to look forward to?*

I dismiss the thought as soon as I have it. That won't be me. I won't give in.

Mikhail stops in the doorway, casting one long look back at me before he closes the door and leaves me and my mother alone.

The air is thick with tension. Somehow, it's even worse than it was with Mikhail in the room.

I never expected Mikhail to help me. I've never had any notions that, in my time of need, he would rise up and save me. But my own mother? Some deep, childlike part of me refused to believe that she would really turn me over to my enemies on a silver platter. Yet that's exactly what she did.

"Well," she sighs, clapping her hands together, "I can get your dress out and steam it if you want to get in the shower and—"

"I want a maid to help me," I interrupt.

"What?"

"A maid," I repeat. "Um… the woman who served me tonight. I liked her hair. The blonde woman. Maybe she could fix my hair for me."

My mom frowns. Then recognition crosses her face. "Oh. *Oh.* No, that won't work. She's fired."

"But she was just here tonight."

"Until Alexander caught her messing with the security cameras," she says. "He fired her on the spot. She's gone."

My only ally inside the house is gone. My connection to Ivan is wedged so deeply under my mattress it might as well be in Timbuktu. I'm alone. Completely alone.

And I have no idea what I'm going to do.

"Go get in the shower," my mother cajoles. "I'll iron your dress and get it ready. We don't have much time."

"No," I mutter softly. "We don't."

I pad into the bathroom and close the door behind me. Captivity is a state of mind. And I can feel the bars rising up around me.

I grab my necklace and look up at the sky, praying for a miracle.

"Help me," I whisper. "Someone, please. If I don't get out now, I never will."

33

IVAN

I lie back and stare up at the ceiling. It's impossible to sleep knowing Cora is in another bed.

On the phone with her, there was a moment where I imagined it was all real. Where the scene played out in my mind the way I wanted it to, with my hand doing all the work while Cora fell apart underneath me.

Then we had to hang up and the reality of my empty room came crashing down on me.

Based on what I overheard from the dinner conversation, we have mere weeks to get Cora out of Alexander McAllister's house before she's going to be married to Mikhail. Yet I can't shake the feeling that something isn't right.

Since I can't sleep anyway, I pull out my phone and open up the live audio feed.

Cora has been wearing the necklace to bed. In the silence of her room, I can hear the soft thud of her heartbeat and her deep, even breathing. It's like white noise. The sound of her continued life, even if she isn't with me, is calming.

I close my eyes and listen to her inhales and exhales, to the staticky murmurs as she shifts beneath the blankets or rolls over.

Slowly, I settle. My eyes close and I match her breathing pace, letting my body sink into the mattress and drift closer to sleep.

Then the peace shatters.

There is banging and voices. Cora is panting and panicked. I'm out of bed and slipping into pants before I even know what is happening.

Whatever it is, it's wrong.

Screw the thoroughly drawn-out plan and the mitigation of risks. Fuck it all.

I'm going after her. *Now.*

Cora is talking to her mom, but I know there are more people there. I can hear it in Cora's voice that there is a bigger threat.

Finally, that threat reveals itself.

"If you can't control your daughter, then I will," Mikhail spits.

I clench my teeth as I tear through the mansion towards the security wing. Since Jorden has all but recovered, Yasha has taken to sleeping in the security wing of the house. He has been monitoring the situation here with Francia and working with me in every spare second to map out exactly how to get in and out of Alexander McAllister's mansion with Cora in tow without getting anyone killed.

"It's actually great news," Mikhail continues. "You and I are getting married. Tonight."

It takes all of my restraint not to hurl my phone at the wall.

"Fuck," I hiss.

Tonight.

For all I know, there's a minister standing directly behind him, paperwork in hand. This wedding could be seconds or hours away, I have no idea.

But that doesn't change the goal: I need to get to Cora *now*.

I listen as Cora argues and fights back. Pride swells in me as she refuses to leave with them, but it descends into panic. There is more banging and shouting. I have no idea what is happening. Is she being attacked? Is she okay?

I break into a jog, the phone held close to my ear so I can hear every second of audio.

Finally, I hear Cora's voice again.

"I'm not going with you. You can't force me into this. You can't drag me out of bed in the middle of the night and have a wedding."

"Can't I?" Mikhail hisses. "I'm not sure if you heard me the first time, but I can do whatever the fuck I want."

"The fuck you can," I growl.

I don't bother knocking on Yasha's door. There's no time. I throw it open and crash into his room.

"Cora is in trouble. We have to go. Now!" I bark.

Yasha yelps and yanks his comforter up, covering himself...

And Jorden.

On any normal day, I'd comment on the fact that Jorden is naked in Yasha's bed. I'd have a good time giving him shit about it. But right now, I have no interest.

"Cora is in trouble," I repeat. "We have to go."

Jorden hugs the comforter to her chest. "What's happening?"

Cora answers for me, the audio picking up her muffled cries. "I can't breathe! Get off of me!"

My stomach churns painfully. She's in danger and I can't help her. I'm still fifteen minutes away.

I should have grabbed her when we were in that bathroom and ran. Fuck the guards. Fuck everything else. I should have risked it all and taken her then.

Now, it might be too late.

Yasha curses and jumps out of bed. I turn away as he pulls on clothes and then reaches for his phone. Without saying anything to me, he makes a call.

"Rooster," he says, "it's Yasha. We need backup."

Through the necklace, I can hear Alexander demanding that Cora cooperate. She promises him that she will.

I'm going to kill them. Alexander, Mikhail, Konstantin... Hell, even Cora's mother. I'll kill them all and leave their heads on pikes in the lawn. I'll go medieval on their asses. Let everyone know what happens when you mess with Ivan Pushkin's woman.

Yasha turns back to the bed, grabs Jorden's face, and presses a quick, tender kiss to her lips. "I'll see you later."

Then my best friend strides towards me, purpose in his every step. "Let's go get your girl, Ivan."

34

CORA

"Whoever would have thought the two of us would be here?" my mother asks.

I've been avoiding my reflection in the mirror since the moment I stepped into the white dress. But I risk a look up to see my mom standing behind me.

"Do you mean lacing up a wedding dress in the middle of the night for a forced marriage? Because if so—yeah, not me."

Her smile falls. "I know you think this is the worst thing that could ever happen, but we were living on the street. We were in the gutter. Alexander saved us."

"We jumped out of the pan and into the fire as far as I'm concerned," I mutter.

She pulls harder on the laces, making me jolt. "Don't say that in front of Alexander. You've made things complicated enough."

They are the ones who made things complicated. *They* woke me up in the middle of the night. *They* are trying to wed me to a psychopath. What did they expect would happen?

But there's no point in fighting back.

My mother stands back and smiles. "I think that's it. You're done."

My heart quivers. I want there to be more laces to tie. More pins to stick into my already overdone updo. I'm not ready to step out of this room and face whatever is coming next.

Ivan said captivity is a state of mind, but it's a place, too. It's hell.

Hell is what waits for me outside that door, and while I swore to myself and to Ivan that I will fight tooth and nail to make it through this never-ending nightmare… I desperately wish I didn't have to.

I'm just so tired.

Tears well in my eyes as my mom moves around me. She reaches up and dabs at them with a white handkerchief.

"Every woman cries on her wedding day," she reassures me.

I snort. "Usually for different reasons."

"Yes, well…" She shrugs. "Mikhail doesn't need to know that. As far as they know, you're overcome with joy."

"He won't believe that."

"Then *make* him believe it." Her voice has a surprising edge to it.

I look in my mom's eyes. She and I have never looked too much alike. She is shorter and softer and, ever since she met

Alexander, her wavy hair has been tamed into low buns, her makeup subtle and nude.

"*Make* him believe it," she repeats. "Because as bad as you think things are now, they'll only get worse if you keep fighting. Let Mikhail take care of you. Let him keep you safe."

"Is that what you did with Alexander?"

She holds my gaze for a few more seconds, something unspoken passing between us. Then she turns away. "Of course not. I love him."

"Very convincing."

Suddenly, my mother whips around me, her voice low. "You don't seem to understand the danger you're in now, Cordelia. Mikhail has put up with your protests so far, but he won't forever. If you want this family to survive—if *you* want to survive—you'll learn to take the hand you've been dealt."

It's the first time since I got here that I've seen a glimpse of my actual mother. A peek at the woman behind the facade Alexander has crafted.

She's scared.

Maybe some of her fear is for me. The daughter in me would sure like to think so. But I know most of it is for herself. If I'm difficult, it might reflect poorly on her.

Before I can say anything, she steps back and smiles. "You look lovely, Cordelia."

She's receded back behind her mask. I don't even recognize her.

Is that what I'll have to become? A shell of my former self who tucks all of her thoughts and feelings and fears out of sight?

I want to keep fighting. But I'm not sure I can. Because she's right: Mikhail will kill me if he doesn't get his way.

My mother turns towards the door and panic washes over me. "Are you ready to get married, sweetheart?" She has the audacity to ask the question with a smile on her face. I'm not sure if she's that deep in denial or if it's an example of how I should behave. *Smile. Pretend. Do what you must to get through.*

I can't bring myself to respond, so I just hike up the skirt of my dress and make my way across the room.

What is Ivan going to do when he finds out? This was never part of the plan. He promised he would stop this from happening.

More tears start to burn the backs of my eyes and I blink them away.

I can't think about what was promised or what could have been. There isn't time for that. The only thing that matters is now. And right now, I'm being married off to a lunatic.

A lunatic who will probably keep me under lock and key after we're married. There won't be any more need to convince the public of our relationship. Actually, keeping me out of sight will work in his favor. We'll look like stereotypical newlyweds, too busy between the sheets to come up for air.

The lie makes my stomach turn.

Mostly because it isn't all false. Konstantin was clear that he thinks I'm past my prime. I'm sure item number one on Mikhail's to-do list will be *me*.

My mom opens my door and steps out into the hallway. For just a second, she ducks out of view. I hear her moving something in the hall, probably to make room for the long train of my dress. And that's when I see it.

The letter opener.

Alexander didn't take it with him after he knocked it out of my hand earlier. It's still on the floor, half-hidden by the shadow of my bed.

I don't think or hesitate. I lunge for it.

By the time my mom reappears in the doorway, her placid smile firmly in place, the letter opener is tucked under the neckline of my dress.

The next time I pull it on Mikhail, there will be no warning. He won't see it coming.

I hope to God it hurts.

35

CORA

Mikhail and Alexander didn't use the last hour to get ready the way I did. When my mother and I walk into the sitting room, the two of them and a third man who I can only presume is the minister are lounging on the sofa.

There are no candles or flowers. No attempt to arrange the furniture into an aisle or play some music. Mikhail isn't even wearing a suit. He's in a pair of dark wash jeans and a dark gray button-down. I look ridiculously overdressed in comparison.

"Finally," Alexander mumbles, rising to his feet.

Mikhail follows suit. He keeps a half-step behind my stepfather, but his eyes are glued on me.

I thought taking the time to put on the dress would give me a chance to get out of this. Instead, I'm in even deeper. There is nothing in Mikhail's eyes that makes me believe I can convince him he shouldn't touch me tonight. I told him I was getting dressed for the occasion, and now, he has some seriously perverted expectations.

His pale eyes go dark with twisted desire. Finally, he looks away. "Let's get this over with."

"The words every bride dreams of hearing on her wedding day," I mutter.

Alexander grabs my arm and hauls me to the open space in front of the fireplace hearth. A TV hangs on the wall above our heads with an infomercial for kitchen knives on the screen. At least they had the decency to put it on mute.

A few guards linger in the hallway. I hear more patrolling the entryway.

Mikhail steps into place across from me. He reaches for my hands, but I keep them flat at my sides. I won't run screaming from the room, but I'm not going to hold his hands and pretend this is all hunky-fucking-dory.

"Where is your father?" I ask. Not that I care. The only thing that would make this already gloomy wedding even worse is Konstantin Sokolov's appearance.

"Probably in bed," he admits. "He's more interested in the outcome than the destination. I'll fill him in later."

"Okay. We've got a bride, a groom, a minister, and witnesses," Alexander says. He snaps at the third man. "Let's get on with it."

The minister is a middle-aged man with dark circles under his eyes and what looks to be a tattoo peeking out of the collar of his neck. He looks like exactly the kind of person who would perform a middle of the night wedding ceremony with an unwilling bride and then hop over to his 4 AM appointment of harvesting black market kidneys.

He opens a book and begins reading. "Welcome. We are gathered here today to join—"

"Move on," Alexander barks.

The man nods and skips a page. "Love is the joining of—"

"Nope." Alexander circles his finger in the air. "Skip that shit. Get to the meat."

The officiant looks flustered as he skips ahead even more. Then he looks up at Alexander, a question in his eyes as he continues. "Do you, Mikhail, take Cordelia to be your lawfully wedded wife?"

Mikhail looks into my eyes, his chin raised. "I do."

Holy shit. It feels impossible that this is happening. Should I stab him now? I feel the tip of the letter opener pressed against the spot above my heart. If it starts beating any faster, I might accidentally impale myself first.

There are too many people. Alexander is standing behind me, probably to make sure he can sneak attack me if I try to fight. Plus the guards outside the room. They can be here in a second.

It's happening.

And I don't see a way out.

The officiant clears his throat and turns to me. "And do you, Cordelia, take Mikhail to be your lawfully wedded husband?"

No. Hell no.

The words ring in my head loud and clear, but my mouth stays closed. I stare at Mikhail, silently begging for him and the rest of this situation to just disappear.

But he doesn't.

"Come on, Cordelia," Alexander whispers. His words hiss against the back of my ear. "Don't leave us in suspense."

This is it.

There is no way out.

I don't have a choice.

I squeeze my eyes closed and swear to myself that I'll be free again… one day.

Then I open my eyes and meet the gaze of the monster I'm being forced to marry. "I—"

Before I can finish, the ground quakes and the French doors behind us rain glass.

36

IVAN

The explosion is bigger than I expected.

I peek over the concrete half-wall I took cover behind and see the double doors from the patio to the house are now blown out. Alexander McAllister is looking into his backyard to the smoldering motorcycle parts laying in his singed grass.

"Rooster really knows how to rig a bomb," Yasha remarks.

"I hope he can fight half as well," I add as McAllister's security guards flood the backyard.

I catch a glimpse of white through the shattered door frame. *Is that Cora?* I don't have time to find out before Yasha and I are surrounded by guards.

Yasha takes out a guard in front of him with a single shot to the head. Then he ducks, lands a blow to another guard's stomach, and presses his gun to the man's neck.

The men in front of me hesitate, wondering whether they should focus on me or help their colleagues. I quickly solve the dilemma for them. I fire two weapons at once, bringing both men to their knees.

"Keep moving. I'll finish them," Yasha barks.

So much for sneaking in and out without bloodshed.

We carve a path to the back of Alexander's house. Rooster has a team watching the front of the house to make sure Mikhail can't escape with Cora and I have my own contingent flanking the sides of the property.

My only goal is to get inside and find Cora.

But there are more guards than we bargained for and the going is slow. Luckily, they aren't heavily armed. They probably didn't expect much of a fight in the middle of the night.

That was their mistake.

I fire wildly to keep them at bay. One by one, they start to topple and die.

Distantly, I hear another loud boom. Rolling the motorcycle bomb into Alexander's backyard had been Rooster's idea. The man was practically giddy when he suggested it.

"I've been waiting for an opportunity to use my invention," he said. "This is it. Let me try."

When I agreed, his wife, Legs, rolled her eyes. "I swear, he won't be happy until he dies in a fiery blaze."

Based on the whoop of celebration I hear coming from the front of the house, she isn't so far off.

A new wave of guards come sprinting around the side of the house. I hear Yasha curse behind me. This might really be it. We can't fight all of these men alone.

Then I realize why they are running.

A motorcycle engine roars around the house, and I see Rooster driving while Legs sits behind him holding... *holy shit*, she's throwing Molotov cocktails. Behind them, a guard is rolling in the grass to put out the flames engulfing his body.

"They are fucking crazy," Yasha laughs. He's panting and bloody, but he pushes me towards the patio. "Go get your girl. We've got it out here."

He doesn't need to tell me twice.

I sprint for the patio and then slow down as I approach the blown-out doors. We have the exterior handled, but what's going on inside is a mystery. The maid I hired as a spy was fired for trying to gain access to the interior cameras. Mikhail could be holding Cora hostage. Maybe she's already...

No.

I'm going to find her. Alive.

I step through the door gun first. Glass crunches under my boot. It's wild how much quieter it is inside. I can still hear Legs screaming and the whine of the motorcycle, but it's muffled and far away. My senses have narrowed in on the space in front of me. On the only goal that matters.

Then I see it.

A glimpse of white lace from behind the sofa.

"Cora." I speak her name without thinking. It's a reflex. She's here. She's moving.

She peeks around the back of the couch, eyes wide. "Ivan?"

It's really her. She's alive. She's here. I have her.

Then her voice cracks. "Ivan, watch—"

A guard jumps in front of me with a battle cry, cutting off Cora's warning.

He isn't large or particularly skilled, but he has the advantage of surprise. I should have cleared the room first, but I was so set on getting to her.

Now, he is too close for me to safely take a shot. Especially with Cora in the room. I haven't come this far just to let her get taken out by a stray bullet.

The man charges me back into the fireplace. The hard edge of the stone cuts into my spine.

I use the moment to holster my second gun, freeing up one hand. Then I launch myself at the *mudak.*

He focuses on securing my gun hand, holding it back above my head while I kick out at him. The heel of my boot connects with his ribs and I hear a satisfying crack. He cries out and twists my wrist. Pain flares, but I'm able to get out of his hold before anything is broken, spinning around so I can drive a knee into his stomach.

He groans and drapes a heavy arm around my back. We grapple with each other, jockeying for control. Twice, I could shoot him, but knowing Cora is right behind keeps my trigger finger steady. I won't risk hurting her.

Not when we're this fucking close to the end.

Finally, I get the man back on the couch, but he still has my body pinned in with his arm. I have the upper hand, but only barely. And if I don't get Cora out of here soon, there's no telling what could happen to the battle outside. More guards could be in this room any second and that would be it. Game over.

I roar and drive an elbow down into the man's throat. He gasps and starts to choke, but his grip doesn't loosen. If anything, it tightens. He holds me harder, struggling for air.

Just as he starts to breathe normally again, an angel rises over his right shoulder. I don't even have time to look up before there's a flash of white... and then a wooden handle is protruding from the guard's neck.

His eyes go wide. Then they go blank. Then, pulse by pulse, they close.

Blood pours from the wound, staining the beige sofa beneath him. When he finally lets me go, I'm not willing to take any chances. I press the gun to his forehead and pull the trigger to put this dog down forever.

Only when his eyes roll back in his head and his limbs go limp do I finally look up.

Cora is standing next to the couch, her hair falling around her face and blood splattered on her dress.

"Beautiful," I breathe. "You're fucking beautiful."

She blinks and then looks down at herself. Her mouth tips into a half-smile that wobbles and disappears again. She's proud, terrified, stunned—too many things at once. I cross the distance between us in one step and haul her into my arms.

I need her weight against my chest. Her breath against my neck. I need to hold her and convince myself that this is real. She is with me.

"Time to get you home."

She can't even speak. She just nestles her head into the side of my neck and nods.

So, with her bloodstained veil dragging on the floor behind us, I carry Cora out of Alexander McAllister's house and into the night.

37

IVAN

The front of the house is cleared out. Aside from two cars burning in the driveway, there is no one to stop Cora and me from climbing in my car and peeling out.

I call Yasha the minute we're through the gates. "Get out of there as fast as you can," I tell him. "I have Cora. We're gone."

"We're working on it." I hear faint yelling and commotion behind him, but it's quieter than I would have expected. "Mikhail must have called off his guards. Either that or they abandoned him."

Cora can hear Yasha on the speaker phone and she leans forward. "Mikhail and Alexander both disappeared the second the doors exploded," she explains. "They left me with a guard, but I think they went into a panic room or took another exit or something. I don't think they wanted me to see where they were going."

"I wouldn't be surprised," I say to both her and Yasha. "On either account. They're all fucking cowards."

"Yeah, but if those cowards did escape, they'll be coming straight for the mansion," Yasha warns.

"I'll take Cora somewhere else until things settle."

"Copy that. See you on the other side, brother."

The line goes dead and the car is oddly silent. Especially after the chaos of the last... shit, how long has it even been? Thirty minutes? An hour? My sense of time is warped. I have no idea how much time has passed since I first heard Cora's scream through the necklace.

"Are you okay?" I ask.

She looks down in her lap. Her hands are folded together and there's blood all over her knuckles. "In the last couple hours, I was woken up in the middle of the night, forced to get married, survived an explosion, and killed a man. Safe to say I've had better days."

Cora takes a deep breath and turns to the window.

For a few quiet minutes, we just drive. Streetlights illuminate the car in red, yellow, and green. People living very different lives walk down sidewalks with their friends.

If things had been different, Cora could be with them. She could have been out there, just a normal girl. I want to ask if she's thinking the same thing, but she's clammed up with shock. The only thing that will fix that is time. Even though I want to scrub it all away from her. To take the pain myself.

I can't. I just have to fucking *wait*.

Suddenly, she sits up. "This isn't the way to the mansion. Where are you taking me?"

"My old penthouse in the city. It's where I lived before my father handed the mansion over to me."

She turns to me. I don't look at her, but even in my peripherals, she's too much. Her soft curves and strawberries-and-cream scent. Being this close to her after living without is intoxicating. It's a fucking miracle I can even drive straight.

"You'll be safe there," I vow. "I won't let anything happen to you."

She settles back into the passenger seat and the tension consumes us once again.

I lead Cora inside and bolt the door behind us.

"There's a security team downstairs monitoring everything." I point to the wall of windows opposite us. "And that is bulletproof glass. Just in case a shooter climbs twenty-five floors."

She blinks at me, her green eyes taking in my expression for a moment before she quickly turns away.

Again, the sense that something is wrong gnaws at me. Something beyond the fact that she is wearing a bloodstained wedding gown from a ceremony with another man.

Which is fucking infuriating in its own right.

I turn on the electric fireplace in the sitting room. Flames lick across the screen and heat immediately blows out of a recessed vent.

She looks from the fireplace to the couch and hesitates in the middle of the room. That hesitation, that fear—that rips me apart inside. I want to reach out and smooth the wrinkle in her forehead. I want to rip the wedding dress off of her and wash away every trace of what Mikhail and Alexander did to her.

But this shit is a fragile situation. What she did, what she had done to her... Pushing her too far now might ruin what's left of her spirit.

So as much as it agonizes me, I need to keep my distance.

For now.

"There's a guest room if you want it," I rasp. My heart throbs uncomfortably in my chest. "I'll show you."

I lead her down the hallway. When we pass the master, I duck in and grab her a pair of shorts and a t-shirt, then keep going to the next bedroom over. It's only ten steps away from mine, but it might as well be a mile. A light year. I don't know how I'm supposed to sleep with her so fucking close, yet so impossibly far away.

When I let myself imagine saving Cora, it went so differently. We reunited like we did in the bathroom at the restaurant. In a tangle of lips and limbs, clawing at each other to get closer.

But this Cora looks like a ghost in front of me. Her eyes are vacant and her skin is pale. She looks like she's barely staying on her feet.

She tiptoes into the room, her head swiveling from side to side as she takes in every corner. She's scanning for threats.

"You're safe in here."

She jumps at the sound of my voice and then flushes. "I know."

I'm not sure she does.

"I'll find something to eat while you change," I say, backing towards the door. "You can sleep if you want or come and join me. It's up to you."

She chews on her lower lip and nods. "Thanks."

I close the door and linger there, my hand resting against the wood. I'm going to eviscerate Alexander and Mikhail and the entire Sokolov family for what they did to Cora.

Sighing, I put the violent thought aside and start to walk toward the kitchen. I'm halfway there when I hear a yelp. I don't hesitate for even a fraction of a second—I just spin around and charge right back into Cora's room, ready to wreak havoc on whichever *mudak* was stupid enough to follow us here and—

But there's no one else in there aside from Cora.

She looks like she's fighting ghosts. Grunting and cursing, banging into the dresser and the corner of the bed.

"I can't get it off!" she gasps. Her arms are bent behind her, her fingers working frantically at the stuck zipper in the center of her back. "It's—The stupid thing is stuck. I can't… It won't come off. Ivan, it won't—"

I cross the room in two strides and peel her hands off of the garment. "Take a deep breath, Cora." I hold her face and force her eyes to mine. "I'm here with you. You're okay."

Her green eyes go glassy. "Get me out of it, Ivan. Please."

My gaze drops to the material. I could undo it one hook at a time. Unravel the knots. Tease open the laces.

Or I could just rip it to fucking shreds.

I go with Option B.

Seizing a fistful of this cursed fucking fabric in each hand, I snarl and tear it apart. Stitches pop and explode.

I'm tearing it apart for her, but it's also for me. Cora was wearing this wedding dress for another man. I don't just want to tear it off of her; I want to burn it to ashes.

I don't stop until it's fluttering in scraps around her like white petals. It's an eerie echo of the night we met, when she stood surrounded by a very different kind of ruined dress.

Her arms are folded over her bare breasts when she turns to me. Color is coming back into her face, turning her cheeks a delicious shade of pink. I have to fight not to drink in every gorgeous inch of her.

Now isn't the time.

This isn't what she needs.

But I'm about to go insane with how bad I want her. I want to reclaim her from head to toe. With kisses, with lip and tongue and fingers and breath. I want to make her feel safe again. Whole again. To come undone in my arms again. She's so close and it'd be so easy to reach out and drag her into bed with me…

Time. Give her time. She needs time.

"You should get dressed."

I grab the shirt from the corner of the bed and unfold it for her. She keeps her hands over her chest while I slide what might as well be a two-person tent over her head. The hem settles midway down her thighs and, when she stretches her arms through the holes, the sleeves hit well past her elbows.

I force myself to take a step back. "I'll let you get some sleep. I'm sure you're tired."

The decision has already been made: Cora needs to leave my life. I need to get her far away from this city and this world... from me. Blurring that line tonight will only make things harder.

Maybe this is for the best.

I swallow down the desire lodged in my throat and turn for the door.

Cora's voice stops me. "I'm alive."

I frown and look over my shoulder.

"I'm alive," she repeats. "And we're here. Together."

I don't need the reminder. I know down to the centimeter how close she is: *very*. How long it would take for me to span the gap: *no time at all.*

"And I don't want to sleep," she adds softly.

I turn around fully now. Cora is standing much closer. Too close. Close enough that all I'd have to do is reach out and she could be in my arms.

I fist my hands at my sides. "What do you want, Cora?"

She grabs the front of my shirt in her fists and gently presses her body against mine. "I want you to make me feel like everything is going to be okay."

38

CORA

Heat pours out of him, soaking through the thin material of the worn t-shirt he dressed me in. I loosen my hold on his shirt and let my fingernails scratch over the hard planes of his body.

"No." Ivan shakes his head and grabs my wrists. He puts distance between us. "Not tonight."

I blink up at him. "Don't you—? I thought you wanted—"

"You're traumatized. I'm not going to take advantage of you after everything you've been through." He bites his lip. "You have—*God*, you have no fucking idea how much I want... But I'm not going to fuck it up."

His eyes are stormy as he studies me. Ivan wants this, too. I know he does.

"I know what I want," I tell him. "But I also know what it's like to be forced. I won't do that to you. If you don't want me, then—"

The words die in my throat as Ivan spins me back against the wall. He places a finger under my chin and forces my face up to his. His breath is hot and heavy against my skin.

For a moment, we're back in the shadows of his office. It's the night we first met, but this time I know it's not just a fling. I can see everything waiting ahead for us.

I'd do it all over again just to end up here with him.

He lowers his face to mine, our foreheads pressed together. "Of course I want you, Cora," he growls. "I have always wanted you."

I curl my hand around his wrist. "You don't scare me, Ivan. I'm not traumatized. Not with you. Not with this."

I brush my lips over his jaw. Every part of him is clenched and straining.

"You don't have to hold yourself back with me," I whisper. "Whatever you want to give me, I can take."

Ivan comes alive in an instant.

He grips my hips and wraps me around his waist. His hard erection presses against my belly. He squeezes my cheeks as he claims my mouth with his. It's a hot flash at first, one burning second of need. Then he settles and slows. Gentle. Tender and thorough.

It's luxurious, this kissing. *There's no rush*, he's telling me. *I'm going to take my time with you.*

He carries me over to the bed and lays me down on my back. "Stay put," he says, dropping to his knees. "I have you exactly where I want you."

He pushes his shirt up my thighs and trails kisses up the sensitive insides of my legs. The exhale is enough to send goosebumps racing across my skin.

I want to tell Ivan he doesn't have to do this. The other day in the restaurant bathroom, that was enough. It's his turn.

But the way he settles between my legs and sighs keeps me quiet. He wants this.

He wants *me*.

He starts slowly, flicking his tongue against my slit, teasing me open. But the restraint doesn't last long. Part of it is my fault—I can't stop myself from working my fingers into his hair and holding him fast against me.

I moan as he explores me. The flat of his tongue applies toe-curling pressure and his lips suction around my clit.

Embarrassingly fast, I clamp my legs around his ears and grind against his mouth. I chase and chase and chase until I flop back on the mattress and absolutely fall apart.

"Oh my god," I gasp. "That was—"

"That was only a fraction of what I intend to do to you."

He drags his tongue up the center of my stomach. I grab his face and try to bring him to my mouth, but Ivan wrangles me back onto the bed and pins me down with a strong arm.

He grabs my hips and fills me in one slow, steady thrust.

"Oh my…" I hook my legs behind his back while my body adjusts. "Ivan."

A growl rumbles through his chest. "You feel so fucking good, *solnishka*."

He lets his hands roam over my stomach and my chest. He palms my breasts and circles the pointed peaks of my nipples all while he thrusts into me again and again.

"I don't want this to ever end. I want to stay here forever. I want you inside of me for the rest of my life."

"You can't talk to me like that, Cora." His voice is strained.

His jaw clenches and something dangerous flashes in his eyes. Then he slowly, *so slowly* slides out of me… and slams back in.

I arch up the bed from the force, but Ivan brings me right back and does it again. And again.

I cling to him, wrapping my legs around his hips and my arms around his neck. I meet his thrusts halfway and whisper breathy nothings in his ear.

Unlike the first orgasm, this one crashes over me suddenly. There is no build—just a sudden drop into blissful oblivion.

"Fuck, fuck, fuck." I kiss his neck and his face. I devour every inch of him I can reach until the pulsing in me slows. "Ivan, that was—"

Ivan flips me onto my stomach before I can finish the sentence and hauls my hips up. He fills me with one thrust.

He fills me again and again and I gladly take it. I lower onto my elbows and arch my hips higher.

There is no way I can possibly climax again, but I don't care. I'm happy to be used by him. I'm more than content just to touch him.

Then Ivan slips a hand around my hip and finds my center. I was so sure I was finished for the night, but all of the sudden—

"I'm coming. I can't believe I'm… Fuck, Ivan, I'm coming."

He roars as my body squeezes around him and I know he's close, too. But I can't hold myself up long enough to help him finish. I collapse to the mattress and he smooths his hand up and down my spine.

I peek over my shoulder at him. He's silhouetted by the bedside table, a golden halo ringing his dark hair. Then he rolls me onto my side. His body curls around me easily, like we were made for this. He settles behind me and slides back in tenderly, nestling so deeply inside that I can't tell where he ends and I begin. I can feel his heart thundering, matching pace with mine.

Somehow, this is different from the sex before. It's slow and sensual. It's peaceful.

It's home.

"Cora," Ivan moans. His lips whisper my name against my shoulder blade again and again. Until his breath catches and he spills into me.

39

IVAN

I tried to be careful. I fucking tried to go slow and be gentle. But having her close, smelling her, *tasting her*—it was too much.

Did I push her too far? Is she hurt?

Fucking hell, I should have sent her away immediately. The moment we left Alexander McAllister's, I should have driven her to the airport. She isn't safe in my life. She isn't safe with me. Not when being near her turns me this feral.

Then she looks back at me. Just a little peek over her shoulder…

And I know, if she keeps looking at me like that, there's no goddamn way I can ever let her go.

That's why I turned her around and finished in her from behind. Because those eyes will be the death of me. Worse yet, they'll be the death of *her*.

If she stays in my world, she'll die. One way or another, I'll lose her.

At least, if I send her away, she lives.

When it's over, Cora rolls to face me. "Thank you for saving me."

"You're the one who stabbed that motherfucker in the neck. You saved yourself."

She shakes her head. "No. No, I—You gave me hope. With the phone call that showed me you weren't an enemy. The bathroom. The texting. The necklace. Everything you did was a little ray of light. I needed all of it."

"Anything for you," I whisper back. "I'll always be there for you."

It's a lie. Or, it should be.

Tomorrow, I'm going to let her go.

Tomorrow, I'm going to set her free.

But for tonight, let me lie.

Cora nestles her head against my chest and closes her eyes. Her breathing slows and evens out quickly, but I don't let go. I hold her while she's asleep, delaying the moment I have to let her go for as long as I can.

But dawn comes too quickly. Birds sing outside the window. The sun cuts through the shades. Time marches on and reality invades dreams.

Gently, I disentangle myself from Cora limb by limb. As I go, I take my heart with me.

Our time together is done. Soon, she'll understand why it had to be that way.

40

CORA

I smell him before I open my eyes. Woodsy, musky, pure Ivan. I roll over and swipe an arm across the silky soft sheets…

But he isn't there.

The bed is cold.

Slowly, I peel my eyes open. Golden morning light streams through the white curtains. The room looks like a dream.

But if this was a dream, Ivan would be here.

"Ivan?" My voice is raspy. I tug the sheet around my naked body and sit up. "Ivan?"

He steps silently into the doorway. There's a look in his face I can't figure out. Something unsettled. Raw.

"Is everything okay?" I ask.

Was last night not good for him? I came over and over and over again. More times than I thought was humanly possible. I'm still buzzing with the afterglow.

"Fine." His mouth turns upwards, but the mask doesn't reach his eyes. "You should get up. We have a lot to do."

I pull the sheet up to my collarbone. I wish I was dressed right now. I feel far too vulnerable. "Like what?"

"You can change into these." Ivan lays a bundle of clothes on the dresser next to the door. I didn't even realize he was holding anything.

"Why?" I sigh. "I mean, I know why I need clothes. It's not like I can walk around naked all day."

Except I could. If he wanted. All it would take is one look from him and I'd stay in this bed all day. All week. For the rest of time.

"What do we have to do?" I ask again.

"I spoke to Yasha this morning and everything has been quiet as far as the Sokolovs and your stepfather are concerned. We figure this is the best time to get you out of the city."

It takes a few seconds for his words to sink in. I blink at him while my brain buffers.

"We're leaving?"

Ivan's expression hardens. His jaw clenches and his gaze shifts from above my shoulder to the opposite wall. "*You* are. As soon as possible."

"For how long?"

"Forever."

The word is finite. Immovable. In it, I hear what he's actually saying: *goodbye.*

"What if I don't want to go?"

"This was *your* plan," he says. "I saw the pro and con list you made while you were staying at Jorden's house. You two were planning to leave. You were going to run off and start over somewhere new."

It was only last week that Jorden and I sat in her small kitchen and made that list, but it feels like a lifetime ago. I was a different person living in a different world. One I thought I could control. Now, the idea that I could boil down everything about my relationship with Ivan into a few pro and con items is laughable. As if it's not infinitely more complex than that.

"That was before—"

"I know. So now, you have even more reason to leave."

"That was before I realized I was wrong about you," I finish.

His mouth works side to side. Then he picks up the clothes from the dresser and tosses them onto the bed next to me. "This has nothing to do with me. You can't stay here. You knew that before and I'll remind you if I have to. It's not safe, Cora."

"Nowhere is safe."

"If it's about money, I'll make sure you're taken care of," he continues as if he can't hear me. "I told you I'd pay you for your time and I will. I'll include the last week and give you overtime. You've earned it."

"This isn't about money! I don't care about money. I care about—"

"I have a private jet waiting for you," he plows ahead. "There are going to be several different legs of the trip to shake anyone who might be tailing you. It will be a lot of travel, so I ordered you some clothes and got a suitcase packed. All you need to do is get dressed and then we can—"

"No!"

It's hard to feel powerful and in control when I'm wearing nothing but a bedsheet, but I do my best. I stand up, hand pressed to my chest to keep myself covered, and lift my chin.

For half a second—maybe even less—I consider just listening to Ivan.

Maybe starting over fresh would be a good idea. It's what Jorden and I decided on originally. One man can't possibly change my plans that much, right?

I look at him now. His stubbled jaw. The trace of bruises on his cheeks. The scratches and scrapes on his forehead from shrapnel and fighting last night. Fighting that he did *for me*. To rescue *me*.

"You can't force me out," I say. "I have a choice here, don't I? It's finally my turn to decide my future. I deserve the life I want." I jab a finger into my chest. "The life *I* want. Not the one *you* decide for me."

He drags a frustrated hand through his hair. "I'm making a decision that gives you a life. I'm helping you survive."

I take a deep breath and look Ivan directly in his eyes. "I don't want to be safe somewhere far away. I want to be here with you. I love you, Ivan," I whisper. "I love you whether you love me back or not."

"You can't be fucking serious."

I'm not sure what to say to that—which works out nicely, because Ivan doesn't give me the opportunity.

"'*Whether I love you or not.*'" He scoffs. "Would I have done anything I've done in the last couple weeks unless I loved you?"

It's my turn to frown. "Um… I don't—"

"Why would I allow a woman as disgusting and vile as Francia into my house unless it was to save the life of the woman *I* love? Why would I have risked myself and my men rescuing you last night if I didn't love you?"

With every question, he takes a step towards me, closing the gap between us.

"Do you think last night could have happened with someone I wasn't head over fucking heels in love with?" he snarls. "I mean, for fuck's sake, Cora… That doesn't happen for just anybody."

He's close enough now that all it takes is one step for me to be pressed against his chest. For my cheek to land over his racing heart.

He strokes fingertips through my tangled hair. "Of course I love you, Cora. That was never a question. There isn't anyone else. There never will be."

41

IVAN

Cora is a fucking angel.

She's wearing a long floral sundress that Anya sent over for her. I've considered pulling the car over twice to fuck her absolutely silly before we even made it to the house.

Through sheer force of will alone, I made myself wait so we could do it in bed for once—except, as soon as we reach the porch, Yasha bursts through the front door to meet us.

"So good to see you again, Cora. Really. Glad you're back." Then he turns to me. "Good to see you, too, brother. But there's something you should know before you go in there."

Instinctively, I shift Cora behind me. "Tell me now."

"It's fine. The house is secure. Neither the Sokolovs nor Cora's family have made any moves to contact us or anyone else in the house."

I frown. "Okay. Then what the fuck is this about?"

I'm getting impatient. I need to christen every surface of the mansion. A sexual exorcism to purge Francia's essence from every goddamn nook and cranny. I'll fuck Cora in the garden, in the eighth guest bathroom, hanging from the chandelier—it'll be like burning sage to get rid of the demons.

"They haven't contacted *anyone* in this house," he repeats with emphasis. "Not a word all of last night or this morning."

It takes me a second before my eyes pop wide. "Are you fucking telling me that Francia is still in there?"

Cora gasps as Yasha nods.

"She has no clue what happened last night." He smiles in wild disbelief. "After the attack, I figured Mikhail would call and warn her. But I got back here and she was still in bed. Then she woke up this morning and… business as usual."

"She's *here*?" Cora hisses.

"Why didn't you get rid of her?" I demand.

Yasha gives me a shit-eating grin. "I thought you might enjoy the honors."

When I process what he's suggesting, my grin spreads wide to match Yasha's. "You thought right." I turn to Cora. "Stay behind me."

I kiss her hard and fast before I step into my own house, slamming the door behind us to make sure the sound echoes. Cora stays tucked away between me and a pillar in the foyer.

It only takes a few seconds before I hear the click-clack of heels on the tile. Or maybe it's cloven hooves. Who can really say?

"Where in the hell have you been?" Francia snaps.

Her nostrils are flared in frustration and her top lip is curled. She isn't attractive on a good day and today is *not* a good day. Not for her, at least.

Fuck, I can't wait until she's out of my house.

"I went out."

"Where? For what?" Her eyes narrow. "Who were you with?"

"That's my business."

She shakes her head. "That is not how this works. If we are going to live in this house together, I have to know something about what you're up to. I'm not going to be married to a ghost. Plus, you said you wouldn't be unfaithful. You can't touch anyone else while we're together."

"Luckily," I say, reaching behind me to turn the doorknob slowly, "you and I aren't together. Not anymore."

Francia goes deathly still. "That's bad news for Cora then. Or have you forgotten? I control what happens to her."

Her threat is lifeless. Based on the way she's staring at the front door and the way her throat bobs, I have a feeling Francia can feel the shift in the air, even if she doesn't quite know it yet.

"Is that right?" I smirk. Cora slinks out from behind me. I feel absolutely fucking giddy to have her right here. The warmth of her body along my arm, the tingle of awareness that she is finally, mercifully close to me... "What do you think, Cora? Does Francia have any control over you?"

"Not anymore," Cora says with surprising viciousness.

Her eyes gleam and her fists knot up. It's hot as hell, actually.

Cora squeezes my hand as Francia takes in the two of us. She digs frantically into her pocket for her phone, but I can tell as soon as she looks at the screen that there's nothing there. No missed calls. No messages.

Her shoulders sag and she takes another step back. "Did you kill them?" Her chin is wobbling, but she's fighting back tears. "Is that why they didn't call?"

"It would almost be better if I killed them. Then you could believe they abandoned you because there was no other choice. But no, I didn't. As soon as I showed up, Mikhail and Alexander ran like cowards without even a word of warning to you. So much for your 'allies.'"

She looks even paler than usual. Her lips are white and her eyes dart from side to side, looking for an escape.

Francia stares at Cora for one beat, two. Then she turns to me. "I assume our deal is at an end."

I snort. "Fuck yes. Your life is at an end, too. Unless Cora decides to spare you."

I walked through the door with every intention of killing Francia for everything she'd put me through in the last week. But Cora is the victim. If either of us should decide what happens to Francia, it should be her.

Slowly, Francia shifts her gaze back to Cora.

"You're interested in what I have to say now?" Cora asks, a smile on her face.

"I won't apologize for wanting to live."

"Fine," Cora snaps. "Don't. But do apologize for almost killing me and Jorden in the process."

Francia's thin lips seal together. Finally, she exhales. "I'm sorry."

"That's cute. Try again. This time, on your knees."

"You're not serious."

Cora points down at the floor. "Drop to your knees and beg me for forgiveness, Francia."

Holy hell, I didn't think it was possible to be more turned on than I was last night, but here it is. Francia thought Cora couldn't be a Bratva wife, but look at her now. She is ruthless.

It's incredible.

"What if I refuse?"

"Then you die," Cora says simply. "Your call."

Francia looks at me, which just makes me laugh out loud. Never in my life have I been looked at as the more merciful of two options.

I just shrug. "I'd do as she says."

She wobbles between a sneer and a sob as she gingerly lowers herself to her knees. "Cora, I'm sorry for—"

"Closer." Cora curls a finger. "I can't quite hear you. Crawl closer to me."

Another pause. Another hopeful glance in my direction. Another absolute failure to find anything close to salvation there.

So, with another grimace, Francia slides across the tile floor on her hands and her knees, her gaze fixed on the floor.

"Look at me," Cora barks.

Francia's face is burning with shame. Her eyes shimmer with tears.

I'm loving every fucking second of this.

Cora holds up a hand to stop Francia once she's close enough. "Good. Now, look at me and speak clearly."

Francia bends her neck back to look up at Cora. "I'm sorry."

"For what?"

"For… for planning to kidnap you."

"And?"

"And moving into this house with Ivan," she continues.

"And?" Cora prods.

"And… and I'm sorry for kidnapping Jorden, too?"

"I don't know. Are you sorry? It's not a Q&A; it's an apology."

"I'm sorry for kidnapping Jorden," Francia states. "I'm sorry for everything I did that hurt or upset you."

Cora looks back at me, a small smile playing across her lips. "Was that everything, Ivan?"

I step up behind Cora, her back pressing firmly to my front. I'm sure she can feel my hardness against her lower back. I lick the curve of her ear and then whisper, "Make her beg."

Cora shivers, but it's subtle. Just for me.

"What do you want to happen now, Francia?" Cora asks. "What should I do with you next?"

Francia hasn't looked away from us. She was transfixed by us. At the sound of Cora's voice, she blinks and looks back down at the floor. "I want to live."

"Then show me."

She sits back on her heels and shrugs. "How? I'm on my knees. What more do you—"

"Show me!" Cora snaps. Her voice echoes off the high ceilings. "Show me how much you want to live. Show me what your life is worth to you."

For the first time, Francia doesn't look angry, she looks scared. That's because she never saw what I saw in Cora—her fire is what drew me in. Francia underestimated her.

She drops back onto her hands and knees and crawls closer. Then she lowers her forehead to the floor. "Please don't kill me, Cora. I want to live. I'm... I'm begging you." Her voice cracks. "Please don't kill me."

Cora looks down at her, expression icy cold. "God, that was pathetic. Worse than I thought it would be."

Francia starts to sit up, but Cora quickly puts her foot on Francia's shoulder and pins her back to the floor. "I didn't say you could get up."

Francia yelps but then falls quiet again.

"I don't want to ever see you again," Cora snarls. "I don't care where you go, but I suggest you make it far—because if I do ever see you again, I'll kill you myself."

Francia nods. "Okay. Okay, I'll disappear."

Cora removes her foot. "Stand up."

Francia rises, unsteady and afraid. Still, it isn't enough. She deserves more than embarrassment. She deserves pain. Lots of it. What I wouldn't give to let loose on her and—

Suddenly, Cora jerks out of my grip and lands a punch directly in the center of Francia's face. There's a nasty cracking sound and blood spurts down her lip.

Francia screams and recoils back, both hands clamped over her nose. More blood wells between her knuckles.

"Now," Cora says, shaking out her fist, "get out of my fucking house, you psychotic bitch!"

Even after the blow, Francia doesn't hesitate. She leaves a trail of spattered blood droplets as she runs around us and disappears through the front door.

I turn and look at my woman. "Cora…"

"Sorry about the power trip." Her cheeks are pink and she chews nervously on her lower lip. "I should have let you handle that, but I just… I got so mad when I saw her. I wanted to make her pay."

I grab Cora's shoulders and look her in her eyes. "Cora, that was the sexiest fucking thing I have ever seen." I grab her hand and place it over the bulge in my pants. "I have never been more turned-on in my life."

Her mouth tips into a shy smile as her hand strokes up and down the length of my zipper. "Now what?" she asks.

I smirk. "I have an idea."

42

FRANCIA

She thinks she is better than me.

That worthless bitch thinks she deserves that life more than I do? Just because Ivan is willing to show up and save her again and a-fucking-gain?

She'd be nothing without him. *They* would be nothing without me. I'm the reason they met. I'm the reason they're together.

And I am going to be the reason they lose it all.

There is no car waiting for me outside, so I walk through the front gates and down the road for a few minutes before I pull out my phone.

Then I call the only person left to call.

It rings and rings and rings before Mikhail finally answers. "What?"

"Funny. You're questioning me, but I'm the one who didn't get a warning about what was going on. *I could have died.*"

"So could I," he hisses back. "We bumped up the wedding on *your* advice, Francia. *You* told us we needed to hurry and that you would keep an eye on Ivan."

"I had it on good authority that he was planning an attack." It's not entirely true, but the fact he refused to touch me was evidence enough that something was up. His loyalty to Cora would be sweet if it wasn't so pathetic.

"Next time, details would be nice! Like, '*Hey, Mikhail, Ivan is going to send a crew of motorcycle-riding pyromaniacs to try and kill you all. Just thought you should know.*' I almost lost my eyebrows."

"Yeah, well, I just got surprised by Cora and Ivan coming home together. I would have loved to miss that reunion. The only reason I made it out is because I—" *I begged on my knees in front of them both*. The memory is too horrible to repeat. I shake my head and bury it. "A warning would have been nice next time."

"There won't be a next time. This plan went off the rails as it is, Francia. You don't have anything left to offer and we're done with—"

"I have plenty more to offer."

"You should offer your life," Mikhail snaps. "That's all you have left to give me. Men are dead because of your incompetence. Why should you get to live?"

"Even more will die without me. Maybe even you, Mikhail."

There's a long pause. He could be taking a long time to think it over, but I doubt it. Alexander is probably there, too, listening in. I'm sure they're looking at each other, silently going back and forth on what to do with me. God forbid Mikhail make a single fucking decision on his own.

In that way, he and Cora are perfect for each other. Neither of them can take care of themselves. Neither of them knows how to survive.

Not the way I do.

"Well?" I press.

"What do you know?" he asks with a sigh.

I laugh. "It's cute that you think I'd tell you on the phone. Before I say a word, I need some assurances from you. From *both* of you."

There's another pause before Alexander speaks, confirming my theory that he's been listening. "I've taken too many chances on you, Francia. Will this one pay off?"

"That depends. How much do you think the location of Katerina Sokolov is worth?"

There's what I have to presume is stunned silence on the other end of the line.

"We'll meet in an hour," Alexander says. "This is your last shot, Francia."

I smile. "That's all I need."

43

CORA

Jorden starts talking to me before the patio door can even close behind her.

"I think Niles puts something illegal in this lemonade." She holds up her glass to the light and squints as she studies it. "Do you think it's drugs?"

"Good morning to you, too."

She gives me a quick wave and then swirls the drink with her stainless steel straw.

Apparently, being kidnapped is only novel for a day. Because it's now day four of being home and I'm losing to a glass of lemonade.

"To answer your question, I don't think Niles puts anything in it that shouldn't be there. He's too proper to drug people without asking first."

"If that's true and there are no drugs in here, then explain why I would be willing to barter my firstborn child to have one of these in my hand for the rest of time."

"Maybe it's the fresh fruit frozen in the ice cubes. That's a nice touch."

She wrinkles her nose. "Maybe. But since I'll never know for sure, I'll just have to come over here every single day and get a glass straight from the source."

"And talk to your best friend."

She lounges in the chair across from me and winks. "Obviously. You're the real reason I'm here, Cora. The lemonade is a delicious perk."

Lies. She and I both know Jorden isn't here for me. She isn't here for the lemonade, either. She is all about one blonde, right-hand man.

Whenever Yasha is in the room, it's like no one else exists. I've taken to slipping silently away whenever they happen upon each other and can't help but gaze into each other's eyes like they're being hypnotized. I have it on good authority that they have been going at it like rabbits any chance they get. Ivan spilled the beans to me a couple days ago, after we participated in some rabbit-like activities of our own. Of course, we did that in our bedroom, not the linen closet next to the den.

"What's with that look?" Jorden asks suddenly.

"What look?"

She circles a finger in the direction of my face. "That dopey smile."

I dip my fingers in my ice water and flick some at her. "My face isn't dopey."

"Fine. What is with that blissful look of radiant joy on your incomparably beautiful face?"

"I don't appreciate the sarcastic way you said that." I laugh. "And it was nothing. Just smiling about you and your lemonade."

"Good. Then it's bringing you just as much joy as it's bringing me. Ever since this lemonade has come into my life, I've been walking on sunshine."

I'd bet her very fulfilling sex life has a lot more to do with her sudden joy than lemonade, but I keep my thoughts to myself.

Since we've seen each other every single one of the last four days, there isn't much to talk about. Jorden and I sit and look out on the lawn. At the butterflies fluttering around the marigolds. At the hummingbirds hovering near the feeder at the edge of the patio.

Locked away in my stepfather's house, I forgot what it felt like to just *be*. To sit in silence without plotting or planning. To enjoy the fresh air.

"How are you doing?"

I startle at the sound of Jorden's voice.

"Sorry," she laughs. "Did you forget I was here?"

I wave her off. "It's okay. I was just thinking."

"About…?"

"Nothing." I shrug. "Everything. I'm not sure. I've had a lot of time to think recently."

She frowns. "Is that a good thing or—"

"It's not bad. Ivan is letting me rest. He wants me to relax. And I need to. The last few weeks have been a lot. I'm happy to have a second to breathe."

"But…?" Jorden presses, eyebrows raised.

There are pros and cons to having people around you who can read your every facial expression. I'm not sure which one this is. "I guess I feel like I should be doing something," I concede.

A male voice calls over, "As far as I'm concerned, you *are* doing something." I turn around to see Yasha strolling across the patio, his eyes fixed on Jorden.

"Oh, yeah? What's that?"

He reluctantly turns to look at me. "Ivan has been in a helluva good mood since you came back. Thank God, too, because I was about to smother him in his sleep."

"I didn't really have to *do* anything for that to happen, though," I argue.

Yasha snorts. "I disagree. The two of you '*do*' plenty."

"Ew! Like you can talk."

"We're talking about you, not me," he corrects sternly. "But Francia is also gone. That was all you. The household staff is in love with you for it. Ask four of them to carry you around on one of those beds that royalty use and I bet they'd do it."

"A litter," Jorden says.

Yasha turns back to her, his eyes going starry. "What?"

"A litter," she repeats. "That's what the bed thing is called. I sometimes fall asleep with the History Channel on."

"I wouldn't have pegged you for a history buff." He takes a step closer to her and I can already feel myself fading out of their notice.

She smiles, her cheeks tinting pink. "I like to watch the conspiracy shows about ghosts and aliens."

"I've never seen those. Maybe we can watch them together. When are they on?"

"Late," Jorden says softly. "*Really* late."

They are looking deeply into each other's eyes when I clear my throat. "Well, I'm glad the staff still likes me. After everything, I thought maybe they'd think I was more trouble than I was worth."

"No way," Yasha insists. "They like having you around. It's nice for them to have someone they can go to with household operations questions. Ivan hates that stuff."

"I thought Niles handled all of that."

"He does it because Ivan refuses, but it would usually fall to the Bratva wi—lady of the house," he corrects quickly. "But no one expects anything of you right now. You've earned some time to rest and relax."

"Amen," Jorden agrees.

"Speaking of…" Yasha lays a hand on Jorden's shoulder, and I can practically see the sparks flying between them. "Maybe you want to nap? I can escort Jorden out if you want to be alone."

I start to shake my head. "No, that's okay. I'm actually—"

Jorden jumps up quickly. "You do look sleepy. You know, sleep is one of the most important factors in overall health. You need to bank some to catch up, I bet."

I narrow my eyes at her, but she won't be shamed.

"I'll get out of your hair." She turns to Yasha. "You can escort me out if you—"

"Yeah, okay." He gives me a tight, guilty smile. "See you later, Cora. Goodbye."

The two of them run into the house like the patio is on fire. I can't even be mad at them. I'm glad they've both found someone. Jorden deserves a good guy and I know Yasha will take care of her.

I'm smiling when I feel strong hands massage my shoulders from behind.

"Niles, what strong hands you have," I moan.

Ivan bends down and nips at the very top of my ear with his teeth. "That's not funny."

I jolt playfully, throwing my arms over my chest to cover myself. "Oh, Ivan! It's you. I thought it was... someone else."

He walks around my chair, his woodsy scent wrapping around me as I take in every climbable inch of him. Maybe I'm no better than Yasha and Jorden. He's been here for half a second and I'm molten.

He sits in Jorden's chair and then deftly pulls me onto his lap. "I like Niles. It would be a real shame to have to kill him."

I hook my hands behind his neck and kiss him. "Don't kill Niles. I think his lemonade is the only reason Jorden keeps coming to visit me."

He laughs and my heart squeezes. I still can't get over how nice it is to see him like this. *Free.*

"What's so funny? Are there really drugs in it? Jorden thought maybe he was dosing her, getting her hooked."

"Niles buys lemonade by the gallon from the store. He pours it into pitchers and then takes the bottles to the recycling."

I gasp. "No way! He uses fruit ice cubes."

"Those are all Niles. But the rest?"

"Liar!"

He rubs his nose against mine and lowers his voice. "Don't tell him I told you. He doesn't even know that I know."

I shake my head with faux disappointment. "I can't believe the kind of loose ship you've been running here, Ivan. I thought I was signing on for the life of luxury, but I've been drinking store-bought lemonade like a common peasant."

"What can I say? I'm a heathen."

His eyes have flecks of yellow and green in the sunlight, and the sight of him here—smiling and in my arms—is almost too much for me to take. My heart hurts from happiness.

"Then it's a good thing I'm here to keep you in check."

He presses a slow kiss to my neck. "You can certainly try."

I'd like to. If he keeps those teasing fingers moving up my thigh, everyone just on the other side of the wall of windows is going to get quite the show. And yet suddenly, I don't give a damn.

I'm about to tell him that we haven't had sex in this particular chair yet and that seems like a terrible mistake we should correct immediately, but before I can, his phone rings.

"I really don't want to get that," he murmurs against my lips.

I catch my breath. "And I really don't want Niles to see me naked."

Sighing, he answers and heads inside to take the call. I lie back in the chair with a dreamy exhale. If Jorden thought I looked dopey before, she wouldn't know what to make of the smile on my face now.

When I hear the patio door open, I'm ready to get Ivan right back to where we were. Then I turn around and see his face.

When I do, I sit up and spin to face him. "What is it? What happened?"

He hasn't even said anything and my heart is racing. Underneath my calm facade, I've been waiting for the other shoe to drop. And here it is. My little slice of paradise is going to be snatched away, I just know it.

"Nothing." Ivan pulls me to my feet and guides me through a deep breath. "Everything is okay. You're safe."

I inhale and exhale slowly. "Okay. Then why do you look like that?"

"Because there's someone here to see you."

"It can't be anyone good if you look like that," I say softly.

"Jury is still out on that one," a voice says from behind Ivan.

A *familiar* voice.

It's been over ten years since I've heard it. But it's hard for a person to forget the voice of their own parent.

Ivan steps aside so I'm standing face to face with my father.

Marcus St. Clair raises one hand in a small wave. "Hi, Cordelia."

44

CORA

"No." I shake my head and spin around so I'm facing Ivan, my back to my father. "I'm not doing this."

"I told you she wouldn't be interested," my father mumbles.

I hate that he's talking to Ivan like they have some secret connection. I hate that he is here.

I hate *him.*

I'm about to turn around and tell him all of that when Ivan puts a hand on the back of my neck. His touch is firm but gentle. "Hear his side of the story before you decide."

"I know his story," I hiss. "I know what he's going to say."

"Maybe. Maybe not."

I frown. "Why do you care, Ivan? How do you know him?"

"I was desperate to find you. Yasha reached out to your dad and he met with us. He helped."

My eyes go glassy. Not because my dad showed up to a meeting—that's the literal least he could do for his only daughter. No, it's because, while I was stuck in Alexander's house, forced to play at marriage with Mikhail, Ivan was looking for me.

He never gave up.

I nod. "Fine. I'll hear him out. But I'm not doing it for him; I'm doing it for you."

Ivan presses a kiss to my forehead. "That's a good enough reason for me."

When he walks away from me, I want to wrap my arms around him and hold him in place. But I calm my racing heart and turn back to my father.

Marcus St. Clair looks exactly like I remember him and nothing like it at the same time. I almost forgot how similar we are. We have the same dark hair and green eyes. I now remember where I got my pointed chin. It certainly wasn't from my mother.

But he looks different, too. There are gray strands speckled through his hair. His jawline is less sharp. I remember him being a tall beanpole—even as a little kid, I could get my arms most of the way around his legs. Now, he's rounder. Softer. He hides most of it behind a sharp suit, but it's easy to notice those kinds of things when you haven't seen each other for…

"Well, how long has it been?" I ask, a surprising amount of venom in my voice. "A decade? Longer?"

"It's good to see you again, Cordelia."

He sounds so calm. So level-headed. I hate that, too.

"My name is Cora," I grit out.

"That's right. Ivan said something about that. Sorry. Old habits and all."

I snort. "Not much of a habit if you haven't seen me since I was a pre-teen."

His mouth twitches. "There were a lot of years where I was there."

"You know, when you put it that way, there were a lot of years where I didn't know Mikhail and Alexander wasn't trying to force me into marriage. Maybe those few pesky weeks were just a blip."

"Don't compare me to him, Cordel—Cora. It's not fair."

"Don't talk to me about what's fair," I spit. "If life was fair, I'd tell Ivan to kick your ass out on the curb and I'd never see you again."

Marcus glances over his shoulder towards where Ivan's silhouette is visible just behind the glass. "You could. He'd do it, too. I think he'd do just about anything for you."

If he thinks complimenting Ivan is going to put him on my good side, he's wrong. It just makes me want to push him farther away. What I have here is good. I don't need anyone from my past coming along to ruin it.

"Maybe that's why you should hear me out," he adds. "If he thought I was a bad guy, would he have let me into his house?"

"You don't know anything about us. Don't talk about him. This is about you and me. This is about whether I want you here or not."

"You're right. I'm sorry." He looks down at his feet.

Is that shame? Does he feel guilty? Did he think of me while he was gone? I'm not sure if any of it makes any difference.

He looks back up with a sad smile. "I guess that's all I can say: I'm sorry. I want to know you. Who you are now. Who you've become."

"Convenient that you decide you want to know me now that life is finally good. I'm living in a big mansion and then *boom,* here you are."

"This has nothing to do with where you're living. I didn't know where you were before this or I would have come to you then."

"You knew we were in a homeless shelter," I interrupt. "Didn't you? After we left, you knew we were living on the street. Mom said you refused to help us."

He looks away from me. It's as good as an admission. Neither of us have ever been able to lie for shit.

"That's what I thought. You didn't care what I was up to back then," I sneer.

"Your mother took you and ran. I didn't know—"

I want to plug my ears, but I settle for shaking my head. "*You* left! *You* abandoned *us.*"

"No! No. She ran away. She met Alexander and didn't want anything to do with me. I wanted to help you, but I didn't know if the money would go to him or… I just wasn't sure what to do."

"She met him after we were already on the streets. The only reason she is with him is because she was poor and desperate."

"I know that's what she told you, Cordelia, but the truth is—"

"Cora," I grit out. "For the last time, my name is Cora."

He runs a hand down his face. He looks as exhausted as I feel. "Your mother told you a lot of things, Cora. My guess is a lot of them weren't true. I didn't abandon you. She was cheating on me and she left to be with him. What happened after that, I don't know for sure. But I know I didn't leave."

I remember being huddled next to a bench one night, trying to blend in so none of the beat cops on patrol would bother us. My mom fell asleep crying. *"He won't help us, Cora. He's going to leave us out here to die."*

I thought she meant my dad, but maybe…

My head is swimming. He's telling a much different story from the one I've known the last ten years. But even worse, I know he's lying. At least about one part of it.

My chin wobbles. I work hard to keep it steady as I meet his eyes. "Whatever happened with her and Alexander and you, you *did* abandon me. You disappeared. You left me with them even when they…"

I can't make myself say it. I haven't seen this man for almost half of my life. What kind of explanation do I really owe him?

Still, his face crumples. He lifts a hand like he wants to reach for me, but he thinks better of it and lets it fall to his side.

"You're right," he says finally. "I wasn't the one who left first, but… I still left. I should have fought harder to see you and to get custody. I thought your mom would come back once you'd been on the streets, but she didn't. Then she was with Alexander and I thought you were happy there. I thought— never mind. It doesn't matter what I thought. I fucked up, Cora. Big time. But I want to try to make up for it starting now."

I have half a mind to ask him what he wants from me. Everyone else seems to want something. My mom and Alexander want to use me like a bartering chip. Mikhail wants me to be his thoroughbred breeder. Francia used me as a decoy.

Ivan is the first person in my life who wants me for me. I'm not ready to believe there are other people like him.

Not yet.

"Can you forgive me?" my dad asks. "Could we try to start over?"

At one point, I would have lied. Out of fear that he would get upset and never see me again, I would have lied about what I wanted. What I needed.

Not anymore.

"I don't know," I admit. "This is a lot. I'm not sure what to make of it all. I need time. Maybe a lot of it."

Disappointment flashes across his face, fast and furious, but he wipes it away and nods. "Okay. That's understandable."

We stare at each other for a few seconds before he takes a step back towards the door. "I guess I should… I'll leave."

"That's probably for the best," I say softly.

"Ivan has my number if you need anything. Or if you don't need anything. Just… if you want to talk."

I can't meet his eyes as he walks away. I don't want him to see me cry.

45

CORA

Ivan walks my dad out. I retreat into our bedroom and try to keep myself from crumbling.

I'm not that scared little girl living on the streets with her mom. I'm not that terrified teenager trying to disappear into the wallpaper at Alexander McAllister's house.

I'm a different person in a different world. I've changed.

But that doesn't make any of this easier to process.

I curl up on the bed, hugging my pillow to my chest. Sitting outside felt like being in a fishbowl. I don't want to be on display. I want to be alone.

At least, I think I do. Until I hear the door open and feel a familiar dip in the mattress behind me. Suddenly, all I want is to be wrapped in Ivan, cocooned in his scent and protected from the outside world.

He drapes his arm over my hip. His warmth soaks through my shirt, melting away the chill my dad left behind.

"Are you okay?" he whispers.

The tenderness in his voice makes my eyes water. I squeeze them closed and nod. "I'm okay."

"I knew you were, but I needed to make sure you knew it, too."

I roll over so I'm facing him. Even when I'm prepared to be close to him, it always takes me by surprise. The scent of his skin, the feel of him against me, the closeness of his mouth—all of it is intoxicating in a way I've never felt before. It's a struggle to think straight.

"What does that mean?"

He tucks a strand of hair behind my ear. "It means that you're strong. You've been through a lot worse than a meeting with your dad. I wouldn't have brought him here if I didn't think you could handle it. I'm glad you know how strong you are, too."

I hear my dad's voice in my head. *If he thought I was a bad guy, would he have let me into his house?*

"You could have told me he was coming." I sigh. "I'm not mad, but I'm not *not* mad. I've had enough surprises for a lifetime."

He runs a finger down my spine. "If I'd told you, would you have agreed to see him?"

"The only reason I agreed to it is because of you. If you'd told me and then asked me to meet with him, I would have done it." Ivan arches a skeptical brow and I wilt slightly. "I would have… considered it."

He snorts. "You would have flat-out refused. And I understand that. My dad didn't abandon me and I still avoid him whenever possible."

"Speaking of which, I would love advance warning when he's coming over. I have enough parental drama without dealing with yours, too."

"Fair enough." He traces a path under the slope of my jaw. "I just knew how much him leaving hurt you, *solnishka.* And I knew that the version of events you were told wasn't completely accurate."

I blow out a breath. "I almost forgot about that. Apparently, my mom knew Alexander before my dad left?"

"That's what he says. He told me that your mom cheated on him. When she left to be with Alexander, Alexander refused to take you all in. But she was so in love with him that she bounced around from shelter to shelter with you rather than go back to your dad."

I shake my head. "I want to say it doesn't make sense. I mean, if Alexander was already in the picture when we were living on the streets, why wouldn't he have stepped in?" I pause and reconsider. "Actually, when I say it out loud, it makes perfect sense. Alexander has been a sadistic manipulator from the very beginning. I'm not surprised at all."

We're quiet for a while. Ivan watches me, his finger still swirling, our breath mingling.

Finally, I look up at him. "He asked me to forgive him."

"You don't have to."

I arch a brow. "You're the one who brought him here. I figured you were on his side."

"I'm on your side." He wraps his arm around me and pulls me close. "I'm always on your side."

"Even if I don't know what I'm going to do yet?"

"Even if you know exactly what you're going to do and decide you will never forgive him and want to key his car."

That surprises a laugh out of me. "I had no idea committing petty crimes was a date night option."

"Petty crimes, misdemeanors, just about any felony you can dream up. I'm open for anything as long as you're with me." His smile softens and the moment between us softens, too. "I'm not going anywhere, Cora. You have plenty of time to figure out what you want to do with your dad. I'll be here when you're ready."

I've done a good job of holding back my tears, but one slips free.

Ivan brushes it away. "Don't cry."

"No, it's good. It's a happy tear. Knowing that you'll be here, that we have time—it means everything to me."

"We have so much time, Cora. A lifetime." He brings my knuckles to his lips and presses a long kiss there. "We are going to make it through all of this. We are going to live our lives together and start a family. And we aren't going to pass any of this bullshit family drama down to them. We're going to give them the lives we never had: parents who are there for them and a dad who is head over heels obsessed with their mom."

Those pesky tears are burning in my eyes again, and I swipe them away. "That sounds like a good plan."

"That's the only kind I make."

I roll my eyes and laugh. "So cocky."

"If you want cocky, I can show you cocky," he growls.

In a second, he's on top of me, his mouth on my neck and threatening to venture lower.

I thread my hands through his hair. "Don't get me wrong: I want you to stay right where you are, but... don't you have a meeting today?"

He growls, the vibration rumbling through my chest. "A meeting I'm already late for, yeah."

My disappointment is immeasurable, but I slowly push him back and sit up. "I don't want anyone to think that I'm a distraction for you."

"You aren't a distraction, Cora." He strokes his long finger under my chin. "You're my woman. My reason."

I turn my face and kiss the center of his palm. "Keep talking like that and I'll change my mind and beg you to stay."

"They should see that."

My eyes go wide. "They should see the two of us in bed?"

"Fuck no. That sight is all mine." Possession flares in his eyes. "But they should see who you are to me. Come with me to the meeting."

"Really? You want me there?"

"I want you with me," he says. "Always." He strokes his chin as he thinks about it. "But let's save that for another day. I'm fucking famished and I don't want to go to this meeting anyway. So here's what's going to happen: right now, I'm going to fuck you to within an inch of your life. We're going to shower and get ready to leave, then I'm going to get horny and do it all over again. Then, when you're sweaty and wrecked and you smell like me, I'm taking you to get the best burger you'll ever have in your life."

Let no one say that Ivan Pushkin is not a man of his word.

He does indeed fuck me to within an inch of my life. He does indeed carry my still-trembling body to the shower, rinse me off with the gentlest touch I've ever felt, then carry me right back to bed and devour me until I'm a melted puddle of goo on the sheets. Then, with a smile on his lips, he dresses me in sweatpants and a baggy t-shirt and walks me out the door, down the stairs, and into his Range Rover.

We pull up outside the most rundown-looking burger joint I've ever seen in my life.

"Are we getting hamburgers or hepatitis?" I ask nervously.

He rolls his eyes. "Back home in the mansion for one day and you're already a snob."

I thwack him on the arm. "I'm not a snob!" Gesturing at myself, I add, "Would a snob be about to waltz into this place like the most slovenly peasant who ever lived?"

Ivan's eyebrow perks up and his tongue darts out. "You look pretty good to me, *solnishka...*"

I push him away and recoil to the far side of the car, even as a smile plays across my lips. "Nuh-uh. No way. Hands to yourself, mister. You made me come way too many times already this morning. If I let you at it again, you're going to break me permanently."

"Don't threaten me with a good time," he growls.

Laughing, he lunges toward me. I shriek and jump out of the car as fast as I can, his hand pawing over my hip but not quite close enough to reel me back toward him.

I hit the pavement and dance away. I'm still looking back at the vehicle when I collide with something solid and warm. The impact makes my head spin and I stumble backward, dizzy. It's only when my vision clears and I realize what—or rather, *whom*—I just slammed into that every trace of laughter vanishes.

Because Mikhail Sokolov is staring down at me.

46

CORA

For a split second, I convince myself I'm hallucinating.

How many nightmares have I had the last few nights that featured the pale face in front of me? Maybe this is another one of those.

Except no. Ivan is never there in my nightmares.

But he's here now.

Before I can even process that this is real, Ivan grabs my arm and jerks me behind him.

"Is it a trap?" I whisper.

I look around in horror. If this is a trap, Alexander will be waiting just outside. I don't see anyone out of the blue, though. Just a few couples and families like us. Some construction workers on lunch break. Nobody who doesn't belong.

"Master let you off your leash today, Mikhail?" drawls Ivan.

I peek around him in time to see pure rage flicker over Mikhail's face. His neck is a violent red color.

If this is a trap, he looks just as surprised as we are.

"No one controls me." He looks pointedly at me. "I would never let myself be dragged into a war for another man's woman."

"I didn't do it for another man's woman," Ivan snarls. "I did it for *mine*."

The customers standing between Mikhail and Ivan shift nervously. A man in a janitor's jumpsuit steps out of the way, glancing back over his shoulder to watch this altercation play out. So much for not having all eyes on us.

Mikhail doesn't seem to notice. He doesn't have eyes for anyone beyond Ivan. Not even me.

"You fucking Pushkins think you own everything. Cordelia was always mine. She was promised to *me*."

Ivan snorts. "We don't all play by the rules your daddy made up for you, Mikhail. He can promise Cora to you all he wants, but she was never his to give away."

Mikhail's eyes flick down to where my hand is clutching Ivan's forearm. I see rage turning his face a dangerous shade of violet.

Without warning, he rears back… and charges.

Ivan shoves me back, farther away from the mayhem. The other customers in the restaurant shout and slide back. Over the scraping of chairs on the concrete and worried voices, I hear one sound rising above the rest: the thud of Ivan's fist connecting with Mikhail's blood-red face.

The hit rocks Mikhail, but he manages to stay on his feet. His eyes narrow into furious slits—or maybe it's just that they're already beginning to swell shut.

"The bitch is nobody. *Nobody.*" Mikhail spits blood onto the floor. "You could have anyone, but you stole what was mine. *You* started this war, Ivan. And for what? I guess I need to get between the whore's legs to figure out what you see in her."

Ivan doesn't bother with a reply. This time, he takes the fight to Mikhail.

Mikhail sees it coming and dodges to the side, but not fast enough. Ivan lands a glancing blow that sends Mikhail toppling into a nearby table. The customers there have already abandoned their lunch to cower along the wall, but their burgers and shakes crash to the floor.

"Someone call the police!" a woman cries out.

Ivan waves a hand in the air, dismissing the woman. "Not necessary. I'm going to put the dog down myself."

He grabs Mikhail by the front of his shirt, lifts him off of his feet, and slams him back down on the table he was just gripping for support.

His back ripples with strength. The veins in his arms are raised, adrenaline and blood and vitality coursing through him.

"Cora does not belong to you or anyone," Ivan growls. "It's her choice. It has *always* been her choice. And she chose me."

Mikhail screeches and springs up off the table with all of his strength, but Ivan just uses the momentum to spin him around and slam him against the wall. His chest caves in, the air rushes out of him in a huff, and the color drains from his face. His eyes go wide with panic.

Ivan leans closer, though I can still hear every word. "I should fucking kill you for what you did to her."

"Do it," Mikhail gasps. "You might as well. My name is ruined."

Ivan shakes his head. "I can't torture you the way you deserve here. Not with all these people around. No, your end will have to wait until I'm ready. Right now, I don't have the time for this."

Mikhail swings out again, but it's a weak attempt. He lightly connects with Ivan's ribs and, an instant later, Ivan slams him against the wall a second time and punches him in the eye.

He is sliding down the wall, nearing unconsciousness, when water sprays across the room.

Mikhail blinks and Ivan steps back as the chef walks out as far as the sprayer from the sink will allow. "Break it up!"

The water seems to revitalize Mikhail. He stands up, swaying slightly, before he jabs a finger in Ivan's direction. He seems to want to say something, but the words don't come.

Then he turns to me, his pale eyes burning with a furor I've never seen before. "This is not the end," he spits.

For a moment, it's just me and Mikhail. Fear overrides everything else. I can't move. Can't breathe. Can't think.

Then Ivan grabs him by the back of his shirt and hurls him down the street. Mikhail lands hard with a grunt and the whole gathered crowd sucks in a shocked breath. We all watch as he climbs to his feet, gives us one more skewering look, then disappears around the corner.

47

CORA

I don't realize how tightly I'm gripping the edge of the trash can until Ivan's hands smooth over mine. Gently, he pries my fingernails away from the wooden lip.

"Are you okay?" he asks, voice low and serious. His right sleeve is dripping water. A droplet carves its way down his bicep and rolls off his elbow. I watch it go in what feels like slow motion.

"I'm okay." My voice is shaking. My entire body is shaking. I wasn't even the one fighting.

"I'm going to take care of you, *solnishka*. I won't let anything happen to you."

"I know."

And I do know that. I believe him.

So why can't I stop shaking?

"You've got to go, man!" the chef bellows from the kitchen. "I'm calling the cops."

Ivan starts to let go of me, but I cling to him. I twine my fingers through his so he can't escape. I need him close to me. He scrutinizes me for a moment, then sighs and leads me back out to the car.

He helps me up and buckles me into place before walking around and claiming his spot behind the wheel. We take a circuitous route through the city to make sure we shake anyone who might be following us. Based on Mikhail's face, that run-in was a surprise for him, too. But still—better safe than sorry.

Finally, we move beyond the last of the residential streets until we're winding through the hills. Only then can I let myself relax.

"Are you okay?" Ivan asks again.

He's still holding my hand over the console. I squeeze his tighter. "Yeah. I'm okay."

"You were shaking." Ivan readjusts his grip on the wheel. The whites of his knuckles are visible. "I can't stand that he scared you like that."

"Really, I'm okay. I knew you would protect me."

His jaw clenches. "He deserves worse than he got. If there hadn't been so many people, I would have—"

"Ivan, I know. I—" The vibration in me seems to have reached my chest. My heart is racing and I realize all at once that I wasn't shaking because I was scared. This hum in my chest has nothing to do with fear or Mikhail Sokolov.

It's for Ivan.

I need him. Now.

"Pull over."

"Right now?" He checks his mirrors. The road is empty.

I shift in my seat and press my thighs together. "Right now."

Ivan pulls into the next dirt driveway and follows it until there's an overgrown alcove in the woods. Huge trees cast shade over the car and block the view of the main road. It's perfect.

Before Ivan can ask what is going on, I unbuckle my seatbelt and crawl into his seat. I straddle him, pressing the beat between my legs against his body.

"Seeing you back there was really, really hot." I hook my hands behind his neck and roll my hips against him. "That's why I was shaking. It was adrenaline from seeing you in action like that. But now, there's nowhere for all that adrenaline to go."

Ivan's eyes have been eaten away by the black of his pupils. He grips my waist and drags me against him. "I have an idea or two for where it could go."

He captures my mouth, nipping at my bottom lip while he throws his seat back as far as it will go. I yelp in surprise and Ivan slides his tongue past my lips.

We are a mess of teeth and tongues and limbs as he lifts my hips high so I can wiggle out of my sweatpants. Somehow, I manage to get them off and straddle him again. Ivan tugs down the neck of my shirt and pushes my bra aside. He takes my breast in his mouth and I arch my back.

"Ivan," I moan. His hair is silky soft between my fingers. "You're killing me."

He smirks up at me. "Well, we can't have that, can we?"

His pants are a lot easier to deal with than mine. A button and one zipper and my hand is wrapped around the long, thick length of him.

He curses under his breath as I slowly explore him from top to bottom. "*You're* going to kill *me*, Cora."

I'm fine with that, but he isn't. He presses me back against the steering wheel, grips my hips, and pulls me down onto him in one devastatingly steady stroke.

We crash together until I'm sticky with sweat and panting. All I can do is lay my head on his shoulder as he seats himself deep inside of me again and again.

"Come for me," he growls. His fingers dig into the soft flesh of my hips. He's on the edge, holding himself together long enough for me to fall first. Sacrificing for me yet again.

I throw my head back and cry out.

"Good girl, Cora. Just like that." His lower lip is caught between his teeth as he works me down his cock once, twice, a third time. Then he crashes down with me.

I kiss his creased forehead until his arms band around my back and we're lying together, limp and sated.

And safe.

Most of all, we're safe.

48

CORA

I push open the doors of the gym. Yasha immediately slides his headphones off and slows his treadmill. "What are you doing here? Did Jorden send you to see me?"

"No… Should she have?"

"No!" he answers a bit too fast. He downshifts into a grimace. "It's not a big deal. We just had a little disagreement. I figured she sent you in to mediate."

"Ah," I say. "Hence the running. If you two are fighting, I'm sure you have a lot of excess energy to burn off."

"On the contrary: when we're fighting, I'm even more exhausted than usual, if you catch my drift." He grins and waggles his brows—as if I needed the nonverbal explanation.

"Gross." I wrinkle my nose. "Moving on. So why are you two fighting?"

"We aren't fighting. She just wanted me to come to her place last night and I told her I couldn't."

"Why couldn't you?"

"Because."

I raise my brows. "Because… why?"

"Because of *you*," he says, like it's totally obvious. "You're back and Mikhail and Alexander are still out there. I need to be here in case anything goes wrong. To keep you safe."

"That's actually what I came to talk to you about," I say. "I want to be as safe as possible, too. After the other day with Mikhail, I haven't been able to stop thinking about how useless I felt."

"Ivan had Mikhail handled, Cora. He didn't need your help."

"No, I know that. I get that. But there might come a point when I need to fend for myself."

Just the thought of a point like that brings back memories I'd rather forget. *Mikhail cornering me in my bedroom at Alexander's house, pressing me against the wall while his hands crept lower and lower and...*

I blink the images away and find Yasha studying me. He swipes the sweat off of his forehead. "I don't know what you're saying."

"I want you to teach me how to fight."

"No. Correction: *hell* no."

His answer is so fast that it takes me by surprise. I'm sure I must have misheard him.

"What?"

"No." He shakes his head firmly. "I can't." He pulls out his phone, ignoring me entirely.

I'm still standing there, wondering if I'm the butt of some joke I don't get. "You *can't*? What does that mean?"

"Listen, CorCor—can I call you that?" He pockets his phone. "CorCor, I basically view you as a sister at this point. You are a sexless, shapeless blob in my eyes."

I wrinkle my nose. "Somehow, I'm both grossed out and offended at the same time. What are you talking about?"

"Fighting is close and personal." He does a little bob-and-weave to prove his point. "For you, grappling would probably be the best use of your learning time and that can only take place in close quarters, you know what I mean? I'm not going to do that without talking to Ivan first."

"You're kidding. What is this, like, some kind of 'bros before hoes' thing?"

He snaps and points at me with a pleased grin. "Exactly! You get it."

I gasp in mock horror and pull out my phone. "I'm going to tell Ivan you called me a 'hoe.' How do you think he'll feel about that?"

"Woah! It's just a phrase. He knows that. He won't care." Yasha watches me pace while I dial and the phone rings. Just before Ivan picks up, he whispers, "But don't tell him… just in case."

"Hello, *solnishka*," Ivan answers. "Everything okay?"

"I want Yasha to teach me how to fight."

Again, I expect a few moments of consideration and a discussion. I've got my argument ready, an extremely convincing PowerPoint already cued up in my head. But just like Yasha, Ivan answers immediately.

"No."

My mouth falls open. "What? Why?"

"He said no, didn't he?" Yasha crows. "I knew it! He would have killed me if I'd done it without asking."

I ignore him and focus on Ivan's deep voice. "Yasha is not going to teach you how to fight."

I frown. "You already said that, but *why?*"

As I ask, the doors to the gym open up and Ivan walks in. He lowers the phone from his ear and slides it into the pocket of his gray sweatpants. "Because I am."

Ivan is in a black tank top that is molded to every ridge and valley of his body. I stand stock-still and ogle him. His broad shoulders, muscled arms, and tapered waist. I haven't even gotten below the belt yet and I'm already giddy and squirmy.

I've never seen Ivan in casual clothes like this in the light of day and, good God, I think he was created for athletic wear. He is broad and solid and the idea that I should learn to defend myself seems silly in the face of everything that he is.

"Okay," Yasha says, creeping forward one step at a time. "That is my cue to leave before something physical goes down."

Ivan blinks away from me to look at his best friend and I am forced to acknowledge once again that we are every bit as bad as Yasha and Jorden. Fifteen seconds in the same room with us and Yasha is sprinting for the exit.

As he passes Ivan, he pats him on the shoulder. "Good luck. And if Cora says anything about me calling her a name, it was a misunderstanding. You know how women can be."

"Hey!" I call after him. But it's too late. Yasha is already hightailing it for the doors.

And then Ivan is in front of me. Every hot, chiseled inch of him.

I blink away from his chest and look into his eyes. That doesn't help much. He's got them cranked up to full power today. I'm a helpless deer in the headlights. "Where were you?"

"I was planning to get a workout in when Yasha texted me that you were here."

"Can I do anything in this house without you knowing about it?"

"Probably not," Ivan admits. "Not until things cool down. The only reason I agreed to leave for my meeting this morning is because Yasha swore the security team would update me on where you were every fifteen minutes."

The oppressive surveillance has an echo of being trapped in Alexander's house under lock and key. The difference is, Ivan is doing all of this to keep me safe—to keep me free. He's looking out for me. I get that and I love him for it.

I just want to be able to look out for myself, too.

"So," Ivan starts again, "you want to learn how to fight?"

I nod. "Will you teach me?"

"Of course. For a price."

"A price?"

He grins wickedly. "I scratch your back, you scratch mine. Quid pro quo. That sort of thing."

"Well, I don't know how to fight. Even if I did, you don't need me to teach you that. I can teach you how to French braid hair if you want?"

He chuckles. "Tempting, but I'll pass."

"Then what do you want?"

He leans in, bringing his woodsy scent with him. "I'll decide later."

I have to exhale away the haze in my mind. "You want me to agree to conditions I don't know yet? I think every lawyer in existence would tell me that's a bad idea."

Ivan spreads his arms wide. "I don't see any lawyers in here, *solnishka,*" he says. "It's just you and me."

I sigh. I'm one thousand percent positive I'll regret the words that are about to come out of my mouth. I'm also one thousand percent positive it's the kind of regret I can live with.

"Fine. I'll pay your extortion price, Ivan. Teach me to fight and I'll do whatever you want."

49

CORA

I lift my arms to try to pull my hair back into a ponytail and my shoulders scream in pain. I drop them to my side and turn to Anya. "Your brother is a sadist."

She floats up behind me, looking and smelling like a spring flower even after the two-mile jog we just did. "You're the one who asked him to teach you to fight. If you were smart, you would have come to me first."

"He said he wouldn't let anyone else train me. 'Anyone who lays a hand on you will suffer my wrath' were his exact words."

But it feels like *I'm* the one suffering his wrath right now. Ivan brought out the dumbbells at the end of our session yesterday and I feel like every muscle in my body is still crying.

Anya laughs as she twists my hair up into a perfect messy bun on the first try. "I'm not afraid of big, bad Ivan. You should know that. Plus, look at the two of us right now. I'm training you, aren't I?"

"Well, yeah. But he gave you permission, didn't he?"

"He was going to skip your training session this morning because he's busy being *Pakhan* Pushkin and reigning over his lands, so I volunteered to pick up the slack. Don't worry." She pats my shoulder, drawing another wince out of me. "You're safe in my hands. Well, safe-ish."

Anya leads me away from the weights and machines and stops in the center of a large blue mat.

"Sparring?" I balk. "Already? It's only my second session. Am I ready for that?"

She nods. "It's what Ivan had on the schedule and we both agreed it might be best for you to try sparring with someone your own size first. Less intimidating. In theory."

I'd agree with Anya—except, in her pink satin boxing shorts and matching gloves, she looks like *Beat My Ass* Barbie. I never noticed how many muscles she has. What is in the water in this mansion? Whatever it is, I'm not getting nearly enough of it.

Anya smacks her gloves together. "Okay. No more procrastinating. Get your gloves on and let's do this."

I clumsily struggle into the red leather gloves she brought for me. Once they're on, it takes me three tries to finally get my arms up and into position.

"I'll take it easy on you since you're recovering today," Anya says, bouncing from one foot to the other. "No hard hits and I'll move slow. This is just practice."

I bite down on my mouthguard and nod. "Okay. Thanks."

Then Anya's smile vanishes from her face. She drops into a stance and takes one powerful lunge in my direction. I flow effortlessly with the motion, let it scythe harmlessly past my face, then turn and unleash holy hell on her for daring to think I was so weak.

Just kidding. That's what I wish I did. In reality, I shriek and fumble out of the way, trip over my feet, and land hard on my face on the mat.

Anya looks down at me with scorn in her eyes. "What the hell was that?"

"No." I roll over and gesture up wildly at her. "What in the hell was *that*? That was not slow and easy, Anya!"

She laughs at first, but quickly bites it back when she sees the frown on my face. "Sorry. Okay. We'll go again. This time, it will be slower and easier. I'm just used to sparring with Ivan, I guess."

"Well, I am not Ivan." At this point, I think that's apparent to everyone here. And to whichever lucky security guard is monitoring the cameras today. I'm sure I'm giving the security shack a real treat right now.

Anya helps me to my feet. We square up again and, on her signal, we start. She approaches me again, still moving fast, but more "relentless Terminator" and less "enraged bull." My muscles burn as I try to keep a safe distance between us. Somehow, Anya still manages to weasel her way in and land a few soft jabs.

"Keep your arms in!" she orders. "Protect your ribs!"

I adjust and then she strikes and taps the side of my head. "Keep your hands up. Protect your face."

Again, I adjust. Again, she hits my ribs. "Ribs, Cora!"

The lesson goes about like that for the next thirty minutes. Anya tells me to protect some part of my body, I do it, and then another part of me is exposed enough that she gives me a love tap that really isn't so loving.

By the time we finish, I'm dripping in sweat, my muscles burn with exhaustion, and I already have a few purple bruises spreading on my arms.

"That was really good for your first try," Anya says.

I look up at her from where I've collapsed in a pile of limbs on the floor. "Are you just saying that so you can assault me again tomorrow?"

She laughs. "You probably don't want to hear this, but that was not exactly exciting for me. If I wanted to assault you, I could have done it four times faster and already be showered by now."

"Great." I throw my arms over my eyes. "Now, you've wounded my body *and* my pride."

Anya grabs my hand and yanks me up to standing. I wobble, but she holds me steady. "You are truly pathetic when you're tired."

"And hungry," I add.

She chuckles and then slaps my butt. "Go shower and rest up. I'll meet you here tomorrow, same time."

With that torture lying ahead, I practically crawl down the hall to my bedroom and then shuffle into the bathroom. I'm so sore that I think I black out at some point after starting the shower and peeling off my sweaty clothes, because the next thing I know, I'm standing in the steaming hot shower spray, moaning out a litany of curse words.

"Does that feel good?" A deep voice asks from the doorway.

I'm too exhausted to be startled or self-conscious. I just nod and whimper. "This is the best and worst moment of my entire life."

Ivan laughs. That deep, growly sound would start a fire low in my belly if my body wasn't currently using all of its reserves of energy to keep me upright.

He leaves his clothes in a pile on the floor and slides into the shower behind me. When his arms wrap around my middle, I give myself over to him.

"I'm so tired," I whimper. "You Pushkins are going to break me."

"No. We're going to make it so no one can break you. It just takes time."

I groan, but the sound quickly shifts to a moan as Ivan works his hands down the aching muscles of my arms.

"Oh my God, Ivan." I almost sink to the shower floor, but he presses one hand flat to my stomach to pin me against him. "I'm... You're... Good God."

Another laugh rumbles through him as he keeps coaxing his massage lower and lower. Over my stomach and lower still, until his fingertips graze over my center.

I thought I was on the verge of death—but as soon as he teases at my pussy, I'm burning. Aching. Yearning.

Funny how that works.

He comes and goes. Teases and retreats. "What are you doing?" I whimper the fourth time he gets so close to the promised land before disappearing again.

"Pelvic massage." The words shouldn't send a shiver down my spine, but with that voice, he could read a phone book to me and I'd have no choice but to straddle him.

"Feels more like you're taunting me because you know I can't fight back."

"I don't want to hurt you," he explains. "Over-massaging the muscles can be just as bad as overworking them."

I shake my head and lean back against him. His body is warm and sticky from the steam in the shower. "No, no. Over-massage. Overwork. Do your worst. Especially right *there.*"

He chuckles again. A few minutes ago, all I wanted was to shower and sleep, but I have very different plans now. Ivan presses a kiss to the side of my neck… and then slips away.

I blink my eyes open and watch him climb out of the shower. "Where are you going?"

"You need to be ready for tomorrow. I don't want to tire you out."

I start to argue, but then I see the mischief shining in his amber eyes. He knows exactly what he's doing. And he's doing it on purpose.

"Is this my punishment for asking Yasha to train me before coming to you?" I groan pitifully. "Are you trying to torture me?"

He smiles and leans into the shower. "If you think *this* was punishment, you aren't going to know what hit you when I finally claim my payment."

With that, Ivan walks his toned, naked ass out of the bathroom.

Even when I'm this mad at him, I can't help but watch.

50

IVAN

It's only been a few days of training, but Cora is already improving. Her form is better, she's moving a bit faster while she spars, and she isn't ending every day near tears.

My body now aches at the end of every session—but for very different reasons.

Cora bends at the waist and stretches both hands down to her ankle. She extends her leg, pressing her hips to one side and straining her already thin leggings. She does it all *sofuckingslowly* that I want to roar and rip the mirrors right out of the walls.

At least, I think she's doing it slowly.

I might just be fucking horny.

The shower massage with no happy ending started as a way to get her back. Then Cora kept "falling asleep" before I could get to bed every night as a way to get *me* back.

She thinks she's winning.

She doesn't have a fucking clue.

"Enough with the stretching, Cora," Anya calls from the sparring mat. "He can't take his eyes off of you. Your job is done."

Cora stands up and spins around, doing her best to look innocent. But she knew what she was doing.

"Very classy, Anya," I mutter.

"I wasn't the one staring at my…" Anya turns to me with an arched brow. "What is she to you now? Your girlfriend? Fiancée? I can't keep up."

"She's mine to look at whenever the fuck I want," I snap back. "I don't need your permission."

Anya holds up her hands and backs away, a smug smile on her face.

Meanwhile, Cora sashays her way to the sparring ring. I know she's safe with Anya. Still, I can't shake the feeling that *I* should be the one standing between Cora and anyone who wants to hurt her.

Then again, I want her to feel like she can take care of herself. I want her to be confident. And learning a few techniques and getting stronger—all of it is helping her regain the confidence Mikhail and Alexander stripped from her.

That's worth its weight in gold.

"Good dodge," Anya coaches as they circle each other. "Don't forget to keep your hands up so I can't—"

In the middle of her advice, Cora feints with her right hand and then lands a blow above Anya's brow with her left.

Anya is stunned for a second before she grins. "Holy shit. I guess I'm the one who needs to keep my hands up. Nice shot!"

Cora glances over at me. The pride in her eyes is plain to see. She's ecstatic. I don't even have to check the mirrors to know that my face shows the exact same things.

She's my queen. Anya wanted to know what Cora is to me and that's the answer. Cora is my queen.

As they continue, I can't stop myself from watching the way her body shifts and bounces with every step. Her sports bra holds her chest in tight, taunting me with cleavage I want to bury my face in. Her stomach is tight and glistening with sweat. Her hips curve wide and I can see the indention on her lower back where my thumbs fit perfectly. Where I can hold her steady and fill her until we're both out of our minds with need.

Anya shouts out a few more corrections, but I don't hear a thing. I'm lost in a fantasy, growing harder by the second. I'm so lost that I barely catch Cora unbalancing Anya and taking her to the floor.

"How the fuck did you—" Anya taps out and sits up, arms resting on her knees. "I didn't see that coming. How did I not see that coming?"

Cora is still on her hands and knees on the mat, panting as sweat drips down her neck. I have the perfect view down the top of her sports bra. And when she looks up at me, a pleased smile tugging the corners of her mouth, I know the game is up.

It's time for my reward.

Cora takes a long shower.

After the way she sauntered up the stairs and stripped naked in the bathroom doorway, I know she's waiting for me to break down and join her. If I didn't already have other plans in mind, I would.

Instead, I sit back in my armchair, hands folded over my stomach, and wait.

Finally, the shower turns off. I hear frustrated stomping across the tile floor. I'm barely holding back a smile when the door slams open and Cora comes out looking like Aphrodite. Her hair is wet and falling over one shoulder, her skin is flushed from the heat of the water, and she's barely covering herself.

"Is that a hand towel?" I ask.

She opens her mouth to respond when suddenly, she stops. Her brows pinch together as she takes in the scene—all of it.

Directly in front of my chair is an absurdly expensive sex toy sitting on a platform. A little stage arranged for a private performance.

"Is that... is that a saddle?"

"Something like that. With a few modifications." I lift the remote control in my hand and tip my head towards the not-at-all subtle attachment rising out of the center of the seat. It's purple and ribbed and it looks very, very dangerous.

A slow, persistent blush rises up her chest and neck. "What is this?"

"You said you'd pay my price. Payment time is here, *solnishka.*"

She ventures closer. The lamplight glints off the moisture clinging to her skin. When she's close enough to touch, she traces a finger down the length of the dildo and I have to repress a full body shiver.

"I don't see how riding a sex toy is a sacrifice." She looks up at me with lowered lashes. "Isn't this a treat for me?"

I shrug one shoulder. "I guess we'll see. Drop the towel."

Cora hesitates for only a moment. Then, shoulders back and chest forward, she lets the towel fall away into a pile around her feet.

Fucking hell, she's gorgeous.

She's always been gorgeous, but there's something beautiful about the small ways her body has been changing since she started training. The little curves of new muscle. The proud posture—head up, shoulders back. The gleam in her eyes.

I hold out my hand to help her onboard. With delicate fingers, she grips my hand and puts her feet in the stirrups, but she stays hovering out of reach of the purple rubber cock.

"What do I—How do I—"

"Lower yourself onto it."

Cora looks up at me, a quick flash of nerves. Then she maintains that eye contact as she carefully positions herself and lowers down, inch by agonizing inch. With the lube I put on before she emerged, she slides on with no problem, though she bites back a tender gasp.

"This is nowhere near as big as some of the toys you bought me before. Is that the punishment?" She arches an eyebrow.

Instead of responding, I hold up the remote and shift the dial.

It buzzes to life instantaneously. It's on the very lowest setting, so it does little more than vibrate and pulse a quarter of an inch up and down. But it's enough to get the reaction I want. Cora jerks with a yelp of surprise and squeezes the daylights out of the saddle grips. Once the initial shock passes, she screws her face up into as serious of a mask as she can muster.

"So is this—*ah, fuck*—is this it?" She leans back and arches her spine with another soft exhale. "You don't touch me for days and now, I'm going to get off while you sit in that chair and *watch*? I thought you were some big, bad Bratva boss, but now, I'm wondering if you've just been making it all up."

I just smirk. She won't be able to form words here in a little bit, so I'm fine with her trying to taunt me now.

I turn up the intensity on the dial and enjoy the show.

Another quarter-inch of penetration ramps up as the vibration intensifies. A moan she tries hard to hold back slips out of her. I can see the fight in her body. The pink tint to her cheeks. The way she pinches her lower lip between her teeth. The soft whimpers that slip from her, so quiet I can barely hear them.

When I turn up the dial another notch, though, there is no more hiding a goddamn thing.

"Oh, *fuck*." She rocks forward again, all of her weight resting on her hands. Her mouth is open, eyes glassy as she rolls her hips. "Oh, oh… oh my—"

I shift the dial ever-so-slightly higher and Cora falls to pieces. Her stomach tightens as her thighs clamp around the seat. I can hear the relentless chugging pulse and groan of the machine as it splits her apart.

Then she releases. I see her let go all at once. She cracks wide open.

My cock is so hard it's throbbing. I want her. I want her so fucking bad.

"Oh my God." Cora moans and starts to lift herself off of the seat.

Before she can, I stand up and grab her thighs. Her legs tremble beneath my fingers. Gently, I push her back down until she's fully seated on the attachment.

She blinks up at me, her eyes still glassy from her release. "What are you doing?"

"It's not time to get off yet."

"But... But I just came. I really, *really* came."

"Once." I hold up a finger in front of her. Then I trail it down her neck, over her peaked nipples, and down her quivering stomach. "But you've got a long way to go yet, my love. You're going to stay here and come until you can't walk. That is the price you're going to pay."

51

CORA

Overstimulation is hot in theory. In reality, it's a seesaw from torture to ecstasy and back again.

My body is still clenching around the dildo attachment, my first orgasm ebbing away, when Ivan forces me back down onto the machine.

His eyes are black with desire. It's almost scary. *Almost.*

Mostly, though, the way he's looking at me makes me want to throw this machine in the trash and get Ivan inside of me as soon as possible.

"You're going to stay here and come until you can't walk. *That* is the price you're going to pay." His voice is hoarse, thick with need. I can see the large bulge in the front of his pants.

"Wh-what about you?" I stutter.

He steps back and drops down into his chair. "I get to watch. That's *my* prize."

Before I can open my mouth to renegotiate, he flicks his large thumb over the remote and I cry out.

I'm still sensitive from the first orgasm and this machine is a beast. Suddenly, I'm terrified. I was all talk, all bravado coming out of the shower. But this is not the fight I was ready for.

"I won't come again so soon," I tell him. I'm practically begging. "I need more time. I need—"

He turns up the power and my words are lost to a crackling groan I didn't know I was capable of. I toss my head back and rock my hips. My whole body is moving on its own. I'm helpless to do anything but go along for the ride.

"Like that," Ivan coaches. "Grind down on it."

I want to do as he says, but in reality, I have zero control here. The machine takes what it wants. Well, actually *Ivan* takes what he wants, kicking up the power so I have no other option than to come again.

I open my eyes just long enough to see Ivan leaning forward in his chair, his eyes locked on me. I have his full attention even if I can't give him mine. I'm a little busy drooling and coming while my brain turns into pudding.

"I'm coming. I came," I say. Truth be told, I'm not really sure which tense to use. I just came down from one wave, but a slight shift of my hips has the attachment working me right back up.

"Touch yourself," Ivan orders.

I sit up and slide my hands over my chest. My nipples are pinched to hard, sensitive points that I let slide between my fingers.

Ivan watches my hands with intense focus. He isn't missing a moment of this.

"It feels so good," I whisper.

"The machine?"

I shake my head and look at him. "Your eyes on me."

"You like when I watch you."

It isn't a question, but I nod anyway. "I like seeing what it does to you."

My eyes slip lower to the evidence of how much Ivan enjoys watching me, too.

He stands up and eases towards me, lowering the intensity on the toy as he does. Then he sets the remote to the side and slips his waistband down low. His cock springs free.

"You can do a lot more than see it," he growls.

I don't need an invitation. I take him in my hand and wrap my lips around his head.

At this rate, I'm going to be a pile of goo before the night is done. It's nice to take control of something while I still can. To give Ivan a fraction of the pleasure I'm feeling.

I circle my tongue around him and then dive deep.

Ivan lets out a low curse, which is all the encouragement I need. I wrap my hand around the base of him and stroke, meeting my mouth in the middle.

Without really meaning to, it becomes a competition with myself to bring him to his knees. I want to make him lose control the same way I have.

He places his hand at the back of my head, thrusting gently into my mouth. My name falls from his lips like a prayer. "Cora."

I feel him tensing. I know it's close.

Then fireworks flare behind my eyes as the toy kicks into high gear.

I fall back with a cry, using every bit of my strength to stay seated and not fling myself onto the floor.

When I look up, Ivan is holding the remote again. I didn't even see him grab it.

"Cheater!" I pant.

He laughs and stands back, turning the dial higher and higher.

I clench my teeth and think about taxes. About grandmothers in hand-knit cardigans and counting how many tiles there are in the floor. I pull all of my muscles tight and, when that doesn't help, I give up and just flop silly and let this thing have its way with me.

It promptly obliterates me yet again. Three orgasms? Four? I'm losing count. Numbers don't seem to hold much meaning anymore.

"You're still fighting it," Ivan says with a frown. "Why?"

I feel the intensity pick back up and I moan. I can barely find words. My mind is melted. Rational conversation is for the birds.

Somehow, I manage to gasp out, "I want you inside of me. When I come, I want you... I want it to be you."

Ivan reaches out and places a hand on my stomach. Gently, he shifts my body back, angling me so the focus of the vibration shifts. Then he slips his hand lower, circling his finger over my clit.

I open to him, moaning wordlessly because I am so far beyond human speech that it is straight-up laughable.

He kisses my forehead and my cheek. Then his lips find my ear. "It's been me this entire time, Cora. Inside of you or not, your pleasure is mine. I own you."

And just like that, I crash.

The most powerful orgasm yet rocks through me. I cling to Ivan's arm to keep from pitching sideways. It's a miracle I can sit up at all.

As I come down from yet another climax, Ivan finally turns the machine off.

The silence in the room is deafening after the nonstop vibration of the toy. I'm positive he can hear my heart thundering in my chest. The blood coursing through my veins. He grips my waist and lifts me off of the toy as if I weigh nothing.

"Am I done?" I whisper, wrapping my useless legs around him.

"That depends. Can you walk?"

He pretends like he's going to set me on the ground and I cling to him even more tightly. "Definitely not. Don't even try it."

He chuckles and lowers me onto the bed.

As I spread out on the mattress in front of him, his smile fades. The dark desire I saw in his eyes earlier is back and entirely focused on me.

I'm not sure where I find the energy, but I spread my legs and run a hand up my stomach. I trail my finger over my skin and around each of my breasts.

Before I can slide my hand back down between my thighs, Ivan snatches my wrist and pins it to the mattress. Quickly followed by my other hand until I'm wrapped around his waist with my hands bound above my head.

"Mine," Ivan whispers, his gaze tracing every inch of me.

I arch my hips, brushing the tip of him. "Yours."

He slides his cock into me easily. I thought he'd be an inferno of intensity, but he's actually slow and tender. Each stroke is a balm to my frazzled nerves, an antidote to the buzzing in my veins.

He stretches and fills me with just the tip until I'm sure I can't take anymore. Then he slides in deeper.

"This." I strain against his hold on my wrists and arch towards him. "This is—I want this. You."

The words are nonsensical, but they're everything.

The toy took whatever it wanted from me. Ivan is different. He hears me. Moves *with* me, not *in* me, if that even makes any sense.

He fills me in long, steady thrusts until I unfurl in a wash of heat and pleasure and love.

I know he feels it, too, because his breath picks up. He releases my wrists and grips my thighs, holding me fast against him.

"Perfect," he breathes, watching me come undone one last time as he follows close behind. "You're so fucking perfect for me."

It's a long time before Ivan slides out of me and carries me into the bathroom. I just took a shower, but my skin is sticky with sweat and my new muscles hurt in all the best ways. He lathers soap over my body and his own. Then he wraps me in the softest, fluffiest towel and lays me in our bed.

"Tell me what you need, Cora."

"You."

His eyebrows rise. "I don't think you can handle any more of me tonight."

I smile, my skin warming with a blush. "No, not that. Just… lie here with me. Stay here with me."

He nods and starts to lower himself into bed when I hear my phone alarm buzzing. He grabs it from the nightstand and holds it out to me. "What is 'BC'?"

"Oh. That's the alarm for my pill."

"Pill?"

I struggle upright and pull the circular pill container out of the nightstand. "*The* pill. I was off of birth control while I was at Alexander's, but I'm back on my schedule now."

I drop a small blue pill into my hand and am about to toss it back down the hatch when Ivan lays his warm fingers on my wrist. "Do you want to be back on your schedule?"

"What?"

He tips his head towards the pill.

I frown and blink. Apparently, five—God, maybe *six*—consecutive orgasms make me a little slow because it takes me way too long to understand what he's saying.

Finally, I look up at him, eyes wide and stunned. "Do you want me on my schedule?"

"I want what you want," he says. "But I also want a future with you."

It's the most direct conversation we've had about our relationship since… ever. Sleeping in the same room, doing a whole lot of *not*-sleeping in the same room—it all pointed towards this being an actual relationship. But neither of us had said it out loud.

Until now.

I blink back a flood of emotion. "I want a future with you, too, Ivan. I want all of it."

"Kids?"

Leave it to Ivan Pushkin to be direct about life's big questions. "Yeah," I admit. "I want kids. I want to be a better parent to them than either of mine were to me."

"That won't be hard. For either of us," he says.

I chew on my lip. "I hope so."

His thumb brushes over my mouth, untucking my lip from between my teeth. "I know so, Cora. You're going to be an amazing mother whenever the time comes."

My heart races. "I haven't really thought about—I mean, the timing is—There has been a lot going on and I guess I don't know what you are—"

"I'm not going anywhere." He curls his hand around my neck and presses his forehead to mine. "I'm here with you, *solnishka*. No matter what. Whenever you're ready."

I press into his steady touch. He's solid and dependable. I've never felt safer than when I'm in this man's arms.

I know our kids will feel the same way.

"I'm ready."

He pulls back to look in my eyes. "Ready."

"Ready," I repeat. "I'm not going anywhere, either. So why not just… let fate decide?"

His eyes are a bright amber when he smiles. He's so handsome that I want to look away. It's too much.

"Fuck fate," he says, plucking the pills out of my hand and tossing them back into the bedside drawer. "You and I will choose our own future."

52

IVAN

Cora is still asleep when Yasha texts me a warning. *Your dad is on his way to the house.*

Not exactly the start to the morning I was hoping for. My hopes were firmly wedged somewhere between Cora's sleep-warm skin and the top sheet.

I could have the guards lock the front gates and refuse to see him. It's my house; I can do whatever the fuck I want.

The trouble is, laying out my future with Cora felt good. We're going to start a family and build a life together. As much as I'd love to stay here and get a head start on building that family, I also need to make it clear to my father that the window of time when he could barge into my house and call the shots is long over.

I quietly slide into a pair of dark jeans and a t-shirt and head downstairs. I get to the entryway with just enough time to open the front door and intercept Boris on the porch.

Based on the way he stumbles back a half-step, I can tell he wasn't expecting me. Surprise drop-ins have always been his favorite. I'll have to thank Yasha for the heads-up later.

"You put a tracker on me or something?" he grumbles, lowering his shoulder like he's ready to push through me to get inside.

I fucking wish he would.

I wave him in with a stiff arm. "I pay the guards to tell me when visitors arrive."

"I'm no 'visitor.' I'm your father. I was your *pakhan!*"

"You were," I agree. "Not anymore."

His eyes narrow. The wrinkles around his eyes are deeper than I remember, the blue veins across his cheeks more visible. He looks worn. Tired. A lack of power does not suit him.

"I'll be *pakhan* again if shit keeps going the way it's going around here." He paces across the tile floor and then spins back to face me. "I hear your latest little fiancée is gone."

"Francia was not my fiancée."

"Oh, excuse me. Your *whore*," he spits.

"Insult Francia all you want. I couldn't care less. If you want to get a rise out of me, try complimenting her. That might do the trick."

"This isn't some joke, Ivan. You may think this world is your playground, but the way we present to our enemies matters. The way we present to our allies matters even more. Right now, we look weak."

"*My* enemies. *My* allies. None of it belongs to you anymore."

He snorts. "Call it what you like! I wouldn't want my name on this mess, anyway. Your allies include biker gangs now, apparently. Everyone is talking about the stunt you pulled the other night."

Yasha has kept an ear on the ground the last few days. We hoped the attack at Alexander's house would skate by unnoticed, but exploding motorcycles and suburban fires aren't exactly lowkey.

It doesn't matter. I'd do it all over again to have Cora here with me.

"I pulled that *stunt* to make sure people know they can't walk all over my Bratva. To make sure they know Cora is my woman and she will be protected as such."

"I'm sure it was an honest mistake on their part. You have so many women coming and going; who could even keep count?"

"Would it be better if I just had one woman that I beat into submission?" I fire back.

The words land exactly like I hoped they would.

Rage ripples across his face and his lips twist into a hideous sneer. Any calm he possessed when he showed up here is long gone. "Your mother knew what she was getting into with me. I never made her any promises I couldn't keep. I gave her a life and children and she brought her wealth and status with her. She made the Bratva stronger."

"She made the Bratva stronger while you broke her apart, one slap at a time," I growl. "That's a fair trade?"

"She also raised you and your sister to be soft. You think that what you want should be more important than what the Bratva needs. You and Anya are more focused on your useless fucking *feelings* than what is best for the Family. When you think about it," he says, "your mother tore me down, too. Child by child."

At one point in the not-too-distant past, this conversation would have made me livid. Now, I'm just finished with it.

I gaze down at my father. He looks so old these days. "I feel bad for you, Otets. Actually, no—if I wasted even a moment of my time thinking about you, I'd feel bad. Because, despite spending your entire life giving up everything for the sake of your legacy, you've lost it all. Your wife, your children, your Bratva—it's all gone and you have nothing left. There's not even anyone to pity you."

He puffs out his chest. "You are in *temporary* control of the Bratva, son. If you think I can't take it all back at the snap of my fingers, then you're—"

"You talk too much." I sigh and rub my chin. "If you want things to change, stop jabbering and fucking do something about it."

My father stares at me, his jaw set and grinding together in frustration.

"Well?" I press. "Are you going to challenge me? Or are you finally realizing that I could have you relegated to the motherland with nothing but the clothes on your back within the hour? One word from me and you would live the rest of your life shivering in fucking Siberia and looking over your shoulder, wondering if I'll come do to you what you did to my mother."

Silence like nothing he and I have ever experienced before descends on us. He clears his throat and shuffles in place.

"And here I thought family loyalty meant something to you," he mutters at last.

"It means *everything* to me. Which is why I'll kill you or anyone else who threatens mine." I take a step towards him, voice low and razor sharp. "You may call love useless, but my love is what I will live, fight, and die for. It's my reason. If you think you're more powerful than that, I welcome the challenge. But if you're smart, you'll either bend the knee or disappear."

"And if I don't?"

"You will live just long enough to see your family and former allies turn their back on you. Then I'll kill you with my own two hands."

I can count the number of times I've seen my father speechless on one finger. He meets my eyes for a long moment. When he sees that I mean every last word, he turns on his heel and leaves.

I stand there for a while after he's gone. The entryway smells like his old man cologne and, beneath it, the tang of his sweat. I used to work to make my father happy. I was raised my entire life to be the kind of leader he was, the kind of man he was. Now, he's gone, and I'm the one calling the shots.

I have everything my father never knew he wanted.

Soon enough, I'll have it all.

My dad has only been gone for five minutes when another text from Yasha pings. **The Sokolovs want a meeting with you.**

Very funny, I text back. I haven't even been awake an hour and he's already giving me shit.

I'm heading into the kitchen to get coffee when he answers. *I'm serious, Ivan. They want to meet. What should I tell them?*

Fuck. He's not kidding.

I forget the coffee and turn towards my office.

53

IVAN

I tap the screen in front of me and watch a tiny hourglass flip and turn three times before it connects. Then three video windows appear.

"What the fuck is she doing here?" I growl.

Francia is sitting in front of the camera with one leg tucked up into her chair and a steaming cup of coffee in her hands. She looks way too casual and way too alive for my liking.

"I'm not happy about this, either," she snaps.

She's obviously not talking to me. So I shift my attention to the third screen: Mikhail and Konstantin Sokolov.

They look like ghouls lurking in the dark. The two men are so pale the camera doesn't quite know what to do with them. The brightness shifts and flares, trying to find something to focus on until Mikhail flips on a light behind the camera.

The light highlights the bruise I left under his right eye. I can practically see the outline of my knuckles along his eye socket. There's a long scrape on his nose and chin from where he skidded across the concrete.

Serves the motherfucker right.

"Things have changed," Konstantin says. "I thought it would be a good idea to touch base and make sure everyone understands what is at stake."

"Nothing has changed. I'm going to kill you all."

Allowing Cora to make the call to let Francia live was the right choice. I stand by it. But I'll still fantasize about choking the life out of her until the day she is dead.

"And there is why we can't meet in person," Francia sighs. "All this violence is bad for negotiations, Ivan."

"I have no intention of negotiating."

"We don't want to negotiate, either," Konstantin agrees. "The time for that has passed."

Francia frowns at the screen. "Then what is this? The last time we talked, we were going to—"

"The last time we talked, Francia, you brought some information to our attention. Some crucial information."

"And you returned the favor by not prepping me for this meeting," she snaps. "I'm not feeling real 'crucial' over here."

They can bicker all they want, but I'm not interested in sitting in on their group therapy session. "Get to the point, Sokolov. What the fuck does any of this have to do with me?"

"This has everything to do with you." Konstantin nudges Mikhail, who shifts out of frame. "This all started, for me, when my Katerina was promised to you. That deal was never finalized and I lost what would have been a solid investment."

"Then I suggest you keep your kids on a tighter leash next time you want to exploit them for your own personal gain."

Through the video call, it's hard to tell if he's fazed by the anger crackling off of me like toxic radiation. "This wasn't just for my personal gain. A marriage to Katerina helped you, too. Your father wouldn't have agreed to the match otherwise."

"My father and I don't always see eye to eye. He wanted a partnership with you; I want to bury you alive."

Konstantin grimaces and folds his hands in front of him. "Regardless, your father and I made a deal and you agreed to it. You gave me your word that my daughter would be your bride."

"Then your daughter disappeared. I can't marry a missing person poster, so I don't see why you're wasting my time."

"*Did* she disappear, though?" Konstantin muses.

He gestures to someone off-camera and suddenly, a figure barrels into the frame. There's a dark pillowcase over their head.

A creeping feeling of dread rips through my gut. *What the hell is going on?*

"Well," Konstantin presses when I say nothing, "did she? That's what everyone said. You would know best, though. Was she missing, Ivan?"

He is bluffing. It's a trick. He wants me to admit something, but I'm not stupid. There's no way that he—no, I won't even let myself think it.

I sit back in my chair. *Breathe, motherfucker,* I say in my head again and again, trying and failing to make myself relax even as everything inside of me goes rigid.

"I don't have time for this, Konstantin. Say what you dragged us all here to say or I'm leaving."

He just tuts and purses his lips again. "Well, you no longer have anyone to funnel money to via secret offshore accounts. Hopefully, that frees up enough time for you to listen to what I have to say."

The dread doubles.

No. He didn't find her. There's no way.

Except there is always a way. If someone knew where to look… If they had a nudge in the right direction…

No. Even if he followed the money, he doesn't have her. I would have heard by now. I would have known. I would have prevented it.

The cloaked figure next to Konstantin is shivering now.

"I could have all the time in the world and I still wouldn't have time for this, Konstantin. Spit it out or I'm hanging up."

He smiles acidly. Then, with a melodramatic flourish, he rips the pillowcase away from his prisoner. First, it's nothing but a mess of long, tangled hair. Then Konstantin grabs the person by the neck and forces them into the camera.

There is no background visible now. No adjustment for the lens to make.

The entire screen is filled from corner to corner with the bruised, terrified face of Katerina Sokolov.

"Katerina," I breathe. It's so soft that the microphone doesn't pick up the sound, but they can see my face.

She's thin and pale, even considering that she shares the Sokolov family genes. Her hair is a riot of knots fanning out around her head. The mottled color in her face is half-bruising, half bags of sleep deprivation piling up beneath her eyes.

Suddenly, she's jerked back. Mikhail appears, hovering over her shoulder.

"My Katerina has come home at last," Konstantin croons. He drapes an arm around his daughter's shivering shoulders. "I thought you two should be the first to know."

"What the fuck, Konstantin?" Francia shrieks. Somehow, she looks even more shocked than I am.

"Joyous day, isn't it?" Mikhail squats down looking just as smug as his father.

"This wasn't—" Francia shakes her head and leans towards the camera. "I didn't pass information along so you could— You weren't supposed to bring her home. This ruins everything!"

It all clicks together. Truth slapping me in the face with a cold, hard hand. Francia delivered information about where the Sokolovs could find Katerina and, instead of rewarding her, they cut her off.

Now, Katerina will take her place at the altar with me. Whether she wants to or not.

"For *you*," Mikhail corrects, shifting around so his smug face is between his father's and sister's. "It ruins everything for *you*, Francia. But you were always just a means to an end. Now, we have a new means. We have a new end. We don't need you."

"What do you want?" I grit the words out between clenched teeth.

Katerina won't even look at the screen. Her eyes are locked on the table in front of her. Every time her father or brother get close, she flinches.

What did they do to you, Kat?

I gave her money and sent her away. She's supposed to be off in her new life, away from all of this shit.

"I want what was promised to me," Konstantin says sharply. "I want you to marry my daughter."

"That's not what we agreed to!" Francia shrieks.

I ignore her and shake my head. "That's not going to happen."

"Then she dies."

Konstantin shrugs like it doesn't matter either way to him. Like it's not his *own fucking daughter's life* that he's tossing in the middle of the table like a poker chip.

"You wouldn't fucking dare," I snarl.

"I'm a businessman first and foremost, Ivan. If an asset isn't serving me—if it's dragging me down—I cut it loose." He reaches over and tucks a lock of Katerina's blonde hair behind her shoulder. "Not only did Katerina not marry you and bring an influx of cash and connections into our family, she fled. She disappeared and embarrassed us all. So either you make good on your deal and she becomes a benefit to me —or I kill her just to rid myself of the shame."

"It would be easy," Mikhail adds. "Everyone already thinks she is missing. No one knows she's back. We could slit her throat and no one would know a thing."

Francia waves her hand in the air. "I'd know. I'd tell everyone what you did."

"You'd die, too," Konstantin says. "No one would miss you."

Francia tries to come up with a response, but there isn't one. He's right. She handed over all of her cards and now they don't need her. Not when they have Katerina.

"You're a sick fucking monster," I rumble.

"I am a man making things *right!*" he roars, suddenly enraged. The blood in his cheeks turns him a sickly purple. "You think the world is yours. That you can give and take as you fucking please. But you will take what *I* give you. And my son will take back the woman you stole from him."

I stiffen. "Cora does not belong to him."

"She did!" Mikhail seethes. "Cora was promised to me the same way Katerina was promised to you."

Konstantin nods. "As it stands now, you're robbing me of two good matches for my children. I can't take that kind of loss on the chin, Ivan. It has to be dealt with."

I can't give into this shit. Can't show weakness. If the Sokolovs smell blood in the water, they'll come for my throat. The Bratva is already in a tenuous position with the transfer of power from my father to me. There's no telling what might happen if this shit breaks loose.

I lift my chin. "I refuse to be extorted by a *mudak* like you, Konstantin. So there—it's dealt with. Why should I care if you kill your own daughter?"

At that, Katerina finally glances up. It's only for a second, but her eyes flash towards the camera.

And there's *so much fear* in them.

I hope to God she knows I'm bluffing.

"Maybe you don't care," Konstantin ponders. "Then again, if you didn't care, you wouldn't have made sure Katerina stayed hidden for so long. You wouldn't have kept sending her money after she vanished. That's how we tracked her, you know? We followed the money overseas. Breadcrumbs from you to her, laid out so neatly. Nice place you put her up in, but the doorman couldn't keep my soldiers from breaking down her door and dragging her out by her hair."

If I didn't have decades of training, they'd see the emotion on my face. The fury. The guilt.

"You marry Katerina and Cora comes with me," Mikhail chimes in. "All will move forward as it's supposed to."

I clench my fists under my desk. "Cora isn't going anywhere with you. Ever."

"Cora is *mine*," Francia interjects.

She's been quiet the last few minutes, but now, her teeth are bared and her eyes are dangerous slits. She looks every bit as crazy as I know she is.

"I'll kill her for this," she adds. "No one will get Cora except for me."

Mikhail shrugs. "That could be fun to watch, too. After everything that bitch has put me through, it's probably better for my reputation that I don't marry her, anyway."

He's pretending to be cavalier, but I saw the rage in his eyes the other day. Mikhail is pissed. If he gets his hands on Cora, it won't end well.

Konstantin slashes a hand through the air, cutting everyone off. "All that matters is that Ivan has to make a choice. Either he stays with Cora and I kill Katerina. Or he honors the promise he made, leaves Cora, and marries my daughter. What will it be, Ivan?"

It's like choosing which gun I want to be shot with.

Either way, someone dies.

I know what I want to do, but the way Katerina keeps looking up at the camera... I can hear her voice in my head. Same as it was the day she came to me and begged to be set free.

Help me, Ivan. Please.

I'm trying to drum up a plan that can solve all of this when I hear a squeaky floorboard in the hallway outside my office.

"I need time to think," I snap.

Konstantin shakes his head. "You've had enough time. Decide now or—"

"Tomorrow."

"Ivan," he growls. "We aren't playing games here. We will kill her if you don't—"

"I'm not playing a game, either. If you want to do this right, let's do this right. We'll finalize details tomorrow. Over dinner."

The doorknob to my office starts to turn and I don't wait for a response. I slam the laptop closed just as Cora steps inside.

54

CORA

I told myself everything was fine when I woke up alone. *Ivan is busy. He can't lie in bed all day. He's probably working in his office. Don't freak out.*

I got dressed and brushed my teeth. I focused on the soreness between my legs as I walked down the stairs to his office. He asked me to stop taking my birth control last night. We might have a kid together! He's committed.

Don't freak out.

Then I walk into his office and see his face.

He's looking at me, but he isn't seeing me. His eyes are unfocused and his body is tense. His hand is shaking from the force he used to slam his laptop closed.

Never mind. This is the end.

Something is wrong and I should definitely be freaking out.

Instead, I smile. "Good morning."

"You're up early," he says in a low monotone.

"After last night, I wasn't sure I'd ever be rested again." I try for a laugh, but it sounds hollow.

He hums a vague response and nods. But he doesn't look at me.

"You're up early, too. What are you working on?"

"Nothing."

I hesitate for only a second before I walk around his desk and lay my hand over his. "I'm worried about everything you're worried about, Ivan. Whatever is going on in your life, it matters to me. I want to help."

He flips his hand over and closes his fingers over mine. "You can't."

"Then let me be unhelpful *with* you." I spin his chair towards me and settle on his lap. "What's wrong?"

"You've dealt with enough already. Let me handle this."

I run my hand up his forearm to squeeze the swell of his bicep. "I know you can handle it. You've been carrying the weight of the world on your shoulders for most of your life. But I haven't been doing all of this training for nothing. Let me carry some of it. I want to."

His hand spreads across my ribs like he's trying to shield me from whatever's out there. "It was Konstantin."

I know no one is standing behind me, but I still feel the urge to glance over my shoulder. "You were talking to him?"

He nods. "He wanted to have a conversation with me... about Katerina coming home."

"Katerina," I breathe, my mouth moving before my brain can catch up. "She is... She came back?"

No, she's gone. Ivan sent her away. His ex-fiancée is half a world away.

"She didn't *come* back; she was *forced* back." His fingers tighten on my side. "They found her and *dragged* her back. It was Francia's little parting gift."

My stomach twists. Ivan's arm around my waist is the only reason I don't crumple to the floor. "Me. I—It was me. My fault. When they first kidnapped me, I thought Francia was… She made me think she was my friend. I told her you sent Katerina away so she would trust you. It was all a trick. It's my fault that they found her. It's my fault that—"

"Look at me." Ivan pulls me closer and forces my eyes to his. "None of this is your fault, Cora. None of it. The only people responsible are the Sokolovs, Alexander, and Francia. I'll make sure every last one of them pays."

I suppress a shiver and a gallon of guilt I'll definitely have to wade through later. "So why did Konstantin call to tell you Katerina was back? What did he want?"

"The same thing he has wanted for years." His jaw clenches before he can force the words out. "He wants me to marry her."

I know this. Konstantin hasn't exactly been subtle about how much he wants Ivan to marry into his family.

What I don't know is why Ivan looks like this is a death sentence.

His hand fists in the fabric of my shirt. "Konstantin wants me to choose. He wants me to pick between Katerina and…"

"Me," I whisper as understanding finally sinks in. "And if you choose me… she dies."

He leans forward so his forehead is resting on my chest. "I got her out of this city in the first place because I knew they'd kill her. She didn't want any part of this world, of this life. I knew Konstantin would kill her rather than lose her, so I sent her away. Now, he has her back."

I stroke my fingers through the hair at the back of his neck. That bit of silky friction is the only thing keeping me tethered to reality instead of blasting off into a full-on freak-out. "I don't want someone to die because of me."

"This isn't because of you. This is because of *me*. And I'm fucking stuck," he growls. "If I choose you, Katerina dies. And if I choose—"

Before he can even say it, I grab his stubbled face. Our eyes meet for only a second before Ivan tightens his arms around me and our lips crush together.

I shift so I'm straddling him in his desk chair, my feet on the floor. My sleep shirt slips up my thighs and Ivan strokes his calloused fingers over my skin. Just that little touch has me on fire.

I can't give this up. I can't walk away.

"I can't even hear you say you *could* be with someone else," I whisper, breathing heavily. "How am I supposed to let it actually happen?"

He grips my hips and settles me over his waist. "If I choose you, they'll come after you even more than they already have. And if I *don't* choose you, they'll *still* fucking come after you. So much has happened that they want revenge. They can't take it out on me, so they want to take it out on you."

I twine my fingers together behind his neck. "Sounds like it doesn't matter either way then."

"It does matter. It is the only fucking thing that matters, Cora! I could choose Katerina and then get you out of the city the way I wanted to from the start. I'll make you disappear. You'll be—"

"Dead. I'll be dead. If you send me away, I won't survive it. I've been away from you before and I can't do it again." I kiss his jawline, trailing my lips to his ear. "I'm yours, Ivan. Please don't make me leave."

He growls and his hands tighten on my heated skin. My nightshirt is around my waist and I yank it over my head so only the tiny scrap of fabric between my legs separates us.

His eyes trail over my body possessively. "That's why I have to send you away. Because you're mine, Cora. I have to protect you." Ivan kisses my chest and circles his tongue around my nipples until my toes clench.

"You can't. I'd... I'd... I'd marry someone else."

His fingers dig possessively into my hips. "Excuse me?"

"I'd find some man I don't really love," I continue, "and I'd marry him. It would be out of *loneliness*. Because I needed a distraction. Being without you and knowing you were with Katerina would drive me insane and I'd marry someone else. It would be like none of this ever happened."

With every word, Ivan's hold on me grows tighter. He's crushing me against his chest so I can barely breathe.

"Is that what you want?" I pant.

He doesn't answer. Instead, he lays claim to every bit of my skin he can touch and taste. I lift myself up and reach between us. His breath is hot on my neck and my collarbone as I unbutton his pants.

We're barreling towards something. A cliff, a waterfall, a breaking point. We're going to go tumbling over—that much is guaranteed. The question is whether I fall alone or we fall together.

I wrap my hand around his dick and he catches his breath.

"Do you want to send me away?"

His eyes darken. "I want to keep you safe."

"So you're willing to give me up to someone else?" I slide my hand up and back down. "You're going to let me marry another man? You're going to let me touch another man like this?"

Before the words are even out of my mouth, Ivan stands up and sits me on the edge of his desk. He wraps my legs around his hips, shoves my panties aside, and fills me in one thrust.

I can't give this up. I won't.

When he's seated deep inside of me, Ivan grips my chin and looks into my eyes. "You can't be with anyone else. Ever. You're *mine.*"

"I'm yours." Tears burn in my eyes. I blink them back. "I'm yours and you're mine. There isn't anyone else. There can't be."

Ivan kisses me until I'm lying flat on the desk in front of him. Splayed and vulnerable, he drives into me again and again. He circles my clit with his thumb and palms my breasts. The sex is fast and greedy and desperate. He touches me like he owns me, heart and soul.

Because he does.

I fall first, clenching and crying out until Ivan follows a minute later. When we're finished, he scoops me up off the desk and holds me in his lap again. "We're back where we started," Ivan says, kissing my bare shoulder.

"Yeah. Except I think I might know what we need to do."

He arches a brow. "You were thinking of a plan through all of that?"

"I'm a great multitasker." I grin. "I just need to know one thing. Do you still have my engagement ring?"

55

IVAN

I meet Katerina at the top of the driveway in front of the mansion. Just like I told Konstantin I would.

She's wearing a satin gown that must have fit her at some point, but it hangs off of her frail shoulders now. Her arms are thin and her cheeks are sunken in. It is definitely Katerina walking towards me, but all I see is Cora.

And not Cora as she was just a few hours ago when I fucked her on my desk like I'd never get to do it again. The Cora I see superimposed over Katerina is Cora as she was in that photo of her from the paper, her bony arm wrapped around Mikhail's. A wilted Cora. A dying Cora. It was like touching him drained the life from her.

I see that same mute horror in Katerina's face.

One day, I'm going to kill them all for what they've done to these innocent women.

"How did you convince him to let you talk to me alone?" Katerina asks when I'm close enough to hear her quiet murmur.

I ignore her question. "If you have a wire, tell me now."

"I don't have a—"

"Give me a signal," I demand, stopping a few feet away. "One he can't see."

She glances over her shoulder, looking back at the car idling at the base of the drive. I know Konstantin is inside watching our every move. It was a condition of this meeting. The other condition was that we wouldn't be recorded.

She holds out her arms and lets them fall to her sides. "I don't have a wire. If I did, I'd wink or something. But I don't. It's just the two of us."

Just the two of us and the dozen-plus Sokolov soldiers hiding in my bushes.

"How did you convince him to let you talk to me alone?" Katerina asks again.

"I didn't need to *convince* him," I growl. "No matter what your father tells you, I have the upper hand. He needs this deal more than I do. I can do whatever I want."

She shakes her head sadly. "If that was true, neither of us would be here right now. I'd be an ocean away from these people."

Tears well in her puffy eyes. She's done a lot of crying the last few days; that much is obvious. I reach out and squeeze her shoulder. I never wanted to marry Katerina, but I always liked her. She was a hell of a lot better than anyone else in her disgusting family.

"I'm going to get you out of here and back home. You just have to trust me."

"I do trust you, Ivan. Or at least, I trust that you're better than the men in my family. You tried to do the right thing by me even when you didn't have to. But here we are again and I'm not sure even *you* can get me out this time."

"My plan doesn't depend on you being sure. I just need you to stay out of my way."

"What plan? What are you going to do?"

"There is more than your life on the line here," I say softly. I trust she doesn't have a wire on, but I'm not going to take any unnecessary risks. Not with this. "Follow my lead and I'll get you where you want to go. Do you understand?"

Katerina stares at me for a few seconds, pondering. Then she leans in. "I'm not marrying you or anyone else. I never wanted that. I want to be on my own. Independent. Whatever your plan is, take that into account."

I nod. "Already done."

"And when I leave, I'm taking my sisters with me," she adds in quickly.

Harder to manage, but not impossible. Given the way Konstantin keeps trying to sell them off to the highest bidder, it's probably a good idea. "I'll do my best."

She obviously doesn't love that answer, but it's all she's going to get. "Thank you, Ivan."

I press a hand to her lower back and walk her towards the front door—the sign to Konstantin that our conversation is over. "Don't thank me yet. Save it for later. When you're free."

Katerina and I are standing in the entryway when Konstantin and Mikhail walk through the front door.

Mikhail's face twists into a smirk. "Well, aren't you two a pretty picture? Together at long last."

On second thought, fuck the plan. I'll skip dinner and kill him now.

"Enough." Konstantin elbows past his son and looks from Katerina to me. "Have you made your decision, Ivan?"

"I told you I'd have an answer for you at dinner, didn't I?" I snap.

His brows raise, waiting. "And?"

Before I can tell Konstantin that I'll gut him before I let him come into my house and demand answers from me, the doorbell rings. Mikhail is closest to the door, so he spins around and throws it open... to reveal Francia.

Mikhail's eyebrows hit his hairline. I just sigh. I've stopped being surprised when she pops up. She's like a fucking cockroach.

"Oh. Mikhail..." Her eyes narrow before she struts past him into my house. "Am I late?"

"You can't be late if you weren't invited."

Konstantin steps in front of Francia to box her out. "You aren't part of this deal."

"I was until you cut me out. You broke your word, but I won't break mine. I said I'd be here until the end, so here I am." She picks lint off the shoulder of her black dress like everything is la-di-fucking-da, but her hand is shaking. "What happens here tonight concerns me. I'm staying."

"Get out, Francia," Mikhail barks. "You lost. It's over."

Francia is ready to face off with the Sokolovs in my foyer, but it's a waste of time. I know how this ends for all of them. As far as I'm concerned, the more the merrier.

Besides, none of them should be here. If the Sokolov Bratva was just a touch more inexperienced, I'd kill them all where they stand and be done with it. But they are a genuine threat, even with their meager resources. I won't throw my men into a war if I can avoid it.

"Everyone is staying," I announce. "Go to the dining room. Grab some champagne."

"What are we toasting to?" Francia asks.

I slide my arm around Katerina's shoulders and smile. "A new beginning."

Katerina goes rigid, but her family and Francia are all too thrilled to notice. Konstantin thinks I'm marrying his daughter. Mikhail and Francia are both looking around like they expect Cora to be wheeled out to them on a silver platter.

You better celebrate now, I think. *It won't last long.*

Katerina and I lead the way to the dining room, where flutes of champagne are waiting on a tray. I take one and gesture for everyone else to follow suit.

It's a hell of a scene. A room full of enemies sitting in a circle and sipping champagne. Completely unaware of the noose tightening around their necks.

I stand at the head of the table, glass in hand. "I know we've all had our troubles. There's a lot of history here. Betrayals and partnerships alike. Secrets and lies aplenty. I brought you all here because I want to start this next phase of my life on the right foot."

Konstantin raises his glass in cautious agreement. "I like the sound of that."

"Good. I'm glad you agree with me." I step back from the table just as the doors behind me open.

I don't need to see Yasha and Lev to know they're there. They're standing on either side of the kitchen doors, waiting. Konstantin's eyes dart between them and me, trying to get a read on the situation.

"Not that it matters either way," I continue. "I don't give a fuck about your feelings or whether you agree with me. It would just make things simpler if you did."

Mikhail points to the door behind me. "What are they doing here? You said security would stay outside."

"*Your* security would stay outside. This is my house. If you thought I'd be unarmed while you walk in here making demands, you're even dumber than you look."

Konstantin lurches to his feet. "This is against the spirit of the arrangement."

"And kidnapping the woman I love was *in* the spirit?" I snap.

Konstantin frowns. I can practically see the gears churning in his head. Am I talking about Katerina? Or someone else?

So many people kidnapped. Who could possibly keep track?

"If you can't honor the conditions you required, then we'll leave," he spits. "You can't marry my daughter and treat her family like this."

Katerina is doing exactly what I asked her to do. She's sitting quietly and staying out of my way. If only her father and brother were as accommodating.

They both step toward the door as if there is a chance in hell I'd let them walk away.

"Sit the fuck down, both of you. You're not going anywhere. I haven't even made my announcement yet."

"With the way things are going, I don't think I want to hear it," Konstantin seethes. "I've waited a long time for this, Ivan. For you to follow through with your commitment. If we're going to be family, then—"

"*That* is where I'll stop you, Konstantin. You're wasting your breath. We will never be family. I won't marry Katerina."

Konstantin exhales sharply. "You've made your decision then."

"There was no decision to make. I can't marry her."

"Can't?" he asks. "Or won't?"

Konstantin is looking at me like he wants to impale me on the wall. Mikhail is searching for an exit. The rat wants to flee, but there is nowhere to go. Not until I release them. *If* I release them.

"Can't," I repeat. "I can't marry Katerina—or anyone else, for that matter. It's too late."

I extend my arm out, champagne flute held lightly in my hand. I only have to wait a few seconds before delicate fingers slip around the stem.

I revel in their stunned silence.

Cora does, too. I can see her out of the corner of my eye, head held high, shoulders back. She is sheer grace as she presses the glass to her lips and drinks. Just like I told her to.

She tips the champagne back slowly, letting the light reflect off the glistening diamond on her ring finger.

I take her other hand in mine and face my guests. "I'm already married."

56

IVAN

The announcement is still settling over the silent room when a chair scrapes away from the table.

It happens quickly. Francia is staring open-mouthed one second; the next, she throws her chair back and sprints at Cora.

Arms flailing, mouth open in a scream, Francia looks like she's possessed. Maybe she is. It would explain a lot.

I don't think—I just react. I shift over to block Cora and Francia slams into my chest instead. But it's like trying to hold a rabid raccoon. She's so focused on her goal that she barely notices me. She just reaches over my shoulders and keeps clawing, screeching, scratching.

I shove her back, but before I can take a swing, Yasha beats me to it.

My second-in-command grabs Francia by the collar of her little black dress and flings her to the ground. She immediately tries to crawl back up, but he plants a foot in her chest and kicks down *hard*. Her head bounces off the tile with a nasty crack and she goes limp.

"Damn it," Yasha mutters to himself. "I hoped that would last a little longer."

More chairs scrape as Mikhail and Konstantin move closer for a better look.

"She's breathing," I tell them. "Not for much longer if she wakes up and runs for Cora again. But for right now, she's breathing."

"I don't care about her," Konstantin hisses, glaring at Francia's crumpled body. Then his rage shifts to Cora. "This is about *her*. We had a deal, Ivan."

"So did we," Mikhail grits out. His beady eyes are fixed on Cora. "You belong to *me*."

An animal sound I can't control shudders through my chest. It's the only response I can manage that doesn't involve cracking their heads open.

Cora squeezes my hand. "I never belonged to you, Mikhail. I never will."

Konstantin snorts. "This won't stand. Katerina has been ruined by her connection to you. No one will marry her now. Not with this trail of drama behind her. She's useless to me."

Katerina doesn't flinch. If anything, she's probably thrilled. She never wanted to be used by Konstantin.

Lev walks calmly past me and offers a hand to Katerina. When we were up late last night choreographing how this dinner would go, I suggested another man for the job. But Anya wouldn't hear of it.

"Lev is a gentle giant who saved another Bratva daughter from a terrible fate." She squeezed her husband's hand, tears shining in her eyes. "It's a nice, full-circle moment for him to escort Katerina away from her father, too."

Katerina must agree, because she takes Lev's hand without a second thought and starts to follow him out.

"Where are you going?" Konstantin calls after her.

He starts to reach for her, but I block his path. "You said she's ruined. She's useless to you, remember? It doesn't matter where she's going."

"That is my daughter!" he cries. "I deserve to know where she is going and who she will be with. I deserve—"

"You deserve to be executed," I tell him flatly. "You deserve to be made an example of. I suggest you shut your fucking mouth and be grateful I'm offering you a way out."

His face is red and the vein in his neck is throbbing. "I don't need you to *offer* me anything. I'm not surrendering."

"Then you'll be obliterated." I shrug as if I don't care either way. Truthfully, I don't. "Cora was always going to be my choice. There is not a single reality in this universe or any other where I end up with anyone else. You can fight me on that and die or you can bow out gracefully and still get a reward."

Konstantin's eyes narrow, slicing from me to Cora and back again. "A reward?"

"It's a mercy, really," I correct. "Cora is my wife, Katerina goes free, and I offer you a business merger that gives the Sokolov family more power than any marriage ever would have."

Before Konstantin can respond, Mikhail barks out a laugh. "Why the fuck would we trust you after everything you've done? You've gone back on your word too many times to count. You've broken up two different marriages to stand here with Cordelia and you want me to—"

"Her name," I bellow, the rage in my chest flaring bright, *"is Cora Pushkin."*

Mikhail falters a step. I claim the lost ground, striding closer until I'm towering over him. "And my decision is final. Nothing you say can or will change my mind, except in how I choose to deal with you. Either you graciously accept this handout or you keep talking and I'll slaughter you here and now."

"We have soldiers outside." Mikhail raises his chin, but doesn't move any closer. "We are ready to fight."

"So am I. I'll kill you and command my men to slaughter every last one of your soldiers before your lifeless, useless body even hits the floor." I turn my focus to Konstantin. As much as I want to end Mikhail, I have other affairs to handle first. "If you aren't my allies, then you're a threat. And I won't let any threat to my wife survive."

My wife. The title singes the tip of my tongue. It's a pleasant burn. I plan to repeat it over and over and over again until I'm used to it. Preferably while I'm buried deep inside of her.

"What are the details of this merger?" Konstantin croaks.

Mikhail whips around, eyes blazing. "You can't be serious, Father! We cannot accept his terms. He's throwing shit at us and waiting for us to lick it up. We're not pathetic."

I smirk. "I beg to differ."

"Shut up, Mikhail." Konstantin's voice echoes off the high ceilings. He looks back at me, and one look into those beady, calculating eyes is all I need to see to know that he gets the picture here. That he takes this deal sight unseen or he gets crushed beneath my boot. "I accept your terms."

"No!" Mikhail is shaking. "We don't accept. *I* don't accept. What about me? That bitch was promised *to me!*"

He jabs an accusing finger in Cora's direction. I don't hesitate —I grip it and twist, not stopping even when I hear the crack of splintering bone.

Mikhail drops to his knees, his screams echoing off the tile.

I lean down and whisper in his ear. "Talk about my wife like that again and next time, that will be your neck cracking."

Konstantin grabs his quivering son by the arm and hauls him up. "There won't be a next time. We're leaving."

I could say a lot of bad things about Konstantin Sokolov, but at least he knows when he's in over his head.

The old man is trying to wrestle his son towards the door when he loses his hold on him. Mikhail has been an obedient little dog for years. Now, he's off the leash.

"We aren't leaving anywhere." His top lip is curled and his teeth are bared. "I'm not walking away with my tail between my legs. Not after everything I've been through to get *her*. Cordelia fucking St. Clair, you are *nothing.*"

"Mikhail!" Konstantin grabs for his shirt, but Mikhail pulls away.

"You think you are better than everyone else. But you are nothing but a powerless little whore who needs to be put in her place. You are—"

I stopped hearing Mikhail the moment he started speaking. It doesn't matter what he's saying. He's insulting my wife and that's more than enough reason for me to knock his head off his shoulders.

His face is the only thing I can see in my narrowed field of vision. My fist is hurtling toward it—when, suddenly, he's gone.

I blink and look down. Mikhail is sprawled on the floor a few feet from Francia, his arms and legs limp.

It takes me a second to realize what happened. Glancing to my side, I see Yasha grinning and shaking out his knuckles. "Two for two," he brags.

"You beat me to him," I realize, blinking out of my daze.

He's cheesing from ear-to-ear. "Sorry, brother. Hate to steal your thunder. But you already got to hit the son of a bitch once. I've been dying for my turn."

"I wasn't going to hit him; I was going to kill him."

"Don't." Konstantin stands over his son, his eyes pleading. "Please. Let me deal with my boy. I'll get him out of here. Don't kill him."

Suddenly, Cora's hand loops through my arm. She doesn't say a word, but her touch is enough.

She's okay.

We survived.

We're here.

"Don't let him near me," I growl. "Keep your son away from me and my family. This is the last time I show you any mercy. Do you understand what I'm telling you?"

Konstantin lowers his head in a grim nod. Then he drags his son's unconscious body out of my dining room.

57

CORA

This is over. We're done.

I don't let myself believe it until Konstantin has dragged Mikhail through the front door and it slams closed behind them.

Is this war finally over? Am I free?

Ivan is still staring at the door like he is waiting for the Sokolovs to run back in, armed to the teeth. It's not such a crazy idea. They aren't easy to put down.

But the house stays quiet.

I reach out and squeeze Ivan's hand. I run my thumb over his thick knuckles. I soak up the warmth of his touch.

We made it.

We're okay.

"Well, that went about as well as I thought it would," I observe wryly.

Ivan turns back and starts to smile. Then he sees me—and his face falls.

I almost duck down. With a look like that on his face, someone must be behind me. Maybe Francia regained consciousness and is coming in for round two.

Then Ivan grips my chin and tilts my face up to the light. "You're hurt."

"I'm—What?"

"I didn't see it before. You didn't say anything. You're bleeding."

"I am?" I try to reach for my face, but he pushes my hand away.

"I need bandages," he barks towards the kitchen. "*Now!*"

I'm not in pain. I don't see blood dripping anywhere. Am I in shock? Maybe it all happened so fast that I didn't feel it. I've heard about that happening with stab wounds. People don't realize until minutes later that they were stabbed at all.

But Francia didn't have a knife in her hand, did she? If she stabbed me in the head, I like to think I'd know.

"Is it just a cut? Do you think I need stitches?"

Ivan pushes me back to my chair. My knees buckle when they hit the seat, and I drop down. "I'll take care of you. You'll be okay."

A maid rushes out of the kitchen with a first aid kit. Ivan snatches it out of her hands and tears through the contents like I'm moments away from bleeding out.

"Hold this in place." He presses a piece of gauze to my forehead and then searches for a bandage. Ivan shakes his head. His jaw is set and his eyes are a stormy gold. "You're hurt. Francia *hurt* you."

"She barely even touched me. You stopped her."

"Not soon enough."

He pulls my hand holding the gauze away. I reach up and feel the tiniest cut on my forehead. "*This*? This is what you're worried about? Look at the gauze, Ivan. There isn't even any blood. I'm fine!"

"Stop saying that," he growls. His lips brush against mine and I slide towards him. My thighs open, straddling him where he kneels on the floor in front of me.

"I'm fine," I repeat softly.

Ivan doesn't seem convinced. "No one was supposed to get close to you. The only reason I went through with your plan is because you were supposed to be safe."

"And I *am* safe, Ivan. Look at me. I'm safe right now. With you." I grab his hands and press them to either side of my face. He strokes my cheeks with his thumbs and then lets his hands slide lower. He traces every inch of me, taking stock.

"I'm okay," I say again. "I'm perfect."

He can't stop running his hands over me. Even when Yasha and Lev appear, Ivan doesn't stop touching me.

"What's the word on this one?" Yasha pokes at Francia's limp leg with the toe of his shoe. She is still face-down on the tile. "Drag her to the dungeon?"

"How about the bottom of the ocean?" Lev suggests.

"That's too easy of an ending for her." Ivan scowls, glancing at her only briefly before he turns back to me. His hands slip over my hips and around my waist. His fingers massage into my spine as he gives them an answer. "Francia told me she wanted to be a Bratva wife, so let's make her one. Send her back to Moscow. Let the old-school Bratva members watch over her."

Yasha winces in something very close to sympathy. "We might as well put her in a hole and let her rot. It'll have the same outcome. They'll eat her alive."

Ivan reaches up and brushes his finger over the supposed "cut" on my forehead. "Good."

Yasha and Lev haul Francia out of the room by her hands and feet. As she dangles between them, I try to feel *something*. Anger or vindication. Maybe even sympathy.

But there's nothing.

We spent countless hours together in the kitchen at Quintaño's. We used to open together on Saturday mornings and we'd play ABBA on the jukebox while we wiped down tables. On slow nights, we'd split our tips.

She was my friend. And now...

"I thought that would feel more...momentous."

Ivan is stretched up on his knees now, his face level with mine. "What?"

"Francia being hauled away. Dragged out of my life forever. I thought I would care more."

"You don't?"

"I'm glad she's gone. I just thought it would matter more, but..." I shake my head and run my hands over his shoulders. "The only thing I care about is this. You."

Ivan hums as he squeezes my ribs, his thumbs dragging over the lace detailing of my dress. "It's hard to care about anything when you're wearing this. It was distracting."

"You didn't look at me once when I walked out," I laugh.

"I didn't need to." He nuzzles my neck, his stubble scraping over my pulse point. "I could feel you. That was enough."

Goosebumps erupt across my skin and I shiver. "I think it might be a wedding dress. It seemed appropriate given... well, everything."

Ivan kisses my collarbone and my neck. He trails his hot mouth over my skin, setting me on fire piece by piece. "You know what else seems appropriate?"

I'm breathless, eyes closed and heart thundering. "What?"

His lips find the shell of my ear. "Claiming you on this table. Celebrating that you are mine and now, everyone fucking knows it."

I've lost the power of speech. Instead, I circle my arms around Ivan's neck and nod.

He kisses me with bruising force as he scoops me up and sits me on the edge of the table. Untouched champagne flutes topple over and spill. I feel the liquid soaking into my dress, but I don't care. I'm going to beg Ivan to rip me out of it in a second anyway.

Turns out, I don't even have to ask. Ivan grabs the neckline of my gown and shreds the bodice from my collarbone to my waist with one solid tug.

It's so hot I can't even bring myself to care that the dress probably cost thousands of dollars.

"You're perfect," he growls. His eyes are dark with desire as he shoves the shredded fabric to the side and swirls his tongue over my breast.

I arch against his mouth. "I'm yours."

Ivan finishes ripping his way through the skirt while I fumble with the button on his pants. The lace is soaking up some of the champagne. The rest of it forms a sparkling waterfall that flows off the edge of the table and splatters to the tile floor. But it doesn't matter.

Nothing matters but this.

When I finally get Ivan's pants out of the way, I take him in my hand and press him to my opening. He doesn't ask if I'm sure or tease me half-mad.

With one thrust, he gives me exactly what I want. He gives me everything.

I cling to him with my arms and sticky legs. His hands wrap around my butt, pulling me even tighter against him. Grinding into me until there's no more space. Until I have nothing left to give.

"Oh, Ivan. I want you this deep all the time," I gasp as he pulls out and thrusts back in. "Right there. Please."

He drags out of me and pulses back in until I'm practically crawling up his body to get closer. Until I am delirious with need and begging for him to let me come.

Ivan slips his hand between our bodies and circles his thumb exactly where I need him.

Then he holds me together as I shatter.

An embarrassing number of people are probably listening in from the kitchen. Yasha will give both of us shit about this later. He'll definitely tell Jorden all about it and I won't have a leg up in getting to tease her about all of her secret trysts with Yasha. But this moment is worth all of it. Nothing matters more than this man and the way being pressed against him feels.

I wrap my body around him, holding him tightly. "Never let me go. Stay here."

"I'm not going anywhere." He kisses my temple and lifts me off of the table as he fucks me relentlessly. "I'm staying right here."

I don't question how Ivan is able to carry me from the dining room to our bedroom without ever once slipping out of me; I just enjoy it. I kiss his neck and roll myself down his length until he has to stop on the stairs, a steadying hand on the wall.

"Keep that up and you'll kill us both," he warns with a laugh.

"I can't decide if that would be the best or most embarrassing way to die."

"Both," he decides. "But I'm serious: quit it. I have plans before I die."

Hopefully, plans that involve finishing what we've started here. And then starting it up again the moment we're done.

To make sure we both live to see that moment, I pivot to kissing his neck and sucking on his earlobe while he walks us up the stairs, down the hall, and into our bathroom.

Ivan sets me on my feet in our shower and pushes the shredded remains of my dress from my shoulders. Then, before I can get him out of his clothes, he spins me around and presses my palms flat against the tile. His fingers thread through mine slowly. He kisses my shoulder blade and my spine. He moves lower, licking and sucking his way across my skin.

"You taste sweet," he groans.

I can feel him hard and throbbing against my thigh, I squeeze my legs together and stroke him. "I think that's the champagne."

"No," he groans, thrusting into my thighs. "It's you, Cora. It's all you."

He shifts his hips and, without letting go of my hands, he fills me again.

"Fuck," he whispers against my neck. "How do you feel this good? How is it like this?"

I shake my head. I truly have no idea. Every time Ivan touches me, I'm amazed at how well we fit together.

There's been so many lies and charades from the beginning of our story. But this... *this* is real. This heat building between us means more than a ring and a sheet of paper ever could. It's a commitment. Because nothing will ever be better than this. After being with him, how could I ever settle for anything less?

It *has* to be him.

Now. Later. Forever.

His hands clench around mine and I know he's close. I arch back, meeting his thrusts so the sound of us coming together echoes off the tiles. The new angle leaves heat pooling low in my belly.

"Right there, Ivan," I beg. "Don't stop. Right there."

He growls in my ear. "Come for me, Cora. Come for me again."

And I do.

Ivan's hands twined through mine are the only reason I don't melt to the shower floor. He holds me firmly, thrusting through my orgasm until he finds his own. When we're finished, the evidence of it dripping down my legs, Ivan finally takes off the rest of his clothes and starts the shower.

Together, a tangle of lips and limbs, we let the hot water wash away the day.

58

IVAN

"I thought the end of all this war doom and gloom would mean you had more time for me." Yasha swaggers into my office and plops down across from me. He's trying to frown, but he can't quite hide his amusement with himself. "I'm a mess without you, *compadre.*"

I roll my eyes. "Cora hasn't seen Jorden around much lately, either. You have any idea where she's been?"

The most obvious grin spreads across his face as he shakes his head. "Nope. Haven't seen her."

Yasha isn't fooling anyone. Cora and I know exactly what kind of debauchery our best friends are up to. But bring it up and it's *deny, deny, deny.*

"I guess it's hard to see clearly when the lights are off and you're tangled up in sheets together."

Yasha faux-gasps. "The fact that you think I'd have sex in the pitch dark like a teenager is… it's insulting. *If* I ever had the pleasure of a night with Jorden—which I'm neither admitting nor denying—then I would do it in full daylight with the windows open and enjoy every delightful second."

He'd be describing those details to me at painful length if Jorden wasn't making him keep their relationship on the down-low. Left to his own devices, Yasha isn't discreet enough to keep anything secret, let alone when he's having copious amounts of sex.

My second-in-command blinks away his thoughts and looks at me, a dopey smile still plastered on his face. "Anyhow—*if* I could do that, then I would. But since I can't, I'm here in your office, wondering why *you* are here in your office. I thought everything was settled."

"Everything is settled. Mostly." I power down my computer and lean back in my chair. "But there's always more to do."

"Later," Yasha says sternly. "Right now, we celebrate. The Sokolovs agreed to the terms you sent them. We split profits from gunrunning, one of our least profitable sectors, and otherwise, they are going to fuck off. Mikhail wasn't wrong: we threw shit on the ground and they licked it right up. That is a major win deserving of a few weeks away from your computer, at least."

"It's not finished yet. There still hasn't been any word from Alexander."

Cora hasn't said it, but I know she's worried about how her stepfather is going to react to the fallout of everything. So far: silence. He could be gathering his forces for retaliation as far as we know. I wouldn't put it past him. The man is desperate. Cora was his only real asset, so without her, he'll have to succeed based on his own merits.

Which means he doesn't stand a fucking chance.

Yasha waves away my concern. "Alexander is a nobody. Konstantin told me he'd relay the details of the arrangement to him, including your 'marriage' to Cora. Beyond that, he doesn't matter. His only power was in working with the Sokolovs, but now, the Sokolovs work for us."

I waver. "They don't work for us; they work *near* us. We aren't partners and we have to be ready for them to find a better deal somewhere else and betray us."

"I am ready for that. I'm looking forward to it, actually." Yasha grins. "I want another crack at those assholes. Let's give them what they deserve."

"If it wasn't for Cora, they'd already be dead. But I can't risk having the Sokolov army out for blood. They'd come for Cora and she has been through enough. I don't want a war."

Yasha lets out a long, low whistle. "She really has changed you." At the sharp look I toss him, he holds up his hands. "In a good way, man. You've always been a strong leader. Better than your dad ever was. For a while there, I was worried you'd burn yourself out fighting every slight against the Bratva. Now, you know what's really important. The men trust your leadership."

It's rare to catch Yasha in a serious conversation, but he isn't smirking or tossing out a secret wink between sentences. He means it.

That means something to me.

"I think we're both made better by the women in our lives," I say.

Yasha starts to nod and then catches himself. "I don't know what you're talking about. I'm free as a bird. No woman in sight."

"Right. Then I guess I won't remind you to tell your woman that you and I have plans tonight. It's our first rendezvous with the Sokolov lieutenants. A gun shipment is coming into the harbor."

"Oh. Shit," he groans, digging his phone out of his pocket. "I forgot. Luckily, I have no one to text and cancel plans with. I definitely won't tell her to come hang out with Cora tonight so she's here when I get back to the mansion."

This is the Yasha I'm used to. Even him keeping things on the down-low is him sharing all of his thoughts, feelings, and plans.

"Good thing, because Cora is busy tonight and can't hang out with anyone."

Yasha's face falls. "Really? You're letting her out of the house?"

"Fuck no. Not yet. But she and Marcus are meeting up here for dinner."

"Wow. That's a big deal for her." He finishes his text to "Definitely Not Jorden" and pockets his phone. "Is she nervous?"

"She said she wasn't, which is a lie. But she'll be fine."

Yasha stands up and saunters towards the door. "I'm sure she will. She has a lot of practice with this."

"Practice spending time with her dad for the first time in ten years?"

"No. Practice dealing with emotionally-closed off men who are desperate to get to know her."

Yasha barely darts out of the door frame fast enough to dodge the pen I chuck at his face.

The warehouse on the harbor has been in Pushkin control for decades Once upon a time, it was used as a front for illegal poker games and clandestine drug dens.

Now, it's a storage facility on the harbor filled with construction equipment—and, for just a few hours once a month, weapons.

A unit of my men scour the property for any sign of betrayal. They scan the building and the surrounding warehouses searching for the slightest hint that Konstantin Sokolov is planning to push back against our arrangement.

Finding nothing, Yasha and I go in.

"I feel like a recruit again," he says, checking the gun at his hip. "I haven't been out on a run like this in years."

"We're just here tonight to make sure things go smoothly. Once I trust the Sokolovs are going to uphold their end of the deal, we'll pull back and let the rank-and-file handle the transfer."

Yasha snorts. "You say that like you'll ever actually let yourself trust those slimy fucks. I'm going to be handling the weapons trafficking until I'm dead. Or until the Sokolovs are dead. Whichever comes first."

"Let's hope that doesn't happen tonight," I mutter out of the side of my mouth. "I'd hate to get blood on this shirt."

We step through the door to see Konstantin's men waiting in front of pallets of boxed firearms. I approve everything, then they get to work. Half an hour later, the Sokolov soldiers are done repackaging the weapons shipments and have started taking their cut of the supplies.

"Look at this," Yasha proclaims, his voice echoing off the metal walls. "Who would've thought we'd all be here like one big, happy family?"

There are a few too many suspicious glances being tossed around for me to feel like we're a family. But this whole arrangement has gone a lot more smoothly than I thought it would.

No weapons have been fired and no one is dead. If the Sokolov gunrunners are pissed about the deal I made with their boss, they don't show it. They toil in grim silence.

"Cats and dogs," Yasha continues. "Oil and water. Yet here we are, working together. I'm inspired. Someone put me on the cabinet of foreign affairs. I think I'm ready to create world peace."

Everyone has been letting Yasha ramble for a few minutes uninterrupted, but suddenly, a voice cuts through the nonsense. "You really love to hear yourself talk, don't you?"

My gun is in my hand before I even turn around. Because I don't need to see who it is. I already know.

I turn to face Mikhail Sokolov.

"I told your father to keep you far, far away from me."

He's standing in the doorway, flanked on either side by guards who don't stand a chance in hell of saving him from me.

"My father is my don, but he isn't my keeper. I can go where I like." Mikhail walks slowly into the warehouse, arms extended like he's a fucking circus ringmaster.

Yasha groans. "Well, so much for peace on earth."

The Sokolov men have finished loading the weapons, but they're all standing around watching their future leader question me. It's not the end to the evening I imagined.

But I'd be lying if I said I wasn't excited about where this might end.

Mikhail running his mouth and showing up where he doesn't belong... If that isn't a reason to put this *mudak* down, then what is?

"If you or your boss were going to kill me, you would have done it already. You know what I think it is?" He smiles. "I think Ivan's little wifey asked for mercy for me." Mikhail isn't talking to Yasha or to me anymore. He's giving a speech to the gathered men. He's trying to rewrite history. "Cordelia plays the sweet and innocent part well, but no one bags men like the two of us without some ambition."

"The fact that you think you and Ivan are in the same category is hilarious," Yasha interjects. "The funniest thing you've said all night. But I suspect whatever you're about to say is going to be even more asinine. Please. Keep going."

Yes. Please. Every word out of his mouth is yet another reason to pull the trigger.

Mikhail clears his throat. "Let me be blunt then: your wife is a gold-digging bitch who jumps to gobble up whatever opportunity lines her pockets the best. When you drive your Bratva into the ground, she'll come crawling back to me." He lifts his chin, looking down his crooked nose at me. "She'll beg for me to forgive her, and I will—for one night. But when I'm done fucking her senseless, I'll snap her neck and throw her away like the trash she—"

The guard to Mikhail's right goes down with one shot to the shoulder.

Mikhail ducks down, arms over his head, while Yasha takes down the man to his left. The guards are only wounded, not dead, but they don't rush back to their feet to sacrifice themselves in front of Mikhail. Neither do any of the other Sokolov soldiers lining the room.

I have a feeling they'll thank me once he's dead.

Mikhail is still cowering when I grab him by the front of his shirt and throw him back against the wall. His head bounces off the metal, the vibration shuddering up the wall.

"How is this for 'face-to-face'?" I growl. "Am I close enough for you, Mikhail?"

His eyes are wide, searching the room for anyone willing to step forward and help him. He comes up empty.

I slide into his line of sight and shake my head. "You wouldn't have come here without all this backup. You thought they were going to rush in to save you. *You thought you were safe.*"

"My father will start a w-war over this," he stammers. "You'll lose more than it's worth."

"More than *what* is worth?" I ask. "More than *you're* worth? Definitely. You aren't worth the breath I'm spending explaining myself. But if you mean that I'll lose more than killing you is worth... Well, I have to disagree. Because killing you is going to be fucking *priceless.*"

I press my gun to his temple. He flinches away. Tears well in his eyes and sweat beads on his forehead. He's shaking from head to toe like the spineless coward he is and always has been.

"Tell me you're sorry, Mikhail."

He looks up at me quickly, a spark of hope in his eyes. "I'm sorry, Ivan. I shouldn't have come. I'm—"

I shake my head. "No. Tell me you're sorry for what you did to Cora. Apologize for everything you did to her."

He hesitates for only a second before the press of my muzzle to his skin reminds him what is at stake.

"I'm sorry I forced her into marriage. I'm sorry I kidnapped her and held her hostage. I'm sorry I kept her from you. I'm sorry I—I'm sorry for everything. I... I don't know what else to say."

"That's enough. That's more than enough." I let go of his shirt and he sags against the wall in obvious relief. "I'll tell Cora those were your last words."

I let that sit for half a second. Just long enough for Mikhail to understand what is happening.

Then I shoot the motherfucker in the head.

59

CORA

"Maybe I should sit at the head." I stand back and try to imagine the place setting there. "Do you think it would be too formal to have the whole length of the table between us?"

Niles has endured an hour of my fidgeting and fussing already, so the poor man just shrugs. "Whatever you decide will be fine."

That's nice and all, but I've never doubted my own decisions more than I have today. Gold or silver cutlery? Should I wear a pantsuit or a dress? Full face of makeup or keep it minimal?

"Your dad doesn't care about any of that," Ivan told me this morning before he climbed out of bed. "He is just excited to sit down and get to know you. So let him see you. Be yourself."

The trouble is, I don't know who I am.

A month ago, I was a waitress at a cheap Mexican restaurant. I lived in a dinky one-bedroom apartment and spent my limited free time watching reality television until my eyes bled.

Then I was a target, bait, Ivan Pushkin's fake fiancée, Mikhail Sokolov's forced fiancée (again), and now... Now, I'm building a life with the man I love. I know how to move forward with Ivan. I know how to leave Alexander and my mother and Mikhail and Francia behind me.

What I don't have a single fucking clue how to do is merge my past and my present.

My dad *was* firmly in my past. Where does he fit in now?

My thoughts are spiraling out of control when Niles lays his hands on my shoulders. "If you want my honest opinion, Mrs. Cora, I think you two should take your dinner at the kitchen island."

"What?" I spin away from the table and face Niles. He's only a foot away, which is the closest we've ever been. He's always struck me as a rich, formal grandpa. You know he loves you, but he isn't going to say it. "But you spent so much time getting the dining room ready!"

"I did. And then you spent twice as much time moving it all around and rearranging."

I drop my face into my hands. "Ugh. I'm sorry. I'm being the worst. You worked so hard and I undid all of it. You're better at this than I am. I should have just left it the way you had it. Maybe I can move it back and—"

I'm already halfway turned around when Niles stops me. "No."

I blink at him, too stunned and frazzled to find any words.

"You need to take a deep breath, dear."

I inhale and exhale slowly. "I'm freaking out."

"You are," he agrees. "Which is why you're going to stop touching everything and trust that it will all work out. You like to eat at the kitchen island, so do that. Do what you are comfortable with and forget about appearances or what anyone else will think. Be yourself. That is enough."

I'm obviously teetering on the edge of a nervous breakdown, because Niles' little speech has me holding back tears.

"Niles, I—just, thank you. I appreciate everything you've done today. But therapy sessions are probably outside of your job description. You can go. I'll figure this all out on my own."

"Anything Mr. Pushkin asks me to do is within my job description."

It takes me a second to register what he's saying. "Hold on—did Ivan ask you to help me?"

"He was worried about you," he says by way of explanation. "And he told me that if you were spiraling, I was supposed to grab your shoulders and tell you to take a deep breath."

I'd be mad that Ivan thinks I need to be managed if it hadn't worked so well.

"Did he tell you to give me a pep talk, too?"

He shakes his head. "No. That was my choice. Did it help?"

I smile. "Yeah. It did. Thank you."

Sometimes, I forget that along with Ivan, Anya, Lev, and Yasha, I also gained an entire Bratva. A family who will support me and take care of me. Including Niles.

I'm almost at ease when the doorbell rings. As soon as it does, I stiffen and my anxiety ramps right back up to eleven out of ten.

Then Niles lays a hand on my shoulder once more. "You'll be fine, madam. I'll answer the door and escort him to the kitchen."

I'm too nervous to do anything more than nod and head in the direction Niles points. It's my own dad. No one should be this nervous to see their own dad.

Then again, no one should be forcefully separated from their dad and live on the streets as a teenager. But shit happens.

Dinner is keeping warm in the oven and, as soon as I step into the kitchen and the swirling aroma of roasted meat and potatoes, I know Niles is right. This is the gathering place. Where Ivan and I make coffee in the morning. Where Anya paints her nails while Lev and Ivan talk out on the patio. It's the heart of the house and I'm comfortable here.

I'm also very glad I swapped out my dress for a pair of dark wash jeans at the last minute.

Be myself. I'm enough.

I repeat those words to myself over and over again, but I'm still standing awkwardly by the island when Niles walks into the kitchen with my dad right behind him.

"I'll get you both some drinks and then come back in a few minutes for dinner." Niles ushers him into the room and then tosses me a subtle wink before he disappears.

My dad and I stare at each other for a second before he holds out the bouquet of flowers I didn't even register he was holding. "These are for you."

"Oh. Wow. Thank you." I fumble with them for a second, our hands brushing awkwardly.

I can't believe I used to hug this man and let him read me stories before bed. He's a stranger now in every way that matters.

"Niles keeps the vases… somewhere." I gesture vaguely towards the pantry. "He'll put these in one later."

"Before he does, make sure you get this out." He reaches out and plucks something out of the center of the bouquet. "It's my poor attempt at an edible arrangement of sorts. I remember you liking those."

I'm not sure what he's holding until he flips the white bag over.

"Is that saltwater taffy?"

He smiles. "From that shop we used to go to. Marina's Confectionery. It's still open. They moved to a bigger location, but they still make taffy. Isn't that wild?"

Instantly, crystal-clear memories of hopping down the sidewalk hand-in-hand with my dad flood back to me. Every so often, he'd take me with him to the hardware store. Afterwards, we'd walk down the block and buy a bouquet from the flower stand and a bag of saltwater taffy from Marina's. I'd ration out the taffy for weeks afterward, eating only one piece or half a piece per day to make it last.

All at once, the anxiety I've felt all day shifts to something else. Something raw and painful that I've tried to squash down for years.

"Are those okay?" he asks, misunderstanding my sudden tears. "Do you not like them anymore? I should have guessed.

It was years and years ago when you used to eat those. I just thought—"

"I love them." I swipe at my eyes and put on a smile. "I do. I love them so much that I… I haven't had them since you left. Er, since we left. It was too hard to remember the old days."

His face pinches with sympathy.

I shake my head. "I'm sorry. I wasn't going to do this. We were going to have a normal dinner, but I already made it weird. I didn't mean—"

"You didn't make it weird. You made it honest." He blows out a breath. "All of this is hard, Corde—Cora. But we're here and I'm glad we're trying to figure it out. No matter how uncomfortable it is."

"You're uncomfortable, too?"

"Oh God, yes," he groans. "Don't get me wrong—I'm happy to be here. I'm so glad you agreed to have dinner with me. But I guess owning up to your shit is never easy. No matter how much you want to. And I *do* want to. That's what I'm here to do. I want to tell you how sorry I am about not reaching out to you sooner. And for being angry."

Niles hasn't even come back with drinks yet and we're already diving into the deep end. It feels nice, though. I'm tired of putting up a facade.

"I was angry, too. I still am a little bit," I admit. "Not at you, necessarily, but at the situation. And, yeah, partly at you."

He shrugs. "That's okay. Hopefully, we'll spend enough time with each other that we can sort through all of it. Because I don't want this to be our last dinner. I don't want to go another ten years without seeing you."

I lay the candy on the counter and grab his hand, holding it loosely in mine. "Then we won't."

He smiles and we sit down at the island.

It becomes clear very quickly that I spent all day worrying about nothing. My dad isn't here to judge the house or my hosting abilities. He isn't nitpicking and looking for cracks in my story. He is here to get to know me. To make things right.

He even tries to make things right between me and my mom. "I'm not saying you should forgive her, but I think you should understand her," he says at one point.

He tells me about her life growing up. The reason she was so good at living on the streets is because she'd done it before. Her entire childhood was in constant flux. No stable house, no guaranteed meals, no one to depend on.

"When you and your mom left, things weren't great for me at work. We were struggling financially. It wasn't anything too serious, but even the whisper of problems sent your mom spiraling. I'm not surprised she ended up running to Alexander. All she wanted was stability."

"Financial stability," I clarify. "Because that man is not mentally stable. I don't think Mom is anymore, either."

I tell him about the last few weeks and what Mom and Alexander tried to do to me. I cry and he looks murderous, but we talk each other down. Then, somehow, we start laughing.

The conversation ebbs and flows effortlessly. We reminisce on good memories, talk about the hard times, and, best of all, talk about absolutely nothing. The weather, television, our favorite music. We talk until I forget why I was nervous in the first place.

When he's done with the apple turnover Niles made for dessert, my dad sits back and smiles. "You seem really happy here, Cora."

I can't help but smile back. "I am happy. I'm... I'm in love."

I haven't fully admitted it to Ivan yet. Not in the exact words. But he knows.

"He loves you, too. The way the two of you are with each other... Well, anyone can see how you feel. I'm glad you've found someone."

A new wave of tears threatens to flow—*who knew one person could be this happy?*—when I hear the front door open.

I glance at the clock. "Wow. I didn't realize it was already after ten." Ivan told me he'd make himself scarce until my dad was gone, but he probably didn't think our dinner would go this long.

"It's a lot later than I thought." He stands up and stretches. "I should get going and let you get to bed."

"Or you could stay for a few more minutes? Ivan is here. Maybe we can all... talk?"

Like a real family, I think.

I know one night is not enough to fix everything, but it's a good start. And Ivan is the one who pushed me to even being open to this idea in the first place. I want him and my dad to get along.

"Yeah, sure," he agrees. "I can do that."

"Amazing. I'll go grab him before he sneaks upstairs. He's probably trying to give us space."

I lightly jog out of the kitchen and down the hallway towards the entryway. "Ivan! You can come back here if you—"

I slam to a stop in the entryway as Francia turns to me and smiles.

"Were you expecting someone else?"

60

IVAN

"Was that really necessary?" Yasha groans when he comes back over.

I step back to avoid the puddle of blood forming around Mikhail's head. Or what's left of it.

"He challenged me. I didn't have a choice."

Not that I would've chosen any differently.

"No, I know." He sighs. "I mean, I could have done it. It would have been a real clean shot, too. But you charged in and got your poetic justice. It makes for a better story, but I just would have liked a shot at him. Maybe not even the kill shot. Just a graze."

"You can shoot him now if you want." I toe Mikhail's limp leg. "He won't shoot back."

Yasha wrinkles his nose. "Thanks, but no thanks. It's not the same."

"What did you tell the rest of the Sokolov soldiers?"

"What you told me to tell them: if the police come sniffing, none of them were ever here. They've never heard of the place, never heard of you. They won't have a single fucking clue to offer up to solve this mystery."

"And if Konstantin asks them what happened?"

Yasha knows the drill by now. We've cleaned up enough messes over the years to anticipate what needs to be done. But now is no time to get sloppy.

"Mikhail challenged you," Yasha says. "He showed up unannounced and threatened your wife, questioned your authority, and refused to back down even when you gave him the opportunity to walk away. You didn't have a choice."

I didn't. No one gets to treat me like that and live.

That doesn't mean I'm looking forward to the wrench this is going to throw in my relationship with Konstantin.

I sigh and turn away, walking back towards where I parked at the back of the warehouse. Yasha trails along behind me. "Make sure the body is cleaned up and disposed of," I tell him. "Let a couple of recruits deal with the hands-on work if you want, but I want you to oversee everything. I don't want him washing up on the beach tomorrow morning."

"Done. Maybe disposing of him myself will scratch the murderous itch the asshole gave me. Or maybe not. I'm getting a little old to be hauling bodies around."

His phone rings and Yasha turns away to answer it. He's the point man for so many different things that he's always on the phone. I don't pay any attention to it.

Until he grabs my arm and pulls me to a stop.

"Say that again," he orders into the phone.

"Who is it?" I ask.

Yasha stares at me, his eyes getting bigger with every word being said on the other end of the phone. Words that I can't fucking hear.

I growl and grab his phone, switching it to speaker.

"—*days, maybe four. We just found them this morning. But they were fucking ripped to shreds. Shot and stabbed beyond recognition. Whoever did this enjoyed it.*"

"Tell me who's dead," I bark.

"Who is—Is that—" The man on the phone splutters.

"Yes, it's Ivan," Yasha says. "Skip the fangirling and tell the *pakhan* what you told me."

The man clears his throat. "Every guard at the safehouse in Moscow is dead. No one had heard from them in a while, so I went to check. All three of them were goners. Smelled like they'd been dead for a few days already."

The last message I received from the safehouse was a notice that Francia had arrived and would be "taken care of." Usually, that would mean she'd be offered food, clothes, and a bed. In this case, it meant Francia was going to be bunking with the men who were deemed too unpredictable and reckless to live Stateside.

She was in for hell.

Or so I thought.

I look to Yasha as I ask, "And Francia? Where is she?"

"There's no sign of her. She disappeared. We have men looking for her but—"

I don't need to hear anymore. I run for my car and call Cora at the same time. I told her I'd make myself scarce while she had her dinner with Marcus, but this is bigger than that. Her safety trumps everything else. I need to hear her voice. *Now.*

The phone rings and rings and rings. Then her voicemail picks up.

"Fuck!" I roar.

Yasha is right behind me. "I'm calling Jorden to see if she's heard anything from either of them."

"If Jorden has heard from Francia, she's already dead."

Yasha's jaw clenches, but there's no point in sugarcoating the reality. If Francia is back, there's only one thing on her mind: revenge.

I call Niles, but I'm not getting anything. My only hope now is that it's a signal jammer. If it's not, then they're all—

I can't sit and think about possibilities for another second. I need to do something. I need to get to Cora.

"I'm going to the mansion."

"We have no idea what's happening there," Yasha protests. "Give me a second and I can—"

"I'll call you when I know something. Or you call me when you know something. But I'm not leaving Cora alone right now."

Yasha waves. "You go. I'll see you soon."

I hope like hell he's right.

61

CORA

I need to run.

I need to scream.

I need to tell Ivan.

But there isn't time for any of it. For a second, it's like I'm back at the dinner last week. I'm having déjà vu. Francia hurls herself at me exactly like she did before.

The only difference is, no one is here to stop her this time.

There is nothing between me and Francia except empty space and she's closing it quickly.

When she smashes into me, my lungs compress. I can't scream. I can barely even breathe.

We collapse on the tile floor and every training session I've had with Anya and Ivan falls out of my head. All I can do is throw my arms over my face and try to protect myself from Francia's nails and fist and teeth.

She grabs a handful of my hair and yanks. I swing out at her, but I hit dead air. Then she smashes my head against the floor. Stars explode behind my eyes.

"You ruined everything, you fucking bitch!" Francia screeches. Her breath is hot on my neck. I drive my elbow back in the general direction of what I think is her face and yelp when her teeth dig into my bicep. She's fucking *rabid*.

Then Francia splutters. She lets go of my hair and slides back, and I realize, my bicep smashed into her teeth.

She didn't bite me. *I* hit *her*.

That one success is enough to wake me up. It's enough to pull me out of the shock of her showing up and lunging at me so that I can see what I need to do.

When I was sore and exhausted from training, I told Ivan that he and Anya were going to break me. He swore they were training me so no one would ever be able to break me.

I guess it's time to put that to the test.

Francia is still trying to reclaim the little bit of ground she just lost when I flip onto my back and kick out. She's practically on top of me, so all I manage to do is kick her shins. But it's better than lying on the ground defenseless.

"Don't make this harder than it needs to be!" Francia is panting and scrabbling for grip on my arms.

I know if she pins me down, I won't get back up. So I throw all of my weight to one side and roll. It gives me enough space to pull my right leg up and then kick straight back with the heel of my foot.

Francia's knee snaps awkwardly under my foot. Things that aren't supposed to move go *pop-pop-pop*. Even *I* wince.

Her shriek echoes off the high ceilings as I crawl away on my hands and knees. My head is still spinning from the blow earlier, so standing up isn't an option. I just need to get far enough away to—

Then there's a cold hand around my ankle.

Francia rakes her fingernails into my skin. I try to kick, but she throws herself on top of my legs, pinning me down to the floor.

Francia's breathing gets louder as she scrambles over me. Ivan is going to find me dead on his entryway floor. Maybe Francia will lie in wait and attack him, too. He'll drop to his knees next to my corpse in horror and that's when she'll strike. He'll still probably be able to fight her off, but he'll never forgive himself for letting me die.

That thought is scarier than realizing I'm about to die. And I muster up one last burst of energy.

I haul myself up onto my arms, pull my legs in as fast as I can, and throw myself forward. It only puts a few feet of space between me and Francia. It's not enough, I know that.

But at least I tried.

I hope Ivan knows I tried.

Francia rears back to launch herself at me again... just as shots ring out.

She drops flat on the floor, but I spin around looking for the source. Yasha? Ivan? Maybe even Niles? Ivan told me his household staff is trained for emergency situations like this.

Maybe someone came to save me.

Then I turn and see my dad standing in the hallway, his gun pointed at the ceiling.

"Stay the fuck away from my daughter."

There's a hole in the ceiling and plaster dust raining down in a white haze.

A few hours ago, he showed up carrying flowers and taggy. Now, he's holding a gun. It's hard to reconcile the two sides of him. But it doesn't matter. He's here. I'm safe.

So why doesn't it feel that way? Something still seems wrong. Francia is still lying flat on the floor. My dad is sighing with relief and setting the gun down on the ground. A hole in the ceiling is smoking.

It takes me a second to put together the pieces.

Then it hits me. *He fired a warning shot.*

Which means he didn't hurt Francia.

Which means she shouldn't be lying motionless on the floor.

My dad is moving towards me, leaving the gun behind. I see it all happen in slow motion. He's holding a hand out to help me up, but behind him, Francia lifts herself up. She doesn't stand all the way up because she doesn't need to. She can reach what she needs to while lying down.

She picks up the gun in her hand and, unlike my dad, she isn't pointing at the ceiling. She's pointing it at his back.

Without a word, she fires.

Unlike him, she doesn't start with a warning shot. No remorse. No chance to give up.

Francia pulls the trigger and my dad jerks and crumples to the floor.

"Dad!" I reach out for him, but my head spins. I think I have a concussion, but if I don't get to him, things are going to be so much worse.

I can't put one foot in front of the other, but I try anyway. I lift myself to my knees and the world is yanked out from under my feet. I fall sideways with my shoulder pressed to the wall.

Francia's shadow falls over me. She scoffs. "What Ivan sees in you, I will never fucking know."

Then something heavy hits my temple. The world goes dark.

The last thing I see is the blood on my father's shirt.

62

IVAN

I hear the gunshot before I'm even out of the car.

I slam the car into park and throw the door open without turning the engine off. *Please, for the love of fucking God, let it be Niles fighting back. Or Marcus. Or a guard. Anyone but Francia.*

But the shattered remains of the gates at the mouth of the driveway were enough of a hint as to how this is going to go. The empty guard shack made it a near-certainty.

Francia is here. And somehow, she found her way to Cora.

Knowing that doesn't change the full-body ache that ripples through me when I make it inside and see Francia with her arm around Cora's neck... and a gun pressed to her head.

"Don't take another fucking step," she hisses.

Cora is alive. Her eyes are closed and there's a bump on her forehead, but I can see her chest moving. Francia wouldn't be threatening to kill her if she was already dead.

As long as her heart is beating, there's a chance.

"Let her go and you can walk out of here intact." My voice is tight, but it isn't shaking. A miracle, given the adrenaline pumping through me.

If I don't save her, I'll never forgive myself.

Francia cackles. There are dark circles under her eyes. It doesn't look like she's slept in days. Actually, it looks like she died and came back from the dead. Whatever happened to her in Moscow before she killed the guards and fled, it wasn't pretty.

"We've been through too much to lie to each other, Ivan. We both know I'm not walking out of here."

"Fine." I nod. "If you back away from my wife right now, I'll give you a quick death."

It's way more than she deserves after all of the carnage and chaos she has caused.

If Cora can get the gun away from her head, even for a second, then I can take my shot. But right now, the risk that Francia takes Cora down with her is too great.

"Your wife." Her lip curls in disgust and I watch her hand tighten around Cora's throat.

Wake up, solnishka. *Fight back.*

Cora doesn't budge. But her chest is still moving.

"*I should have been your wife,*" she hisses. "I should have been *someone's* wife. Anyone's. I went to the fucking parties and wore the fucking dresses. I did what I was supposed to do and it didn't work. You didn't want me."

"That isn't Cora's fault. Cora didn't do anything wrong."

"She didn't do anything right, either! Cora had everything. *Everything.*" Francia looks down at Cora for a second, hate burning in her eyes. "She was living with Alexander and engaged to Mikhail. Cora was going to live the life I wanted. The life I deserved. And she threw it away."

"You wanted to marry Mikhail Sokolov?" It's hard for me to imagine any woman that desperate.

"I wanted to marry someone like him! Someone who could crush people like my parents under their heel without a second thought. I hated the Sokolovs for what they did to my family, but I didn't want to kill them; I wanted to *be* them."

I frown. "Your parents were lawyers for Konstantin Sokolov, weren't they?"

"How else do you think they got introduced to the people who destroyed their lives? Konstantin Sokolov passed my parents' business card around to his friends. Next thing I know, my parents are gone every night. They come home out of their minds on drugs. We never had much money, but they spent all of it and more. They dipped into Konstantin's money, too. Until he caught them. And killed them for it."

"How did you manage going to private school with dead parents?"

"Konstantin took me in." She brushes her tangled black hair back over her shoulder. "Since my parents couldn't repay their debt, he took me as payment. I worked for him. I kept an eye on Katerina. I know you and Kat like to think you pulled one over on Konstantin by sending her away, but he always knew his daughter was a flight risk. So he gave me a position in his house and in her school. I kept an eye on her. I had a front row seat to your entire engagement... and Katerina's disappearance."

How many times must I have walked past Francia while she was working at the Sokolov estate? How many times did I look right past where she was lingering in the shadows? I never noticed her. Not even once.

Not until it was too late.

"When Katerina went missing, I struck a deal with Konstantin," she continues. "I told him that I would help figure out what happened to Katerina. But as time passed, my plan changed. I was tired of living *near* the upper crust. I could mimic their dainty, prissy voices and I had enough of Katerina's hand-me-downs to play the part to perfection, but I was on the outside looking in. Where you were considered, Ivan... I wanted to be up close and personal."

Even now, there's a purr to Francia's voice. There's an attempt at seduction being made even while she's holding the woman I love at gunpoint.

The woman is fucking unhinged.

"After trying to get your attention again and again with no luck, I thought I'd send in Cora." Francia strokes a hand down Cora's dark hair, her face puckering in disgust. "She's pretty, but she doesn't belong in this world. Even better, she didn't *want* to be in it. I wanted to get your attention with her and then pivot to me. But even when Cora ran from you, you chased her. You pursued her. *You liked her.* And the more Cora tried to get away, the more I hated her. She had everything at her fingertips and she had no fucking clue."

My voice comes out in a rasp. "If you want to be mad at someone, be mad at me. If you want to punish someone, punish me." I hold my hands out to the side, practically begging Francia to shoot me.

If she turns her gun on me, I'll take my shot. I'll end this. Even if I die doing it.

Whatever it takes to save Cora.

A slow smile creeps across Francia's face. "That is exactly why I'm going to kill her, Ivan. To punish you."

This is why I wanted to send Cora away. I wanted to get her out of this city and away from me. Because my love for her is reason enough for my enemies to come after her. This nightmare is playing out exactly like I knew it would.

And I don't know how to stop it.

"You're going to watch the woman you love die." Her hand tightens on the trigger.

"I'll kill you. The moment that gun goes off, I'll shoot you."

Francia shrugs. "I'm dead either way. At least, this way, I know you're as miserable as I am."

"Cora," I croak. My voice is broken, desperate. *Wake up.*

"It's too late for her." Francia smiles. "Say goodbye."

She pulls the trigger and a gunshot pierces through the quiet.

63

CORA

"Cora."

The desperation in Ivan's voice makes me want to weep. My dad was right: it's obvious he loves me. It's the only thing he wears on his sleeve.

I want to open my eyes and tell him that I'm awake. I'm okay.

But I can't. Not yet.

"It's too late for her," Francia says. "Say goodbye."

I've been waiting for the right moment. Really, I've been waiting for the buzzing in my ears to ease and my balance to return. I'll be dead long before that happens, though. Unless I act now.

I feel Francia stiffen. I know this is it.

She's going to kill me.

All at once, I slam both hands up and swing her arm and the gun away from me... at the same moment she pulls the trigger.

The sound of the shot pierces my eardrums, but I power through the pain. The time for rolling over and waiting for someone to save me is over. Ivan and Anya didn't train me for nothing. They trained me for *this*.

"What the—" Francia is frozen for a few precious seconds. The still-smoking gun is in her hand, aimed at the front door instead of my head. And I lunge.

Distantly, I hear Ivan laugh in surprise. I tune it out. I tune out everything except Francia's hollow, angry face. I focus on her sunken-in eyes… so I can scratch them out.

She tries to swing the gun back at me, but I grab her wrist and twist. She elbows me in the ribs and knees me on the inside of my thigh, but I don't let up until the gun clatters from her hand and falls to the floor.

"Push her back!" Ivan yells. "Get away from her and I'll shoot."

I try, but Francia is clinging to me. She knows I'm the only thing standing between her and being shot dead.

Francia wraps her hand around my neck and spins behind me. My head is already fuzzy and her pressing on my windpipe isn't helping.

"You can't fight me, Cora," she whispers in my ear. "I'm stronger than you. I'm tougher than you. *I want this life more than you do.*"

I claw at her arm.

Ivan moves closer, but then I feel it. A blade pressed to the side of my neck.

"She has a knife," I gasp.

Ivan stops in the middle of the room. I've never seen him so tortured. Torn between keeping me safe and wanting nothing more than to rip Francia's head from her body.

"That's right. I have a knife." Francia cackles. "Cora here keeps destroying all of my plans, so I came with plenty of backup. It's time you learn that you can't steal from other people and get away with it."

"You think *I* stole something from you? You're the one who stole my life. My husband!"

"The only reason you know Ivan is because I dressed you up and pushed you in the right direction," she snaps. "If it wasn't for me, the two of you would have broken up once Ivan completed his little mission. You'd be back waiting tables at Quintaño's, pretending you don't regret letting Ivan get away. Maybe that would be better than how things are going to turn out for you. At least you'd be alive."

I shake my head, talking more to Ivan than to Francia. "No matter what happens, Ivan is worth it. He's worth every insane thing you've put me through. We aren't together because of you. We're together because we love each other. Because we are meant to be. You had nothing to do with it."

The tip of the knife twists in my neck. I feel a warm trickle of blood running over my skin. "One thing is for sure, even if you think I had nothing to do with getting you two together: I'm going to have everything to do with keeping you apart. In the end, Ivan's future is in my hands. His fate belongs to me. *Ivan is mine.*"

She's insane. Francia is certifiable.

But hearing her claim Ivan with so much conviction is all it takes to send rage burning through me.

Suddenly, I'm back in the training room with Anya. She's behind me, her hand wrapped around my neck.

"Destabilize," Anya instructed. "That's your only goal in this position. You want to get the person off balance long enough to escape. Slam them against a wall, kick their kneecaps, rock back and forth—whatever it takes to loosen their grip."

Without another thought, I grab Francia's wrist and pray my grip is strong enough to keep her from stabbing me in the throat. Then I throw all of my momentum backwards and slam her spine against the wall.

I feel the air whoosh out of her, hot on my neck.

Ivan rushes forward, but I'm not waiting for him. Not when I have her exactly where I want her.

I spin around, grab her wrist with my other hand, and drive Francia's own hand still holding the knife straight up into her jugular.

Her eyes go wide as hot blood pulses from her neck and pours over our interlaced hands. Her lips move, but no words come out. I'm glad. The time for her to explain and rationalize is over. She was a crazy bitch, and now, she's a dead, crazy bitch.

"The only person's fate you should have been worried about is your own," I say, stepping back as she slides to the floor. "Ivan belongs to me."

64

IVAN

Cora is swaying over Francia's body, blood dripping from her fingertips onto the tile floor.

She looks like hell, but she did it.

Cora killed Francia.

Since the moment I got the call at the warehouse, all I've wanted to do is get to Cora. Now, I take a moment to admire her. Bloodstained and breathless and fucking *fierce*. My queen.

Then she takes a stumbling step away from Francia and I can't wait another goddamn second. I need to hold her and feel her, warm and alive, in my arms.

Cora keeps backing up until she thuds against my chest. I catch her with an arm around her waist and press my lips to her ear. "I've got you. You're okay."

She jolts for only a second before she sinks against my chest. "Ivan."

"You were fucking incredible," I whisper. "You did everything right. Everything we taught you. You were amazing."

If I had things my way, Cora would have never learned to fight. It wouldn't have been necessary. But I'm glad she did. She took care of herself and I could not be prouder.

Her head lolls back against my shoulder. "I'm tired. My head... I'm dizzy."

I press a kiss to her temple—the same spot where, just a few minutes ago, Francia had pointed a gun. I'm not sure the image of Cora on the ground at Francia's mercy will ever fully leave my head. That is the kind of shit that haunts you.

I'll remember it forever.

And make sure it never happens again.

"You're okay now," I tell her. "I'm going to get you to the doctor. You'll rest and be fine."

She sighs. "Thank you, Ivan."

I'm so focused on her heartbeat fluttering in her throat and the way her lips part around a sigh that I don't hear the footsteps behind me until it's almost too late.

At the last second, I push Cora forward and spin around, positioning myself between her and the threat.

In this case, the threat is Alexander McAllister. And he's pointing a gun directly at my chest.

At this point, I'm more annoyed than anything. *When are these bastards going to give up?*

"I knew you weren't going to disappear. That would've been the smart thing to do."

He grimaces, his face screwed up in rage. "Francia told you she had a backup plan."

"*You* are her backup plan?" I almost laugh. "You hitched your horse to that crazy bitch? You must have been desperate."

"You left me no choice! Konstantin made his deal with you and cut me out. After everything I did—for him, for Mikhail —they... they all abandoned me. Me and Francia. Because of you. *Both of you.*"

As Alexander has been talking, I've edged ever so slightly away from Cora. One half-step at a time, I've moved so the gun isn't aiming at Cora at all. She's off to the side, staying quiet and still. Alexander is fully focused on me.

"You could have left Cora alone. You didn't have to drag her back home and marry her off."

"I needed that arrangement with the Sokolovs to—"

"You weren't starving in the streets. You didn't *need* anything. You wanted it. You got greedy and you took a risk. I never would have bothered you if you hadn't taken her from me."

"*You* took her from *me*," he rages. His face is red and sweating. "She was promised to Mikhail and I was going to make sure that deal happened. Then you showed up. It ruined everything. Konstantin Sokolov was going to sink me if I didn't complete the deal. And now, my name is trashed. No one is going to come to me. What good is a fixer with an endless trail of scandals in his wake?"

Yet again, I could take a shot at Alexander, but he might shoot back before he falls. He could kill me where I stand.

I'd rather it be me than Cora, but if there's any way we can both make it out of tonight together, I'm going to take it.

So I wait for an opening, gun clutched in my right hand.

"About as good as a fixer who is charged with double homicide in the death of his stepdaughter and her husband," I tell him icily. "You say you're ruined, but *this* will ruin you, Alexander. Right now, you could walk away and make a life for yourself. But if you pull that trigger, it's over."

He leans in close, the gun still aimed at my chest. "It's over for Alexander McAllister either way. After tonight, he's going to disappear. I have enough money left to start over. I'll kill the two of you, kill Evaline, and then leave the country. Everyone will assume I died and I'll start over fresh. Far, *far* away from the influence of the Pushkins and the Sokolovs."

Cora is staring at him, open-mouthed. I don't want her to say anything to draw his attention, so I ask the question I know is on her mind.

"You'd really kill your own wife?"

"Evaline was a means to an end," he spits. "Every man needs someone to keep their household running and their dick wet. You know something about that, don't you, Ivan? Why else would you choose Cordelia when you thought she was nothing more than a waitress?"

Fuck it. I'll take my chances and shoot him dead right now.

Before I can even raise my gun, Cora flies out of nowhere and throws herself on Alexander's back.

"You selfish son of a bitch!" she screams, clawing at his face and his neck. "You ruined my life, you asshole! I won't let you kill my mother, too!"

Alexander is too busy trying to stay on his feet to remember he has a gun in his hand. He stumbles back and forward, trying to shake Cora off.

Finally, he bends forward and Cora slips. She ramps up to jump on him again, but Alexander raises his arm and cracks the back of his hand across her face.

Cora's head jerks to one side. She falls to her knees and slides across the tile floor.

"You fucking bi—" Alexander starts to hiss.

But the first half of the word is barely off his lips when I press my gun to his head and pull the trigger.

No last words. No hesitation. Blood sprays and Alexander crumples to the floor in a useless heap.

"No one puts hands on my woman and survives," I snarl over his lifeless body.

One last victim of my fucking rampage.

65

CORA

My face burns, my ears are ringing, and my head feels like it's packed with wet sand. As I look from Ivan to Alexander's body and back again, my brains slosh from side to side.

His eyes are dark and menacing. He is pure wrath.

Then he shifts towards me and everything about him softens. Ivan drops to his knees next to me and cups my face in his massive, gentle hands. "Tell me you're okay."

As long as you're with me, I'm perfect.

"I'm okay," I rasp. My throat is clogged with emotion. "Is it over? How many more are there?"

Ivan looks over his shoulder, scanning the doors. "I think it's over. Fuck, I hope so. I killed Mikhail and then ran here to stop Francia. Then Alexander shows up. They are coming out of the woodwork tonight."

"Wait—you killed Mikhail?"

He winces. "You don't need to worry about that now."

"Are you hurt?" I smooth my hands down his broad shoulders and over the firm plane of his chest. He feels like the most solid thing in the world right now.

He grabs one of my hands and presses it to his lips. A bit of blood rubs off my hands and smears across his chin. I look back at his shoulders and realize I was spreading Francia's blood all over his shirt. "Cora, don't worry about me right now. If you're okay, I'm okay."

I close my eyes and take a deep breath. "I'm okay, I think. I'm sore and I might have a concussion, but I—I just don't understand how this all happened. I was having a really good day. Dinner with my dad went well and I—"

The words lodge in my throat at the same time my heart drops to my stomach.

I forgot. How could I forget?

"What is it?" Ivan stiffens, looking around for danger.

There isn't any more danger. Just the wreckage of what already happened. The carnage littered all around the entryway.

Including the body of my father.

"Dad!" I push away from Ivan and crawl across the floor.

When Francia shot him, he fell backward into the hallway. Everything that happened after that was a whirlwind of fear and survival. I didn't have time to check on him or look to see if he was moving. I couldn't worry about him and make it out alive.

Now, I'm alive…

But my dad might be gone.

Ivan makes it to my dad's side before I do.

"Is he alive?" I don't want to hear the answer. For just a second, I want everyone I love to be safe and okay. I want my world to be right.

I crawl past Ivan and look down into my father's face. He's pale. There's too much blood soaking through his cotton polo. I can't even remember what color it was when he got here tonight. Green? Maybe blue? It's a muddy brown now.

Ivan has his fingers pressed to my father's neck.

"Ivan?" I whisper quietly enough that even I can barely hear myself.

"There's a pulse," he says finally. "It's faint. If he's going to survive, we need to move fast."

Ivan bolts up and grabs his phone, but I can't leave. I can't walk away. Not again.

I grab my dad's hand and try to ignore how cold his fingers are. The tips are turning blue. "You're going to be okay, Daddy."

I'm not sure if I'm saying it for him or myself. Probably both. God knows we both need some comforting lies right about now.

"You have to be okay. I just got you back." My voice breaks and I press my cheek to his shoulder. Tears stream down my face and drip onto his already-ruined shirt. "I'm so sorry I dragged you into this. This is all my fault."

In the background, I hear Ivan on the phone. He's telling Yasha what happened and arranging an off-the-record ambulance ride to the hospital. I don't know when I'll stop being amazed at how much control and power he has in this city, but it isn't today.

"You're going to be okay," I say again. He still isn't moving, but I believe my own lie a little more.

Ivan is here now.

If he's here, I know everything will be alright.

66

CORA

The hospital waiting room is empty except for me and Ivan.

We've been here for two hours already. The first hour passed quickly. It was eaten up by Ivan barking orders at every doctor in the vicinity to double- and triple-check me for any injuries.

"If something happens to her because any one of you motherfuckers didn't do a thorough enough examination, I'll burn this hospital to the ground," he growled after I'd been x-rayed and examined at least three different times.

Beyond a mild concussion, I must be fine. Because, even with that threat hanging over their heads, each doctor cleared me to go home with Ivan as soon as I was ready.

But we didn't go home. We came to the waiting room to wait. And wait. And wait.

"He should be out of surgery by now, right?" I drop my face into my hands and press my palms into my aching eye sockets. "He's been back there for hours."

"Two hours. That's not that long for a gunshot wound." Ivan massages his heavy hand between my shoulder blades. It eases the tension in my body, but I don't think anything can help the ache in my heart.

"It feels like a long time. Someone should be coming to update us more often. Like, if he dies on the table, will they even tell us? They might not even know he's my dad. I didn't tell them. Did you tell them?"

He squeezes my shoulders until they ease down from around my ears. "As soon as there is something to know, they'll tell us."

I know he's right, but this is torture. Sitting next to my father while he bled out on the floor was terrible, but at least I could watch his chest rise and fall. I knew he was alive.

Now, I'm powerless. And it's all Francia's fault.

"I can't believe she shot him." The tension Ivan rubbed away comes back in full force. "He has avoided my mom and Alexander for a decade, but one week of being in my life and he gets shot and ends up in the hospital."

"I don't think it is being part of your life that is the problem," Ivan says softly. "My world is dangerous. It's why I wanted to—"

I turn to him and squeeze his hand. "Don't say it. I know you wanted to keep me safe, but sending me away wasn't an option."

He has been there for me all night—through the attacks and afterward. Every second since he barged through the front doors of his mansion and found Francia holding me hostage has been spent trying to protect me and make sure I'm okay.

"I chose you, Ivan." The light behind him flares in my concussed vision, casting him in a faint glow. If it didn't burn so fucking badly, it would be kind of beautiful. "I chose your life. It's my life, too. *Our* life."

He nods. "It is our life, Cora. You decided I was worth the danger. And I know you're worried your dad is going to get out of surgery and walk away again, but your dad made the same choice you did. When he pulls through, he won't be mad at you. You're worth the nightmare that was tonight and so much more."

I squeeze his arm and lay my cheek on his shoulder. Closing my eyes feels good, but I don't want to sleep. It's the early hours of the morning. Getting a bit of sleep now would be smart. Who knows how late we'll be up by the time this night is over?

I just know, if I go to sleep, I'll dream of everything that happened. Of Francia running at me, red-faced and screaming. I'll dream of my father's body hitting the tile floor. Of Alexander pointing a gun at Ivan's chest.

I'll see myself plunging the knife into Francia's neck again and again.

I don't say anything, but Ivan knows me too well. He can feel me tensing up, trying to protect myself from my own memories. He turns and kisses my forehead. "What's wrong?"

"I killed someone tonight," I whisper.

"You killed Francia."

"Is there a difference?"

"The difference is that everyone who has ever known her will understand why you did it."

I sigh. "I know she was awful, but… by killing her, am I any better than she was?"

All at once, Ivan's shoulder is gone from under my head. But before I can tip sideways, he grabs my face. His thumbs are gentle as they brush along my cheekbones. "There is no comparison between you and her. You are worth a hundred of her. A million. *Solnishka*, you are not a bad person for protecting yourself against a crazy woman. You're a Bratva queen. You did what had to be done."

I shake my head. "Maybe one day, I'll be able to hear those words and believe them. Until then, I might just need you to repeat them to me a lot."

He smiles sadly. "I'll say them as often as you need, Cora. If it helps, I love knowing you can be a little ruthless. It's sexy."

I arch a brow. For the first time in hours, a reluctant smile pulls at the corner of my mouth. "Really? I'll have to remember that."

I'm still looking up at him, letting his smile thaw the ice in my veins, when I hear the door open.

News. It's a nurse coming to tell us how the surgery is going. Maybe a doctor. *Finally.*

It feels like I move quickly, but the concussion slows things down. All I know is by the time I look towards the door and stand up…

My mother is standing in front of me.

I can't make sense of what she's doing here or how she found me. I just stare at her. Ivan is the first to say something.

"Evaline, what are you—"

Before he can ask the question, my mother hauls back and slaps me.

My cheek stings, but the real pain is in my skull. It feels like my eyes are going to bulge out of my head. My teeth rattle together and I have to grab the arm of the chair next to me to keep from dropping to my knees.

Ivan grabs her and pushes her back, barking something at her about not laying a hand on me. But I don't hear any of it.

Her eyes are red and puffy like she's been crying. Mascara runs down her cheeks and her nose is running. She looks like she got thrown in a dryer on high speed.

What is she doing here?

I can't make sense of it until my mom's screams cut through the roar of blood in my ears.

"—have no idea what you've done, Cordelia! You killed him, but you ruined me, too! Where am I supposed to go? *What am I supposed to do?*"

I feel like I'm on stage for a play I haven't rehearsed. And the play is in another language.

"I didn't—" I shake my head, which is a mistake. My vision pixelates and I have to close my eyes until it settles. "I killed Francia. But she was attacking me. She was going to kill me. I didn't have a choice."

Ivan is still pushing my mother back, but she's stretching onto her toes, talking over his shoulder and around his arm. "I don't care about that little bitch; I'm talking about Alexander. You killed my husband and I'll never forgive you."

Oh. I'm not sure how I forgot. In all the chaos, Alexander's death slipped through the cracks.

Probably because I have no regrets about it at all. I didn't pull the trigger, but I know the world is a better place with him gone. Ivan did us all a favor. If he hadn't shot him in the head, I would have. Gladly.

"He broke into my house. He knew Francia was going to try to kill me and he didn't try to stop her." I stare at my mom, but nothing I'm saying is wiping away the anger on her face. "He was going to kill *you*. He said he would kill you and start over somewhere else with—"

"Don't lie to me," she snaps. "Everything Alexander ever did was for our family. He was trying to take care of us."

I snort. "He was taking care of *himself*. He never cared about you. He said every man needed someone to take care of his house and keep his—"

I stop myself. I've crossed a lot of lines tonight, but telling my own mother her dead husband only kept her around as a sex toy is too far.

"He was a bad person and he was going to kill us all."

Suddenly, she takes a step back. Ivan doesn't budge. I know he's going to stay planted between her and me until she leaves. But she calms down.

For a second, I think she's going to listen to me. My mother will recognize that *I* am her family. I'm the person she was supposed to take care of and sacrifice for, not him. Maybe tonight will bring both of my parents back to me.

Then her top lip curls in disgust. "Alexander was right about you, Cordelia. You're selfish. You don't care about me."

If my jaw could hit the floor, it would.

"*I* don't care about *you?* You can't be… You're fucking serious right now." I don't need to ask the question; I already know. I shake my head. "I'm never going to be a priority for you, am I? There will always be some man who comes along and—"

"He wasn't just 'a man'—he was my husband!"

I continue on, ignoring her. "There will always be some man who means more to you than I do because he pays your bills and keeps you in comfort. I was nothing more than a burden, wasn't I? You probably liked when I ran away. Then you didn't need to worry about me anymore."

"I didn't *like* when you ran away," she says. "You abandoned us mid-deal with the Sokolovs and we had to scramble together enough money to—"

I can't stop myself from laughing. None of this is funny, but it's all just so absurd.

"I'm done with you," I tell her. "You will never care as much about me as you do yourself, so I'm done. Forever."

There's a single second of stunned silence before she launches herself at Ivan again. If he wasn't there, I know she'd be screaming directly into my face.

"As if I'd want anything to do with you! You're a murderer! You're some criminal's whore and a murderer! I never want to see you again!" she shrieks. "You're no daughter of mine."

"We're done here." With far too much ease, Ivan picks her up and carries her out of the room.

A ridiculous end for a ridiculous woman. It's an oddly fitting goodbye.

67

IVAN

Evaline tore into the waiting room like a wild animal, but there's no fight left in her by the time we get to the sidewalk outside. I shove her through the automatic doors and she stumbles towards the curb.

"Where am I supposed to go now?" she whispers again and again in a hollow, broken voice.

I don't think she's talking to me, but I'm happy to answer anyway. "I don't give a fuck. Anywhere but here would be a good start."

I want her as far away from Cora as possible. But I also know if she stays here, I'll kill her. And I've done enough of that for one night.

Her husband tried to force Cora into marriage and then, when she refused, kill her. And Evaline doesn't give a damn. She never tried to save Cora. She never tried to make things right. She is more worried about her life than Cora's.

Part of me once thought Evaline was like my mother. She was trapped with a monster and didn't have another choice. But now, Alexander is dead. She is free to make her own choices. And with this newfound freedom, her first thought was to get to the hospital and scream at her daughter for having the audacity to save her own life.

This bitch doesn't deserve Cora.

"Alexander was all I had." Her shoulders sag. It looks like she's caving in on herself. "I have nothing left."

"You could have had your daughter."

Her eyes are dark, shadowy caverns when she looks up at me. "Cora hates me. She has hated me for years. It's why she killed Alexander. She wants to punish me for—"

"*I* killed Alexander." I pause and let the confession sink in. "Cora didn't pull the trigger; I did. And I did it because, just like you, he slapped Cora. I'll kill anyone who hurts her."

Her eyes go wide and she stumbles another half-step back.

Good. She should be scared.

"And just so you know—so you can spend the rest of your days thinking about all the many ways you've fucked up—he hit her because Cora attacked him after he said he was going to kill *you*. She was defending *you*."

Evaline's jaw drops. "He didn't say that," she whispers. But I can tell she doesn't believe it.

"He sure as fuck did. After everything you've done to her, Cora was still trying to protect you. Your daughter was looking out for you even though you have never once looked out for her."

A tear rolls down her cheek. "I didn't know. I thought—I need to talk to her."

She takes a step towards the front doors and I shift in front of her. "You are never going to talk to your daughter again."

"We're family. We need to—"

"*You* need to get away from me right now. Before I decide to kill you for hurting my wife."

She inhales sharply. "You wouldn't kill your wife's mother."

I chuckle darkly. "Then you don't know a fucking thing about me. If you touch my wife again, I'll end you. If you so much as breathe the same air as her, I'll pop your lungs like balloons and watch you choke. If I even hear your name whispered by anyone in my vicinity, I will hunt you down and make you wish you had never been born."

She's pale now. She takes another step back and falls off the curb. Only barely does she catch herself on the bumper of a parked car to keep from spilling into the street.

"I don't care where you go," I tell her, "but it better be far away from here. Do you understand?"

As much as I want Evaline to run into the night and disappear forever, part of me would respect her for pushing back. I'm estranging her from her daughter forever. She should fight against that. She should rage and beg, whatever it takes. That's her *daughter* she's letting go. Show some goddamn heart.

But in the end, Evaline nods weakly and then shuffles into the darkness.

Maybe she'll end up on the streets again. Maybe she'll find another rich man willing to take her into his house. Either way, I don't care.

I watch her turn the corner and disappear. Hopefully for the last time.

"Do you think that was a good idea?"

I saw Yasha crossing the street towards us a few minutes ago, but I was a bit too busy ridding Cora's life of yet another soul-sucking leech to pay him any mind.

I turn to him now. "I think it was one of my best ideas, actually. I should have done it a lot sooner."

He nods. "Good. If she stuck around, I was going to have to keep an eye on her and any future boyfriends she had to make sure they weren't plotting anything. It would have been annoying."

"That's why I did it," I say sarcastically. "So you'd have less work."

He grins. "I appreciate that. You're always looking out for me, boss."

I roll my eyes. "What are you doing here?"

"Came to make sure you survived without me having to bail you out of trouble like always." He nudges me in the ribs and sighs. "Seriously, though, I'm glad you both are okay. The house was fucking wrecked. I found Niles locked in a closet. If you hadn't already killed Francia, I think he would have."

"Is he okay?"

"The first thing he did when he got out was find a ladder and start patching bullet holes. It should be back to normal by the time you get home tonight."

"*If* we get home tonight. Cora's father is still in surgery."

Yasha winces. "Is he going to make it?"

"I think so. I hope so." I run a hand over my head. "Cora is tough. She can get through anything... but she's been through enough. She needs this."

Yasha gently pushes me towards the doors. "You should go be with her then. I'll make sure Mommy Dearest stays gone."

"She'll stay gone. I think I scared her thoroughly enough. You should get some rest. Or go find your woman."

Yasha smiles, but still wrinkles his forehead like he's confused. "Who?"

"God. When are you two going to give up this stupid game? Everyone knows you're fucking."

"Obviously, I fuck. I mean, look at me, Ivan. *Of course I fuck*."

I groan. "It's been a long night. Go find Jorden and let her deal with you."

"Jorden? Huh, there's an idea," he says, still grinning from ear to ear. "I never thought of her before, but maybe I will go see her. Since you're letting me off for the night and she is Cora's friend and all. I'll go check on her and make sure she's safe. Because I'm a very nice guy."

Yasha is still talking to himself, his voice fading out, when I walk back through the automatic doors and into the hospital.

I turn every corner expecting someone else to show up. Hell, after the night we just had, maybe my father will make his final stand with whatever old guard lieutenants he could scrounge up. Maybe I'll have to kill him to cement my place as *pakhan* of the Pushkin Bratva.

But no one shows up. I walk the quiet halls back to the waiting room.

It's empty.

Panic grips me for a single second before a young nurse clears her throat behind me. I whip around, and the girl jolts. "Sorry, I—Your wife told me to tell you that she's in Room 408."

"Is Marcus St. Clair out of surgery?"

She nods. "I just wheeled him into the recovery room."

"What's his prognosis?"

She gives me a nervous shake of her head. "I'm sorry. That's something you'd have to talk about with the doctor. I wasn't in the operating room and I haven't seen his charts. But you're welcome to go in and see him for yourself."

I want Marcus to pull through for Cora. So some piece of her old life—the life she lost—can come back to her. She deserves it.

As I approach Room 408, I hear voices. Laughter.

I knock on the door and find Cora standing next to her father's hospital bed, smiling wider than I've seen in a long time.

She turns her smile to me and almost knocks me back on my ass. She's so fucking beautiful.

"Oh, here he is!" Cora says. "Ivan is the one who called the ambulance and got you into surgery so fast."

Marcus is still pale, but he's cleaned-up and conscious. "You look a lot better than the last time I saw you," I remark.

He turns to me slowly, his eyes heavy. "You saved my life."

"Yeah, well, you bought enough time for me to get to the house and save Cora's life. For that, I owe you mine. This was the least I could do."

Cora fluffs his pillows and holds a cup of water to his lips so he can drink. She talks to him about nothing for half an hour until he drifts to sleep. Even when he's snoring gently, though, Cora stands by his bedside, looking down at him.

"You should sit down," I tell her. "You need to rest, too."

She nods, but doesn't budge. "I just can't believe he made it."

I grab her by the waist and pull her into my lap. "Believe it. You made it, too."

"I wasn't sure I'd get to talk to him again. I thought it was all over."

"It's not," I whisper. "You can both talk tomorrow. So for now, rest."

She curls against my chest. "Tomorrow. I like the sound of that."

I hold her even tighter. "You have a lifetime of tomorrows, Cora."

Her cheek curves as she smiles. "You'll be there, too?"

I kiss her forehead. "Until the very end."

68

CORA

TWO MONTHS LATER

I'm trembling so hard I can't even scratch my face without almost poking an eye out.

"Stop doing that!" Jordan grabs my hands and pins them to my sides. "You'll ruin your makeup."

"My makeup is already ruined."

I've been crying on and off all morning.

When I unzipped the garment bag that held my dress: tears.

When Jorden and Anya came out in their bridesmaids dresses: tears.

When I asked for a latte and Yasha brought me decaf because "you do not need the extra energy. You're about to buzz out of your skin": tears.

In my defense, I was so nervous last night that I couldn't sleep. I'm exhausted and anxious and—

"I don't know if I can do this." It's the first time I've let myself say the words out loud.

Jorden frowns but, with her smokey eyeshadow and bronzer, it looks like she's posing for a magazine. "Can't do what? Scratch your eye?"

"Get married!" I blurt. I spin away from her and immediately trip on the train of my dress. It takes me a second to extricate my heel from the lace and stand tall again.

When I do, Jorden is gaping at me. I wonder what lipstick she's wearing. It's flawless. "You don't want to marry Ivan?"

"What? Yes! I mean—No. Er, I do want to marry him. Of course I do! I love him."

She presses a hand to her chest. "Oh, thank God. I would *not* want to be the person who had to deliver that news to Mr. Tall, Dark, and Felonious."

"I want to marry him; I just don't know if I can. I mean, I can't walk in this dress. It's only been an hour and I've already smudged my lipstick, cracked a nail, and lost a pin in my hair. I'm just not made for all of this." I pick up the layers of intricately embroidered lace that cinch around my waist and fall to the floor in delicate ripples. "I'm not a princess."

"Uh, yeah, you are. You're as close as most people are ever gonna get, anyway. Plus, you picked all of this—the dress, the hair, the makeup. Ivan told you he'd get married in the kitchen with Niles as officiant if you wanted."

"Maybe I should have taken him up on that," I mutter.

A small ceremony would've meant fewer witnesses when I inevitably faceplant in the aisle or recite my vows with lipstick on my teeth.

Jorden steps in front of me and grabs me by the shoulders. "Let's break it down. Question one: do you love him?"

That's an easy one. "Of course I do. More than anything."

"Excellent." She smiles. "Question two: are you sure you want to marry him?"

That's a slam dunk, too. "I've never been more sure about anything in my life."

"Then, *girl*—" She spins me towards the full length mirror behind me, her head peeking over my shoulder— "stop freaking out and enjoy what should be the best damn day of your life."

All at once, the fears and worries fall away.

Maybe I will land on my face in front of everyone. Maybe all of my nails will chip and I'll lose an eyelash and my dress will get stuck in a door. As long as I end the day married to the man I love, nothing else matters.

Suddenly, Jorden pecks my cheek and whispers in my ear, "I'm going to make myself scarce. I'll be back before the ceremony."

I frown. "What? Why? Where are you—"

But she is already hustling away… past Ivan, who is standing in the doorway.

Jorden ducks out behind him without a peep. I've never loved her more.

"You aren't supposed to see me in my wedding dress," I protest weakly.

Somehow, Ivan looks at me even harder. His eyes are shining as he traces every line of me. Is it suddenly extremely hot in here or is it just me?

"We were engaged before we even started dating. It's in our nature to do things a little backwards." He arches a brow and stalks towards me slowly. His smell invades the room ahead of him. I inch backwards before I bump into the vanity and almost scream at the unexpected contact.

"Like, maybe we should have cake and then say our vows?" I suggest.

"No," he growls. "Not like that at all." He unbuttons his jacket and drapes it on the arm of a chair. There's a lot of talk about men in suits, but I don't think we've given proper consideration to men working their way *out* of suits. He undoes the cufflinks and drops them to the floor with a *clink-clink.*

I recognize the heat in Ivan's eyes. I've seen it more than enough times to know where this is going. I may have been nervous about the wedding all day—but this? I don't have any doubts about how to do this. We've known how to do this since before we even knew each other's names.

I swallow, my mouth suddenly dry. "Then what?"

Ivan slips his bow tie off and drops it in the trail of clothes he's shedding. Little by little, he's going from billionaire boss to dangerous don. Tattoos reveal themselves. Muscles. Harshness and sexy brutality in the slope of his lips and the flame in his eyes. "I think you have an idea already of where I'm going with this, *solnishka.*"

He's only a foot away from me now and he's right—I do know. I also know that I can't stop myself. I reach out and undo the top button of his shirt. He's still playing the game, but I can't wait. I know where this is headed and I want to get there.

Now.

"Ah, now, you're getting it," he breathes. He takes the final step and his hips arch forward to come rest against mine. I hate every layer of lace keeping us apart.

I undo the final button and then stroke my hands up the hard plane of his bared stomach. His skin is tan and warm and I want to drown in the woodsy smell of him.

It doesn't help that I hear the voice of tradition screaming in my ear. The groom seeing the bride before the ceremony? *Wrong.* Ivan being here with the door closed and that look in his eyes? *Very, very wrong.*

Too bad that only makes it all that much hotter.

"Jorden will kill me if I ruin my makeup." It's true, but I don't care. A second ago, I was worried about lipstick on my teeth, but now? I'll walk out there with wild sex hair, smeared lipstick, and a wrinkled dress if it means I get *him.* Hell, I'd tap-dance down the aisle naked for one single kiss. One single touch.

Ivan tips my chin up and leans close. Not quite all the way, but almost there. I stretch onto my toes, lips already parted. *Kiss me. Ruin my makeup. Destroy me.*

"No," he sighs again mournfully. "Not like that. Like *this.*"

With a sudden blur of motion, he puts his palms on my hips and whips me around until my back is to his front and we're both facing the mirror.

His breath is hot in my ear. "I want to watch you fall the fuck apart when I make you mine."

He undoes the buttons at the back of the bodice and roughly peels the dress down my torso until it's a puddle of white at my feet. I love how he hisses, how his face contorts when he sees the bridal lingerie I'm wearing beneath.

It was supposed to be a surprise for tonight. *Whoops.* I guess Christmas came a little early for Mr. Pushkin.

I catch his reflection behind me—his dress shirt open over his bare chest, his eyes dark with need. I've never wanted anything more.

"We… we have to walk out of this room right now," I argue in a limp croak. "Because I think I'll die if I don't get to marry you today."

"Oh no," he breathes, pushing my panties to the side and stroking a finger over my aching pussy. "We can't have that."

My whole body trembles at just this little touch. I reach back and hook my hand around his neck. "Then—oh, fuck me, just *hurry up.* I'm dying here."

He smiles and unbuttons his pants. When he presses his dick against my opening, his fingers dig into my hips. I arch my back and all it takes is one shift for him to slide home inside of me.

Then Ivan's lips are back against my ear. "You can forget all about *walking* out of here. When I'm done with you, you won't even be able to stand."

Ivan drives deep into me at the same time his fingers circle my center. Fireworks explode behind my eyes. I'd collapse in a heap on the floor if he wasn't holding me upright with a hand on my hip and another at my throat. I can see the lines of desire stretching my face in the mirror.

My parted lips matching his.

Those eyes, amber and bright.

He strokes into me slowly. Lingers for a moment. Then he draws out almost entirely before starting all over again.

It's painful how slow he's taking this. Straight-up *torture.* He knows what he's doing, too. Every time he thinks my eyes are fluttering closed, he lets his smirk tip up just a bit more.

"Oh my God, Ivan," I cry out. My hands press against the glass. "There. Right there."

I clench around him as I come. Ivan's breathing picks up, but he doesn't join me. His hands just tighten around my waist, dragging me against him as the orgasm wrings me dry.

"Come with me," I plead between moans. "Come."

But instead of moving faster, Ivan slows. He eases farther and farther back until he lets go of my waist and steps away entirely.

I'm still panting when I catch his eyes in the mirror. "Wh-what are you doing?"

"Walk to me."

"What are you—?"

"*Walk.*"

My insides are still pulsing softly, coming down from his touch. But I stand up and walk towards him.

My legs shake, but I place one foot in front of the other. I feel like a newborn giraffe, but Ivan's looking at me like I'm the sexiest thing he's ever seen.

My orgasm is still ebbing away, but I already want more. I don't think I'll ever get enough of him.

When I reach him, I reach out to balance against his chest. "What was that for?"

"I'm checking to see if I'm done with you yet." He kisses my cheek and my neck. Then he dips lower, flicking his tongue over my lace-covered nipple. He drops to his knees and kisses each of my hip bones and the soft spot low in my belly.

It's like worship the way he touches me. Like every inch of me needs his full attention. Like he'd spend a fucking lifetime kissing his way up the stretch of skin between my knee and hip.

I stroke my fingers through his hair. Partly because I want to touch him, but mostly because I might fall over if I don't hold onto something. "And? What's the verdict?"

He looks up at me from where he's kneeling. His lips are tipped into a smile I want to taste. "You can still walk. So I'd say the job's not quite finished."

That's all he says before that smile slips between my legs. At first, I half-scream like he's branding me when his lips tug at my clit. Then, quickly, the heat digs deep and settles. I curl my hand around his neck and pull him closer.

If this is what it feels like to burn, I never want to be put out.

His tongue pulses into me while he circles his thumb over my clit. As heat unfurls inside of me, I stumble back. The world is tipping and I can't stand upright.

Right on cue, Ivan stands, sweeps me right off my unsteady feet, and lowers me to the floor in front of him. My legs drape over his shoulders as I clamp my thighs around his ears and grind against his mouth.

"Right there—Yes—I need—Want—" Nonsense words tumble out of me as the orgasm swells and then breaks. I fist my hand in his hair and scream to the ceiling.

Guests could be arriving downstairs right this second. Maybe they can hear me through the walls. But they could be standing in the doorway and I wouldn't change a damn thing.

They're here to witness our love, right?

Might as well give them something to witness.

I laugh in my head at the thought—that's something Ivan would say.

My thighs shake and tremble as he lowers me gently to the carpet and crawls up the center of me. He presses kisses to my feverish skin as he goes.

"This is all mine," he whispers, tasting my ribs and nipping at my collarbones. "Fuck the minister. Fuck the ceremony. You are already mine."

Love swells in my chest. I follow a drop of sweat down his neck and over his muscled chest with my finger. "I'm pretty sure that's blasphemy."

"If this is blasphemy," he whispers, "then send me straight to hell."

He fills me completely in one stroke. I tuck my legs around his body and hold his head against my shoulder.

We slide together like it's the most natural thing in the world. It's easy and slow and right.

I'm exactly where I'm supposed to be.

Here. With *him*.

Pressure builds slowly. I scrape my nails down his back and whisper in his ear, "Please come inside me."

This time, Ivan doesn't argue. He spills into me with a groan and then stays there. We hold each other on the floor, letting our hearts ease back to a normal rhythm.

Finally, he lifts his head and kisses my chin. "Can you walk?"

"I can barely *talk*," I correct. A smile I can't contain spreads across my face as tears well in my eyes. "We really are doing things backwards, aren't we?"

Ivan brushes a fallen tear from my face and shakes his head. "No. We're doing things exactly right."

Jorden takes one look at me as I walk down the stairs and shakes her head. "I don't even know why I bothered."

She's not wrong.

I'm *wrecked.*

Fifteen minutes ago, I was naked and splayed open beneath Ivan. Now, I'm about to head down the aisle on legs that are still quivering from all of our scandalous pre-ceremony activities.

My updo has become a loose braid down my back and my eye makeup is a total loss. Jorden pulls out a makeup wipe and scrubs it away while cursing me and my husband-to-be under her breath for wasting all of her hard work. When she's done, my face is pink and flushed, my lips are swollen, and the evidence of what Ivan and I did is still dripping down the insides of my legs.

But it all feels right.

Even the fact that when the double doors open and I head down the aisle, Ivan looks as good as ever. Not a hair out of place. The man is unrufflable.

From the outside, anyway. Only I know the truth.

I like that.

When he looks up at me, he's seeing me in my lace lingerie and heels. He's remembering the way I felt wrapped around him and dreaming about being back there again tonight.

I love being the only person who gets to see him fall apart. The only person who can bring him to his knees.

He smiles at me and the rest of the world falls away. The Bratva, our families, our friends—nothing else matters. The man I love is waiting for me. Why should I care about my ruined cat-eye?

"You look fucking incredible," he whispers in my ear when I reach him.

I meet the minister's eyes and then immediately look away. "Behave yourself."

He looks me up and down. "Never."

During the ceremony, I ignore the guests and the minister and the way Jorden and Yasha are blatantly ogling each other intensely enough to cause a scene. I ignore everything and everyone except the man in front of me.

It passes in a blur of tears and joy, capped off with a kiss that knocks me so thoroughly off my feet that Ivan has to scoop me into his arms and carry me down the aisle while our guests cheer.

He carries me straight through the house and out the double doors to the patio where our reception has been set up in the backyard.

String lights hang over the lawn and there is a stage with an orchestra playing music into the evening. It looks almost exactly like it did the first time I ever saw it.

Ivan and I cut our cake on the patio where he saved me from being assaulted by one of his guests all those months ago.

I point out the eerie full-circle feeling as Niles swoops in to finish cutting and serving cake to the guests. Ivan and I head to the dance floor for our first dance.

"Saved you?" He snorts. "You didn't act like I 'saved you' at the time. I remember you not being very thankful at all."

Our guests are in a wide circle around the lawn while cello music swells against the warm night. My dad is dabbing at his eyes with a white handkerchief. He's been a blubbering mess all night. I guess I know where I get it from.

"It was only because I could have handled him on my own. That guy was a sloppy drunk. He was handsy, but I could have fought him off."

"Thank God for that," he breathes.

I frown. "Excuse me?"

"That sloppy drunk destroyed your dress. I have him to thank for finding you naked in my office." Ivan's amber eyes undress me, turning darker by the second. "It set a lot of things in motion."

I roll my eyes even as a blush spreads over my skin. "Maybe you should have invited him here tonight. We have him to thank for our relationship."

Ivan swirls me out and then back against his chest, holding me close. I'm not a good dancer, but Ivan is graceful enough for the both of us.

He presses his cheek to my temple, his words soft in my ear. "No. This is all us, Cora. You and me. We got ourselves here."

I look over his shoulder at Jorden and Yasha standing shoulder to shoulder, smiling like two idiots in love. Anya and Lev are sharing a piece of cake, feeding each other little bites and laughing. Even Ivan's dad looks marginally happy from his perch at the table in the far back corner. Boris Pushkin probably still doesn't approve of me, but he's smart enough to stay quiet about it.

Then there's the gifts I saw on the gift table earlier. A card from Katerina without a return address. She's on the other side of the world, single and happy. Even Konstantin sent a gift. Ivan told me it was his peace offering. The elder Sokolov knows Ivan killed Mikhail, but he also knows his son was a reckless asshole. Ivan didn't have a choice.

All around us are the signs of a new beginning. A future we've carved out for ourselves.

I can't wait another second to get started.

"You're right." My voice is shaking, but I power through. "We got ourselves here. All three of us, actually."

Ivan spins us with ease, but I feel the moment he falters. His hand tightens around mine and he draws back to look down at me. I've never seen him so still.

"The three of us," he repeats, taking in my fresh wave of tears and the smile I can't bite back another second.

"We're having a baby," I blurt. "I'm pregnant."

Ivan crushes me into a hug just as the song ends. The guests cheer, but they aren't in on our little secret. It's just for the two of us.

As the orchestra plays on, everyone shifts onto the dance floor. But Ivan drags me away in the other direction.

He hauls me by the hand upstairs, down the hall, and into his office. I can hear the hum of the party and see the glow of the lights through the French doors as my husband wraps my legs around his waist and presses me against the wall.

Unlike the first time, this isn't a fantasy I accidentally let myself get lost in. Being with Ivan isn't a break from reality that I will try to enjoy as long as I can before he is gone forever.

Ivan is my real life fairytale.

This is our happily ever after.

EPILOGUE: CORA

TWO YEARS LATER

Ivan parks and kills the engine, but I can't bring myself to get out of the car. I sink down in my seat and stare up at the house. The porch steps might as well be Mt. Everest.

"I feel terrible," I mumble.

"We'll get you inside and you can lay down."

I shake my head. "Not physically. Emotionally. I feel bad."

Ivan chuckles and tucks a strand of hair behind my ear. "There's nothing to feel bad about. The night got cut a little short, but we didn't have to go out in the first place. I was fine staying home."

"It's our second anniversary, though. We have to celebrate."

"Yes," he agrees, leaning in and kissing my shoulder. "Which we could have done from our couch. Niles would have loved to order us an anniversary dinner."

He's not wrong. Niles made little inquiries all week about what our plans were and if there was anything he could help with.

I groan. "Now, I feel bad about that, too. I already pulled out of the trip he tried to surprise us with. The least I could have done is let him make us some dinner."

"Niles knows why you pulled out of the trip. He isn't mad at you."

"You don't know that. Niles would never admit he's mad in a million years, even if he is."

"Because he knows I'd string him from the chandelier by his ankles."

I snort. "You would never hurt Niles."

Ivan arches both brows. "I'll hurt anyone who makes my pregnant wife feel bad about being too sick to take a trip. You are growing a person and taking care of a toddler. You deserve to do whatever you want when you want it."

He's rubbing my shoulder. I reach up and grab his hand, then hold it in my lap, my thumbs tracing his knuckles. "You're really not upset? Because I'd understand if you are. We were supposed to go to Bora Bora. Instead, I couldn't even make it through the entree at our favorite restaurant before I felt like I was going to hurl."

"If I'm mad at anyone, it's the bitch next to us who ordered the seafood."

I laugh. "That 'bitch' was at least ninety."

"She could be nine hundred and I still wouldn't give a shit. I should've punted her to the curb."

I know he's not serious, but I love being the person Ivan will always fight to defend.

I also love being the person who can calm him down.

Slowly, I drag my hand up his arm. "It's okay. The nausea has passed now. But I'm still suffering from other first trimester symptoms."

"I'll get you whatever you need. Just tell me."

I turn to him, our eyes meeting in the dark. "Do you remember what things were like when I was pregnant the last time?"

I'm trying hard to feel sexy, but it's a chore considering that, fifteen minutes ago, Ivan was holding my hair back while I threw up in a planter box by the curb. My teeth are brushed —all pregnant women should keep an emergency kit of toothbrushing supplies in their purse—but I'm not sure mint toothpaste is enough to recover the mood.

At least, I think so. Until Ivan understands what I mean.

He gently wraps his hand around my throat and tips my head to one side. His eyes are black in the lights from the car's console. "You were fucking insatiable, Cora. I thought you were going to wear me out."

"But I never did," I grin. "You were always up for the challenge. Are you up for it now?"

He chuckles darkly and slides my hand down to the front of his pants. He arches a brow in challenge. "I'm up for it if you are."

The mix of pregnancy hormones racing through me are most definitely up for it. I can already feel the dampness pooling between my legs. I can also *definitely* feel how rock-solid Ivan's erection is.

He strides around the car and opens my door. Then we creep up the front steps.

"Matvei should already be asleep," Ivan whispers, slipping his key silently into the door. "If we can creep past Yasha and Jorden on the couch, they can stick around and make sure he stays asleep while we take care of you upstairs."

Between Yasha and Jorden and Anya and Lev, Matvei has no shortage of aunts and uncles who are dying to take care of him. Not to mention Grandpa. My dad is an absolute softy for my baby boy. But I'm glad he's not here tonight. With the way I'm feeling, the last person I want to run into on my way upstairs is my dad.

My body brushes against Ivan's arm. "If you want to *fully* take care of me, they might need to stay the night."

Ivan smiles and the soft curve of his lips paired with the square line of his jaw is almost enough for me to throw myself at him right here. Forget sneaking upstairs—we can do it on the porch.

But propriety and a little mercy for whoever on the security team is manning the cameras tonight wins out. I tuck away my inner freak and follow Ivan inside.

The house is dark and quiet. Usually, Jorden and Yasha put Matvei to bed and then post up in the den and watch movies. But I don't hear a sound tonight.

"Maybe they are upstairs in his nursery?" I whisper.

Ivan nods like it's a possibility, but his brows crease together. He tiptoes into the sitting room. When he finds it empty, he stands tall and spins around.

My chest tightens. "Is everything okay?"

"I'm going to call the security shack and see if they've heard —" A soft thud interrupts him and Ivan whips around. He's staring at the closet in the hallway, every muscle in his body tense.

"Ivan?" I hiss.

"Go check on Matvei," he orders. Then he inches towards the closet.

I'm suddenly terrified. Whatever is going on, I want to know that my baby boy is okay.

I pull out my phone and open the baby monitor app. The live feed loads up for three excruciating seconds before I see Matvei lying on his side in his crib, perfectly safe and asleep. His room is otherwise empty.

For the moment, he's safe.

So I turn my attention back to Ivan and watch him glide across the room. My anxiety spikes higher with every step. I'm not armed, so I grab a key from the ceramic bowl on the foyer table and hold it between my knuckles like I'm Wolverine. It's not much, but it's better than nothing.

There's another thud and clatter from inside the closet. It sounds like something falls off one of the shelves.

Ivan hesitates outside the door for just a second before he yanks it open. "Who the fuck are you and what are you doing in my—"

His voice is lost in a chorus of shrieking. One male, one female.

Then Ivan jumps back with a scowl twisting his face. "For fuck's sake! Put your ass away, Yasha!"

My heart is hammering from the anxiety and the noise, but I storm into the sitting room. "What?"

The closet door is open and now, I can see exactly what Ivan was talking about.

Yasha's bare ass is framed in the doorway. His pants are around his ankles. Also around his ankles... my best friend's feet.

Jorden is pinned against the game shelf in a position that looks eerily similar to the one Ivan put me in on our wedding day.

"Don't look!" She reaches over Yasha's shoulder and tries to close the closet door, but she can't reach. "Close the door, Yasha."

"I'm a little busy here! If I close the door, Ivan is going to see a lot more than my ass."

Even in the dim light, I can tell Jorden's face is beet red. She meets my eyes and seems to wilt in embarrassment. "Oh. Hi, Cora."

"Ivan, close the door," I say. "Yasha and Jorden, get dressed and get out here."

Ivan closes the door and then walks towards me, shaking his head. "So much for sneaking upstairs."

"What the hell were they thinking?" I snap. A second later, I have the chance to ask the sexual delinquents themselves. "What the hell were you two thinking?"

Yasha is dressed, but his shirt is buttoned wrong and his hair is sticking up in every direction. Jorden looks fine except for her swollen lips and the beginning of a hickey on her neck.

"We were thinking it would be awkward for the two of you to come home and find us on the couch," Yasha retorts. "We were being courteous."

"'Courteous' would've involved *not* getting hot and heavy in a closet when you're supposed to be babysitting," Ivan rumbles.

"I made sure Matvei was asleep first!" Jorden protests.

Yasha arches a brow. "For someone who lives in a glass house, you are throwing a lot of stones, boss. I had the pleasure of walking past the sitting room last week when Cora was on the back of the couch with her legs spread and Ivan was—"

I scream before he can even finish. "We were home alone!"

That day was actually one of my first hints that I was pregnant. I'd followed Ivan into the shower that morning and then, just a few hours later, I was aching for him again. The memory of his beard stubble scraping my inner thighs sends heat flooding everywhere.

"Not quite." Yasha smirks. "So I thought the closet would be a better choice than that public display."

Oh, God. Kill me now.

Ivan looks at me and then spins back to Yasha. "Forget you ever saw that. And next time, if you want to be courteous, wait until you're at home. You aren't a fucking teenager. You can wait."

"Actually, we couldn't." Jorden bites her lower lip and then holds up her left hand. There's a cartoonishly large red diamond on her ring finger. It takes me a second to realize it's a Ring Pop.

I look from the ring to her and back again before it clicks. "Holy shit! You're engaged!"

Jorden grins and nods. "Yasha just proposed to me."

"With a Ring Pop?" Ivan asks under his breath.

Yasha elbows him hard. "It's all I had on hand, okay? I was being spontaneous."

I pull Jorden into a hug while Ivan claps Yasha on the back.

"You two are cheesy and disgusting, but we're happy for you," Ivan says.

I nod. "So happy. Beyond happy! Especially since you two tried to keep it a secret that you were even dating for months. The fact I know the same day that you're engaged is a shock."

"It would have been hard to keep it a secret," Jorden says.

She looks at Yasha and something passes between them. When Yasha turns back to us, his smile is so big it looks like he's going to burst. He's bouncing from heel to toe like a kid waiting in line to meet Santa.

Ivan breaks the tension. "Whatever it is, say it. You're shit at keeping secrets."

Yasha looks to Jorden and she rolls her eyes, but waves him on.

"The engagement was kind of a rush job because Jorden just told me... she's pregnant!"

My jaw drops. "What?!"

Yasha looks nothing but relieved to have these two secrets off his chest. For working in a criminal organization, he really is terrible at deception when it comes to stuff like this.

"I'm pregnant," Jorden confirms, wiping tears from her eyes. "I just found out last week, but you made your announcement and I didn't want to step on your toes. So I was waiting until the time was right, but—"

"You could never step on my toes!" I squeeze her hands and pull her in close. "I am pregnant at the same time as my best friend in the entire world! How could I ever be anything but thrilled about that?"

"I'd be a little more thrilled if I could open the closet without seeing Yasha's bare ass for the rest of my life," Ivan growls. Then he smiles and wraps an arm around Yasha's shoulders. "But I'm still thrilled."

It's hugs and congratulations all around. Then we all sit down on the couch in a haze of happiness.

"I'm going to be a dad," Yasha finally says, shaking his head. "Can you believe that?"

"I can honestly say I can't believe it," Ivan says. "But you're going to be a great one."

"Yeah?" he asks.

Jorden lays her head on his shoulder and looks up at him with nothing but adoration. "Yeah."

Yasha kisses her forehead and Ivan looks over at me. He's beaming with pride for our friends and there's no other way I wish this night had gone.

Especially since I know we'll still make our way upstairs eventually.

We have all the time in the world for that.

EXTENDED EPILOGUE: IVAN

SIXTEEN YEARS LATER

Check out the Extended Epilogue to take a sneak peek
sixteen years into the future! Learn about Yasha and
Jorden's daughter, Ivan and Cora's heirs, and a glimpse of
what love looks like almost two decades after "I do"!

CLICK HERE TO READ IT NOW!

Printed in Great Britain
by Amazon